Codename Pandora

Codename Pandora

KJ Graham

ISBN-13: 9781517465957
ISBN-10: 1517465958
Library of Congress Control Number: 2015915666
CreateSpace Independent Publishing Platform
North Charleston, South Carolina

ACKNOWLEDGMENTS

Hugh S Peoples

Callum McMeekin

George Kean

Val Moir (VM Photography)

TABLE OF CONTENTS

CHAPTER 1

ESCAPE

It was late February 2009. Inside the Porton Down research facility, MI6 had its own little version of Guantanamo Bay. Here they kept prisoners they did not want the rest of the world to know about. Cell One was occupied by the former Mossad agent turned assassin, Areli Benesch. She had been captured while on a mission to assassinate MI6 assets who were due to give evidence against a secret military facility in Scotland. She had been commissioned by a shadowy figure high up in the American military ranks. MI6 wanted to know all about this and also her previous employer, Mossad. Because Mossad would demand its wayward agent back, Benesch had been spirited away so no one could ask for her deportation. Unfortunately for Benesch, this also meant that she was at the mercy of her interrogators.

She was subjected to water torture, electric shock treatment, and truth drugs. Areli kept sane by thinking of the things she would do to her captors when she eventually broke free.

Areli watched the wall of her cell, never taking her eyes off the shadow cast by the sunset. Her plan had taken weeks to prepare. Earlier, she had thrown the guard off his usual routine by spitting in his face like a demented wildcat as he was locking her cell door. The broken piece of spoon Areli had managed to jam in the door check stopped the locks from engaging properly. Had the guard not been assaulted at that exact second, he would have known right away the lock had not clicked shut.

The shock of an assault by a normally model prisoner knocked him off his routine, and he staggered back to the office to wash from his eyes the urine that the Israeli bitch had spat at him and report to his supervisor. The supervisor screamed at Areli, but she was happy that he never had the presence of mind to check the door lock.

The supervisor had decided he did not want to end up smelling of urine for the rest of the shift and backed off after seeing the bedpan in handy reach, lifting his colleague's dropped keys during his departure.

Areli washed her mouth out and waited patiently for the sun's rays to hit the line she had scribed on the wall with the handle of the broken spoon. Soon it would be payback time for the last year of torture she had endured at the hands of the British secret service. In time, she had given up most of her secrets, but she had drawn the line when it came to her motherland. No matter what they did, Areli refused point blank to divulge Mossad secrets. Her time as a freelance assassin was out in the open now, but state secrets were locked away so deep in her head even the drugs were unable to unlock them.

Areli was meditating, channelling the fury of her captivity into a controlled and determined state of mind. The footsteps in the corridor brought Areli back to the present. She checked the wall. The sun was on the mark, and it was time to unleash hell.

Mary the cleaner had just started her shift and as usual had started by mopping the corridors. She had just drawn level with the first cell when the door burst open. Areli charged her down, stabbing her in the neck with the handle of the spoon. As she fell, Areli grabbed the broom and, with a quick leg action, snapped the mop head off, leaving her with the handle.

Andy had just returned to the wing after a quick shirt change and scrub up to remove the last of the urine when he heard the scream.

He turned the corner into the corridor just as a sprinting Areli hit him in the stomach with the broken shaft of the mop. The broken, ragged end pinned him to the wall like a cherry on a cocktail stick. Areli knew he was finished and wasted no more time on him. In the office, Jake, the supervisor, was just in the process of getting out of his swivel chair to see what all the commotion was when the door burst open. He was hit in the chest by a charging madwoman. The chair toppled backward as the force carried them both over. Areli knelt on his chest and rammed the broken handle of the spoon up through the soft area of skin below his chin, cutting through windpipe and spinal cord, killing him instantly.

She may have dispatched her captors, but escape was not on her mind, not yet. She was going to make the British pay a terrible price for their treatment of her. Her lightening attack had been so fast that no alarm had been raised. The Porton Down complex had no idea that one of the most dangerous women in the world was loose in one of the most sensitive and secret military locations in Britain.

Areli retraced her footsteps, checking on all three of her victims. Only the woman was still alive, but Areli could tell by the loss of blood it would not be long until she succumbed to her wounds. She was barely conscious and no threat to Areli's escape.

Areli Benesch had studied the comings and goings of the facility's staff. She knew on night shift there was very little chance of an unwanted visitor.

She headed for the shower to get rid of the blood spatter and find a guard's uniform that fitted. Fifteen minutes later, Areli returned to the office sporting a crisp new uniform that, other than the legs being too long, fitted her perfectly.

She had tied her uncut mane into a tight bun. Although she was dressed, she still felt naked. She needed a weapon. After a search of the supervisor's belt, she found the keys for the locked cabinet in the corner of the room. Areli was not impressed by what she found in the cabinet—two CS gas canisters and two revolvers so old that Areli had never seen the model before. She busied herself loading both guns, placing one in the holster she had just pulled on, tucking the other into the back of her trousers. It was time to get out of here, before her escape was discovered. Areli followed the corridors until she came to a T-junction.

To the right was reception and freedom. Then Areli read the sign on the door to the left, and it changed her mind. Instead of turning right, she turned left, heading to the door marked "Biohazard." The door was keypad entry. Beyond the door, two people were working away, oblivious to Areli who observed them for a few seconds before knocking on the door.

Professor Colin Ferry was in a foul mood. He had just discovered his young protégé had been stealing test material from the lab's supplies. That wasn't the main reason for his mood, however. He knew he had to report the theft, and he knew when he did, Gary, his trainee, would be finished. Once Gary had a criminal record, no one would touch him. Ferry was upset. Gary Harding had the makings of at worst, a talented scientist, and at best, a genius.

The knock at the door brought him back to reality. Colin climbed down from his stool and shuffled toward the door. His arthritis was playing up badly. He was glad he was in his last year of work. Then he could head out to Florida where the weather was kinder to his condition. Colin arrived at the door to find a young female guard standing outside. She smiled at him as he entered the code and opened the door.

"Why can't you lot remember the code? This is the third time this week we have been interrupted. It's not on." Colin stopped speaking as Areli pulled her hand from behind her back and pointed the revolver at Colin's chest.

She pushed Colin back and closed the door. "Both of you, put your hands on your head." Areli spotted the CCTV camera above the door. One pull of the cable, and it was disconnected.

Colin spoke up. "There is nothing here for you. Please leave. You are frightening my assistant."

Karen Lowe had backed herself into a corner and was shaking like a leaf. Areli noted that the old guy seemed to be hovering in front of something. "Move across to your assistant, old man, if you are so worried about her."

Colin stood his ground, not moving. Areli was now sure he was trying to hide something. "I told you to move, old man. Do it now." Colin's face was glowing as the situation pushed his blood pressure through the roof, but he stood his ground.

Behind Colin stood a sealed chamber that contained two of Colin's previous projects—Vokxin and Diavokxin, both derivatives of the same chemical reaction. Diavokxin was a chemical warfare nasty, which, when exposed to the air, reacted with oxygen, changing its composition. This, although it could be inhaled, could not be absorbed by the blood, and thus it caused hypoxia and death within a few seconds of inhalation. A thimbleful was enough to take out the equivalent of an office block before the reaction died away.

Vokxin, on the other hand, was the stuff of nightmares. It was what scientists called a global killer. Unlike its cousin, Vokxin's reaction did not die away—it multiplied as it mixed with oxygen.

Once Vokxin was let loose, every living thing that relied on oxygen would be doomed within a matter of hours.

It was hard to believe that the only thing that stood between life and death on planet Earth was a sixty-four-year-old arthritic man called Colin.

Areli could almost smell the fear from the elderly scientist. Her sixth sense told her there was more to his fear than just a madwoman waving a gun about.

Then Colin made the second biggest mistake of his life. The first had been creating Vokxin. The second was trying to tackle Areli. He tried to grab the gun in Areli's hand, and the inevitable happened. Areli sidestepped his charge and hit him hard on the back of the head with the barrel of the gun. Colin collapsed to the lab floor. Arthritis was the least of his problems now.

Karen Lowe, Colin's personal lab technician, stifled a scream as Benesch spun round, pointing the gun in her face. "Shut up, woman. The only thing that is keeping you alive is the fact a gunshot would be heard, so if you scream and raise the alarm, I have no reason to keep you alive, and you will die. Do you understand me?"

Karen tried to assist her fallen work colleague, but Benesch pinned her in the corner while she checked out the chamber the old man had been trying to hide. "Tell me what is in the chamber that the old fool was willing to give his life for."

Karen was chalk white. She was hyperventilating and close to passing out. The terror of what had just happened, mingled with the terror of what could now happen, was too much for Karen to comprehend. She tried, but no words would come out. Areli crossed to a wall cupboard and started pushing containers around while she watched the assistant out of the corner of her eye. She returned with a sealed glass beaker that sported the label H_2SO_4—sulphuric acid. Karen watched in horror as Areli undid the metal pull-down seal on the neck of the bottle and stood above the fallen body of Colin Ferry. The horror of what Areli was about to do struck home with Karen. "No, please, leave him. Please don't do this."

Areli knew the girl was hers to command from that point onward. "Then tell me the truth about what is in the chamber. Tell me quickly, for my grip on the acid is poor. Who knows how long I can hold it for."

Karen had no option except to tell her something. She did not lie—she was just sparse with the facts. "The chamber contains two chemicals for use in experiments. Nothing more."

Areli was no fool. She knew when she was being played. "Enter the code on the access panel and take out the chemicals so I can see them."

Karen tried to stall her, but Areli tipped a drop of acid out. It landed an inch from Colin's nose and started to bubble and hiss as it tried to eat its way through the concrete floor of the lab. Areli made eye contact with Karen. She did not have to say anything. Karen busied herself opening the chamber.

The chamber contained a test tube contained within a square, vacuum-sealed glass box about the size of a compact camera. Also, there was a rack of ten small glass vials, each the size of a bottle of nail varnish. Karen made a show of displaying them to her, then started to load them back in the chamber. "Not so fast. Leave them out."

The colour drained from Karen's face. Areli watched the terror in the girl's eyes. She walked over to the bench and studied the square container. Karen recoiled, moving to the far side of the lab. It was as if the grim reaper had stepped into the room and put his hand on the girl's shoulder. "Enough of this nonsense. You will tell me the truth now. If you don't, I will break this little glass box on your friend's head." Areli picked up the square container. Karen let out a gasp and went to step forward but checked herself.

Areli was starting to get worried herself. What was in these glass containers that could drive an old man to risk his life and a girl to the brink of a nervous breakdown? Areli decided to change tactics. She needed the girl to talk, and the way things were going, there was more chance of the girl passing out than anything else. She checked out the girl's lapel badge. "Karen, I am not a stupid person, so let's be adult about this. You want me to leave the old man alone, and I want some information from you. You tell me where I am and what is in the containers, and I will leave you to call for some help with your old friend here. If you don't, and he dies, you will never forgive yourself."

Karen was puzzled by her captor's first question. How could she not know where she was? She must be some kind of escaped mental patient. Karen had heard rumours that the far side of the building contained some type of detention facility. She had to try and humour this madwoman until help arrived. "You know my name, but what is your name? You have no identification on your uniform."

The girl was wasting time, but Areli knew she had to be patient if she was to get the girl to open up to her. "My name is Areli, and I have no identification because the uniform is stolen. I have been detained here against my will for a long time, so if you tell me where we are and what the containers are, I will leave you in peace."

Karen did not want this woman to know the truth. She needed to get the containers back in the chamber before any harm came to them. "Areli, the containers have harmful chemicals in them. We need to get them back in the sealed chamber. We can put them back. Then I will give you money from my purse and directions to a train station or an airport, wherever you want to go."

Areli was still getting nowhere, and time was running out. She needed to get away from this place before she was found out. "Karen, of course they are dangerous chemicals. Don't treat me like an idiot. You are a scientist, not a cleaner. Tell me the exact composition of both chemicals and the precise location of this facility, or your boss will need a new face if he lives. Also, I will test one of those small capsules by making you drink it. Look at my face. Do you think I am joking?" Areli backed up her threat by putting the acid down and taking one of the small vials from the rack. Karen shrank into the corner, but she had no place to retreat to. Areli grabbed her by the throat and lifted the vial to her lips, putting pressure on the end cap with her thumb. Karen screamed at her to stop, and Areli relieved the pressure but held Karen tightly by the throat. "Last chance, Karen. Talk or I pour this down your throat."

"OK, OK. The chemicals are called Diavokxin and Vokxin. They are Cold War relics and were to be used against the Soviets if nuclear war broke out.

They bond to the oxygen in the air, creating something unbreathable, which causes hypoxia and death within minutes of inhalation."

Areli released her victim's throat and stepped back. She was digesting this latest news. "Good girl. Now I need to know more. Why two chemicals? What is the difference, and why are the chemicals here?"

Karen did not want to go further, but she knew Areli would fulfill her promise if she did not reply. "They are both derivatives of the same chemical. Diavokxin is in the small capsules. Each capsule, if opened, will kill every living thing for one square mile. Vokxin is unstable and cannot be opened." Karen left it at that. She felt like a traitor. She had given official secrets away to a madwoman.

Areli was pleased at what she had found out, but there was a nagging doubt that there was something the woman was still trying to hide from her. "Karen, if Vokxin is unstable, why keep it? What is its value to keep it for so long?"

Karen had been put on the spot and had no answer but the real one. "It cannot be destroyed. If released, it would wipe out every oxygen-dependent organism on planet Earth in seven hours, fourteen minutes, and thirty-two seconds, give or take a few seconds, depending on the state of the ozone layer at that particular time."

There was silence in the lab. Both women contemplated their next move. Areli was trying to work out what to do with her newfound power. Karen was wondering just how mad her captor was. Surely she would not attempt to take the chemicals from the lab. Karen did not have to wait long to find out. Areli made a beeline for the lab door. To Karen's horror, she took the two chemicals with her. At the door, Areli punched in the numbers she had watched the old scientist use earlier. Karen made a run for her but stopped dead in her tracks as Areli removed one of the small vials and flung it as hard as she could toward Karen's feet.

The vial exploded with a popping noise just as the lab door swished shut behind Areli.

Karen had about four seconds before the chemical entered her lungs and started converting the oxygen in her body into something her blood could not absorb. Karen had been present only once when Diavokxin was administered to a chimpanzee in an attempt to see if an antidote would stop the chemical reaction in the body. It had failed, and as she watched the poor animal had died an agonizing death. This terrible image flashed in front of her eyes as she fled, holding her breath and searching for the only thing in the room that could save her life. If she was quick enough, there was a chance.

Karen flung equipment out of the way in her headlong charge to save her life. She found the oxygen cylinder and mask under the bench nearest the door. She pulled it on and hit the top to start the flow of oxygen. Karen had the good sense to realise she was not out of the woods yet. She charged for the door. She had seconds before the sensors picked up the Cold War chemical and set off the alarms and sealed all exits. The room was airtight, as was the rest of the building. Karen knew from drills and discussions with Professor Ferry that it would take hours for help to arrive, and further hours for the building to be made safe. She had a fifteen-minute supply of oxygen. If she did not escape now, she would die a horrible death in this gas-filled tomb.

Areli could see as she exited the lab that the corridor led past the entrance to the cell wing that she just escaped from. She could see the reception desk in the distance. Most of the desk was obscured by the wall, but Areli was sure due to the nature of the facility that it would be manned by at least armed security. She knew that time was not on her side. It was only a matter of time now until the alarm was raised. The facility must have some sort of warning system for when chemicals escaped. She moved swiftly down the corridor, taking extra care not to make any noise.

The security guard was about to take a sip from the steaming mug of tea he had just made for himself when the chemical alarm sounded. He punched a code into the computer, trying to find where the alarm had been triggered. The map showed the schematic of the whole site. They were housed in a small annex to the side of the main complex. The guard was praying it was the main annex and not his building. He did not want the hassle of finding the faulty sensor or the extra paperwork it would cause.

Movement to his right caused him to look up just as Areli fired. The shot hit him high in the chest, knocking him off his chair.

❖ ❖ ❖

Private Bennett had just relieved one of his unit and was settling in for a long night on guard duty. The guardroom by the entry barrier had no heating, and Bennett was not looking forward to the next four-hour shift. He was not in a good frame of mind. He had not busted his arse to get into 42 Commando to end up a glorified car-park attendant. He could not understand why a commando unit had to do this; surely, it was a job for a squaddie.

Two things happened in quick succession. An alarm started to sound. Private Bennett picked up his SA80 rifle and started to head toward the entrance when the gunshot drowned out the alarm for a second.

Bennett stopped. He was in the process of taking his weapon out of safety when the door sprang open. Areli and the soldier spotted each other at exactly the same time. Bennett had no chance. Areli's gun was ready to fire while Bennett had only just clicked off the safety catch. He started to raise the weapon, but Areli fired before he managed to bring the gun to a firing position. Areli had aimed for the heart, but her weapon was old and outdated. The shot hit Private Bennett in the stomach, causing him to curl up. He fired as he fell, but his shot was compromised, and it kicked up a chunk of concrete two feet in front of Areli. She brought the pistol up, aiming at the soldier's head but checked before pulling the trigger. She had had enough of the slaughter for tonight. He was no longer a threat. She removed the rifle and radio from the soldier and flung them across the road into the ditch. Areli was wondering what to do next when a set of headlamps suddenly dazzled her. A car swung off the road and pulled up at the closed barrier by the gatehouse. Areli smiled to herself. Her unsuspecting taxi had just arrived.

Gary Harding was late for work again. He had been working on his own private project for twenty-six hours solid and had not noticed the time slipping away. A mad rush by him meant that he was only two hours late for his shift. He was sure Professor Ferry was about to sack him. He did not need to give him more excuses. Between his project and trying to steal equipment without his mentor finding out, Gary's head was full to overflowing. He was close to a nervous breakdown. He was so close to finishing his quest that he had only dozed for the last three weeks. His only meals had been ham sandwiches from the staff canteen and bottles of water. He was busy raking through the contents of his glove box looking for his security pass when there was a tap on the driver's window.

Gary was so intent on looking for the pass that he had failed to notice the woman walking up to the side of the car. He powered down the window with one hand while still searching for the missing pass with the other hand. He was oblivious to the woman pointing a revolver at his temple. Areli leaned in the window and switched the car off, removing the keys at the same time. For the first time since pulling up, Gary turned his attention away from looking for his pass. He was surprised to find a woman guard pointing a gun at him. "Hi, it's OK. I do have a pass. I was just looking for it. Can you give me a second? It's here somewhere."

Areli walked round to the passenger side opened the door and got in without speaking. It suddenly dawned on Gary that all was not well. "Drive away from here. Do it as if nothing has happened and don't try to signal to anyone. If you do not do as I tell you, I will shoot you and take the car. Do we understand each other?"

CHAPTER 2

THE GLASS HOUSE

The low winter sun streamed in through the bedroom window. I screwed my eyes up to block out the bright rays as I searched for the time on the alarm perched on the bedside table next to me. Ten fifteen. I had overslept again. My right arm explored the far side of the double bed. To my disappointment, it found only crumpled sheets. Sam was long gone; her side of the bed was cold to the touch. The woman was unbelievable. There was not a day that passed that Sam had not spent exercising. She was like a woman possessed. Lately, it had started to worry me. She spent more time in the gym and the shooting range than she did with me.

For the moment, I put the thought to the back of my head and busied myself making the bed and getting the kettle on for my much-needed coffee to wake me up. Coffee made, I popped out onto the balcony to survey the scenery, also hoping to catch a glimpse of my missing partner as she attempted to run herself into the ground. She was nowhere to be seen, and the bitterly cold wind from the sea drove me back indoors, leaving me to admire the west of Scotland from the comfort of the upstairs lounge. Again alone with my thoughts, my mind drifted back to the events of the previous year. Sam had been sent by MI6 to guard me from some nasty people. At first, I loathed the girl. But as events had progressed, I had found the real Samantha hiding behind the hard-as-nails image that she portrayed to the outside world. Yes, she was a cold-blooded killer, but there was a lost girl trying to break free inside her.

She had been mentally scarred by the death of her parents and only sister. Many nights since then, I had cradled her in my arms as she broke her heart after waking from terrible nightmares. It was hard to tell if her past career in the secret service or the loss of her family had triggered the nightmares. It was clear to see that the last year spent with me had not cured her psychological problems completely. The thing that was worrying me was her increase in her physical training. I wasn't sure if she was trying to work herself hard so that she could sleep through the night. For sure, it was more than just keeping fit. Had she had enough of me, and was she staying out of my way, unable to find the words to tell me enough was enough? I was a relative newcomer to long-term relationships and was finding it difficult to spot the signals from Sam that someone with more experience would undoubtedly pick up. She was a very complicated lady, but one whom my inexperienced heart had grown to love.

I had found it hard at first to be at ease with this feeling. It was as if my head was telling me this would never last. All my previous romantic encounters had ended in tragedy. This was too good to trust. My train of thought was cut short as Sam glided silently into the room. I studied her as she pulled open the top of a water container and swallowed the contents with huge gulps.

It was clear she had been working very hard. She was dripping with sweat, her T-shirt clinging to her torso. Sam had never been chubby, but she was thinner and had a more chiselled physique than ever before. She looked every bit the Olympic long-distance runner—a fact that did nothing but underline my worries. To me, Sam's figure when I had first met her was pretty much perfect. Gone were her curves and toned physique, replaced with a six-pack and hard, defined muscle. Fine, if you were training for Britain's strongest man but not pleasing to the eye. Sam recovered and broke the silence. "Not bad today. That was thirty miles and the last ten all uphill." Sam was waiting for my response.

"Not bad for a day's work. What do you fancy for lunch, Samantha?"

Sam watched me while she finished her bottle of water. "Do I detect a note of disapproval, Captain?"

I knew I had to tread carefully. I was not good at hiding my feelings, and Sam was getting good at reading my thoughts. "No. If that is what makes you happy, so be it."

Sam got up and strolled into the kitchen area to dispose of the empty water container. I followed her through. "Sam, it's just I can't see the point of all this heavy training. I am worried that one morning I will wake up next to a woman with the physique of a Russian shot-put champion." Sam smiled at me but her grin was an uneasy one.

She retaliated by making a joke of the situation. As she walked past me, she pinched my bum. "I didn't hear you complaining about my body last night. I'm going for a shower. You can make me a surprise for lunch." She turned as she got to the door and gave me a beaming smile before finally heading for the shower.

I lost track of time while I prepared lunch. I finished garnishing the prawn salad, then went looking for Sam to tell her lunch was ready. Sam's en suite shower was empty, and Sam was nowhere to be seen. A brief recce of the property found her in the shooting range. She was busy emptying a full mag rapid-fire into the paper soldier at the far end of the range. Sam was concentrating on the target and was wearing ear defenders. She had not noticed my entrance. She was counting down the shots as I took my revenge, and as she fired the last shot in the chamber, I pinched her right buttock. The shot went high, just nicking the corner of the paper target. "Lunch is ready, Rambo."

Sam put the gun down and spun round.

For a second, her eyes betrayed her. There was a flash of anger in those grey, hauntingly beautiful eyes. Sam regained control almost instantly. "That was mean. It would have been my best score this week." It was moments like this that reminded me that deep down in Sam's subconscious there lay a killer that Sam tried so hard to suppress.

That also worried me. How long could Sam stay in retirement when this alter ego still lurked in the shadows of her soul?

After lunch the usual routine that we had drifted into continued. Both Sam and I headed for the gym. Sam pestered me to leave the weights and do some sparring instead. Sam had become proficient in most types of martial arts, but I had only practiced the art of tae kwon do. As the sparring progressed, it was clear to see Sam had by far the upper hand. Her speed and agility were greater than mine. Sam landed various kicks and punches on the body protectors we had both suited up with. "Come on, Adam. Get with the programme! You need to move more. Stop taking half-hearted chances. We both have protectors and head guards. Go for it."

As she spoke, Sam leapt into the air, hitting me hard on the side of the head protector with her leading foot. The red mist started to descend, but I checked myself and talked to Sam, trying to get the stars that were floating in front of my eyes out of the way. "Sam, enough, this proves nothing. Yes, you could go on for hours hitting me and scoring points if we were in a competition, but you and I both know, in the big bad world you have lost so much weight, you have no real power behind your kicks. Let's call it a day."

Sam responded by charging at me, hitting me with two side kicks.

The first I blocked, but the second was too fast. Despite the body protector, I could actually feel my ribs flex and crush in on my lungs. It had been about a year since a bullet had broken my ribs, and I was still very protective of them. The red mist had fully descended. Sam knew about my ribs. In my mind, she was bang out of order. I backed away, protecting the side Sam had just scored a bull's-eye with and waited. Sam dummied a couple of times. Then the moment I had been waiting for came. Sam charged in and jumped, aiming for a headshot. I jinked back, just out of range of Sam's kick. I spun round, hitting Sam full in the chest with a spinning back kick. Sam's momentum drove her onto the kick, and for the first time that day, I did not hold back. The kick was one of those kicks you just knew had connected perfectly. Sam stopped instantly, then was driven backward, legs and arms flailing. She hit the gym floor with a thud, and her head cracked off the wooden floor. My first thought was that I had killed her, but she sat up, then promptly fell backward, her knees clamped to her chest.

I flung my headgear off and dived onto the floor by her side. "Sam, are you OK? I am sorry. I shouldn't have done that."

Sam rolled onto her side, trying to draw breath. She spoke through clenched teeth. "I will be fine. Just give me a minute, please."

Sam sat up, throwing her headgear away; she was still having problems drawing breath. I busied myself by untying her body protector and giving her more room to draw breath. "Jesus, Adam, that hurts. I take your point. You win. I need to go and lie down."

Sam headed for her bed, while I took a walk along the beach to clear my head. I was less than proud of myself. I had lost control for a fraction of a second. I reasoned with myself that we were sparring, and we were both wearing protection, but deep down, I felt I had crossed the line. The winter evening had started to descend when I climbed the winding path back to the glass house. A quick check on Sam found her still in bed, fast asleep. I decided a bit of cooking therapy was called for. Why it relaxed me, I was not sure, but for some reason, it cleared my mind, possibly because I had to concentrate on the cooking. I decided my meal would start with a chicken dish and got to work grilling and slicing two chicken breasts. I then stuffed the breasts with goat cheese and wrapped them in bacon.

The main course was ready to serve and the wild-berry crumble was cooking nicely in the oven when Sam appeared by my side. "That smells great, Adam. I will set the table. Adam, we need to talk after supper. I have something to ask you."

The meal was a very quiet affair. My mind was playing tricks on itself, trying to guess what Sam was going to ask me. Sam was also very quiet. She was clearly still thinking of the best way to ask me something. We retired to the lounge area, leaving the dishes for another time. Sam pulled out one of her dwindling supply of Russian vodka bottles and filled two glasses.

"Well, Miss O'Conner, get it of your chest. What did you want to ask me that had to wait until after dinner?"

Sam curled up next to me on the sofa. She was not looking at me, just staring out of the window into the darkness of the night. "Adam, I want you to come to Switzerland with me."

I half turned and stared down at Sam. She continued to watch the darkness. "Is that it? All that build-up for that? Of course I will go with you. You know I would go anywhere with you. I was worried that this was something serious."

Sam was quiet for a few seconds. "Adam, it's not going to be a holiday. Let me explain something before you say anything else." Sam took a slug of her vodka then continued. "Adam, you know that I love you to bits, but I am not a housewife and never will be. I have loved spending time here with you chilling out, but I need to do something. My days with the secret service are over, but I can't just switch off. I need to be doing something that keeps me alive."

Although I was still concerned what Sam might have up her sleeve, I was somewhat relieved. From my point of view, the news could have been so much worse. I had half expected Sam to say she had had enough and send me on my way. Sam pressed on, explaining what she was planning. "I am running low on ammunition for the target range, and you can't just walk into a supermarket and buy that sort of stuff. I need to take a trip to Switzerland. MI6 has a contact there who can supply pretty much whatever you need in terms of armaments."

I digested this information while Sam topped up our vodka rations. "Surely MI6 doesn't buy its weapons from an arms dealer?"

Sam smiled as she returned with the refills. "Adam, you are out of your league. Yes, they do, mainly because Karl Muller has his finger in almost every arms deal on the planet, and he doesn't mind who he sells that information to. MI6 buy their weapons from him to grease the wheels, so to speak. He has given us really good information about our enemies on many occasions. Don't look so worried, Adam. I know what I am doing."

I knew she had her mind made up, and there was no point in trying to change Sam's mind. I had learned from past situations that it would only end up in an argument. It looked like I was going along for the ride. What worried me was that when Sam had done this for a living, she had MI6 to back her up. Get this wrong, and we would be at the bottom of Lake Geneva with cement shoes.

"OK, Sam, you're the boss. Let's change the subject for the moment. Did Peter from Cancer Research call the Invermorroch Hotel to say he had collected the money?"

Sam curled up next to me on the couch. It was clear to see that now the subject of Switzerland was out of the way, she was in a better frame of mind. "Yes, I popped into the hotel on the way back from my run today.

He had left a message with Paul to say he had got the donation, and he had agreed to speak to his superiors to get them to step up testing in the west of Scotland."

Sam and I had made a promise that, after the Machrihanish incident last year, we would try to help. We had watched as the government did little to resolve the radiation problem in the west of Scotland caused by the American base. Just as the MI6 director at that time had predicted, they had tried to brush the problem under the carpet. We could not sit on a fortune in drug money that Sam had found in the glass house, knowing that it could help people with problems near the base. It was hard to believe that only a few years ago, the glass house had belonged to the wife of a Russian drug lord. Sam had been given the mission of eliminating the woman and had come across the papers for the glass house while searching the target's London home after she had been eliminated. Sam had fallen for the house the moment she set eyes on it, and the rest was history. Sam had used the house as a bolt-hole when things got too tough. She had never disclosed the house to her superiors, or the fact that it contained vast sums of Russian drug money. It had been our hideout when the Americans had sent a kill squad to find us and silence the only people who could testify against the wrongdoings at the American air base, and it was now our home.

"Adam, I forgot to tell you. Paul and his wife Margo have invited us down to the Invermorroch Hotel for supper with them sometime. Might not be a bad idea to keep in with the hotel owners as we get all our mail delivered to them."

Sam was right, but we had shied away from local contacts to preserve our secret location on top of the cliff. Paul was a gentleman, but I was not sure that we could keep both our fake identities and past story the same over a prolonged period of contact. No one could find out about my colourful military past with the Special Forces or security services. As for Sam, it was even more important that nobody found out her real identity. She had never returned to the secret service after her vacation, and neither of us knew if we were being hunted by MI5 or MI6. We had been so enchanted with each other's company that we had spent most of the year squirreled away in our glass house by the sea. I had started to reply to Sam when I noticed she was fast asleep with her head in my lap.

Next morning was a cold misty affair. Yet again, I awoke to an empty double bed. At the time, I thought nothing of it until during my morning chores, I noticed that Sam's Beetle was missing from its usual parking space in the ground-floor garage. It was not unusual for Sam to head to the shops herself, but she usually mentioned it or left a note. A quick search of the normal places Sam left her notes proved fruitless. After cleaning the lounge area and kitchen, I headed downstairs to the garage area and gave our two remaining vehicles a coat of wax.

Sam arrived back around lunchtime. She was fired up and desperate to tell me something. "Well, Captain Macdonald, you had better get your bags packed for we are on an afternoon flight to Switzerland tomorrow." It was clear Sam had struck while the iron was hot.

"You didn't let the grass grow under your feet with that one, madam." Sam was watching me closely. She knew she was treading a fine line keeping me on board her project.

"Adam, don't get mad with me. I stopped in at the Invermorroch on the way home and spoke to Paul and Margo. We have a dinner date with them for half past six tonight."

This was typical Sam. I was beginning to realise Sam was always in for a penny, in for a pound. She knew she would probably be in hot water with me for the Switzerland thing so adding the hotel trip made no difference to her.

At six fifteen, we left the glass house to drive the four miles to the Invermorroch hotel on the outskirts of Arisaig. "What's wrong, Adam? You haven't spoken much since I got back. Are you still speaking to me?" Sam half turned in the passenger seat, watching my facial reactions.

"You, madam, are a nightmare at times. Has anyone ever told you your mood swings are out of control?"

Sam thought for a moment before replying. "Yes, as a matter of fact, an Iranian diplomat friend of mine told me that once."

I watched Sam's expression to see if she was kidding me, but she had her poker face on.

"And did you take any heed of your Iranian friend?"

Sam suppressed the urge to smile. "No, I shot him while he lectured me. I don't think he realised how bad my mood swings can be."

Any other person, and I would have said they were pulling my leg, but I knew Sam was telling the truth.

"Adam, we will be fine tonight. It will give us a chance to get used to our cover again before we head for Switzerland and things become more serious."

As with most small communities worldwide, gossip played a major part of village life. As expected, Sam and I were the star attraction in the hotel. People knew of the big house on the coast, and they were very curious as to who lived in it.

Paul was a quiet, polite gentleman. It was clear from the start that Paul wore the trousers in the household, but it was Margo who told him which pair though.

Margo took charge of our interrogation. I marvelled at how Sam immediately fell back into her old ways, putting on an Oscar-winning performance for the benefit of our hosts. Sam's alias, Ann Hunter, was an award-winning artist, while my alias, Alan Hunter, was a freelance journalist who worked away a lot.

I couldn't help thinking to myself this was not a good idea. I just knew that Margo could not leave it at that. It would only be a matter of time until she appeared at the glass-house door. This to me signalled the end of our blissfully peaceful existence.

❖ ❖ ❖

That same evening, in the southern end of Great Britain, Areli Benesch had made her escape from Porton Down, taking with her a hostage by the name of Gary Harding. Her initial intention was to get her bearings, and then, once she had found her way, she would put a bullet in the young guy and head for her adopted home of Monaco. Her initial plan collapsed when Gary Harding spotted the two types of chemical Benesch was guarding jealously.

"Oh my god, how did you…I mean, how could you? You will kill us all. We need to go back. You can't continue. You don't know what you have done."

Areli smiled menacingly at the young man. "I know exactly what I have done. I have secured my escape from this hellhole of a country. You will follow my directions, or you will be the first to die a horrible death."

Gary thought for a moment. There was no point not telling the woman. She needed to know before she wiped out the human race.

"The little glass container must be put back for safekeeping. If you don't, and it gets into the atmosphere, it's the end for us all. Please, you must believe me."

Areli teased him by playing with the vial. Gary could not take his eyes off the Vokxin. On more than one occasion, he almost drove off the road.

"Tell me where you live. Is it close? Also, do you live alone?" Gary was not sure what she was playing at but decided to go along with the questioning, if only to keep the madwoman happy.

"I live with my parents about seven miles from here. They are on vacation in Florida at the moment, so yes at the moment, I live alone."

Areli mulled this over in her head while Gary negotiated the country lanes. She had it pretty much decided that she would let him drive her to his home where she could sort out some type of clothing and get fed and watered.

She would deal with her prisoner when the time came. After twenty minutes, they arrived at the village of Netheravon. A left turn just before entering the village sent them along a dusty farm track. They passed two converted farm steadings before coming to a modern sprawling bungalow complex surrounded by a large hedge. Gary clicked a remote and the wrought-iron gates opened inward, revealing a large front lawn complete with two tennis courts.

Gary watched as Areli surveyed her new surroundings "The tennis courts are there for a reason. They are my mother's. She is a professional tennis coach." Gary pulled up at the front door and switched the car off. "Well, what happens now?"

Areli was still taking in her new surroundings while she talked. "Telling me your name would be a good start. Then you will show me round this house of yours. You will not do anything stupid like trying to contact someone or leaving a message. You will not try to escape, and in return, I will let you live."

Gary was thinking as he opened the front door and let Areli in. All this around him, even his sacred project, they all meant nothing if the crazy woman opened the Vokxin. Gary made a split-second decision. He did not know it at the time, but it was a decision that saved his life.

"My name is Gary, and I have a business proposition for you."

Areli headed for the kitchen. "Gary, you can make us cheese sandwiches while you talk, and I will listen to this proposition." Areli headed for the fridge and downed a full pint of milk while Gary went about preparing the sandwiches. At first, Areli wasn't paying much attention to Gary, but a few words clicked, and she started to listen.

"The Vokxin must go back, and I am willing to cut you in on my discovery fifty-fifty if you give me the Vokxin. My specialty is DNA sequencing. I have been working on altering human DNA to make it adapt to different conditions. I have had some success with this, and I am on the verge of turning the world of biology on its head. Financially, the research is already priceless. We could both be the richest people in the world very soon if you agree to join me and let me take care of the Vokxin."

Areli was struggling to suppress a smile. The kid was delusional, but she decided to play along with his game. "OK, Einstein, tell me how you are going to change the world."

Gary knew she did not believe him, so he pressed on, using plain English to explain in the hope that she would get the rough idea of his discovery. "I have isolated and extracted the DNA chain from two different species that are resistant to radiation. I combined DNA from cockroaches and from these bacteria called *Deinococcus radiodurans* with human DNA to produce human cells that, along with other benefits, are resistant to high doses of radiation."

Areli decided it was time to shoot his fanciful ideas down in flames. "Even if you could prove you have done this, it would still need to go through years of testing before it yielded any profits. That is, of course, if it did actually work."

Gary was young and petulant. He did not like this woman pouring scorn on his obsession. He would show her just how far his research had progressed. He walked over to the knife block and selected a sharp paring knife. Areli clocked this and brought the pistol to bear on the youth just in case he had any ideas of using the knife on her.

"I am already past the test stage and have positive proof my work is a success. One of the spin-off discoveries I have found is that the bacteria named *Deinococcus radiodurans* defends itself from radiation by rapid cell regeneration. This phenomenon seems to have replicated itself in the DNA transfer to human cells. I could not wait for some bunch of old fools in the medical council to grant a test programme. I tested the DNA on myself. I have been stable for the last few months and have seen some amazing results."

The story had now taken the full attention of Areli. "Are you saying you tested your theories on yourself, a real life Dr Jekyll?"

Gary was sure she still did not fully believe his story. "Please watch closely."

Areli watched in horror as the young man carved his name into his own forearm using the paring knife. Gary gritted his teeth. The pain was almost unbearable. The blood ran from the wound, down his upturned arm, and pooled in the sleeve of his sweatshirt. He had to show this woman he was deadly serious, not trying to bluff his way out of a desperate situation. When he could stand the pain no more, he dropped the knife and staggered back to the kitchen table, flinging himself down on a stool before the pain caused him to black out. He curled up, trying to take control of the waves of pain and nausea that threatened to overcome him.

"My god, you stupid young fool! What do you think you are doing? I cannot take you to hospital. You have signed your own death warrant."

Gary could not stand the pain or the woman bleating on in his ear. "Shut up, woman, and watch my arm because I will not do this again."

Areli turned her attention to his name carved deep in the soft flesh of his forearm. The cut had started to go a deep purple colour. The blood had dried and congealed in the open wound and what looked like a ministorm was brewing under the skin of his arm. Areli watched in disbelief as the jagged flaps of skin started to knit themselves together as if someone were pulling an invisible zipper along the joint. Within five minutes, the cut was a pale scar, warm to the touch. Areli was speechless; it was as if she had just watched the hand of god at work before her very eyes.

Gary broke the spell. He was pale and sweating profusely. "Well, I can see from your face you have become a believer. The rapid cell regeneration coded into the DNA repairs the damaged cells a thousand times faster than normal human DNA. If I pull a muscle, it repairs itself almost instantly. I borrowed a quantity of industrial-strength cesium 137 from our lab. It emits high quantities of radioactivity. It should have burned my hands and caused the cells in my body to start breaking down, but it has had no effect."

Gary had run out of steam. His body had worked overtime to repair the tissue damage, and he lapsed into a meditation-like state while his body recovered from the shock. Areli watched as he fell asleep sitting up, his head on the kitchen table. Areli was in a state of shock herself. She had seen some strange things in her life, but this was extraordinary. She sat quietly, contemplating her next move. She had planned to get kitted out and when the time came slit the throat of the youth before slipping away quietly.

Her mind was working overtime. She was no scientist, but she knew what she had just witnessed would turn the world as she knew it upside down. Where things could lead from this discovery...well, it made her head spin just trying to work it out. But the one sure thing she did know was that this young man had to be guarded with her life. There were many governments that would pay a king's ransom for the lad and his research.

Areli contemplated contacting the Israeli government to offer them the young scientist and his research in exchange for a pardon and reinstatement in Mossad. She decided against this. She knew too well how Mossad worked. They would offer her a deal. Then the first time she touched Israeli soil, she would be arrested and flung in jail, and they would take the research anyway. No, she would not fall into that trap. There was a way she could indirectly help her country. Israel's closest ally was the United States, and she knew just the man who would both help her out and take the boy and his research with open arms.

CHAPTER 3

CODE NAME PANDORA

Sir Norman Huntly was digging through a mountain of unfinished paperwork. He was not in the best of humours. His predecessor had retired through ill health and had been somewhat behind on his desk work.

Sir Norman was a control freak. He had run his department in GCHQ with clockwork efficiency. His new appointment to the director's job of MI6 had come as a shock. He had been headhunted by the PM himself. Although he would never admit it, he knew he was like a fish out of water. He would not take the same hands-on approach that the previous director had. His only instruction from the PM was to make sure that Neil Andrews, the previous second in command, was given a task that would ensure he was well away from the helm. Rumours had circulated that a previous case in Scotland that Neil Andrews had headed up had caused the PM huge amounts of embarrassment. Obviously, the PM had not forgotten this.

True to his word, Sir Norman had replaced Andrews with his old second in command at GCHQ. Andrews had been moved to training and development, charged with bringing a below-strength MI6 back up to speed. As he shuffled around papers on his desk a slip of paper broke free and floated down onto the newly fitted deep-pile Axminster carpet. Huntly bent down with some effort and retrieved the slip. His new secretary had handed it to him with some urgency. He had put it to one side. To him it made little sense. He was waiting for his second in command to arrive so he could give him the task of finding out the meaning of the message. He read it one more time, trying to make sense of it.

> CODE NAME PANDORA REPEAT CODE NAME PANDORA. PLEASE ADVISE ACTION REQUIRED PORTON DOWN LOCKED DOWN AWAITING YOUR INSTRUCTION. COMMANDING OFFICER 42 COMMANDO RATED PRIORITY ONE REPEAT PRIORITY ONE.

For a second he thought about leaving it for his number two to deal with but the words priority one stuck in his mind. He lifted the phone and called his equal number at MI5. After all, Porton Down was on British soil so really it was a matter for MI5, not his MI6. Sir Norman did not get the response from Bill Mathews, the director of MI5, that he was expecting.

After repeating the message word for word over the phone, there was a deathly silence. "Norman, I will be there as soon as possible. You should have a file some place safe regarding Porton Down and its codes. Try and find it. Then get the officer who sent that message on the phone. For god's sake man, do you not know that a priority one message means a threat to national security? It has to be actioned immediately, it has only ever been issued four times in the history of this country, and out of those, twice was when we issued a declaration of war."

❖ ❖ ❖

Lieutenant Colonel Patterson had been the officer commanding 42 Commando for the last two years. In that time, he had never been as frustrated as he was at that moment. He had arrived on the scene in the early hours of that morning. After consultation with the duty sergeant, he had questioned the young woman at length. She was in a state of shock but had managed to describe how a madwoman had killed her boss and escaped with chemicals stored on site by the MOD. He had found her story hard to believe, but the fact that the Porton Down unit had sealed itself off from the world, and he had a Royal Marine commando fighting for his life in intensive care, persuaded him to proceed with extreme caution. He positioned the thirty-seven men at his disposal at various points, effectively blocking off all access within a mile radius of the stricken building. After his call to the Ministry of Defence was passed around various offices, it finally landed on the desk of someone who knew a bit about the sealed building. The unknown voice asked questions that Lieutenant Colonel Patterson could not answer.

Eventually he let Karen Lowe, the girl he had quizzed, speak to the voice. He could only hear her side of the conversation, but it was clear all was not going well. "I am Dr Karen Lowe, and no, you can't speak to Professor Ferry. He is in the sealed building, so I suspect he is dead. Diavokxin. Diavokxin, of course I'm sure. Is there something wrong with your hearing? Diavokxin. No, the Vokxin has been taken. OK. Colonel Patterson, he wants to speak to you."

Patterson took the phone from the girl's hand.

"Colonel Patterson, I will contact MI6, and they will be in charge from now on. Under no circumstances should you or any other person enter that building. There will be a decontamination team there as soon as possible. They will identify themselves with the password CODENAME PANDORA. It is imperative that only that team tries to enter the building. You are authorised to use lethal force if required to maintain a secure perimeter around the building."

The last comment surprised Patterson. "Very well, but I need to know your name and rank please." There was silence. The voice had gone.

Colonel Patterson and his men had spent all of the morning and the best part of the afternoon waiting. Eventually, three white unmarked vans arrived at the roadblock. After giving the correct password, they were admitted to the sealed-off building where Patterson and Dr Lowe met the decontamination team. Their team leader was called Captain Smith. He was a no-nonsense type of guy and wasted no time with pleasantries. "Dr Lowe, I need to speak to you in private, if you don't mind. Please walk with me to the main entrance of the building."

Karen Lowe put up no objections. She was physically and emotionally drained from her ordeal. She just wanted to curl up and go to sleep and wake up to find none of this was real, and it was just all a bad nightmare. As they walked, Captain Smith studied Dr Lowe with interest. "Forgive me, Dr Lowe, but exactly what are you a doctor of?"

Karen Lowe had this question put to her before and had been half expecting it. "I finished my studies last year and have a doctorate in biomedical science with a specialist diploma from Cambridge in clinical chemistry. I was the newest member of Professor Ferry's team and was headhunted by him."

Captain Smith gave a low whistle. "Wow, sorry to offend you, but you look very young to have those types of credentials."

Karen didn't hide the fact she was less than pleased with the interrogation. "I am used to it, Captain, but the fact is I am young and bloody clever as well. So what do you want to know from me?"

Smith stopped outside the main entrance and studied the door as he spoke. "Start by telling me the whole story from the beginning."

Karen Lowe had already told her story twice, but hoping that she would get to go home, she started again. She described how the woman had gained entry to the lab, how she had attacked the professor as he tried to grab the gun, and how she had forced Karen to tell her the truth about the forgotten Cold War chemicals. She described how she managed to grab the oxygen mask before the chemicals entered her lungs. She had been lucky; she managed to duck under the chemical-leak-protection shutters as they slammed to the ground in the hope of cutting off the chemical's progress. She had explained that in simulations, she had been taught by the professor to get out the front door fast. She knew there was only a five-second delay between the inner doors being sealed and the front door chemical shutters coming down.

Captain Smith listened intently to her story, letting her tell it without interruption. "Karen, this is very important life-or-death stuff. On the way down this morning, I was brought up to date on the two chemicals we could be dealing with. Are you positive that the vial that was opened in the lab was Diavokxin? There is no way you could be mistaken? Karen, I know you are not a stupid girl, but you had suffered a major shock to your system. In the heat of the moment, could you have been mistaken? You know what will happen if we open this place up and find out it was Vokxin that was spilled, not Diavokxin."

Dr Karen Lowe glared at Smith. She was tired and very close to the end of her tether. "Captain Smith, I and my colleagues have been working flat out to find a way to get rid of this horrific thing that we created. I have been working in close proximity to it every day. I have seen with my own eyes the terrible effects it causes, and it still terrifies me to even enter the lab that houses it. Do you really think I would make a mistake in identifying it? What is in the lab is not the problem. The problem is what is out there in the hands of a madwoman. If she opens it or drops it by mistake, it's over. Mankind has no answer for it. Believe me, Captain. I know. I have tried everything."

Captain Smith was busy checking the seals around the door and window frames. "Karen, do you know when the building was last leak checked? Forget that last statement. If it were leaking, it wouldn't matter. We would all be dead by now. Well, going by your qualifications, I am sure you will already know that there are no records of Diavokxin lasting more than twenty-four hours. So by my reckoning we should be safe to open the place up and hand it over to MI6 by ten this evening. That is, if MI6 ever show up. Bit of a poor show I'm afraid considering this place is now run by them."

Karen was trying to keep her head clear but the conversation had lost her now. "Wait a minute. Go back a few sentences. What do you mean by there are no records of Diavokxin lasting more than twenty-four hours? Diavokxin was never used; it is a Cold War chemical. And come to think of it, MI6 has nothing to do with this research facility. You must be mistaken."

Captain Smith smiled at Karen, the type of smile that told her he knew something she didn't. "My poor Dr Lowe, you are not having a good day, are you? The problem you have is that you are a very smart woman but out there in the real world, life isn't as simple as in your laboratory world. The things you do in the lab actually kill people in the real world. The people that pay your and your colleagues' wages are the people who use them. Karen, this is an MI6 facility, no maybes about it. If you think you are having a bad day now, just wait until they arrive."

❖ ❖ ❖

Sir Norman Huntly and Bill Mathews hadn't yet made it out of the London traffic before the call from Number Ten turned them around. Ten minutes later, they were standing in the prime minister's study. Bill Mathews was just starting to look around the study when the door burst open and a very agitated PM barged in behind them. He wasted no time and addressed Sir Norman first.

"Norman, I believe we have a very grave situation on our hands. What can you tell me about it, and what plan have you put in place to deal with it?"

Sir Norman was like a rabbit caught in the headlamps. He had no answer or real clue what he was dealing with yet.

Bill Mathews was no fool. He knew the PM wanted answers, and he wanted them now. Luckily for him, it seemed to be an MI6 problem, so for the moment he was off the hook. He was content to stand and watch Sir Norman slowly hang himself. "Prime Minister, the Porton Down incident has only just come to light. We were on our way to find out what we could about it."

Far from pacifying the PM, his statement only poured petrol on the flames. "Good god, man. You have had the information since early morning. Thank god the MOD had the good sense to inform me. When were you going to tell me? Or were you going to wait until I had seen it on the evening news? Bill, please wait outside. I have someone you need to talk to. You will be assisting him, and he will be with you shortly." Without a word, Bill nodded and stepped into the next room. "Sir Norman, you have let us all down, I need more from the head of MI6. I require your resignation on my desk now, please. The PM waited until Sir Norman Huntly had closed the door and spoke on the intercom. Two seconds later, there was a knock on the door as it opened. "Come in, Andrews, and sit down."

Neil Andrews had been whipped away from his desk at light speed. No matter who or how many times he asked, nobody would divulge what this rapidly prepared meeting was about. Neil was not easily intimidated, but both men knew that they were enemies, and Neil was racking his brain to think what other punishment the PM had lined up for him.

"Neil, I think we need to clear the air before we go any further. We both know you caused me a lot of problems with the Machrihanish incident. It could have been handled better. I am prepared to forget it—but you must be prepared to hide nothing from me in the future. Do I make myself clear?"

Neil Andrews was no fool. He knew if he wanted to save his career, he had to concede some ground to the PM. "Sir, with respect, it was not my intention to mislead Parliament. You must remember at that time we knew we had a spy high in the government. We could not risk telling the truth at that time."

The PM stood up and started pacing backward and forward. Neil sensed he would do better to keep quiet and let the PM have a moment.

"OK Neil, I can't believe I am doing this, and you won't believe it either. I will give you one chance to prove your mettle. As from now, you are acting director of MI6. If you get the job done, you have my word that you will be the new director of MI6, and if you don't, it won't matter anyway because we will all be dead."

Bill Mathews had waited for half an hour in the adjoining office when the door opened, and Neil Andrews stepped in. "Right, Bill, it would appear we have a bit of work to be catching up with. Are you up for it?"

For a second, Bill was shocked, but then reality dawned on him. "You of all people, my god! The PM must be in trouble if he has had to resort to the person he hates with a vengeance. On the bright side, thank god you're here. I take it Sir Norm got the heave ho then. Should never have been given the job in the first place. Had not a clue. Welcome back, old son."

Thirty minutes later they were taking off from the London heliport after a short police boat trip down the Thames from Westminster Pier.

The military Lynx helicopter lifted clear of the helipad, then swung its nose sharply to the left. The pilot vigorously applied full throttle, and they were on their way. The intercom crackled into life, and both passengers were surprised to find that their pilot was female. "Gentlemen, air traffic have cleared us a direct path to Boscombe Down, where you will be picked up by car and taken to Porton Down."

Neil Andrews thought for a minute, then tapped the pilot on the shoulder. "Forget the car. Take us directly to Porton Down please. You can land this thing on the main road and wait for us."

The pilot hesitated before replying. She knew who she was dealing with. "Negative, sir, it's too dangerous. We could hit a telephone wire or a power cable. Better if we land at Boscombe, sir."

Neil Andrews was having none of it. "Pilot, you misunderstand me. That was not a request. It was a direct order. I will deal with any consequences arising from our change of flight plan."

❖ ❖ ❖

Lieutenant Colonel Patterson had just checked in with his perimeter patrols. His sergeant had just handed out cups of tea to Captain Smith and Karen Lowe when the shrill engine note of the Lynx helicopter broke the eerie silence that enveloped the Porton Down complex. All three watched as the tiny black dot in the distance grew rapidly in size. It was clear to see that the new arrival was in hurry. The chopper banked steeply, did one circuit, then the pilot dropped the Lynx expertly on the T-junction directly outside the complex. No sooner than the engines had been powered down the doors opened and Andrews stepped out followed by Mathews. Colonel Patterson strode forward to meet the new arrivals while Captain Smith remained with Karen Lowe by the stricken research building. "Well, Dr Lowe, here is your chance to meet your real employers. I don't think they dropped in for a cup of tea. This will be a steep learning curve for us all I think." Colonel Patterson introduced the new arrivals to Captain Smith and Karen Lowe.

Neil Andrews wasted no time. "I take it from your attire, Captain, you are our chemical specialist. I need to know when we can enter the building." He turned his attention to Karen. "What level of security clearance do you have, and what is your reason for being here, please?"

Karen had only met the man for five minutes, and already she had formed the opinion he was a dangerous man to cross swords with. "I am Dr Karen Lowe, and I have level one clearance. I was a witness to the attack on the lab. I work in the lab."

Neil Andrews decided that all those present held sufficiently high clearances that he could speak freely. "OK, let's not beat about the bush, please. At any point, if I am wrong, step in and correct me while I go over what I understand happened here. A single person broke into the lab and has got away with what I believe is an undisclosed chemical that has the potential to cause a global catastrophe. During their escape, some of this chemical leaked in the building behind us, and a soldier who tried to stop the perpetrator was shot and wounded. Captain, when you go in, you need to know on the far side of the building there is a holding facility for criminals under investigation by the security services. Normally, there are always three guards on duty at all times, and at the moment, I believe there are three prisoners. Under no circumstances enter the cells without my say-so."

Karen had listened to what Neil Andrews had to say before wading in with her contribution. "Mr Andrews, there are a few things that you have said that need some clarification. There were two chemicals taken—nine vials of Diavokxin, and one vial of Vokxin. The tenth vial of Diavokxin was smashed deliberately to kill everybody in the building. The other thing you need to know is that I am pretty sure it was one of your prisoners that carried out the attack. She identified herself to me as Areli, and she said she had stolen the uniform because she had been held captive for a long time. I hope that sheds a bit more light on the situation for you."

Neil Andrews was trying his level best to maintain the appearance that he was calm and in control. On the inside, it was a very different matter. His heart was racing, and he could feel the beads of cold sweat forming on his back and his forehead. He was the man that had placed Areli Benesch in this detention facility, and he was fully aware that this ex-Mossad agent was very bad news even before she had the means to wage chemical warfare and a very big axe to grind with the British secret service. It was just possible that his actions could cost thousands, if not millions of innocent lives. He needed to regroup. This news had shocked him. "Bill, I want you to stay here and take charge. We need to confirm who is inside once the captain opens the place up. Dr Lowe, you are coming with me as my advisor. I hope you like fast helicopters."

Karen began to protest. "Mr Andrews, I am dead on my feet. I've been up through the night not to mention surviving a chemical attack and an attack by a madwoman. You will need to get yourself another advisor."

Neil Andrews put his arm around her shoulders. "Sorry, doctor, but no is not an option. Being dead on your feet is better than being dead full stop, don't you think? Come. Our chariot awaits us."

Neil Andrews bundled Karen Lowe into the back of the Lynx, then joined the pilot in the front seat. Taken by surprise, she had not had time to put her helmet back on.

Neil took advantage of his situation to speak to her before she fired up the Lynx. "Please forgive my ignorance. I did not ask your name when we first boarded. My name is Neil Andrews." Neil leaned across and shook her gloved hand.

"Captain Fiona Malden, sir. I already knew who you were. I was briefed before takeoff." Fiona started to prep the Lynx for takeoff, going through a quick pre-flight ritual.

"Captain Malden, if you don't mind, I will call you Fiona. Can you first of all take us back to the heliport and arrange for a car to take us to Vauxhall Cross. Then I want you to take this machine and fill her up and do anything else it needs then head back to the heliport. I am commandeering your services for the moment. I need you on twenty-four-hour standby at the heliport. Any problems with that, Fiona?"

Malden smiled as she pulled on her helmet. "None at all, sir, but I am sure my commanding officer will have something to say about it. Buckle up, folks. Takeoff in two minutes."

During the return flight, Neil had time to think of a way to approach this situation he now found himself in. Captain Malden brought her Lynx in to land at the heliport. Her touchdown was sheer precision. Even Andrews, who had spent a fair bit of time being whisked from place to place in choppers marvelled at her flying skills. Andrews and Karen Lowe transferred to the unmarked Range Rover. Ten seconds later, Karen watched as Neil Andrews sprang into action. He called MI6 headquarters at Vauxhall Cross, and a few seconds later, his call was answered. "Hi Jean, it's Neil Andrews here. As you must know by now, I have replaced Sir Norman. That makes you my PA now. Sorry to dump this on you so suddenly, but I need a few things sorted, and they can't wait until tomorrow. Firstly, I have a young lady with me. We are going to have to find her secure accommodation from tonight. Secondly, I need you to stay on, and I need as many analysts who are in the building to remain there until I get in. I need everything you can find on Areli Benesch, and you need to lock down the building. There is a real threat of an imminent chemical attack on our building. You need to get hold of the PM's secretary and tell the PM to expect a call from me very soon. And finally I need to get in touch with either Adam Macdonald or Samantha O'Conner. I have a hunch when you find one, you will have found the other. I would suggest you check Scotland first. I will be with you shortly."

Jean had been the MI6 director's PA for the last ten years. She was a well-oiled machine. The minute the phone went dead she set about the tasks given to her.

❖ ❖ ❖

Karen awoke the next morning to find that there was already a chauffer waiting for her the house she had been dropped off at the night before. She had found out on the way to the flat that it belonged to a MI6 agent called Samantha O'Conner who had been missing for some time. Karen had checked the house for food, but it had been emptied of all foodstuffs. She had eventually given in and gone to bed starving. On the way back to Vauxhall Cross, she had managed to sweet-talk her chauffer into stopping at a corner shop so she could pick up a couple of filled rolls.

The driver popped into the shop, leaving Karen in the car listening to Radio 2. As Karen listened, the eight o'clock news started. Karen listened intently, but there were no stories of mass chemical disasters. It would appear the madwoman was behaving herself for the moment.

On arriving at MI6, Karen was ushered downstairs to the basement. Neil Andrews welcomed her into his spacious new office. "Karen, I think the best way we can do this is if you pull up a chair and just listen to the proceedings, and if you feel you can add something or help in any way, feel free to butt in. All suggestions are very welcome."

Karen didn't have to wait long. The phone rang, and Neil put it on loudspeaker. It was Bill Mathews on the line with the first news of the day. He sounded dead on his feet. He had been up all night checking the lab and its occupants. "OK, I will copy you a full report when I get back to my office, but here is a rundown of the situation in Porton Down. It has been confirmed that the attacker was none other than Areli Benesch. After Captain Smith opened the lab we discovered five dead bodies in the detention wing, one dead body in the lab, and one dead body in the reception. Unfortunately, the marine who was wounded passed away during the night. So that means the only living witness to this mess is Dr Lowe."

There was a pregnant pause. Mathews had more to tell, but it was as if he was reluctant to do so. "Neil, the five dead in the detention centre included two guards and a cleaner who were killed by Benesch. The other two fatalities were caused by the Diavokxin. They were the prisoners. One was a computer hacker, but the other was the son of Khanjar." There was silence in the office.

Karen looked at Neil Andrews for some clue as to who this Khanjar was. "OK, Bill, thanks for that. Any idea where to start looking for Benesch?" Neil was pale. For the second time in two days, he had suffered a nasty shock to his system. The shit had well and truly hit the fan, and he was the man who had to try and sort this god-awful mess out.

"No, Neil, not at the moment. I have every person in MI5 out there looking. We still have some CCTV footage that we requisitioned to analyse. It may provide some clues. I will get back to you ASAP. Speak to you soon."

Karen waited until Bill Mathews rang off and then asked her question. "Can I ask who Khanjar is, or would you have to shoot me if you told me?"

Neil was deep in thought for a few seconds. "Don't suppose it will matter if we are all dead anyway. Khanjar is Al Qaeda's main man in the northern hemisphere. We captured his son trying to set off a dirty bomb in Canary Wharf. We have been using him to ward off any further Al Qaeda attacks on Britain. Tell me, Dr Lowe. What do you think would happen if Khanjar found out his son had died in our custody? We have never been able to track Khanjar down. Even his most ardent supporters only whisper his name. He isn't called Khanjar for nothing. The word is Arabic, and it means *curved dagger*. Anyone who has ever spoken out against him or has tried to inform on him has been found with his throat cut."

The phone rang again. This time it was Neil's PA on loudspeaker. "Mr Andrews, it's Jean. I need to update you on some of your requests, if you don't mind, sir."

Neil Andrews hovered over the top of his intercom as he spoke. "Fire away, Jean. I have you on loudspeaker so Dr Lowe can listen in."

"Very good sir. I have a call for you with the PM in five minutes' time, and we are still at a loss as to how to trace the whereabouts of Samantha O'Conner and Adam Macdonald. They have not used any cards or mobile phones. They have no fixed abode, so that side of the investigation has ground to a halt."

Neil thought for a second. "OK, Jean, get Peter Kent in here right away. He trained Sam. He should be able to track her down."

There was a pause on the other end of the line before Jean came back on. "Sir, that will take a bit of time. He is off the radar in France training the new lad."

"OK, Jean, see what you can do. Put me through to the PM. We better not keep his lordship waiting any longer." Andrews briefed the PM on the present situation and left him the unenviable task of contacting his allies and informing them of the unfolding disaster.

❖ ❖ ❖

The president had just finished a reception for the installation of the new Israeli ambassador to the United States when his chief of staff ushered him to the phone in the Oval Office. "Mr President, you need to take this call. It may be very important."

"Good morning, Prime Minister. What can I do for you this morning?" The president listened, and as the conversation progressed, his mood darkened until he could hold his temper no longer. "Prime Minister, you have some nerve to tell me not to worry, while you have broken god knows how many international laws by keeping this chemical unannounced. Which was bad enough. But now you are telling me you have let someone steal it from under your very noses, and you can't find the thief. Your country's incompetence astounds me. You have one week to find this chemical. If you don't, I will send my own teams across to deal with the threat. It may be in your country, but it affects my country, so you need to keep my chief of staff up to date. Good day, sir."

CHAPTER 4

BASEL

Luke Smith was parked up opposite the café in the centre of Basel. He had been on surveillance for the last hour. He had followed Karl Muller's right-hand man to the café from the chateau on the hill on the outskirts of the town. For two months now, he had followed this giant of a man to and from this café to the chateau as he vetted and ferried passengers to his boss who then concluded whatever arms deal had been arranged. Although to the visitors it would appear Nico the giant was alone, the truth was very different. In a Mercedes parked in the lane was Nico's backup team. They were Triads and had been part of a deal to supply their gang with Heckler and Koch machine guns. Luke had photographed all the visitors in the last two months, and Peter Kent had checked all the visitors, looking for one man or a lead to finding him. Khanjar was their target, but it was not an easy task when you didn't know what he looked like. Luke looked on as the big man ordered a pot of tea. Luke chuckled to himself. How could such a macho giant of a man drink a pot of tea? The image was all wrong.

Just as the giant had poured his second cup of tea, a man and woman sat down opposite Nico. Luke Smith almost dropped the camera when it focused on the woman's features. It had been some months, but Luke knew the pair well. He had been part of the team that had been sent to protect Adam Macdonald. Here he was with his former bodyguard, as large as life.

Sam had lost a few pounds, but it was unmistakably her. She had vanished after the case had been closed on the incident at the American air base.

❖ ❖ ❖

We had flown in that morning. Sam had done all the talking at the airport. With the aid of my sketchy knowledge of the French language, I had got the bones of the conversation with the customs officer. Sam had stuck to the story we had agreed on the flight. We were business partners who were talking to a company in Basel about exporting their goods to England. Sam explained that I was recovering from throat cancer and spoke very little French. I marvelled at Sam's skill in telling the story. She had known that I would not be comfortable with the spy business, and true to form, I was chalk white and perspiring badly. To the trained custom officer's eye, I would be a sitting duck to be stopped and quizzed as to my intentions. Sam's fabricated story covered my physical state beautifully.

The customs officer glanced in my direction but passed us through quickly, apologising for holding us up and wishing us good luck with our business venture. A twenty-minute taxi drive from the airport delivered us to the heart of Basel. Sam said very little in the taxi but held my hand, squeezing it tightly, and giving me a naughty wink when the taxi driver wasn't looking. It was clear to see Sam was in her element. She was completely at ease in her new role. I on the other hand was a complete bag of nerves. If it were not for the fact that Sam was with me, I would have bolted before I even got on the plane. On arriving at the café, Sam led me to a window seat and signalled for us to sit down next to one of the biggest guys I had seen for a very long time. Sam made the introductions, but the big guy seemed less than pleased to see us. It took him all his time to answer Sam's questions. He had taken an unhealthy interest in me and was looking me up and down and asking Sam questions that were clearly about me. After a few minutes more, quizzing Sam this time in German, Nico decided he needed to call his boss for some reason. I had no clue what was being said. Unfortunately, I had never taken German and was relying on Sam, who spoke fluent German, to keep me right.

Sam waited until Nico had stepped outside to call his boss before talking to me. "Adam, he has decided to call his boss because he did not want you to come to the chateau. He does not trust you. He was trying to get me to leave you here and go on alone. I have told him you come or there will be no deal tonight. Nico is Karl Muller's bodyguard and head of security. If he says no,

Karl Muller will walk away from any deal. Nico has saved his life on many occasions. When we leave here, watch out for the Merc parked in the side street. It is full of Nico's backup squad."

Before Sam could say more, Nico returned and started barking demands at Sam while still giving me the evil eye. Sam got up and signalled me to follow her. Nico stood at the door and ushered us out into the street. The minute he set foot on the street, a black Mercedes pulled up at the kerb in front of the café. Nico ushered us into the car, giving Sam the front seat along with the driver and pointing to the back seat where I was to be his travelling companion. I avoided eye contact with the monster as he held the door open for me. No sooner had we sat down then the car sped away, followed closely by the second Merc from the side street. Karl Muller obviously wanted to see us after all. On the trip to the chateau, I went over in my head the discussion Sam and I had while waiting in the airport for our flight to board. Sam had talked at length about Muller's operation. She had warned me that as soon as we were in Muller's chateau, we would be put under the microscope to find out who we were and what we needed the munitions for. Muller's arms sales were only part of his business empire. As soon as he had sold the weapons, he moved onto his second—and almost as lucrative—venture: selling the info of who had bought the weapons and where they were to be used. Muller was well in with all the world's major intelligence agencies.

You could bet ten minutes after the Hamas bought weapons, Muller would be on the phone to his contact at Mossad to offer him intel on the weapons and where they were going and what for—all, of course, at the usual fee agreed to by Mossad.

My hands were cold but sweating badly. I was sure the little gadgets that Sam had placed on my fingers would come off with the sweat. I decided I was not cut out for this type of work. I was dreading the next part of the operation. Sam was still in her element as she chatted away in German to the driver of the Mercedes. As we left Basel, we travelled along a snow-covered valley. Then, after a few miles, we turned left off the main road onto a snow-covered farm road. The road twisted and turned for a few miles, gradually climbing into the hills on the east side of the valley. The two Mercedes cars squirmed their way up the track, sliding sideways dangerously close to a drop-off into a stream far below. It was a relief when we turned up onto the front courtyard of the chateau, which also doubled as a helipad for Karl Muller's Bell Jet Ranger helicopter.

I thought to myself that business must be booming. Muller would have no change out of a million dollars for that baby. Sam caught my eye as I looked out at the helicopter and sneaked me a cheeky wink as our hosts busied themselves getting out of the cars.

We were ushered into the large front hall where our hosts set about checking us for contraband. Nico was dead set on making sure I knew he didn't like me. He started to frisk me down while his wingman, a badly burned Triad who went by the name of Tong, started to frisk Sam. Nico stared into my eyes and used much more force than was necessary, trying to provoke a reaction from me. Sam was staring across the room at me, willing me to stay calm and not blow the contract. I watched as Tong frisked Sam down. He was taking great pleasure in spending far too much time examining Sam's more intimate parts, again trying to provoke a reaction from her. Sam said nothing and stared into space, only the slight flush on her cheeks giving away the fact she was trying to control her emotions.

Although I could handle Nico's childish attempts at trying to wind me up, Tong was a different matter. I was having problems controlling my actions. Tong didn't realise it, but he was playing with fire. If I didn't kill him, for sure Sam would break his neck and not even blink doing it.

After a few more seconds, Muller's henchmen gave up, and Nico somewhat disappointedly led us to a room to the right, leading off from the hall. The room was magnificently decked out with a cream carpet, and there were blue silk drapes hanging from the surrounding walls. The furniture would have made centre stage on the *Antiques Roadshow*—so much so that I was frightened to touch anything in case I damaged it. A few seconds later, a butler in full *Upstairs Downstairs* costume appeared and, in perfect English, offered us drinks or tea or coffee. He proffered a tray of sandwiches cut into tiny triangles and left us alone. Sam wandered round the room examining everything.

I was about to speak, but Sam put her finger to her lips, gesturing me to keep quiet. Sam wandered across to me, still checking out her surroundings. She drew close to me as she wandered past her voice was a low whisper. "Be careful what you say. We are being listened to and probably filmed as well. Make sure all your fingertips are still on."

My prints would not give many clues away as my records had previously been destroyed by MI6 in an attempt to stop the IRA mole in the government finding out who I was. Sam was a different story. If our government didn't have her prints, it was a pretty safe bet some foreign intelligence agency would.

Sam had been, for the last few years, Britain's most active field agent. Careful as she was, there must have been some point in the past when her prints had been linked to her. I did not relish the thought of Muller finding out who she was and handing her back to the British secret service or even worse, handing her to Russia or some other power she had crossed swords with.

Sam's little finger gadgets were thin pieces of latex coated with a chemical that, when in contact with skin, melted into the tiny ridges of the finger, obliterating the fingerprint while still giving the impression that the hand was bare. Hopefully, Sam would remain anonymous to the weapons dealer. As time passed, the tension in the room started to build. What was taking so long? Sam seemed more at ease, but I was like a cat on a hot tin roof. I wanted out, and it couldn't come soon enough.

❖ ❖ ❖

Luke Smith's brain was in turmoil. He was new to the job, and he had been presented with a situation that was not in the handbook. At some distance, he had followed the two Mercedes as far as the road ending at the chateau. He did not want to push his luck and continue up the farm road. He knew from previous trips that it only led to the chateau and no further. He stopped and tried to make sense of it all. He knew he should have reported to his senior officer, but Peter Kent had been recalled to London that morning on urgent business. There was also another reason Luke hesitated to contact his superiors. Sam had saved his life. When she found he was about to be ambushed by an Israeli assassin, although her gun was jammed, she had charged down the assassin and disarmed her, at considerable risk to herself.

Luke had decided to wait and see what Sam and Adam were up to before he told anyone. He felt that he owed her one. Also, during his training at Hereford when he had served in the Special Air Service, Adam had been his instructor and commanding officer for a time. It did not feel right that he should blow the whistle on the missing secret service agent and her partner just yet.

Luke had only been a MI6 operative for the last six months. He had been drafted into MI6 to fill the gap as MI6 had lost some of its team during the Machrihanish incident and was at low strength. Luke had been working with Sam as part of Adam Macdonald's protection detail. After the incident was over, Neil Andrews had been moved to training. When he found out that Luke's cockney family roots actually crossed the water to France, and Luke had spent part of his youth with his aunt and spoke fluent French, he was a man in demand. Although Luke had no desire to join the secret service, he was given little choice. Andrews had contacted his commanding officer and requested his transfer to MI6. The paperwork and training was completed much more quickly than normal due to the manpower crisis at Vauxhall Cross, and here he was, less than a year later, a fully qualified member of the spook brigade.

❖ ❖ ❖

A full hour after being admitted to the waiting room, the door sprung open and Nico, with his usual scowling face, appeared and led Sam and myself up the gilt spiral staircase to the first floor. Nico knocked on the heavy double doors, then entered without waiting for a response. The room had probably been a ballroom at one point in the history of the Swiss chateau. Times had changed. Glass display cases adorned the room. They were dotted around in no order or design. In each case was displayed various state-of-the-art weaponry. As we were led through the maze of military hardware, I spotted a few examples that proved that our host was not just some pawnbroker of military hardware. In one case was displayed the new Remington ACR. In another was the Beretta ARX160. Neither of these weapons had been released for sale and to my knowledge had only ever been seen in the pages of magazines. Muller was no small-time gun pedlar; he was a big-time player in the arms industry. My next shock came as Nico led us to a desk by the window in the top corner of the room. Muller sat at the desk and glanced up from the computer screen only fleetingly as Nico told us to sit down. The picture I had in my head of Muller was about as far away from the real thing as you could get. He could have passed for an accountant or a lawyer but not the pinnacle of an arms empire.

"Mrs Hunter, I am a very busy man, so if we can dispense with the formalities, I would be grateful. Please tell me what you need, and I will tell you if it is possible and the cost."

"First of all, thank you for meeting with us at short notice. My husband and I are in the personal protection business and require some new weapons for an overseas contract. You were recommended to us by a member of the British secret service. I have a list here of the equipment we require." Sam handed the list over to Muller, who lifted a pair of reading glasses and gave the note a quick once-over before tossing it onto the desk and returning to his computer screen.

"Why do you want the equipment delivered to Britain when it is to be used overseas? Where do you plan to use it and when? And what was the name of the person who recommended me?" Muller looked away from the computer and stared over the top of his glasses at Sam, waiting for her response.

I watched Sam with interest. She held Muller's gaze, not flinching or faltering in her reply once. "My dear Mr Muller, we both know I would never give away the identity of a British agent. It's not good for business. The final date for the project has not been set, but it involves a trip to Iran. The reason I need the weapons delivered to the UK is because I need to train staff, so I need the consignment delivered quickly and without the authorities impounding my weapons. I have been told you have the ability to deliver anywhere in the world, no questions asked. So, Karl, can you help us?"

Muller gave a half smile and pushed himself away from the desk and his beloved computer screen, revealing the wheelchair he sat in. "Mrs Hunter, I can supply the Glocks, the assault rifles, ammunition, and grenades, no problem, and as you pointed out, I can deliver them wherever needed, but the cost of doing it all covertly is not cheap. For your list, I would need half a million US dollars. Can your contract cover a cost like that?"

I knew what Sam had on her list: six of the latest Glocks, four assault rifles, four cases of ammunition for each type, and two cases of grenades. I reckoned you would have change out of twenty thousand dollars, even taking into account the cost of smuggling of the weapons into Britain. Muller was making an obscene profit.

With some difficulty, I held my tongue and let Sam handle the situation. "I think we can afford that, but I must insist on cash on delivery. I am sure you will understand that I need the goods in my possession before I hand over such a large sum of money."

Muller had not expected this reply. He had obviously banked on us rejecting the expensive deal. For a second, it had taken the wind out of his sails. He regrouped quickly. "Very well, we have a deal. Now I must ask you to leave as I have a very important business deal this evening and have to prepare for it. Send me the details of where and when you want the merchandise delivered, and I will see to it. Good-bye, Mrs Hunter." Muller pressed a button on his desk, and two seconds later, the English-speaking butler arrived and escorted us back to the waiting room.

Nico did not leave the room with them. Instead he approached the desk and waited for Muller to address him. "Nico, our two guests intrigue me. I have the analysis of the room contents. No fingerprints anywhere and no hit yet on the face recognition computer. I do not like it, my friend, not one little bit. It has to be linked to Khanjar's arrival here tonight. I can take no risks. Take your men, and dispose of them before Khanjar arrives."

The butler told Sam and me that Nico was bringing the car to the door for us. I was desperate to get the hell out of this house and, for that matter, this country as well. I consoled myself with the fact that this time tomorrow, I would be back in my beloved Scotland, and this entire cloak and dagger nonsense would be over. Sam was checking the room for hidden cameras and microphones when my eyes started to water, and I took my first breath of tear gas. I tried to shout a warning to Sam, but it was too late. My entire body was in convulsions. In an attempt to break free from this hellish atmosphere, I threw my full weight against the big bay windows, but my weakened state and the triple-glazed window held me. I fell to the floor, searching for fresh air when the first blow hit me hard—first in the stomach, then my head. I curled up and did as much as possible to stop the blows damaging me further. I tried to fight it, but I took one blow too many to the head, and the darkness descended upon me.

The first thing I heard as my senses started to return was Sam's voice. At first, it was just words, but then my jumbled brain started to bring them together. Sam was in panic mode. We were in the boot of a vehicle travelling somewhere. Sam was freaking out because she couldn't get me to wake up. I was groggy and thinking of something to say when with a lurch the car stopped. After a few footsteps, the boot was opened revealing a star-encrusted winter sky. The chill of the winter night entered the boot and cleared the remaining cobwebs from my battered head. Sam was dragged unceremoniously out of the boot by her hair and flung on the ground at the rear of the car. Her legs and wrists were tied together, as were mine. I sat up and started to shimmy my way to the edge of the boot, but the heel of Nico's boot sent me flying back. I watched helplessly as four of Nico's mates pulled Sam to her feet and started to drag her toward a log cabin by a lake.

Nico was in his element. He leaned into the boot. "Do not worry, my friend. Your wife will join you soon enough, but first my men will entertain her for a little while." Nico slammed the boot closed before I could respond to his taunt. Within seconds, the car was underway again, and I was alone in the boot with my thoughts. I was in no doubt that Sam was a match for any of her captors, but she had been beaten and gassed. She was tied up, and there were four of them. I feared the worst. Somehow, I needed to overpower Nico and then get back to the cabin and help Sam before it was too late.

❖ ❖ ❖

Sam was half dragged, half carried into the log cabin where she was unceremoniously dumped on a large wooden table. Tong, the leader of the group, started to untie her hands while the other three looked on. Sam judged it to perfection. Just as the last knot came free, Sam sprang into action. She hit Tong across the face with a perfectly judged backhand while using her other arm to push herself off the table. The closest Triad charged at her. She could not kick as her feet were still tied tight. She judged her jump, and as he lunged at her, she jumped, hitting the unsuspecting Triad under the chin with both her knees. As she landed, a blow struck her hard on the side of her face.

Her head was swimming, and she was trying hard to regain her senses when she was charged down by the remaining gang members and forced back onto the table. Sam could not move. Both men held her tight while Tong, who had recovered from his blow, tied her arms to the legs of the table, one on either side. Tong inspected his tethers, making sure Sam, who was now spread out across the table, could not break free. Happy with his workmanship, he leaned over the top of Sam, getting so close to her face that his scarred nose was almost touching Sam's cheekbone. "Lady has spirit. That is good, much fun. Tong like woman with spirit. Keep your strength for later. Will need it for four men. Will come back later. We play card game to see who takes you first."

❖ ❖ ❖

I tried to use a sharp edge in the boot of the big Mercedes to cut through the tethers on my wrists, but in real life, it was not as simple as the movies made out. Because my hands were tied behind my back, it was almost impossible to judge where the rope was. Secondly, it did not matter much anyway. Smooth plastic trim covered most metal parts, making it almost impossible to break free. Suddenly, the car started lurching from side to side. We must have moved off the main road and onto a dirt track. I had a feeling I was just about to find out what fate had in store for me.

Once more, the boot sprang open. Nico had been wise and stood to one side. My plan to kick him hard in the stomach failed miserably before it had even started. Nico lifted me out of the boot with ease and dragged me by the feet along a snow-covered wooden pier. Nico was cursing in German to himself. He was mad for some reason that I could not figure out. Nico left me and walked back along the pier. As I lay there, the extreme cold started to seep into my bones. I tried to shuffle, but I slipped on the packed snow covering the wooden pier, and only one of the main supports stopped me slipping off the edge. I looked back to see Nico making his way back along the pier. To my amazement, he was carrying a forty-five-gallon barrel above his head, a feat that any normal man would have found almost impossible. Suddenly it clicked. Nico was going to use the weight of the barrel to break through the ice of the frozen lake. It didn't take a rocket scientist to figure out what he was going to do with me once he had created a hole in the ice. I had one last chance left. I needed to get close to him. Just as he was about to launch the barrel, his balance would be on the limit, and his footing was not the best on the slippery, snow-covered pier. If I could trip him at just the right moment, I could send him over the edge with his barrel. It was almost time. Nico was on the edge, only inches from my tethered feet. He lifted the barrel to its full height.

The strain of this made his huge chest puff out with exertion. I was watching the expression on his face, judging the moment to strike. Then there was a slight rushing noise, and Nico's face froze. Things were happening in slow motion. Nico's checked lumberjack shirt was in tatters, and the white-and-blue pattern was turning red. Nico was falling forward, following the barrel, and I was frozen to the spot. There was a splash, then total silence. Nico was gone. A few seconds later, there were footsteps on the wooden structure. I looked up A man was looking down at me. It took a few seconds to register who the stranger was. He checked the breech of his pistol and then removed the silencer.

"My god, Smithy. What the hell are you doing in this neck of the woods?"

Smithy smiled and bent down, working at feverish speed to free my feet from the rope. "Later, Adam. We need to get you into the car then get back along the lake. Sam is being held at a cabin further along Lake Sempach. She is in big trouble. Her hosts are not known for their manners."

Smithy bundled me into his car after cutting the rope from my wrists. Two minutes later, we were off, flying along a road by the lakeside. If the situation had been less serious, you would have stopped to take a picture. The setting would have made a picture postcard. A huge full moon bathed the frozen lake in a soft blue light, and snowy peaks in the distance topped off the scene.

My brain had started to thaw out, and I quizzed Smithy as he drove. "How the hell did you know where to find us?"

Smithy never took his eyes off the frozen road but pushed the car to its maximum for the conditions. "Adam, you need to get your military head back on for the moment if you want to see your girl back in one piece. Reload the Glock; the spare clip is in the glove box. We need to hurry. We must be ready to move as soon as we pull up. We will be there in a few seconds. I only have that Glock, but we still need to work as a team when we get there. We need to have a quick look at the door, and after we suss which way it opens, you need to work the door to leave both my hands free as we go in. This is important, Adam, so listen. Once you open the door, your job is finished. You hit the dirt as fast as you can, and let me handle the rest. Do I make myself clear, Adam? I know what your track record is like. You may think you are helping me, but the worst thing you can do is break my concentration by moving in my peripheral vision."

❖ ❖ ❖

Sam's wrists were bleeding, but still she could not break free from her bonds. At the far end of the room by the door, the four Triads were deep in conversation. Sam was fine with that. If they were talking, they were leaving her alone. Suddenly the chatter stopped. Tong appeared in Sam's line of sight. Sam was in trouble.

Sam tried to talk to Tong, but he was not in the mood for conversation. He grabbed Sam's ankles and pulled her hard toward him and the bottom of the table. Sam winced as the rope cut deeply into her already swollen and damaged wrists. Her legs now dangled helplessly over the edge of the table. Tong and one of his deputies removed the rope that held Sam's legs together—carefully so that Sam had no chance of kicking her way to freedom. They retied her legs to the table legs, one on either side. Sam squirmed around, but no matter how she tried, she could not close her legs. Sam was concentrating on the ceiling. She knew what was about to happen, and she was powerless to stop it. Tong's disfigured face appeared above her again. He was holding a hunting knife in his hand. "I win. Get to play with you first, pretty one. Tong teach you new tricks before men get leftovers."

Tong's ugly head disappeared from Sam's vision. She could feel him groping around the waistband of her skirt. Sam gasped as she felt the cold blade of the knife slide down the gap between her hip and the skirt. With one sharp tug, the razor-sharp blade cut through the skirt, and Sam heard what was left of the material fall to the floor. Tears of rage were running down Sam's cheeks. If she got out of this, not one man in this room would live. Sam felt the cold air hit her lower body as her underwear was removed.

There was a large cheer from her captors as from the waist down, Sam was revealed to them. Sam steeled herself for the inevitable.

❖ ❖ ❖

Smithy had been watching through a chink in the door. As the shouting started, he nodded to me to open the door. The door swung inward. Any noise we might have made was obliterated by the shouting. Smithy stepped into the room. In the blink of an eye, he had picked his kill order. The Triad on the right centre was first as he presented the most danger. He was within grabbing distance of his pistol on the table. Smithy ducked down, reducing his target area, and fired—one to the chest, one to the head. Next was Tong. He was over Sam and had a knife in his hand. He started to turn, and Smithy hit him between the eyes. As he spun round, Smithy hit him again twice in the chest. Number three was closest. Smithy turned to his left as the Triad stood up—again, one to the chest, one to the head. Number four to the far left had turned to make his escape when Smithy hit him in the back, then put another in the back of his head. All four Triads had died within four seconds of Smithy entering the room. Such was the speed and ferocity of the attack, it took me a few seconds to realise Sam was still tied to the table, naked from the waist down and covered from head to toe in Tong's blood.

I used the knife Tong had dropped in his death throes to cut Sam free. I was wrapping Sam up in a discarded ski jacket I had found when I heard the hiss of the Glock's silencer. Smithy had seen one of the Triads move, and in true professional style, he made sure he was dead by putting another round through his head. Sam was trying hard not to be fussed over, but she knew her little trip had almost got us both killed, and she was very quiet, letting Smithy and me take charge.

There was no point trying to cover up what had happened. The cabin was wrecked. Sam pulled on a pair of jogging bottoms Smithy had found in one of the bedrooms while Smithy and I went about trying to remove any traces of Sam's DNA. Smithy drenched the table in bleach he had found in the kitchen cupboard, while I removed the rope and torn clothing Sam had been wearing. Smithy bundled us into the hire car and set sail for the airport at warp speed. We all knew we had to get out of the country before the Swiss police discovered the deaths and closed everything down. A quick check confirmed that I still had both our passports in a zipped compartment of my jacket. We had travelled south and were around an hour from the airport. A quick check of Smithy's map showed we were just about to pass the town of Sursee.

With a bit of luck, we would be in the air before the bodies were discovered. Sam sat in the back of the car and said very little. After checking we had some cash and our passports at hand, I felt more at ease with our situation. "So, Mr Smith, now are you going to explain how you managed to be in the right place at the right time tonight?"

Smithy smiled as he checked his rearview mirror for any sign of a tail. "Well, Adam, it all started after our last meeting. MI6 were in need of new blood, and I had worked with them. They discovered I had French family as well as my cockney upbringing, so a deal was reached with my CO, and I was transferred to MI6. I have been training with Peter Kent and was given my first solo mission—shadowing Karl Muller. MI6 were tipped off that Khanjar was coming to see Muller about an arms deal. My job was to try to identify Khanjar so he could be tracked down. I was doing fine until you pair strolled onto the scene and made me decide to follow you and see what the hell you were up to. Peter Kent would kill me if he found that I dropped surveillance to save your skins."

"Sorry, Smithy, but Sam and I are glad you did. So who is this Khanjar you are talking about? I have never heard of him."

Before Smithy could answer, Sam replied from the back seat. "He is Al Qaeda. You won't have heard of him because the government have thrown a media blackout on him. They don't want panic or young Muslims being turned to his radical ways. He has been on the scene for a few years now, but the secret service has never been able to pin him down. He is as slippery as an eel. He managed to get into the food-supply chain to our troops in Iraq and poison some of the food. Six soldiers died as a result, and thousands of tonnes of food had to be destroyed as a precaution. He also managed to get into Faslane naval base and plant a limpet mine on the hull of one of our nuclear subs. Luckily, its departure was delayed because its captain fell ill, and the device exploded in port. No one was hurt, but there were tens of thousands of pounds worth of damage to the sub. His son was captured in Canary Wharf attempting to set off a dirty bomb. Make no mistake. He is top of our terrorist list. Bin Laden may be the figurehead, but Khanjar is far more of a threat to our country."

Smithy dropped us at the airport then rushed back to the entrance to the chateau before his boss discovered he was AWOL. I didn't ask Smithy to keep quiet about us. For one, it would drop him in the shit, and two there was no need. We were friends, and I trusted him.

❖ ❖ ❖

Khanjar's Bell 222A helicopter touched down next to Muller's chopper one hour after Adam and Sam were removed from the building. Khanjar and his bodyguard were received at the door by Muller's butler and were escorted by the butler to the old ballroom on the first floor. Muller was waiting for them. As they strode into the room, Khanjar's Arab robes flowed behind him like a sail in the wind. His body man waited just inside the door but close enough to be at his master's side within a few fast strides. Muller was quaking in his boots. If Khanjar ever found out that he had sold him the nuclear waste for the dirty bomb then taken money from the British to inform them of Khanjar's son's attempt to contaminate the city of London, there would be no mercy. But rather than shy away from contact with the Arab warlord, Muller used it as an opportunity to increase his business with the Al Qaeda general. This was his life. He simply could not help himself.

"My dear Mr Khanjar, I hope you had a good flight. Can I get you anything before we get down to business."

Khanjar sat down opposite the arms dealer. His dark eyes penetrated Muller's outer calm. Inside he was a wreck, but he must not let the Al Qaeda warlord know it. "Well, Muller, we best get on with our trading. I am busy so pray continue, my friend."

Muller reached into the desk drawer and produced the latest state-of-the-art Glock. He placed it on the desk in front of Khanjar. He then produced a small laptop, which he opened and switched on. Khanjar looked on, puzzled. "Some months ago, the British secret services, both MI6 and MI5, placed an order for state-of-the-art, individually balanced and sighted Glock handguns to improve the marksmanship of their agents. We supplied them with these. Each handgrip has been fitted with the latest tracking chip from America, which has no way of being detected. On the laptop, you will see there is a world map. Each flashing marker is the location of every British secret service agent in the UK and around the world." Muller spun the laptop round to face Khanjar. "The reason I asked you to come here is this. I felt that it might be useful to you in your hunt for your son."

Khanjar was mulling over in his head the advantages this would give him over his sworn enemy. "Very impressive, Mr Muller. Your genius shows itself yet again to be one step ahead of America's puppets in the UK. But I know to my very great cost, you are also somewhat of a genius with the costs as well. Please tell me, sir, how much this will cost my organisation?"

Muller spun the laptop back round and closed the lid. "For you, Khanjar, I will do a deal, say twenty million US dollars. Not a bad price. You can sell it onto Russia or the Irish when you are finished with it."

Khanjar clicked his fingers, and his body man appeared by his side, attaché case at the ready. "You must forgive me, my friend. I have only brought five million US dollars with me. I will send one of my followers with the other fifteen million next week. No bank transfers. They can be traced. I am sure you trust me, my old friend."

Before Karl Muller could do anything, Khanjar scooped up the laptop and turned with a swirl of his robe. "May your god look kindly upon you. We will speak later." Khanjar was gone as quickly as he had arrived.

❖ ❖ ❖

On the flight back, the plane was almost deserted. Sam and I picked seats at the rear of the plane where no one else was sitting. I could tell Sam was in distress. Our wait in the airport for our flight had been a silent one. I did not want to push Sam into talking. I reckoned she would get round to it in her own good time. Her plan had fallen to pieces. She had been overpowered and almost raped. If I knew Sam, the one thing that would be eating at her more was the fact that she had to be rescued and hadn't sorted it out herself.

We were halfway into the flight, and I was thinking how good it would be to be back in Scotland on our own turf when Sam finally tried to shake herself out of her depression. "Adam, do you think I have lost it? I mean, just nothing went right. And then to end it all, Smithy had to come and save us. What a bloody redneck, saved by the office junior. He has barely got his L-plates off. He's just a kid."

I smiled inwardly and squeezed Sam's hand. "For one, no, I don't think for a moment you have lost it. You had the customs guy eating out of your hand. We were just pushing our luck too far. You're not in MI6 now. You were performing without a safety net. Muller would have never dared to do that if you were still in MI6. And as for the office junior, Luke Smith AKA Smithy was top of his class at Hereford. He didn't get there because he was good at tiddledywinks. He may have a bit to work on before his spy craft is up to snuff, but I bet his commanding officer is cursing MI6 for taking him. Anyway, it's evens. Did you not save his life in Hyde Park last year?"

Sam leaned across and cuddled into my shoulder. "You know, Adam, when you are not kicking me around the gym, you can be a true gentleman. Thanks for covering me up on the table back at the cabin and also for putting up with my moods. You know it wouldn't take much for a girl to fall in love with you."

I squeezed Sam's hand and put my arm around her shoulder. "Excellent! If you find a girl like that, let me know."

Sam sat up, looking into my eyes. "See? There you go again. The gentleman is gone, and the big Scottish idiot is back."

Sam watched Adams chest rise and fall as he slept, she too was shattered but sleep on the flight would not come to her. She was still haunted by what had happened in Switzerland. The thought was made worse by the fact that some weeks ago she had run out of her birth control pills, the thought of falling pregnant with her rapists child made her shiver, Sam made a mental note to pick up her forgotten prescription the minute she got home.

Customs at Edinburgh Airport went without a hitch. No one batted an eyelid that we had just arrived from Europe with no luggage at all.

A quick trip to the boot of the Beetle produced some emergency cash that had been stashed behind the dash. We bought some fresh clothes and a bottle of vodka. We had decided to spend the night in the airport hotel, as it was too late to start travelling north. By ten o'clock, we were both sound asleep, and the Blue Label sat on the bedside table unopened—a world's first, if my memory served me correctly.

❖ ❖ ❖

Areli Benesch had spent the last two days trawling through the news channels. The only thing she could find out was that the Department of the Environment had given a press release to the local news agencies stating that there had been a case of swine flu close to the Porton Down research facility, and as this was being studied at the complex, it had been sealed off and all its staff quarantined, purely as a precaution, until it had been given a clean bill of health. Areli was no fool. She knew the search would have gone two ways. They could have closed all the ports and carried out a massive manhunt for her with her picture in every paper and on every TV screen. But whoever was in charge had decided to keep the lid on things and search for her covertly. Judging by the low-key release, they had opted for the latter.

Areli was relatively happy with this. She would play the British secret service at their own game. She was under no illusions that this was going to be a walk in the park. She was sure that MI5, MI6, and GCHQ were all flat out turning the country upside down looking for her. Areli knew she had already spent too long in one place. She needed to move, and she needed to move fast. Her original plan—to use Gary Harding to escape from the base then dispose of him—was now no use. Over the past few days Gary had pestered Areli to hand over the stolen chemicals. He had explained in more depth his discovery. Although Areli was no scientist, she had picked up the basics of DNA technology. Gary's initial goal of developing a vaccine for Vokxin had taken a different route when Gary had discovered that he could extract DNA from *D. radiodurans* and also cockroaches. His hobby in the evenings was finding a way to reduce the radiation levels of spent nuclear fuel rods. His enthusiasm for this subject was partly due to the fact that a French energy company was paying him a research fee. The one thing that Gary loved as much as science was money. It had always been the driving factor in his career. As his research progressed, his two loves merged. Gary found himself spending more and more time studying the radiation side of things rather than pursing a solution for the Vokxin problem.

In the end, Gary had found a way to combat the effects of radiation and the unforeseen bonus of rapid human cell regeneration thanks to the DNA from the *Deinococcus radiodurans* bacteria. Areli was sure that the kid was onto a winner with the cell regeneration, and she had an idea she knew who might be interested in the radiation fix. During her detention at Porton Down, she had been asked many times what she knew of the radiation problem caused by the American prototype aircraft. Although Areli did not know anything, she had stored this information for future reference. She was sure her previous employer was high in the echelons of power in the United States and would be keen to come to some arrangement with Areli over the young scientist and his discovery. She was going to make contact with her high-powered American friend, but first she must devise a plan to get clear of the area before the British found them. Areli needed to keep her young scientist friend on side, so she decided to feed him a yarn that would keep his attention and stop him trying to escape. Areli found Gary in his room reading. "Ah, there you are. Listen, I have been thinking and have come to the decision that you are right. We will sell your invention and split the profits. When the deal goes through, I will hand over the chemicals."

Gary listened to his captor but did not like the last part. "That sounds sweet, but you need to get rid of those chemicals. Give me them, and I will drive back to Porton and get rid of them safely."

Areli laughed out loud. "And, my young friend, you would come back here with the whole British army behind you. No, this is what you will do, or I will take your invention and give you nothing but a prison cell in return. Listen carefully, my young friend. I have looked around this fine home and found your father's video camera. You will carry out your knife trick one more time and give a detailed explanation of your work and findings on the recording. Then we will drop off the video and wait for the offers to come in. The price for your work will be one billion dollars each. We will take the mobile home that is parked by the side of your garage, and when we have received the money, we will drop the chemicals at a safe location. If we do not have any offers or we are intercepted, I will use the Diavokxin to change a few minds on the subject."

Gary was not happy about the Cold War chemicals still being on the loose, but the thought of the money helped soothe his nerves. Areli had no intention of sharing any money with the young fool. He would be her bargaining chip with the Americans if required. Areli supervised as Gary carried out her instructions and made the instructional video. He was then instructed to e-mail it to the American embassy in London for the attention of the CIA. It would not take long for the Americans to trace the source of the video. Soon the house would be swarming with them. Areli left a note in an envelope on the mantelpiece addressed to "The CIA." Areli took a calculated guess that they would not share the information with the British, and because of the video, they would be here first.

Twenty minutes later, the big camper van pulled out of the drive. Gary had never driven anything as big before and was struggling with the length and width of the big machine. The camper belonged to his aunt, who used their large garden to store the vehicle while not in use. Gary reached the road end then stopped and looked at Areli. "Which way do you want me to go?"

Areli pointed left along the road. "First stop, London. I have a little job to do there."

CHAPTER 5

THE HUNTED

Colonel David Southern sat in the situation room of the White House. He was positioned at the far end of the table from the president. He sat quietly while all in the room gave their views on the best way to deal with the threat evolving from the nightmare scenario on the other side of the Atlantic. One general wanted to flood Britain with troops, while another thought it was all nonsense, that Great Britain had no such chemicals.

The meeting broke up with no clear way ahead. Colonel Southern was asked to hang back. Southern watched with interest as the president left, followed by various generals and high-ranking military figures. Only the president's chief of staff and the chairman of the Joint Chiefs of Staff remained. Although Colonel Southern was probably the lowest-ranking officer present, he was highly regarded in Washington circles as a man who could get the job done. He had made his name the hard way. Toward the end of the Cold War, he had been stationed in Berlin and had fought many covert battles with the KGB. Even the Russian military treated him with caution; he had won many hard-fought battles against them. Even his own military feared him. He was known for his ruthless tactics. If the situation demanded it, he was more than willing to sacrifice his own troops to get the desired result. Unlike some of the officers who had just sat in the room, he was a man of little words. He let his actions speak for themselves. He had refused any higher rank offered to him; he had the uncanny knack of always being in the right. He worked from an office in the Pentagon. His official title was Pentagon Liaison officer, but in reality, this meant little. He refused a secretary and worked alone, mainly due to the sensitive nature of the tasks he was given. The fewer witnesses the better.

"David, I will keep this brief. After your success in averting disaster last year at the airbase in Scotland, the president feels that you are the man he wants to lead a team in recovering this chemical before disaster strikes. You have a free hand to pick as many people as you need for a team, and whatever you need will be provided. The chairman of the Joint Chiefs has been ordered by the president to see to it that you receive full cooperation from all services. The president has told the prime minister that you will be arriving and that he will have no power over your actions. He has lost all faith in the Britons' ability to resolve this problem by themselves. I do not have to tell you we must get across there quickly, so I will leave you to organise your team."

Two hours later, David Southern sat alone in his office. In front of him lay a list of people and equipment. First on his list was his team leader. He picked up the phone and asked the switchboard to put him through to Fort Bragg. The phone rang for a second. When someone answered, Southern asked to speak to Colonel Brent Cussack, ISA division.

Cussack headed up the Intelligence Support Activity section of the army. His unit was responsible for gathering any intelligence for US Special Forces operations. He would be a vital part of Southern's team. Cussack was informed a chopper would be lifting him and his new team in four hours time.

Next on the list was First Sergeant Al Franklyn, a Delta team leader also based at Fort Bragg. The Delta Special Forces worked hand in hand with Cussack's ISA, so they would work well together. Franklyn had also been picked because he had just returned from England, where he had been on an exchange scheme with the British Special Air Service. Southern hoped that the knowledge he had gained in England would be valuable to the team. Franklyn was ordered to be ready for pickup in four hours, along with his top ten Delta commandos. Next on the shopping list was the CIA. Southern called the CIA director and asked him to contact Scott Tomlin and get him to Fort Bragg in the next four hours. The director had been present in the situation room and put up little resistance to Southern taking his best agent away from him. Last on the list was the White House. Southern waited for a few seconds while his contact joined him on the other end of the line. Southern asked for the deployment of SEAL team one to the Machrihanish

Air Base along with a Chinook helicopter and a carrier group to be sent to the Irish Sea.

There was silence on the other end of the phone while everything sank in. "Southern, we have just pulled out of the base. Are you sure we need it and a carrier group to be redeployed? Have you any idea how much this will cost?"

Although Southern was not in the mood to be cross-examined by the president's chief of staff, he continued undeterred. "This is not a budget negotiation. If we do not act now, the cost will be catastrophic."

There was silence for a second. "Very well, Colonel Southern. I will see to it your requests are put in place. The president has one more request. He wants you in the UK overseeing things and reporting back. Good luck, Colonel."

The phone went dead. Southern had had no intention of heading across the pond. He cursed under his breath. If things went pear-shaped, he preferred to work at a distance, but this time he had no option. Southern had just finished with the White House when a message pinged up on his computer. It was from the head of security at the American embassy in London. Southern had been sent the mail because he had headed up the Machrihanish incident. He opened the secure attachment file. Southern watched as the youth went through his DNA theory and watched his demonstration. He was far from convinced until the last few seconds of the clip came up. Areli Benesch walked into the shot and stood so close to the lens that her shape started to distort. "You know who I am, and you know what I have got. I want to do a deal for the chemicals and the technology you have just been watching. I have left you a little present just to prove I am not talking rubbish. We will speak soon my friend, just like Machrihanish, except I will be giving the orders now."

Southern picked up his phone and dialled a number he did not need to look up. "Max, hi. It's David Southern. Listen, Max, this is business, not pleasure. I need you at Boston Logan airport in three hours, no ifs or buts. We need to talk about DNA harvesting. Speak to you soon. Must fly."

A call to Admiral Todd had the desired effect, and fifteen minutes later, a US Navy Seahawk landed on the Pentagons helipad. Southern told the pilot he needed to be in the Boston Logan Airport as quickly as possible. "No problem, Colonel, but we can't do it flat out. We are too marginal on fuel. A speed of one hundred and fifty will get us there in about two hours fifty minutes. That do you, sir?"

Southern nodded without speaking and belted up for the flight. The flight went without any hiccups, and almost three hours on the button after phoning his friend Max, he was in terminal thirty-two at Logan Airport. A quick call to the cell phone of Professor Max Deltorro confirmed he was in the airport and on his way to terminal thirty-two. Southern planted himself down in the middle of a row of plastic, one-size-fits-all airport seats. The corridor he had picked was quiet as the airport was between flight arrivals, and terminal thirty-two was at the far end of the airport. He had just powered up his laptop when Max arrived. Southern had not seen him in the flesh for two years.

As far as Southern could make out, little had changed. Max still looked like he had been pulled through a hedge backward. His blazer was crumpled, his tie squint, his thick black hair sat on his head like an explosion in a wig factory, and Southern couldn't decide if the man was growing a beard or just had overlooked shaving for a few days.

"What the hell is so important that I had to cancel my afternoon lecture?" Max Deltorro stood glaring at Southern like he was a naughty schoolboy.

"Max, sit down and calm down. Watch the video, and then tell me I was wrong to come charging up here." Southern clicked on the start symbol, and within seconds Deltorro was glued to the screen. Max asked Southern on several occasions to rewind the clip. When the clip finished, Max Deltorro sat quietly staring into space.

Southern waited for a few seconds before pressing on with his questions. "Max, do you think the video is real? Could he have done what he says?"

"I would say in my professional opinion as scientific advisor to the president that it is genuine. Our young friend on the video has left out the most important piece deliberately. You see, David, using the DNA to change human DNA is one thing, but finding the correct DNA strains from millions is a different story. Then doing it again is almost impossible. The chances of doing this are roughly the same as hitting a golf ball from the moon and getting a hole in one with it at the first hole of St Andrews."

Southern continued interrogating his friend. "Max, if the research is genuine, would it be possible to use it to manufacture a drug that would counter the effects of radioactive contamination."

Max looked out of the windows to the aircraft parked by the terminal while he gathered his thoughts. "David, what you have just shown me, if it is true, will turn the scientific world upside down. The possibilities are truly endless. Even just off the top of my head boosting cell regeneration could cure cancer or even god forbid slow down or stop ageing. OK, your guy was looking to come up with a radiation fix but he has found much more. You need to get the kid and his work into a lab so you can verify his claims. David, for god's sake, don't tell anyone else about this until you have the kid in a safe place. Whoever markets this will rule the world. Looks like your military connections are going to come in handy, my old friend."

Southern went through the formalities of asking Max Deltorro how his family was doing, but all the time his brain was racing trying to work out the best way to approach this tricky situation. He needed the young scientist back in the States, which could prove troublesome. But worse than that was the fact that Areli Benesch seemed to be calling the shots. She had been missing for some considerable time.

Southern had mistakenly thought that she had come to a sticky end, probably terminated by the British secret service for her involvement in the Machrihanish incident. Southern had read her CIA file before. He knew exactly who he was dealing with. Ex-Mossad, she had been trained in all the black arts of the spy business, and her track record, if somewhat sketchy, was impressive. Southern would have to box clever if he was to outwit her and grab the scientist and the Cold War chemicals. Southern bid his friend good-bye, promising to keep him up to date on the situation.

Twenty minutes later, the refuelled SH60 Seahawk was heading south, back to Washington. Southern used the flight time to work out the beginnings of a plan to bring the young scientist and his work to America. Thanks to the situation caused by the missing chemicals, Southern had pretty much carte blanche to do what he wanted in the UK, as long as it was seen to be connected to regaining control of the missing Cold War chemicals. He had not spoken face to face with Benesch, but she was no fool. He was sure she had no intention of releasing the chemicals. He was somewhat puzzled as to how the scientist and the chemicals had ended up in her grasp. He would have preferred it if he could have stayed in the United States and controlled the situation from there.

The decision had been made for him, and for the second time in two years, he was about to set foot on British soil. He decided against telling his superiors about the situation. The last thing he needed was some do-gooder stopping the operation and losing the United States the chance to lead the world into a new scientific era. It was late evening when Southern touched down on the Pentagon's dedicated helipad. It had been a busy day, but the last thing on Southern's mind was rest. Back in the office, he ordered a sandwich and coffee, then called Langley. The CIA over the years had become used to Southern's nocturnal habits. The head of the computer division listened to Southern's request. "What I am looking for is a trace on the e-mail that was sent to our embassy in London addressed for the attention of myself. Do you think you could pull that off for me?"

Langley's computer expert went off the line for a few seconds. "No problem. It wasn't rerouted or booby-trapped. Looks to me as if the sender wanted you to find it, sir. I have e-mailed you the address in England where the e-mail originated. Happy hunting, sir. Good night."

❖ ❖ ❖

Luke Smith had been in a panic when he got back to his room after saving Sam and Adam. The reason for this was a message had been left on his laptop. "Return to London immediately. Go straight to the office. Priority one."

Luke thought that he had been rumbled. He was sure he was about to be shown the door. On arrival at MI6 headquarters at Vauxhall Cross, he was summoned to the basement where Neil Andrews was holding court. Luke stood with his trainer Peter Kent and listened to Andrews tell the assembled bodies in the room what the latest situation was. He was shocked to find that Benesch was on the loose again. He had helped Sam to capture the woman only last year. He clearly remembered Sam's warning about Benesch's talents. This was still going through his head when Andrews's next sentence struck alarm bells ringing. "I want you all to keep a close eye out for both Adam Macdonald and Sam O'Conner. They know Areli Benesch well and have both crossed swords with her before. If anybody can shed any light on their whereabouts, I want to know. They may know the hiding places of this woman. Remember, if you do find Benesch, you are expressly forbidden to engage her unless we have our clearance from the PM."

❖ ❖ ❖

Sam headed for the car park to warm up the Beetle for our long trip north while I headed to reception to pay the bill. We had both overslept and missed breakfast. It looked like we'd have to stop en route to grab a bite to eat.

I was looking forward to getting home to the glass house, but I was not looking forward to the conversation I was going to have with Sam.

I had made my mind up that this spy nonsense had to stop. We had been lucky this time. Sam had to realise that one of these times our luck would run out. Smithy had saved our bacon, and we owed him big time. Smithy couldn't be there every time Sam got itchy feet and decided to revert back to her secret-service life.

I handed over the key for the room to the spotty youth behind the counter and pulled out my wallet to pay the bill. "No, sir. The bill has been taken care of."

I was somewhat taken aback. I knew I had all our cash so it could not have been Sam. "Are you sure that you are not getting the rooms mixed up? I don't want to get you into trouble, lad."

The spotty youth pointed across the foyer. "No, sir. I am sure. That gentleman took care of your bill." I followed the direction of his pointed finger, and my eyes came to rest on the figure seated in the large wingback chair by the door. Neil Andrews waved at me and signalled me to join him in the adjacent empty chair. My legs went weak at the knees. We had been made. Neil did not travel alone. He would have backup someplace. My eyes darted round the room, looking for his fellow secret-service agents. At a table opposite Andrews sat Peter Kent and Smithy. Smithy looked like he wanted the earth to open and swallow him. Kent was leaning on a walking stick. I strolled over as naturally as the situation allowed.

"Hello, Neil. Fancy meeting you here, I see you have brought Kent and Smithy to Scotland for a holiday."

Neil Andrews stood up warily and shook my hand. "Please sit down, Adam. We have important business to discuss with you."

Neil never took his eyes off me as I sat down. Not really a surprise. The last time we had met I had fulfilled my promise to Neil. I broke his jaw in three places for his part in getting innocent civilians killed—hopefully a reminder to screw the head before ordering a similar situation.

"Adam, before you say anything we must put our differences aside and our heads together. Young Smith has to be commended for leading us to you. Don't take it out on him. He has realised how bad the situation is and acted in the proper manner. Let me bring you up to date. Your friend Areli Benesch has escaped from Porton Down detention facility. Unfortunately, she again has left a trail of bodies in her wake. She has also managed to get her grubby little fingers on one of Britain's forgotten cold-war secrets. She overpowered one of our top scientists and has taken two dangerous chemicals. She is at large in the UK with the means to either inflict massive damage or worst-case scenario, start a chain reaction that will kill every oxygen-breathing organism on the face of the earth. So you see, Adam, we need to pool all our information on the female in order to recapture her. Consider Samantha and yourself reenlisted."

As if on cue, there was a screech of tyres outside the front door, and Sam's Beetle pulled up. She was in a big hurry. I had surmised what had happened. "Please give me a minute, gentlemen." I walked out to the Beetle. Sam was waving at me frantically to get in. I knew in my heart that Andrews was telling the truth. Smithy would never have given us up without a damned good reason.

To head back to the glass house could be suicide. The only person in the world who knew our real identities and where we lived was Areli Benesch.

She had tried to assassinate me at the glass house. Only Sam's timely intervention had saved my life. Sam had played a major part in Areli's capture. If there was one person Areli wanted to get even with, it had to be Sam. Now that she was armed with this chemical, we would be sitting ducks at the glass house. Neil Andrews didn't know it, but he had probably saved our lives by intercepting us.

Sam was screaming at me to get in the car. I leaned in the window and removed Sam's key from the ignition. "Sam, you won't fight your way out of this. I think you better come inside and listen to what Neil Andrews has to say." I turned round and headed back into the hotel foyer, Sam's keys in my hand. I noted in the far corner of the car park, carnage had ensued. One of Andrews's agents was flat on his back and out cold while the other was attempting to get up but was gripping his crotch with both hands as if he expected his precious cargo to fall off at any moment. Sam had obviously recovered from the Swiss debacle and had vented her anger on the unfortunate agents. Sam marched into the foyer and plonked herself down unceremoniously in the chair opposite Neil Andrews.

I joined her and listened while Neil repeated the story he had told me. Sam was not so easily convinced by the story as I had been and bombarded Neil with questions trying to catch him out. "So, Neil, if your story is correct, how did Benesch manage to come into possession of these chemicals, and how are we still in possession of them? How do we neutralize the chemicals if we need to?"

Neil raised his hand and waved across the room to a table in the far corner of the room. At his signal, a woman stood up and started to make her way across to us. "Sam, Adam, this is Dr Karen Lowe. She works in the lab and will fill you in on the technical aspects of the chemicals and also what happened that night."

Sam and I listened as Dr Lowe described in detail her ordeal that night. I listened intently as Dr Lowe described the chemical composition of Vokxin and the difference between it and Diavokxin. I watched Sam's reaction to the doctor's story. From previous experience, I knew she was just about to blow her top. It was only a matter of time.

Sam waited until Dr Karen Lowe had finished. Then she turned to Neil Andrews. "So Neil, you are now the top man at six. God help us all. Did I not tell you to be extra careful with the Israeli bitch? My god, Neil, do you never learn? You put her in a holding cell next to a store for weapons of mass destruction. And coming to that, what the hell are we doing still holding Cold War chemical weapons? Have you never heard of the 1996 Chemical Weapons Act or the Chemicals Weapons Convention we signed at The Hague?" Sam had raised her voice and was in full flow.

"Sam, keep it down. People will hear you." Neil was starting to panic. He had forgotten how much of a wild card Sam could be.

"Keep it down? You stupid man, your incompetence could kill us all. Yet again we have to try and get you out of the shit. Adam should have broken your neck, not your jaw." Sam stood up and marched off to the bar before anyone could speak. I stood up to follow her; she was in a bit of a state.

Neil grabbed my arm and stopped me. "Adam, talk some sense into her. While you are at it, remember to tell her the new head of MI6 has turned a blind eye to her unauthorised absence. As far as the rest of the department knows, you have both been on an undercover mission for the last year. Don't make me change my mind, Adam. Tell the silly cow to get her act together or else."

As I approached the bar, Sam took the vodka and cola that she had just bought and smashed it into the floor directly in front of the bar. Sam turned to march back over to Neil, but I grabbed her arm and stopped her in her tracks. For a second, the coldness in those grey eyes bored through me. I had seen this before with Sam. Just below the surface lurked the killer that had been honed to perfection by her secret-service training. I feared that Neil, director or not, was about to witness Sam's fury at first hand.

"Whoa, girl. Steady! What do you think you are going to achieve by knocking his block off? Come on, Sam. Calm down."

Sam tried to push past me, but I held her tightly. She tried again but gave in when she saw I was not for giving up. She was starting to sob quietly when the head barman started making noises about flinging her out or calling the police. I was torn between two problems. I did not want to let go of Sam in case she changed her mind, but I needed to get to the bar to sort out some damage limitation. The voice behind me startled me. I had been too preoccupied with Sam to notice Karen Lowe approaching from behind. "You go and sort the barman out, and I will wait here with Samantha." I nodded to the new arrival and made a beeline for the bar to head off the barman before he had us all flung out.

"Sam, I know Neil Andrews is not your favourite person, but he truly believes in you. Also, he is sure you are our best shot at catching the madwoman before she releases the chemicals." Sam was still furious with Andrews, but Karen was doing a good job at trying to calm her down. Sam had her first chance to observe her new acquaintance and cross-examine her away from Neil's control. She was not unattractive but did little to show off her natural good looks. At five foot eight, she was reasonably tall for a woman. She was average build with shoulder-length brown hair, which was pulled back from her face and set in a tight bun. She had pale, freckly skin. Sam reckoned she would be in her mid to late twenties. Considering her position as a doctor and her involvement in the case, she had to be one smart cookie. "Well, Dr Lowe, why have you been dragged into this mess, and if you haven't already sussed out the situation, you need to keep an eye on Neil Andrews. He would sell his soul to the devil if he thought it would help his career. That is, if he already hasn't done it."

Karen Lowe smiled at Sam. "It's OK, Sam. You don't have to warn me. I have been his virtual prisoner since this whole thing kicked off. I have watched him in action, and the only person, including the PM by the way, that I think he fears is you. Sam, for everyone's sake, let's just work together until we get this disaster sorted out. Andrews has an army chopper waiting at the airport to take us all south. We need to get our act together fast."

I had just managed to calm the bar manager down and was handing over the cash over that we had agreed upon when Neil Andrews with Sam and the scientist girl appeared by my side. I could tell from Sam's body language that she was still not a happy puppy, but she seemed to have resigned herself to the fact that she was stuck with this situation for the moment. The scientist girl,

Karen, seemed to be focusing her attention on the Sky News channel that was playing on the screen behind the bar. We all turned our attention to the news flash that had just been displayed. It seemed the government was still playing their cards close to their chest. They had just announced that the country had just been put on the highest state of alert for terrorist activity. We watched as the news anchor described how for the third day running, the government Cobra committee had met but were refusing to give any details about the crisis. My first thought was for all the poor people travelling at airports in the UK. They were in for a long wait as the inevitable queues built up as the security checks increased. We all stood glued to the TV until Neil Andrews broke the spell. "Well, standing watching telly won't get it sorted. Let's go. I have a helicopter waiting for us at the airport."

We all traipsed out to a waiting taxi to take us the short journey to the helipad by the side of Edinburgh Airport.

I noted with interest one of Neil Andrews's protection detail being helped into the back of a waiting ambulance by his colleague. No trip back in the chopper for those boys. To my surprise, a military Lynx helicopter sat on the middle of the big H and was attended by its pilot, which was even more of a surprise. Neil introduced Captain Fiona Malden to Sam and me as she was carrying out her preflight checks.

Malden spoke to the tower and was given permission for immediate take-off. "Lift-off in two minutes, folks. Buckle up, please. We don't want any harm coming to you, especially you, Captain Macdonald. Wouldn't look good on my record if I got the Mac damaged while in my charge, now would it? Next stop, RAF Shawbury in Shropshire. Hold tight, folks." Malden throttled up the powerful Lynx for a second. As the power built, it started to vibrate, but as the machine cleared the ground, it smoothed out, and we were off on another one of Neil's adventure trips. To pass the time on the flight, Captain Malden pointed out landmarks and points of interest over the headsets. "Just to let you know, we are stopping at RAF Shawbury to refuel and grab a bite to eat before heading to London. I am based at Shawbury as a trainer with the Defence Helicopter Flying School. My good friend Al is the canteen manager. She will take good care of us before we head south again."

The further south we travelled, the worse the weather became. We were only ten minutes away from Shawbury when Captain Malden was asked to change her flight plan. A few minutes' conversation between air traffic control and Neil Andrews ended up with Captain Malden coming back onto the comms. "OK, folks, a change of plan. I am afraid we will now be landing in forty minutes at Credenhill. No idea what the food is going to be like there." Captain Malden half turned and caught my eye before continuing on the comms. "For the record, Credenhill in Hereford is Captain Macdonald's old stomping ground, so maybe he can tell us what the food is like?"

On approach to Hereford, Captain Malden was not having a good day. Her fuel levels were below the recommended minimum, and she had just been told by Hereford to fly past and circle to await arrival of an inbound flight also landing at Hereford. "Credenhill, this is army flight Victor Charlie one. Negative on flypast, fuel situation critical. I am coming in now. Advise other aircraft to fly past. Thank you." Malden switched her comms off and gave her full attention to landing the Lynx in what could only be described as monsoon conditions. I watched with interest as the green oblong roofs of my old base came into view. Captain Malden seemed to skim over the roofs to the far side of the base.

The lonely looking helipad stood empty and ready for its new visitors. Malden wasted no time setting the Lynx down on her first attempt. Even as she powered down the chopper, a Land Rover was making its way through the blizzard conditions from the closest building.

A red-faced sergeant proceeded to bark at Malden as she exited her aircraft. "No one told you to land. Just who the bloody hell do you think you are? No one lands here without authorisation. I hope they bloody throw the book at you for this, you stupid woman."

We all looked on. Malden, soaked to the skin, had had enough. The stupid woman comment must have been the final straw. "Sergeant, are you something special that you do not have to salute an officer, or are you just too stupid? I do not have to explain my actions to you or even talk to you for that matter. Get some transport out here for my passengers, and do it now. Also, get me your commanding officer. Then we will see who is going to get the book thrown at him, you stupid little man."

There was a pause as the sergeant considered his options. His face was as red as a tomato, and he looked like he was about to explode. He had expected a trainee pilot, not a captain with a full complement of passengers. Reluctantly, he got on his two-way radio and summoned another seven-seater Land Rover Defender to ferry the contents of the Lynx to the main building.

We were just about to transfer to the Land Rover when, out of nowhere, the heavy beat of a Chinook helicopter broke through the howl of the wind. Seconds later, the hull of the big transport chopper appeared and made a slight adjustment to its landing position to make sure it was clear of the Lynx, then dropped the last few feet onto the helipad. A group of men started to disembark from the rear loading-bay doors. Smithy and I waited until the big beast had powered down its engines before getting out of the Lynx. Dealing with the howling wind was bad enough without adding the downwash from the Chinook as well. As we walked to the waiting Land Rover, a shout rang out from the rear of the column of men who had just cleared the back of the Chinook. "Mac, you big Scottish git. What the hell are you doing back here?"

I did not have to look to see who it was. Bob Hunter and I had both served in Kuwait and Iraq and later as trainers here at Hereford. Bob was a good bit younger than me and was still a trainer with the regiment. Bob broke away from the column and made a beeline across the helipad to the Land Rover as everybody piled in leaving Bob and me standing outside, grinning at each other like Cheshire cats in the middle of the worst winter storm to hit southern England that year. Bob peered into the Land Rover and eyeballed its occupants. "Mac, is that young Smithy in the back with the birds and the crabbit-lookin curly haired git?"

I was chuckling out loud at Bob's description of Neil. "Yes, you're right. It is Smithy. He is working for six now, and the curly haired crabbit git is the director, his boss."

Bob's smile vanished. "Jesus, Mac, what the hell have you got yourself involved in now?"

I shook my head. "Bob, you wouldn't believe it if I told you. Look, buddy, I need to get going. Good to speak to you again. The next time you're heading to Scotland, give me a shout, and we will hit the local pubs."

Bob said nothing but gave me a pat on the back as I jumped into the back of the Defender. We were taken to an admin building on the other side of the base and made comfortable while a shout was put out to find the commanding officer. After ten minutes, the red-faced sergeant reappeared with Captain Forbly.

It turned out that at that moment in time, Forbly was the most senior officer on the base. A high percentage of troops were deployed around the world, and a good number of the regiment were involved in a training exercise off base. Neil Andrews took the captain aside while we tucked into sandwiches and mugs of tea. Neil left with the officer saying he would return shortly.

We were all on our second round of tea and sandwiches when Andrews returned with the red-faced sergeant in tow carrying a large box. "Right, ladies and gentlemen, here is the situation. There have been no reports of any chemical attacks, but Benesch is still at large. Some new video evidence has been found. So we need to get back to Vauxhall Cross to have a look at it and plan our next move. Unfortunately, the weather is not playing ball with us, and we cannot travel by helicopter for the present time. Captain Forbly has agreed to lend us two Range Rovers, which are waiting outside. Captain Malden, you will wait here until the weather clears, then make your way back to London, and remain there on standby, please. Sam, I have a present here for yourself and Adam. You are back on the team, so I have borrowed some weapons from our military friends here. Please, Sam, be careful. I have a feeling that we are only going to get one chance at recovering the chemicals. You are both authorised to use lethal force if the situation cannot be contained otherwise."

Outside the howling wind whipped the rain into our eyes as we made the short dash from the admin building to the leather-clad interior of the big Range Rovers. Peter Kent and Neil Andrews headed for the lead vehicle while Smithy, Sam, and I requisitioned the second vehicle. To our surprise, Karen Lowe joined us in the front seat next to Smithy, our driver for the trip.

Karen and Smithy blethered away as Smithy pushed the big 4x4 hard to keep up with Peter Kent, who was driving the lead Range Rover. Sam and I were busy playing with our new toys from Neil Andrews to pay attention to where we were headed.

We had both been given Glock 19s, which were on evaluation by certain units within the British armed forces. Sam complained bitterly that it was not as good a weapon as her custom-made Glock, which she had left at the firing range of the glass house.

❖ ❖ ❖

Khanjar studied the laptop for the twentieth time that day. The vast majority of the little red markers were located in the south of England but there were a few dotted around the country. The three dots that were holding Khanjar's attention were in the north of the country. One appeared to be in the north-west of Scotland by the coast, while the other two were located in Scotland's capital city. For the moment, the two in the city of Edinburgh were going to be Khanjar's targets. He had to find out if his new toy actually led him to British secret service agents. He was worried that the British had discovered the transmitters in their weapons and had set an elaborate trap for him. He lifted his cell phone and clicked on a saved number.

It was answered immediately. Khanjar instantly recognised his comrade's deep, gruff tone.

"You have a task for me, brother. I do not think you call to discuss the weather, although it would seem to be the favourite topic with these English. Tell me, brother. What would you have me do?"

Khanjar took one last look at the laptop. "My good friend, have you found my two friends that I have pointed out to you? Then, if you are happy with their credentials, please give them the welcome they deserve. My friend, do not leave without removing their beacons. I will await good news. Do not contact me until you are safe in the bosom of your good wife."

Khanjar had refrained from offering details over the phone, but Phal had been briefed before entering the capital and had been waiting for the kill signal from his beloved leader. Khanjar knew he would carry out his mission or would die trying. Either way, Khanjar would have his proof on the accuracy of his laptop information.

❖ ❖ ❖

Colonel Southern had only landed at the Machrihanish Air Base two hours ago. In that time, he had secured the perimeter of the base, much to the astonishment of the Ministry of Defence police who patrolled the empty base. Brent Cussack of the ISA and Scott Tomlin from the CIA had been sent south to dig up what they could while Southern was arranging transport for himself, Al Franklyn, and his Delta team. He wanted to be on site at the transmission point of the message he had received from Benesch within the next twenty-four hours. One of the Delta team had been assigned to monitor radio transmissions and keep all the American units linked to him as anchor comms.

Southern was watching two gulls fight their way through the gale-force winds off the Mull of Kintyre when the radio operator approached him. "Permission to speak, sir."

Southern's spell was broken. "Spit it out, soldier. What do you need from me?"

The corporal was looking at a handheld monitor as he spoke. "Sir, are you aware of the Stealth 12 transponder that we developed for use in covert ops." Southern nodded but said nothing, unsure what was coming next. "I have been monitoring multiple Stealth 12 transmissions since we arrived. Looking at the pattern, I would say somebody has managed to tag a large group. And using their locations as a key, I think it could be the entire British secret service!"

Southern let the enormity of this statement sink in for a second before joining the corporal in staring at the handheld screen. There was no doubt that more than a few transmissions were based around the MI5 and MI6 buildings. "Sir, we need to let the Brits know that they have a major security breach."

It only took a millisecond for Southern's military brain to work out all the scenarios. "Good work, corporal. I will inform them of the situation. In the meantime, you keep an eye on their movements for me." Southern had no intention of telling anyone about the transmitters. It might come in very handy in the near future. What intrigued him more was who had planted them, and who else had this delicate information?

❖ ❖ ❖

It had been a very busy day. We had spent most of the day travelling. Looking around our little group, it was clear we were all ready for bed. We had been herded into a corner of the staff canteen at the MI6 building at Vauxhall Cross. Jean was busy dishing out rolls and copious amounts of tea and coffee. Neil was busy with two analysts who had just arrived on scene with reams of paperwork and two laptops. I took the opportunity to talk to Sam, who was still uncharacteristically quiet.

"It looks like those two have hit it off big time, don't you think?" I nodded toward Smithy and Dr Lowe, who were deep in conversation about something.

Sam smiled as she observed the couple for a second. "Yes, you are right! Just look at the body language. Both facing each other and both within the other's personal space. Someone needs to fling a bucket of water over them. Either that or tell them to get a room."

Sam caught my eye as I started to chuckle out loud at her last comment. She searched for my hand as we continued to make eye contact. She was warm to the touch. I relaxed in the knowledge that we still had that vital spark of desire between us. It was nothing you could describe, but it was there, and we both knew it. I was glad to see that the old Sam was still there.

Neil Andrews had to raise his voice to get the attention of our chattering group. But when he spoke, his words silenced the assembled party. His news was not good. "First of all, I have some bad news for us all. It would appear that our number one public enemy has resumed hostilities. One hour ago, two MI5 agents based in Edinburgh were found in an alley with their throats cut from ear to ear. They were not robbed. Only their side arms were missing. At this time, there has been no contact with Khanjar. It is entirely possible that he has found out of his son's death. We have no idea how he was able to identify our two agents but we cannot rule out the possibility of a mole. More bad news I am afraid. It would appear that the United States has got fed up waiting for us to catch Benesch. This morning a US taskforce landed at Machrihanish in Scotland. The PM has been told that any attempt to stop these US troops will result in a request by the US that the UK be punished by NATO for willfully disobeying international law and attempting to conceal weapons of mass destruction. The PM has instructed me to give the Americans a wide berth. He wants Benesch captured immediately. Which brings us to our next task. We have unearthed a security tape that up until now had been lost. Please have a good look at it as it has a huge bearing on where we look for Benesch next."

We all gathered round the laptop as one of the analysts started playing the lost security recording. Neil Andrews pointed out that the area on screen was taken from above the main gate. We watched as a car pulled up. Then a few seconds later, a fuzzy image of a woman appeared by the driver's door. The recording was shockingly bad quality, so much so that it was almost impossible to make out what type of car it was, let alone its registration number. We watched as the car pulled away with the woman in the passenger seat.

Sam was the first to speak. "So Neil, correct me if I am wrong. This is one of the most sensitive military sites in the UK, and MI6 thought it was OK to fit a cheap shit camera that probably cost a tenner. Then you expect us to look at it and come up with all the answers? Just brilliant, Neil, just bloody brilliant!"

Sam's rant was cut short by a gasp from the very pale Karen Lowe. "Oh my god, I know who was in that car. Shit, I can't believe I forgot about Gary."

Andrews was like a man possessed. "Gary who? Karen, we need to know who the driver is." Karen was still thinking things through in her head as Neil Andrews pressed her for more answers.

"Gary Harding was the professor's protégé. He was supposed to be on leave then he changed it at the last minute."

Andrews checked through a bundle of notes. "Gary Harding, Gary Harding. Here we go. The log says that he was on a week's leave. What the hell was he playing at? No wonder no one has missed him." Neil charged off armed with this new information, both analysts in tow, intending to dig up as much as he could find about Gary Harding. Sam and I listened to Karen Lowe as she described her work colleague to her small audience in the canteen.

"Academically, Gary is up there with the very best minds the scientific world can offer. He is something between a genius and a lost child. In a normal laboratory environment, he would not have lasted a week but Professor Ferry knew he had in Gary the makings of a twenty-first century Einstein. God knows how Gary will cope with being abducted."

Sam cleared her throat. I could see her weighing up her next comment in her mind. "Dr Lowe, I don't know how close you are to this Gary character, but be warned. Areli Benesch, as you have already witnessed, is a very nasty piece of work. When she has no more use for your work colleague, rest assured, we will not find him alive. I would advise you to get ready for more bad news."

CHAPTER 6

DIAVOKXIN

Gary Harding negotiated the cobbled back street with difficulty. Areli, who seemed to know the area well, had directed him to the lane through the driving wind and rain. The Blue Mandolin Hotel was only two streets away from the lane and only one street from the Thames.

Situated in the east of the city, the hotel had stood for years as the housing around it had been replaced by industrial sites. Areli needed the attaché case that was stored in the hotel safe. It was her get-out-of-jail-free card for the UK. The attaché case held a Sig Sauer, silencer, and half a dozen clips of ammo, money, a fake passport, and French and UK driving licenses. Once Areli had these, she would be on the home straight.

There was only one problem. The hotel was owned and run by a Jewish couple who had their income supplemented by Mossad in exchange for the use of rooms and the storage of agents' equipment. It was a pretty safe bet that Mossad had been put under extreme pressure by the British government to assist with the capture of Areli. If they had folded, Areli would be walking into an MI6 trap. "OK, my young friend, I am going to leave you for a few minutes. Can I trust that you will not try to do anything stupid? Remember, I have the Vokxin in my pocket. There is nowhere to run. Better to stay and become rich with me, yes?"

Gary nodded he was still thinking what he would do with his billion dollar payout after he had returned the chemicals to a safe place. Areli wasted no time and vanished into the swirling mist that surrounded the camper van. Areli tiptoed round a few street corners before she found what she was looking for.

On the next street corner stood a skinny girl dressed in only a black leather miniskirt and see-through lace top. She was soaked to the skin and stood shivering visibly. Her long, black, straggly hair stuck to her face and neck as the winds battered her fragile body. It did not take a rocket scientist to know what her profession was. Areli approached her slowly, making sure she had no pimp with her. "I think I have the perfect job for you tonight, my friend. If you want to get out of the weather and earn some money, follow me."

Areli led the girl back to the camper van. Gary opened the door to find the two women soaked to the skin. Areli gave the girl a gentle push to get her to climb aboard the camper. Inside, Gary had retreated to the far side of the camper and sat quietly. Although secretly he wanted a girlfriend, he had never been good at chatting to girls and had put all his time and energy into his true love of science and moneymaking projects. He knew if he made it big, he could then concentrate on the opposite sex.

Areli wasted no time with small talk. She handed the girl a towel and proceeded to dry her own hair with another towel while she spoke to the girl. "OK, here is the deal. You get five hundred pounds now. Then you go to the Blue Mandolin Hotel two streets from here and give the reception this piece of paper. They will ask you to wait. Then they will give you a case like this one I have here."

Areli had raided the local shops earlier that day. She had purchased the case, a mousetrap, and sticky tape. Then she had Gary raid the contents of his current account, removing every last penny. Gary had handed the money over grudgingly. Areli explained to him that this would be a drop in the ocean. He eventually brightened up when Areli promised to give him back the five thousand, two hundred, and twenty pounds from her share of the profits. "When you have the case, you will come back here and hand it over. When you do this, I will give you another five hundred pounds. Do you understand the instructions?"

The girl nodded enthusiastically. Her initial thought was that this woman had wanted her to join in on some type of threesome in the camper. She had already set a price in her head for this service at four hundred pounds. Now all she had to do was pick up the case, and she would be a grand better off.

She could pack it in for the night, go home for a hot bath, and still have the money to pay her landlord.

Areli rummaged around in a closet and found one of Gary's aunt's raincoats. She did not want the girl to be kicked out of the hotel for soliciting before she got the briefcase. The jacket covered her see-through top, which left absolutely nothing to the imagination and labelled her as a prostitute.

Ten minutes later, the girl walked into the reception and handed the old man behind the desk the piece of paper. He studied the paper and then the girl who had delivered it. For a second, he did nothing. The girl sensed he was trying to make up his mind what to do. "Wait over there by the fire, child. Warm yourself while I look for your package."

Jasmine skipped over to the fire and sat looking into the embers as they glowed in the poor light of the hotel lounge. The voice startled Jasmine.

"Nothing like a real fire to look at, is there?" Jasmine had not seen the middle-aged man sitting well back in the wingback chair, studying the local paper. She was well used to being chatted up by older men and replied with a twinkle in her eye. "You almost scared me out of my clothes there. I didn't see you. Do you make a habit of sneaking up on poor defenseless girls?"

Before the man could answer, the old man appeared with Areli's case. "Right, luv, that's you now."

The girl gave the man in the chair a saucy wink and headed to the reception desk to pick up the case. She thanked the old man and left. After a few seconds, the old man nodded to the man by the fire, who jumped up and set sail after the girl. Outside, he was joined by his MI5 colleague. The girl had set a good pace, and although the rain had slowed to a drizzle, the fog from the Thames had started to envelop the surrounding streets, aided by the sudden drop in wind speed.

Areli and Gary watched for the return of the girl. Gary had just had a set-to with Areli over the thousand pounds of his money that Areli had just handed to the prostitute. Areli saw the girl first and shouted at Gary to get the camper started and ready to go. Benesch jumped down from the camper and headed along the street to meet the girl. They met in exactly the middle of the alley. Areli placed her case on the ground and held out the wedge of notes for the girl to take. As the girl smiled and reached out for the money, Benesch dropped the money, grabbed her hand, and used it to spin the girl round. With one swift move, she let go of the girl's hand and now with the girl facing with her back to her clamped the same hand over her mouth and jaw, pulling her head back and causing the girl to arch her back. Her left hand was like the strike of a cobra. It appeared from Areli's coat holding a razor-sharp paring knife taken from the cutlery drawer in the camper van. One swift movement sent the blade up under the left side of the girl's stretched-out rib cage. Areli had judged it to perfection. The blade cut deep into the left ventricle of the girl's heart. Areli finished the job by twisting the blade and removing it with the same force as she had delivered the blow. The girl clawed at the hand that Areli had placed over her face. Her nails dug deeply into Areli's hand, but Areli held on tightly, allowing only a small gasp to escape from the girl's mouth as the blade did its terrible work.

The girl's warm breath on Areli's hand slowed, and her knees started to give way, Areli placed her on the ground as gently as a china doll. The blood from the terrible wound splashed on the wet cobbles and threatened to soak Areli's footwear. Areli placed her case next to the dying prostitute and lifted the one from the hotel.

Gary was still in a state of shock as Areli charged onto the camper van. She flung the case on the couch and started reversing back down the street. It all happened in a flash. Gary flung himself at Areli. "You evil fucking witch! You are going to pay for this," Gary screamed at the top of his voice. What he had witnessed had shocked him to the core. Up until now, he had only seen the manipulative side of Benesch. This was the first time he had seen her true colours. And at that second, he realised he had done a deal with the devil.

Areli clocked him in the rearview mirror and hit him hard in the family planning unit with her elbow. As he fell forward clutching his groin, she grabbed his hair and smashed his head off the windscreen. Gary collapsed unconscious over the passenger seat, but Areli had other things on her mind. She had to get out of here, and she had to do it now.

The camper was four streets away and building up speed as the two MI5 officers found Jasmine's body slumped by the briefcase. They had blown their one chance of apprehending Areli Benesch, and an innocent girl had died in the process. In desperation, one officer opened the case to see if it would give any clues to the whereabouts of Benesch. It was a mistake that he paid for with his life. As he opened the case, there was a loud crack and a noise like a breaking tumbler hitting the ground. There was a hissing noise. Then suddenly his throat started to spasm, and his whole chest seemed to turn to stone. He was on his knees gasping for breath. He turned to look for help from his colleague but found him on his hands and knees, his eyes bulging from their sockets. He was clawing at his tie trying to slacken it to allow more air into his throat. His head was exploding, and his strength was ebbing. A great darkness descended on him as his body gave up the fight and his brain gave up the will to live. A terrible weapon that had been designed to kill Britain's enemies had been unleashed on its own people.

Areli drove on, and as the miles clicked up on the camper, Benesch knew her gamble had paid off. She had retrieved her emergency kit from the hotel, and she had set down a marker to the rest of the world.

They knew for certain now that Areli would not hesitate to use the deadly weapons she had at her disposal if she needed to.

❖ ❖ ❖

Neil Andrews was just heading out his office door when the phone rang. For a second, he thought about ignoring it. He had not made it home once in the past week. He had run out of clothes and was heading home for a hot bath and a large whisky. Reluctantly, he picked up the receiver. He listened as the police inspector described the scene, then waited while he put the head of MI5, Bill Mathews, on the line.

Mathews was rattled when he answered the call. He had just lost two of his best agents and was still in shock. "That bitch has to be stopped, Neil. She had just hit this area with Diavokxin. Luckily for us, it is mainly an industrial area, so the casualties are low. So far we have found eight people, including the proprietor of the Blue Mandolin, dead in the hotel. My two agents died.

Two security guards and four homeless men died. Not bad, Neil, if it had been during the day, there would have been thousands dead."

Neil Andrews was only half listening to the head of MI5. The other part of his brain had already started going through the conversation he was about to have with the prime minister. It looked like yet again his hot bath was going to have to wait.

❖ ❖ ❖

The morning sun had just started to rise above the hedgerows in Netheravon when the dawn chorus was silenced by the menacing beat of the rotors. The Seahawk skimmed over the trees, did a circular pass of the target area before coming down to rest in a cropless field next to the Harding household. As soon as the big chopper touched down, Sergeant Al Franklyn and his Delta commandos hit the ground running. Within two minutes, Franklyn reported he had the property locked down and that there was no one home.

Colonel David Southern had been waiting for this information before exiting the chopper. He trusted no one, especially Areli Benesch. It would have been to easy for her to attack his unit with the Cold War chemicals. Southern knew from studying her Israeli military records that she was an accomplished helicopter pilot. If she had breathing apparatus, she could fly the chopper out of the country before anyone knew what had happened. Southern entered the living room and was handed an envelope by Al Franklyn, who departed to check on the positions of his Delta troops.

Alone in the room Southern tore the envelope open and read the note inside.

> *Good day, my friend. We meet again. I have what you are looking for and am willing to do a deal on the chemicals and my young scientific friend. Before we meet, you must show me you have the power to negotiate for your country. You will do this by crashing a helicopter on the White House lawn. Only a person high in the echelons of power in America will be able to do this. I will meet you at the grounds of the British football team*

Manchester United at the first home game after the helicopter crash. You will pick your ticket up from the office. It will be for an American called Richard Nixon. You will take your seat alone, with no help, and wait for me to contact you. If you do not or cannot do this, I will deal with the Russians, my friend.

Southern finished reading the note then set it alight and stormed back to the chopper. Areli was turning out to be a very large pain in the butt.

❖ ❖ ❖

The beat of the helicopter had faded to a low drumming noise before I parted the branches of the tall leylandii hedge. We had made it to the cover of the big hedge by the skin of our teeth. Sam emerged from further along the hedge, followed by Smithy and Dr Karen Lowe. Our luck had changed. We were back in the game. Sam had struck gold with her questioning of Dr Lowe. Neil Andrews had been too preoccupied with the new information about Gary Harding to arrange our accommodation. As it was starting to get late, we informed Peter Kent that we were heading back to Sam's flat. Karen Lowe had been staying there anyway, so it seemed logical that we spend the night in Sam's Kennington flat. Smithy had volunteered to give us a lift there and pick us back up in the morning. En route, Sam had asked Karen if she had any idea where Gary Harding lived. Karen explained to us that Gary still lived with his parents not far from Porton Down in the village of Netheravon. She also informed us that Gary had told her that his parents were on vacation and he had the place to himself. Sam had the idea in a flash. She talked us into leaving at the crack of dawn to have a look at Gary's home before MI5 and MI6 foot soldiers invaded it. Karen had visited Gary before when he had asked her to look at one of his mad experiments. Sam talked Smithy into staying at the flat so that we could leave early and still be back at Vauxhall Cross before Neil Andrews missed us. In the flat, Smithy had been all set to spend the night on the couch with Karen before Sam put the brakes on that idea by ushering Karen Lowe into the bedroom beside her, leaving Smithy and me staring at each other in disgust. We had arrived in darkness the next morning, and Sam had revelled in disarming the house alarm then picking the lock. The note had shocked us all, but before we had time to think about its contents, I caught the first beats of the helicopter in the distance. Sam was the last under the big hedge after sealing the envelope back up and locking the door.

The next fifteen minutes were not good fun as an American soldier had been posted at the end of the hedge only feet from where we were hiding. I was not worried for Sam and Smithy, but Karen Lowe was an unknown quantity. Would her nerve hold out until our unexpected guests left? As I looked around at our small band under the trees, I saw Smithy gearing up while Sam studied the man in civilian clothes who had just entered the house. Silently, Smithy screwed the silencer onto his Glock while never taking his eyes off the grey-and-black camo trousers that stood only feet in front of our position. I was busy trying to imagine what would happen if our American guests discovered us. I was hoping that there would be a withdrawal on both sides, but I would not have bet my life on it. From previous experience, I decided to keep my head down and wait for our uninvited friends to leave. As quickly as they arrived, they were gone, led away by the middle-aged man in civvies.

The minute we climbed into Smithy's Astra hire car Sam took charge. It was as if someone had flicked a switch. The old Sam was back. "Right here's what we are going to do. We are all going to high tail it up the M6 to Manchester. We need to be in position ready to pounce at the stadium as soon as Benesch gets the signal from America."

Smithy pointed out that we needed to speak to Neil Andrews and keep him up to date on the situation. Sam's reply was full of venom." All in good time, I am not about to be put to one side while Neil try's to take all the credit. Anyway I don't trust any other agents to pull it off I will deal with Benesch and Andrews won't stop me."

❖ ❖ ❖

It was eight in the morning when the chief of staff and the chairman of the Joint Chiefs were summoned to the situation room of the White House. They both sat in stunned silence as they listened to Colonel David Southern's report from the UK and his request to crash a chopper on the White House lawn. "Southern, are you mad? The only chopper allowed to land at the White House is the president's own helicopter. You can't crash the president's chopper. You will need to rethink your plan."

There was silence for a second as Southern thought through what he was going to say to his superior officers. "Look, guys. You are not getting it. We need to prove to Benesch that we are serious players, and if crashing a chopper gets me the Vokxin back, then I will fly it to the White House myself."

There was silence for a second as the chief of staff thought over Southern's request. "OK, David. We will work something out here. We will be in contact once we have an answer. The president asked me to remind you that you are in the country of our allies. He wants our troops out of there as soon as we have the Vokxin safely recovered."

Southern signed off, then gave the order to return to Machrihanish. His next call was to Brent Cussack, who answered on the second ring. "Brent, I want yourself and Scott Tomlin to make your way to Manchester. I know that the ISA and the CIA don't normally play well together, but due to the situation, I am expecting the best from you both. I want you both to attend soccer games at Manchester United. You need to know the stadium like the back of your hand. I will be in touch when I have more information for you."

Southern sat watching the English countryside fly past below him. He was deep in thought. What would happen if he had the Vokxin but had not gained control of the young scientist and his discovery? Would he stop and return home? Or would he risk the wrath of his superiors and continue the mission? Deep in the back of his mind he already knew what the answer would be.

❖ ❖ ❖

Unknown to Areli, she was only a few miles in front of her pursuers. The big motor home lumbered its way up the M6 motorway. Inside Gary had been tethered to a gas pipe leading to the van's cooker to stop him making a bid for freedom. He had seen the light as far as Areli Benesch was concerned.

He now knew in his heart that Areli had no intention of sharing any money that was made out of his discovery. Areli had marvelled once more at the recovery rate of the young man. When Areli had smashed his face into the windscreen, he had burst his left eye open on the top of the unforgiving dashboard, closing his eye and leaving a gash on his cheek. Areli had watched over the next twenty minutes as Gary's injuries completely repaired themselves. There was not even a scar to be found on his flawless skin. To Areli, the chemicals had always been purely a means of escape, but this phenomenon she had stumbled across would change the history of the world.

She could ask the Americans for anything, and she would have it. Gary was literally priceless.

❖ ❖ ❖

Our trip had taken us into the afternoon, with Sam using Smithy's phone to call ahead and book us three double rooms at the nearest hotel to the Old Trafford football stadium. Smithy paid for two weeks in advance with the company credit card. I smiled to myself. I could just imagine Neil Andrews going mad when the bill came in for this little lot. The talk in the car had turned back to Benesch and her abduction of Gary Harding. The thing that no one could understand was the American involvement.

I quizzed Karen Lowe about this. "Karen, can you think of any reason that the Americans would need Gary Harding? Is there something that he knows about the chemicals that would be useful to the Americans?"

Karen was shaking her head. "No, definitely not. If that were the case, they would be better with me. I have done more work with Vokxin and Diavokxin than any other scientist other than Professor Ferry. No, if it is scientific, it must be the project he was working on. Although I can't be sure, he did have some way-out theories."

Smithy butted in. "Something smells bad here. I know from speaking to the office that the Americans were threatening to come and sort out the problem if we couldn't handle it. But it still doesn't explain how they were able to waltz in with Delta troops right to the perfect place. Benesch left them a note, for god's sake. I tell you right now, there is much more to this than chemicals."

❖ ❖ ❖

Neil Andrews was in his office brooding over his lack of headway in the Vokxin saga when a knock at his door brought him three pieces of news all at once. He studied the three pieces of paper one at a time. The first note was hard to explain. It would appear GCHQ had been monitoring the White House pressroom. The note stated that the presidential helicopter had had a landing wheel failure, causing it to crash land at the White House.

Normally the White House would try to keep this quiet. But the memo from GCHQ stated that the White House was positively trying to advertise, sending press releases to all the major news networks.

The second memo was deeply worrying. Another MI6 agent had been found dead at his flat in Manchester. His throat had been cut, and his handgun removed. Someone knew how to get to Neil's agents. It was either Khanjar or a copycat killer. The third note made Neil's blood boil. Smithy's hire car was heading north and had been camera-tracked in the Manchester area with four passengers aboard.

Neil cursed openly. He was in no doubt that Smithy had been led astray by Samantha and Adam. What the hell was going on?

❖ ❖ ❖

Smithy's mobile phone rang just as they were pulling up to the hotel. One look at the screen made Smithy's blood run cold. It was the big boss on the phone for him. He did not need to answer the call to know he was in very hot water. Sam saw his reaction and asked for the phone before Smithy had the chance to answer.

"Hello, Neil. It's Sam here. Smithy can't answer as he is driving at the moment. I take it you are calling for an update."

Neil had half expected Sam to answer, but it did not stop him from launching into a rant. "Update, what bloody update? Where the hell do you lot think you are going? I don't recall giving you free reign to swan off without as much as a good-bye. You listen to me, girl, and you listen well. You owe me big. You should be rotting in jail, but I turned a blind eye and even covered for you. You screw this up, girl, and I will lock you up myself and throw the key away. Do I make myself very clear?"

Although Sam did not show it, she was shocked at how wound up Neil was. She had known him for years, but had never seen him in this state. She decided to step carefully for the moment. "OK, Neil, you have made your point. Now do you want to hear what we have found today, or are you just going to keep screaming and shouting until you feel better or drop with a heart attack?"

Neil sat back and switched on the speakerphone while he popped two headache tablets in his mouth and washed them down with mineral water. "OK, Sam, I've calmed down. You are on a secure line, so let's go. This had better be good, for your sake."

Sam had also put the phone on speakerphone, and we all listened as Neil groaned and grunted as Sam divulged the day's goings on. Sam's report's authenticity was proved when Neil heard her describe the signal that was to be used to prove that the unknown American had the power to influence the White House. "OK, Sam, I believe you. There was a press release today to say that the president's helicopter had suffered undercarriage failure and had crash-landed on the White House lawn. It looks as if the unknown American who visited Gary Harding's home is very high up in the power stakes in Washington. Oh, by the way, our checks on Harding have come back clear. Anyone you speak to says that Harding is somewhat unhinged but a true genius. GCHQ noted that Harding's computer a few days ago sent an e-mail to the US embassy. Whatever was in that mail brought the Americans hotfooting right to his door."

I decided to put my oar in the water. "Neil, the signal has been sent, so the meeting will take place at Old Trafford at the next home game. We have the advantage of knowing what is going down. What do you want us to do, and how far do we go to do it?"

"Adam, the Vokxin is the main priority. Do whatever it takes to recover it. If blood has to be spilled to achieve that, then so be it. There are a couple of things you need to know. Benesch was at a known Israeli safe house in London. She used Diavokxin to cover her escape. There have been a number of fatalities. The press were informed that chemicals stored in a warehouse on the Thames had leaked. So far our deception has worked. I will send what agents I can to assist you, but we are a bit thin on the ground. We have had three agents murdered this week. Peter Kent is looking into it, but watch your backs. I suspect that Khanjar has had a hand in their deaths. They all died by having their throats cut. He must have someone on the inside in MI6. You need to be on your guard until we can find the leak."

CHAPTER 7

THE CHASE

Colonel Southern checked his watch one more time. It had been three days since the alleged helicopter crash in Washington. The chief of staff had been given the OK from the president to stage a crash on the White House lawn. In reality, there had been no crash. A team of air force engineers had arrived and removed a wheel from the undercarriage causing the big chopper to list to one side. Hidden behind a security screen with only the upper parts showing, it gave the impression of a crashed helicopter. In the next fifteen minutes, Southern was going to find out if it had all been worth the trouble.

Southern had picked up his ticket and made his way up to the area in which he was seated. A spotty kid had taken his ticket and shown him to his seat before handing the ticket back to him. Southern scanned the surrounding faces, but none of them seemed to be remotely interested in him or his seat. Southern studied his ticket while he waited to be contacted. The local team, Manchester United, were playing a team called Blackburn Rovers. Further up in the last row of the section, Sam studied Southern. She pretended to take a picture of the stadium with her phone but snapped a profile of Southern as he surveyed the crowd.

Sam had bought the phone from the local supermarket the day before. She had already decided the minute the operation was finished, she was going to get rid of the phone as Neil was guaranteed to put a trace on it. Sam transferred the picture of the American to Vauxhall Cross, then put the phone away, and continued her surveillance.

Smithy and I were on the ground floor. Sam had insisted that we wait for her call. She did not want us to give the game away as neither of us had been trained in this type of operation. Smithy's phone started to ring. Smithy checked the screen. It wasn't Sam. It was her boss.

"Mr Smith, I have some information that you need to know. CCTV cameras have identified Areli Benesch driving a camper van in the centre of London just after the chemical attack. You need to check the car parks for any campers. There is a good chance Gary Harding may be in the camper, if he is still alive. Also we have just found out that the picture Sam sent us is an American colonel called David Southern. We have very little on file about him, but he was involved in the Machrihanish incident last year. I spoke to him personally at the time, and I got the impression that he was a very slippery character."

Ten minutes later, Smithy and I were wading through the car park, looking for the camper van. Suddenly, there was a voice behind me.

For a fraction of a second, I froze. Then my brain registered the voice, and I relaxed. I turned to find a very confused-looking Karen Lowe.

Karen, much to her disgust, had been ordered to stay in the hire car until this was all over. "Adam, what is going on? I thought that you were backing up Sam."

Smithy had not noticed Karen and was further to the left, heading for a Volkswagen camper parked three lanes away. I made a split-second decision. Three were going to make the search much quicker. "Karen, you can give Smithy and me a hand to search for a camper. MI6 reckon that Benesch travelled here in one, and Gary may be on board. You take the far lanes, I will take the centre, and Smithy can take the far side."

"Cool. Do I get a gun?"

I gave Karen a withering stare. "You just give me a shout if you get into trouble, and I can do the gun bit, thank you very much, madam."

Karen stuck her tongue out at me and headed off to start her search. I watched Dr Lowe as she made a beeline for the far side of the car park where two large campers were parked. I was amazed at her enthusiasm. She did not strike me as the doctor type, and considering what she had been through, she was holding up very well. I spotted a camper straight ahead and was heading for it when Karen shouted.

She was standing next to a white Ford Transit motor home and waving frantically. Smithy had heard her shouts and was heading her way.

I reached into my jacket pocket and checked the Glock was at hand. I approached the back of the big camper. Smithy and I both appeared front and back at exactly the same time to find Karen banging on the side of the camper just behind the side door. We listened as the occupant responded with a series of three bangs followed by another three bangs, then a final three bangs. We all came to the same conclusion at the same time. SOS. Smithy looked around the car park. Two attendants in fluorescent-yellow jackets were heading away from our direction, some distance away but still too close to risk a shot. Smithy used the butt of his gun to smash the passenger window of the camper, and as if he had planned it, the stadium went into an uproar.

The announcer's voice boomed out over the tannoy, telling everyone that had just watched it and already knew that Manchester United's Wayne Rooney had just scored. I took another quick look around the car park before following Smithy and Karen into the back of the big camper.

❖ ❖ ❖

Areli Benesch did her fourth sweep of the seated area Southern sat in. She was dressed in the uniform of the stadium attendants.

She had picked the lock on one of the basement lockers situated close to the Munich tunnel by the south stand. She now wore the full gear, including the unfortunate attendant's two-way radio. So far she had not been made. She had also picked out two targets other than Southern. The first had shocked Benesch. She had not seen Sam O'Conner for over a year, but the minute she spotted her, the hatred came flooding back in waves. It took all Areli's willpower to keep on walking. All she wanted to do was put a bullet in that woman's brain.

It had been this bitch who had captured Areli by drugging her. So it would appear that MI6 were quicker off the mark than she had estimated. Areli knew for the moment she could do nothing about the MI6 agent without alerting the whole stadium. The English bitch had been clever and had placed herself high in one corner of the seated area. On the other hand, the American agent she had spotted was not so clever. He was seated four rows back from Southern, the end of an aisle. Areli would deal with him first, and if the opportunity arose, she would kill the MI6 woman as she left the stadium.

Southern waited patiently as the game drew to a conclusion. Finally, the home team were victorious, but still there was no sign of a contact. The fans made a headlong charge for the exits, and Southern reluctantly joined them. He had just stood up and was shuffling his way to the exit when he saw Scott Tomlin. He had hoped to make eye contact with the CIA agent to let him know he was leaving, but this idea soon left his head. Tomlin was slouched in his seat, his chin resting on his chest. To the crowd around, he just looked as if he had one too many and had fallen asleep. Southern knew he was dead the minute he set eyes on the unfortunate agent. A pool of his blood had started to form under the seat, and his colour was gone. The only thing on Southern's mind now was to get as far away from here as possible.

Southern had descended one level when Benesch spoke into his right ear. "My friend, we will take the next door on the left."

Benesch had a hold on his right arm. She steered him through the crowd and through a door. Once they were inside, Benesch closed the door and flicked on a light switch. Southern looked round for any other exits, but he was in a large storage cupboard with only one way in and out. "So, my American friend, now that we are face to face, do you have a name?" Benesch started to remove her steward's uniform as they spoke, reverting back to jeans and a sweater.

Southern responded to her question with another question. "I take it you killed my agent in the crowd?"

Benesch rummaged around in her oversized shoulder bag before handing Southern a glass container with a capsule stored inside it. "Yes, my friend, it was me. You needed to be taught to do as I say. You were told to come alone, but you waltzed in here with your dead friend and the British secret service in tow. Your friend's blood is on your hands. Next time I will not be so lenient with your people. Here is the Vokxin. You can go home to your president a hero."

Southern examined the glass container before speaking to Areli. "My name is Colonel David Southern. Are you sure this is the Vokxin?"

Areli nodded thoughtfully as she studied Southern from tip to toe. "Ah yes, it makes sense now. In my homeland, they call you the Berlin Butcher, and yes, it is Vokxin. I will hold onto the Diavokxin just in case anyone tries to cross me."

❖ ❖ ❖

Sam cursed to herself. In the scramble to leave the stadium, she had been held up and had lost Benesch and the American in the crowd. She called Smithy on her mobile and was intrigued to find out that they had found Benesch's transport, along with the missing scientist. Sam, guided by the phone, found the big motor home in no time and climbed aboard to join her colleagues.

I listened as everyone gave an opinion on what should happen next. The young guy was scared out of his mind. He had seen Areli in action and had no doubts that if she were confronted, she would not come quietly. Smithy and Karen were sitting on the fence, while Sam was trying to raise support for ambushing Benesch on her return to the camper van. I decided to stop the madness right there and then. "Sam, no matter what you say, we are not doing anything here. This is not just as simple as grabbing a drug dealer or putting a bullet in an assassin."

Sam butted in before I was finished. "Adam, this may be the only chance we have of grabbing her. We can't let it slip through our fingers."

Sam knew me well enough by now to know that she was not going to change my mind. "No, Sam, not here. Look around you for god's sake. If we get this wrong, and she releases the Diavokxin here, tens of thousands of people will die. I won't let you try, Sam. We need to use our heads here, not our brawn."

Sam was silent but she was giving me the daggers. She was not a happy puppy.

"Listen, folks. Benesch seems to value our young friend here. We need to get away, head to a place where we can lure Benesch into a trap, a place that is not heavily populated where she can do the least damage with her chemicals."

Karen Lowe cleared her throat before speaking. "Has it escaped everyone's mind that if she releases the Vokxin, it won't matter if the area is sparsely populated or not? It will kill everyone on the planet within a matter of hours."

Sam was shaking her head. "No, Karen, if she were going to do that, she would have done it by now. No, she is clever. She is using it as a bargaining chip to get whatever she has planned off the ground."

Gary Harding was starting to panic. He wanted away from the mad-woman. The more they talked, the greater was the chance of her coming back. "Listen, guys. I can tell you exactly what she is up to but not until we get out of here. My aunt has a spare set of keys for the camper, which she keeps in the glove box. We need to get this thing away from here as quickly as possible. Please, can we go now? Please, before it is too late."

I didn't wait for agreement, and two minutes later, the big camper joined the queue leaving the car park. I crawled forward at walking pace while Sam and Smithy kept a lookout in the crowds all around us for any sign of Benesch.

❖ ❖ ❖

Southern and Benesch had just left the stadium when Benesch froze to the spot. The camper was not in the parking lot where Benesch had left it. She scanned the car park in a panic. A large white silhouette far in the distance caught her eye. It was the camper. It climbed up over the bridge that spanned the canal that ran alongside the football stadium.

As Benesch watched in despair, it vanished by the north car park. She had no option but to tell Southern what had happened. Southern pulled out his cell phone and pressed a saved number. "Cussack, I need to be picked up. I am with a female and am heading toward the canal bridge by the north car park. Our target is mobile, so speed is of the essence."

Southern put the phone away and started walking with the crowd toward the bridge in the distance. "Listen, Areli, we have to make this look good. The only reason I have unlimited powers here is because I am chasing the Vokxin. The minute my government know I have it, I will be ordered to stop all activities and return home. So when my colleague, Colonel Brent Cussack, arrives, let me do all the talking and play along with it if you ever want to see freedom again."

It took Cussack twenty minutes to locate them in the mass of fans leaving the stadium. Once in the hired people carrier, Southern started to spin his web of deceit. "Brent, this is Areli Benesch. It would appear we have the wrong end of the stick here. It's the young Scientist that has the Vokxin. Areli was trying to stop him when she was taken hostage by him. The bastard shot and killed Scott Tomlin when Tomlin tried to stop him. He has made his getaway in a big white camper van.

Cussack smiled at Southern. "In that case, sir, I believe I have some good news for you. I had one of my men monitoring the signals we stumbled across. Two traces were in the football stadium, one of which has just left by the north car park."

Benesch put two and two together and almost got it right. "It's that MI6 bitch; it has to be. She was behind you in the stadium. She must have found the camper."

Southern relaxed visibly. He knew they could catch the camper, as it was a slow, lumbering house on wheels. Even their people carrier would be able to catch it. His only worry now was that MI6 were now involved and that would complicate matters considerably.

❖ ❖ ❖

Khanjar had been summoned to the basement of his home. The room lay deep underground in the Scottish home of the Al Qaeda warlord. Faaris was Khanjar's technical genius. Along with a JTRS command-and-control unit that had been captured from the American forces during the Iraqi aftermath, Faaris had managed to obtain detailed information when the Pentagon computers had gone into meltdown, allowing their firewalls to momentarily crash. Faaris knew the JTRS (short for Joint Tactical Radio System) could theoretically link to the British military system, but he had not managed to crack this as yet.

What was getting his full attention at the moment was the unannounced arrival of the American carrier group off the west coast of Scotland, out in the Irish Sea. Khanjar seated himself down next to Faaris and waited patiently as the young man continued to monitor the computer screen. "Well, my young warrior, what have you found that needs my urgent attention?"

Faaris broke his gaze away from the screen to address Khanjar. "My leader, strange things are underway in the sea to the west of Scotland. The Americans are assembling a large force, and by monitoring their communications, I have discovered it is most likely not an exercise. Although I cannot hear the British side of the story, there seems to be tension between the two sides. With the capability to send a message, we could order one of the American ships to open fire on a target in the UK." Faaris was wide-eyed and ready to go.

Khanjar smiled and shook his head at the young man. "My young rascal, you have big ideas. Do not doubt me. I would like nothing more than to see the two rabid dog nations tear themselves apart. You have the right idea, but we must be cunning and patient. If we give your order, the American sailors will question why they are firing on a friend. No, to bring our dreams about, we must chip away at the bond between the two countries. You will continue to monitor the situation. If a stray British warplane gets close to the Americans, we can feed them false information and hope to cause an incident. You continue to monitor the ships and keep me informed before we send anything. Faaris, at the risk of repeating myself, you are sure they cannot trace us, my friend?"

Faaris smiled confidently. "As always, great one, your knowledge has no boundaries. Have no fear. It would take the best IT specialists in the world with the best computers hours to trace the signal to Iceland. My programme watches for searchers and will automatically break the link between here and Iceland fifty minutes before our Icelandic receiver is discovered. We then simply reroute through our receiver in Ireland. The only way we will be defeated is if the Americans alter the JTRS settings."

Khanjar swayed to and fro in the seat while he digested the information he had just received. "You have done well, my brother. Tell me, has the MI6 signal moved from the west coast of Scotland yet?"

Faaris swung round and checked the laptop. "No, I swear there is no agent there, or that chip has malfunctioned and has not recorded further movement. I would forget it if I were you."

Khanjar stood up and started to pace around the stone walled cellar. "But my friend, you are not me. Send Phal a message for me; tell him to come north to us. And remind him to make sure he is not followed here. It is time we had a good look at this faulty signal, I think."

❖ ❖ ❖

We had followed the football traffic for some miles as time had passed the traffic started to thin out I had left the industrial area of Manchester and had found myself on the M62 motorway. At the signs for the M6, a split-second decision had sent me north. I had no plan. In the back of the camper, a huddle had formed round Gary Harding as he began to describe his time in captivity with Benesch. When he told the assembled audience about his discovery, he was treated with a certain amount of disbelief. Dr Karen Lowe asked him about some technical aspects about the DNA recovery and his test programme. She was clearly horrified that he had tested his concoction on himself and butted out of the discussion and sat quietly. I was not sure if she was trying to work out if he was telling the truth, or if she thought he had lost his marbles completely. Smithy was in total disbelief and was finding it hard not to take the piss out of the kid. Sam joined me in the passenger seat.

Since leaving Edinburgh Airport, we had had very little time to ourselves. Sam put her hand on top of mine on the gearstick as she manoeuvred herself into the passenger seat. She smiled at me as I glanced across to see who was arriving by my side. She whispered close to my ear. Her body was so close I could smell her favourite perfume, and it made me long to have her all to myself again, away from this madness.

"Adam, what do you think of the lad's story? I mean do you think he has lost it? He strikes me as a bit of a dreamer."

I placed my hand on top of Sam's and gave it a squeeze. Sam waited while I manoeuvred the camper past two artics fighting for position on the two inner lanes. Then, after returning to the inside lane, I gave Sam my full attention. "There's no smoke without fire, Sam. If it's rubbish, why has Benesch not killed him? Why have the Americans jumped in with both feet? I know it is hard to believe, but there has to be something to the lad's story. Sam, at the end of the day, we can use him to get Benesch and the Vokxin, and that is all that matters. Then we can go home to our glass house on the hill."

Sam glanced at a sign as we passed it. "So, Captain Macdonald, what is your plan? Where are we heading?"

I shook my head. "Honestly, Sam, I'm making it up as we go. But if we have to face Benesch, I would rather do it in an area with low population just in case she tries to give us a taste of Diavokxin. If I have to face Benesch or even the Americans, I would rather pick someplace that gives me the upper hand."

Sam stood up and patted me playfully on the head. "OK, Adam, you get your thinking cap on as to where we are headed, and I will see if I can rustle up some drinks for us all."

❖ ❖ ❖

When Southern and co had left Old Trafford, they were thirty minutes behind the camper van. Cussack drove while Southern listened to the military radio and gave out directions to Cussack about the position of the signal within the camper van. Southern was not just relying on the people carrier to catch the big camper. On the radio, he asked to be patched through to Rear Admiral Holister who was in command of the carrier group assigned to the operation.

Holister listened to Colonel Southern's demands and agreed dryly to put them into action. Rear Admiral Holister knew Southern by reputation, but this was the first time fate had thrown them together. Holister was less than impressed by Southern's attitude and lack of manners. He was deeply worried about the situation that his battle group had been put in. The area he had been asked to patrol was not the biggest sea, and it was awash with ferries and fishing boats, not to mention that it was the return route for the British nuclear submarine fleet. His men would need to be on their toes twenty-four hours a day if they were to avoid a major incident.

❖ ❖ ❖

Sam had just handed out the tins of juice when her phone started to ring. One look at the number was enough; she knew exactly who was waiting on the other end of the line. Sam clicked the answer button but did not have a chance to utter a word before Neil Andrews went off like a machine gun on the other end of the phone. "Sam, listen. It's Neil. I have some important news for you. Tell me, is Luke Smith still with you?"

Sam looked across at Smithy, puzzled by the question. "Yes, Smithy is with us why?"

"We have found out how our agents have been eliminated. The handguns that were supplied by Karl Muller have an undetectable transmitter embedded in the handgrip. Both MI6 and MI5 were issued with the weapons. Someone is using the signal to hunt down our people and kill them. It is also possible that because the transmitter is American, they may be able to track it as well. You need to get rid of Mr Smith's handgun immediately."

Sam had just informed me of Neil's call when I noticed the people carrier coming up alongside the camper. At first glance, it looked innocent enough. As I passed a lumbering truck on the inner lane, something in the mirror caught my eye. I returned my attention to the people carrier. Instead of passing in the fast lane, it was matching my speed. As I watched, the sliding side door opened. I had been taught defensive driving during my time with the regiment, and all the alarm bells were ringing.

I stamped on the brakes, and as the people carrier shot past, I turned the nose of the big camper outward, making contact with the back wing of the people carrier. The people carrier was top heavy, and it did not take much persuasion to cause a spin. Utter confusion ensued. There was a huge scream of brakes as the truck we had just overtaken found a people carrier facing the wrong way directly in its path in the slow lane.

In the camper, confusion reigned. I had given no warning of my avoiding actions. As the people carrier spun helplessly by, the side and back windows of the camper exploded as Benesch opened fire on the camper. She had aimed for the tyres in an attempt to stop the camper, but the spinning people carrier, along with the crash of the truck ploughing into the people carrier, meant that her shots were scattered to the four winds. I watched in the mirror to make sure the people carrier was destroyed before turning my attention to the state we had been left in by the collision. To my huge relief, Sam was up and checking on everyone. Areli's bullets had not hit the tyres, but Smithy had taken a hit on the arm and was cursing quietly to himself as Sam stemmed the flow of blood with a shoelace pulled tight. A wisp of steam passed the driver's window. A quick look at the temperature gauge showed normal.

I decided to pull over and have a look at the damage I had done by ramming the people carrier. Just as I pulled up, Karen Lowe let out a muffled scream. Gary Harding was sitting on the floor with his back to the toilet door. He was transparent and had gone into shock.

In the uproar, no one had noticed him sitting quietly. The reason for this was that one of Areli's bullets had passed through the paper-thin walls of the toilet, entered through Gary's back, and left through his abdomen, shattering his wrist as it left his torso. Sam and I examined Gary. Luckily for him, he was barely conscious. Sam shook her head as I examined the damage, She was right. Even on an operating table, it would have been touch and go. Here he had no chance. I gave him ten minutes at the most before he would be dead.

Sam went through the motions and got Karen to hold a bedsheet firmly against the wound. A quick look at the damage to the camper confirmed my suspicions. The radiator was split along the bottom and was pouring coolant all over the hard shoulder of the M6. I used Smithy's phone to call Neil Andrews. He listened as I told him about the ambush and the state of the camper. He was gone for a few seconds, then came back on the line.

"Adam, your next service stop is Tebay. Get the camper there, and I will arrange help for your team."

CHAPTER 8

RESCUE MISSION

Captain Fiona Malden had just lifted off from her home base at Shawbury heading for London when the tower patched through Neil Andrews. "Fiona, sorry to be a pest, but I need you to pick up my team from Tebay services on the M6, and I need it done bloody quickly. Can you manage that for me, Captain?"

Malden turned the Lynx northward as she was speaking. "No problem, sir. It is a clear night, so I can be on scene in around forty-five minutes. Sir, can you tell me how many and what to look for?"

Andrews was not sure how much to tell Malden, and he hesitated before answering her question. "Fiona, I believe four, maybe five. Two have been wounded, one seriously. Fiona, is your helicopter armed?"

Malden gave a low whistle before replying. Her sixth sense had been correct. Only that morning she had visited the armoury and drawn out a side arm and holster. "Sir, I am carrying a side arm, but my helicopter is a training machine. It is only equipped with night-vision technology."

Andrews was about to sign off when he had one last thought. "Fiona, I am not sure what you are going to find when you get to Tebay. My only command is to get my people out of there safely. Good luck, Captain."

❖ ❖ ❖

The hard shoulder of the M6 was a scene of carnage. The truck that had ploughed into the people carrier sat on top of the people carrier with steam coming from the mangled radiator. The unfortunate driver had not been wearing his seat belt, and he had been thrown through the windscreen of his truck onto the windscreen of the people carrier. At first in the people carrier, there was no movement. Luckily for Cussack and Southern, who were sitting in the front seats, the airbags had deployed and saved their lives.

Southern came to first. For a second, he was disorientated, and then his brain filled with a terrible dread. Not the fact that he had been in a major collision. It was much worse. He was carrying the Vokxin in his breast pocket. With some difficulty, he freed himself from the trapped seat belt and gingerly felt for the capsule. To his huge relief, it was intact. His second action was to check on his travelling companions.

Cussack had a cut under his left eye, but apart from that, he looked to be OK. He was groaning and starting to come to. In the back, Benesch had not fared so well. She was crumpled in the footwell. She had not been wearing her belt as she had been about to shoot the tyres out on the camper when the collision occurred. She had been thrown into the door pillar and had a nasty gash on her forehead.

She was also out cold. Southern leaned over the seat and checked the pulse on her neck. She was alive. Southern had to use both his feet on the passenger door to get it to open enough to slip out onto the road. Cars were pulling up at the scene. Southern knew he had to get out of there fast if he were to have any hope of catching the camper and its valuable cargo. Cussack stumbled out onto the road next to Southern. A couple that had just pulled up asked Cussack if he needed assistance, but he pointed to the figure of the driver crumpled up on the windscreen of the people carrier.

Southern managed to get the carrier group back on the comms and informed them to stay on the line as the situation was changing by the minute. As he spoke, he wandered down to the first car that had pulled up. It sat with its engine running and its hazard lights on. Southern gestured to Cussack, who was trying to get Benesch to come round, to get her into the car. He wanted to get out of there while the gathering crowd focused its attention on the truck driver. Cussack picked up Areli's limp body and carried her to the unfortunate Good Samaritan's car. Areli was dumped unceremoniously on the back seat of the Ford Mondeo, and Cussack jumped into the passenger seat while Southern acquainted himself with the car's controls. When underway, Southern handed Cussack the radio, telling him to arrange a pickup fast. The last thing he needed now was to be picked up by the British police.

❖ ❖ ❖

We had been stopped at the Tebay services for ten minutes. Miraculously, Gary was still clinging to life. Karen refused to leave his side. She was still holding a towel over his stomach wound. Sam and I held a hastily convened meeting outside the camper, out of Karen's earshot. Sam was first to give her opinion on the situation. "Right, guys, we have a number of problems here. First is the young lad. I take it we are all agreed when he pops his clogs, we leave him here for the authorities to sort out." Sam's next statement caught me unawares. "Adam, Neil texted me to say a chopper is on its way to pick us up. We still have the problem of the transmitter in the handle of the gun. We need to split up. I will take the Glock with the transmitter and lead the pack a wild-goose chase. Adam, you take Karen and Smithy and get to safety. And before you say a word, Mr Smith, remember you are still the junior member of the team, and you are wounded."

Before Smithy could protest, the camper van door swung open, and Karen Lowe popped her head out. "Guys, you better come inside." We all traipsed inside, knowing what we would find. Sam put her arm around Karen's shoulder to console her.

Sitting on the sofa seat, Gary was pale and sweating heavily, but to our astonishment, he was alive and kicking. Dr Karen Lowe said nothing but pulled Gary's blood-soaked shirt up to reveal a nasty-looking pink scar. No one spoke.

After a few silent seconds, Dr Karen Lowe was the first to speak. "Well, I think we have discovered why the woman and the Americans are hell-bent on getting their hands on Gary."

Sam lifted Gary's shirt one more time and placed the palm of her hand on the pink scar. She withdrew her hand as if she had been touched by the devil himself. "My god, he is on fire. Sorry, but I am having problems taking this in." Sam was visibly shaken. She had no explanation for the phenomenon taking place before her very eyes.

I studied Gary as he tried to remain conscious. "Gary, can you tell us if you showed this trick of yours to the Israeli woman?"

Gary nodded and pulled himself together enough to string a slurred sentence together. "She forced me to make a video of it and sent it to her friend." Ten seconds later Gary was once more unconscious. His body was using every bit of energy it had to repair his damaged tissue.

Sam's plan was compromised even before I had a chance to object to it. Out of the darkness came the beat of helicopter rotors. The car-park lighting destroyed our night vision. The two dark shapes that passed over us were too high to be looking for us, but they were unmistakably military machines. A cold dread came over me. We had to get out of there and get rid of the gun before we were forced to make a stand. Sam caught my eye and signalled me to go outside. She made the excuse she was going to the toilet, and I followed suit. I left Smithy and Karen trying to get Gary ready for his helicopter ride to safety.

Outside Sam grabbed my arm and led me over to the motorway services building. "Adam, we need to get out of here fast. Please listen to what I have to say before it's too late. I will take the transmitter in the gun and give you guys a chance to make a run for it. Adam, my gun is in our bedroom at the glass house. It is the same custom model Smithy was given and has the same transmitter. They will find out about our home unless I get rid of the gun."

I was about to object, but Sam's face told a story. The thought of losing her beloved glass house was too much to bear. I was racking my brain, confronted with this new situation. I needed to come up with a workable plan that we could put into practice immediately. "OK Sam, here is what we will do. You take Karen and the gun. Drop it as soon as you can, then head for home. Once you have disposed of your gun, head south again. I will get the chopper to drop us at my cottage, and you can head back there. We will regroup and contact Neil from there."

Sam looked relieved but for a second was deep in thought. "Why do you want Karen to come with me? You know I work better alone."

"Once you lose the transmitters, you should be relatively safe, and Karen can split the driving and give you a break. It keeps her safe hopefully." As we were speaking, a guy left the building and was making a beeline for a big white parcel delivery van parked three bays up from the camper van. It was not a hard task to convince the driver to bend the rules and take two passengers into Carlisle. He was happy to oblige once we had agreed on a one-hundred-pound fee. He was over the moon when he saw that his passengers were to be two very presentable women.

Sam broke the news to Karen while I was negotiating with the van driver, and both girls had grabbed their gear and were ready to head for the hills. Sam approached me and gave me a peck on the cheek before heading to the van. To my astonishment, she had tears streaming down her cheeks. "Are you OK, Sam?"

Sam started walking to the van while she wiped her face with a hanky. "You tell Smithy to look after you until I get back."

As if on cue, as the white van pulled away, the beat of a helicopter echoed around the almost deserted car park. I decided to err on the side of caution and helped Smithy to get Gary away from the camper and into the trees that surrounded the car park. I could not be sure yet if this was our taxi arriving or one of the helicopters that had passed earlier returning with some unwelcome guests.

The beat was deafening now, but the car-park lighting blacked out the shape of the helicopter. I removed my Glock and rested my finger on the trigger guard, ready for whatever fate threw at me. Suddenly the fuselage of a chopper appeared in the open space between the fuel station and the main building. To my huge relief, it was a British army Lynx. No sooner had it touched down then its cockpit door was flung open. The pilot was waving furiously at us to get across to the machine.

Smithy led the way, covering the area with Sam's Glock that she had been given by the quartermaster at Hereford. I followed at a distance carrying Gary Harding over my left shoulder, leaving my right hand free to operate my Glock if required. Smithy pulled Gary from my back as I approached the door, leaving me to do a final sweep of the perimeter with the Glock before clambering on board. The area was clear except for a confused-looking sales assistant at the fuel station who had left her post to see what the commotion was in the car park.

The engines had never returned to idle, and as soon as my backside touched the floor of the Lynx, the engines roared as the machine carried out an emergency lift-off. The machine shuddered and vibrated as the airframe came under enormous pressure as the twin Rolls Royce engines lifted the beast into the night sky. I watched the rapidly vanishing faces of three people who had appeared by the main entrance door. The vibrations decreased as the Lynx came into its own high above the service station. The pilot was waving at me and pointing to the helmet on the back of the passenger seat.

I pulled on the helmet and plugged it into the comms system. "We meet again, Captain Malden. Boy, were we glad to see you."

Malden gave her instruments the once-over before replying. "Did I get everybody, and where are we headed?" As we had found before with her, Captain Malden was very much a business-first type of girl.

"Captain, do you think you can get us to the Isle of Arran?"

Malden gave me a quick look over her shoulder before replying to my question. I was sure she was checking to see if I was joking. "Shouldn't be too much of a problem." Fiona Malden studied a chart she had by her side then punched in some information into the choppers navigation system. She then twisted a couple of knobs on her comms system making contact with air traffic control. "Control, this is army flight Victor Charlie two zero one. Have inputted new destination. Requesting confirmation and clearance."

It only took seconds for Malden to receive her clearance. "OK, guys, next stop Arran. I have logged a course for Prestwick Airport. I take it you would like to keep your final destination…private, shall we say?" Fiona Malden gave me the impression she was a very smart lady. I could not help thinking that if she had been a male she would have held a much higher rank than captain.

"Not a bad idea, Captain, especially after almost bumping into your competition earlier." Again Malden looked over her shoulder at me. This time she had a worried expression on her face.

"It's Mac, isn't it? Care to clarify your last comment, Mac?"

"Sure. Just about ten minutes before you arrived, two choppers passed at low level, heading south. I didn't see them, but I am pretty sure they were military machines."

Fiona's head was in turmoil. She could still hear Neil Andrews's words ringing in her ears. *Get my people out of there safely.* For a few seconds, Fiona mulled over what she should do and what the law said she should do.

Fiona made her decision. The Lynx dropped like a stone. Malden used her night-vision technology to guide her Lynx through the hills of the Lake District only feet from the grassy slopes. The combination of her skill and the agility of the Lynx saved the day on two occasions. The first was when power cables cleared the belly by inches. The second was when Captain Malden had to almost put her Lynx on the ground as she ducked under a mast and cables that appeared out of the darkness as she cleared the summit of a steep, dark, forbidding hilltop. Suddenly, a small valley appeared on the left. Malden brought the nose up to slow her machine, then used the collective to swing the tail round so she could have a good look at her perceived hiding place. Satisfied that her rotors would clear the side of the gully, she backed her machine into the gully with millimetre precision.

As the Lynx touched down we all breathed a sigh of relief. I had watched as Fiona Malden threaded her machine through the narrow valleys.

As the big Rolls Royce engines powered down, Malden removed her helmet, carried out a few post flight operations, and put the Lynx to bed for the time being. One look at Fiona confirmed what I had already guessed. Although she was putting a brave face on it, tonight's little flying adventure had taken its toll on her. She was dripping in sweat. Where the helmet had contacted her skin, the imprint still showed. She was as pink as a newborn baby; her flying suit was soaked in sweat. In particular, her armpits and back were soaked.

"Well done, Fiona. I take it that it was not a bad thing that we passengers did not have night vision as well."

Fiona Malden did not reply at first. She was leaning into the passenger seat, retrieving a bottle of water from her kit bag, which had been strapped into the copilot's seat. She took a large gulp trying to hold her hand still enough to stop the water spilling.

"No Mac you are right on the button. That was seat of the pants stuff even I had my eyes closed a few times, only kidding. I wish that I had known about the choppers before I gave away my flight plan on open radio."

We all took turns to nip outside to relieve our bladders before settling down for the night. Smithy was the first to fall asleep after I had a quick look at his wound. He had been lucky the bullet had just nicked his arm he would be fine. It was hard to say what the hell was happening to Gary he had not regained consciousness but seemed to almost be in a coma. No matter how much we tried he would not come round.

I had joined Fiona Malden up front in the copilot's seat and was making an attempt to fall asleep when the beat of a helicopter broke the quiet of the frozen night air. I was instantly wide-awake and reached into my jacket, resting my hand reassuringly on the grip of my Glock.

Fiona's voice startled me as it broke the silence in the cockpit. "Probably search and rescue looking for us. Boy, I hope your boss has got some clout. I am going to need all the help I can get at the court-martial." Fiona checked the luminous dial of her watch. "We will wait for half an hour after sunup before making a run for it."

Sleep would not come for either of us. I wondered how Sam was doing while Fiona was probably trying to plan out her moves for tomorrow. "Penny for your thoughts, Mac." I half turned to look at Fiona. I kept my thoughts on Sam to myself.

"I was just wondering why you are wearing a gent's Breitling watch. I mean, I know you kind of live in a man's world, but is it some kind of statement?"

Fiona looked at her watch. She seemed deep in thought. "Well spotted, Mac. You are the first person other than my mother who noticed it. It's not some kind of macho gesture or anything. It was my husband's watch. When I fly, he is always with me." Fiona smiled, but it was a sad haunting smile.

"I am sorry, Fiona. I didn't mean to pry into your private life."

She shook her head. “No, Mac, it’s fine. Honest, no big secret. I was just surprised you noticed. Paul, my husband, was killed in action during the first weeks of the Gulf War. His Tornado was shot down by anti-aircraft fire over Baghdad. I bought him the Breitling for our first wedding anniversary. He always said it was his lucky watch. Pity he forgot it that morning. He might still have been here.” I watched as a solitary tear gathered in the corner of Fiona Malden’s eye. She brushed it away with a gloved hand before it could escape down her face, betraying her state of mind.

“Don’t worry about anything, Fiona. Neil Andrews will iron out any problems you run into with your superiors. Does this beast have any armaments?”

Fiona shook her head, obviously relieved that the subject had changed. “Sorry, Mac all I can offer is my Browning side arm. She is a Super Lynx 300, but she is a trainer. Your lot at Hereford grabbed the only armed Super Lynx 300s for themselves. You don’t seriously think it is going to come to a dog fight, do you?”

I pointed to the rear cabin. “Fiona, why don’t you ask the guys in the back with the bullet holes that question?”

“Point taken, Mac. We better try and get some shut eye before crunch time tomorrow.”

❖ ❖ ❖

The two US Navy Seahawk helicopters touched down on a motorway flyover several miles south of the motorway service station. Colonel Southern placed Benesch in the second Seahawk with himself. The medics got to work immediately on Benesch while Southern instructed the pilot on the next course of action he wanted carried out. Southern’s chopper headed for the carrier group while Cussack joined the first Seahawk. He instructed the pilot to change his radio frequency to the one used by the Delta commandos. Two minutes later, the Seahawk with Cussack on board was following the directions given by one of the commandos.

❖ ❖ ❖

The van driver dropped Sam and Karen at Southwaite services. Sam wasted no time. She could not be sure how far behind her pursuers were. Karen stood lookout while Sam clambered under a post-office truck. Sam deposited Smithy's Glock on top of the spare wheel, wedging it in place as securely as possible to stop it falling out on the road. Sam and Karen watched as the post-office truck left heading north. Sam had to suppress a wave of anxiety as she watched her only weapon head north. She had given Smithy her replacement Glock for the helicopter trip.

"Sam, how are we going to get away from here? Come to think of it where the hell are we going anyway?" Sam suppressed a smile as they walked toward the main building complex. "Don't worry Dr Lowe we will just use our secret weapon." Ten minutes later they were both standing at the beginning of the on ramp to the northbound M6 motorway. Both girls held a piece of cardboard with the word "Scotland" emblazoned in lipstick on the cardboard.

"So Sam, this is your secret weapon?" Karen shook her head in disbelief.

"Not the card, Karen. Our bodies. That is the secret weapon."

Karen was still shaking her head. "We could be standing here for hours."

Sam smiled and pointed at the truck that was just pulling up. "Well, doctor, I think the secret weapon has just worked. Looks like you need a bit of street coaching."

❖ ❖ ❖

Neil Andrews paced backward and forward like a caged lion. He had been at his desk for the last twenty-four hours solid. His mind would not rest. None of the information he was receiving from his team was making the slightest bit of sense.

Peter Kent was the first to report in with strange information. He had been stationed at the football ground and had witnessed Areli Benesch leaving with two men. He had managed to get within earshot of them and discovered that the men were American. A further search of the football club's CCTV found images of both the men. The images had been run through the Interpol face-recognition system and two names were obtained. The identity of Southern was confirmed for a second time and also a fellow American officer was identified.

Neil Andrews repeated the names again to himself. He was having trouble believing it. Colonel David Southern from the Pentagon and Colonel Brent Cussack, Intelligence Support Activity Unit. These men were high up in the US military chain of command. According to Peter Kent, they were not after Benesch. They were helping her!

The call from Adam had just put the icing on the cake. He had reported that he had been fired on, and then he had rammed the same vehicle that Benesch and the Americans had just left the football stadium in.

Police reports were just starting to circulate that two US Navy helicopters had just airlifted people from a motorway bridge north of Manchester.

There was a knock on his door. Jean, his PA, entered without waiting for a reply. "Mr Andrews, sorry to charge in, but I have just received an urgent message from the control room at Shawbury. Captain Malden's helicopter is missing. She filed a flight plan for Prestwick Airport, but shortly after that, her machine vanished off the radar." Jean waited until the bad news had sunk in before continuing. "Sorry to be a pest, sir, but the PM's office is on the phone again. I have put them off twice already, sir, but this time they won't be fobbed off. Sorry, sir, but I think you are going to have to speak to him."

Jean knew there was no love lost between the two men. She had tried her best to give her new boss some breathing space, but due to the emergency situation, the PM would not listen to any excuses from MI6.

Neil Andrews knew he was in for another long night. He was not looking forward to the conversation with the PM, and he was dreading the conversation he was going to have with the commanding officer at RAF Shawbury regarding the missing Lynx and its passengers.

❖ ❖ ❖

The Seahawk touched down on the deck of the USS *Nimitz*, watched by a small group of officers. Rear Admiral Holister was surrounded by his team of officers who were responsible for the day-to-day running of the battle group's flagship.

The two men met on the deck of the big carrier. Both men regarded each other as two prizefighters would before a big fight. Southern was the first to break the silence. "Admiral, please accept my apologies for dragging you half-way across the world. Please let me assure you that your presence is no waste of time."

Holister regarded Southern through cold blue eyes. He had been around long enough to know not to make enemies of dangerous men. "Welcome on board, Colonel Southern. The requests you made en route have been carried out. If you would like to follow me, I will show you to your quarters, Colonel." Holister led the way for Southern. The group of officers followed at a respectful distance.

"Admiral Holister, I feel that I owe you an explanation for all the trouble I have put you through." Southern proceeded to tell Holister about the two deadly chemicals that were in the hands of a madman. He explained how Benesch had managed to grab the Diavokxin, but the lunatic was still at large with the Vokxin. He explained that he had troops on the ground in the UK hunting down this madman. The rear admiral listened to Southern's story without questioning it until they reached Southern's cabin.

Admiral Holister let Southern finish before commenting. "Colonel Southern, if what you say is true, this is a very grave situation, and we will be here to help in any way. But I have a couple of things running around inside my old head that give me cause for concern. If it's a British problem, why are we going it alone? Both countries should be working as a team to get this sorted. Secondly, I feel I need to put my cards on the table, just as you have done. The safety of my men is paramount to me. If I feel for one minute that your actions are putting my battle group at risk, I will pull them out. And to hell with what Washington thinks. I have two years before I hang up my life jacket. So threatening me will only get you a punch in the mouth and dropped over the side in a lifeboat. Do I make myself perfectly clear, Colonel Southern?"

Southern smiled at the admiral. He had been warned of the straight-talking, no-nonsense, salty sea dog leader who was revered in navy circles. "You're the boss out here. I won't stand on your toes, sir."

Holister explained where everything Southern had requested was and left without further comment.

Southern smiled to himself. The admiral had accepted his twist on the truth. He knew Rear Admiral Holister would report their conversation, and it would get back to Washington. As long as they thought the Vokxin was still on the loose, he was free to continue his quest for the young scientist and his discovery. America must have this technology first if they were to remain the undisputed superpower of the world. Southern removed the Vokxin container from his jacket and placed it at the back of his clothing locker. As requested, his cabin door was to be guarded round the clock by an armed marine. Southern made sure the marine was on duty, then headed for the medical department to check up on Areli Benesch.

Areli Benesch was not happy that she had come round to find herself on board an American warship. She knew it would take very little for the Americans to hand her over to the Israeli authorities. Her fears receded slightly on the arrival of Southern, but she remained cautious. She knew what Southern was capable of. If he thought Areli could not help find the young scientist, she knew he would not hesitate to hand her over to Israel.

Southern wasted no time once on board. On seeing that Areli was up and about, he arranged for Cussack to take Benesch with him as soon as the chopper crews had refuelled and rested. Cussack had spent most of the night searching for a mystery chopper that had been picked up on radar, then vanished as quickly as it had appeared in the area. The Pentagon confirmed that they had picked up a radio transmission in the search area from a British military Lynx helicopter. It had logged a flight plan to the Scottish airport of Prestwick. No further transmissions were picked up from the aircraft, only alerts in the area of Cumbria for mountain-rescue teams and local police helicopters to search for the missing aircraft.

Southern and Cussack debated the finding of the signal thought to be from an agent. It turned out to be a delivery truck. Cussack had drawn the line at stopping the truck and searching it. But he had the chopper sweep the truck for thermal images. Only the driver's heat signature was present. Cussack had concluded it was a red herring and went in search of the phantom helicopter that had been reported to him.

Southern ordered Cussack to take both Seahawks and follow the flight path from Cumbria to Prestwick looking for the Lynx. Southern hoped the trail had not gone cold. He was the master of the gut feeling, and his gut was telling him to find this helicopter before it slipped through their net.

CHAPTER 9

THE CONFESSION

Sam and Karen were dropped off outside the Edinburgh Airport Hotel. Sam was glad to see Herbie was parked in the hotel car park. The hotel had agreed at short notice to put Herbie in the long-stay car park until Sam's return. Sam had phoned ahead to book two rooms and retrieve Herbie from the long-stay parking. Ten minutes later, Sam and Karen were tucking into a full cooked breakfast before heading to their rooms for some well-earned sleep before heading north. Karen watched as Sam emptied her third glass of orange juice in quick succession. "Sam, can I ask you a question?"

Sam drained her glass and nodded without speaking.

"There was a soldier at Porton Down who hinted that we may have used Diavokxin in anger against our enemies. Do you know if this is true?"

Sam refilled her glass while formulating a reply for Karen. "I can't say I heard anything about it, but he is probably correct. Karen, it is a big bad world out there. You wouldn't believe some of the things that go on. All I can say is, if that is all we are guilty of, we will be saints compared to other nations."

Karen watched as Sam polished off the rest of the jug of orange juice. "Sam, do you think Adam and Gary will be OK?"

Sam's rosy complexion paled, and she sat deep in thought. To Karen's surprise, a tear welled up in Sam's eye then tumbled down her cheek. Sam sniffed then wiped her eyes and blew her nose. "I take it Adam and you are an item. Boy, I never thought that secret agents had any feelings. Boy, was I wrong there!"

For a fleeting second, there was a flash of anger in Sam's red eyes. Then she controlled it and continued to blow her nose. "Yes, Adam and I are partners. Please ignore my moods. I am not myself at the moment."

Karen sipped her tea, studying Sam as she emptied the last glass of fruit juice. "It's OK, Sam. Pressure can do funny things to your mind." Sam choked on the last mouthful of juice, trying to laugh and swallow at the same time. "What is so funny, Sam? I was being serious."

Sam composed herself and became very serious all of a sudden. "Karen, in my life, I have had more stresses and pressure than you would believe. No, it's not pressure. I know that for sure. Karen, I am pregnant."

Karen Lowe was lost for words. She sat staring at Sam. Finally she spoke. "Eh, does that not impede on your effectiveness as a spy just a tiny bit?"

Sam smiled at that comment, even although her thoughts seemed far away. "Karen, I don't know how to tell Neil Andrews. He will go berserk."

Karen poured herself another cup of tea and sat back. "So I take it that this was not a planned event then. Have you told the dad yet?"

Sam's rosy cheeks lost their luster, and she studied the carpet, avoiding eye contact with Karen Lowe. "No, I haven't told Adam yet. To be honest, I'm not sure I want to tell him. That's why I told you. I had to tell someone."

Karen stopped and stared, holding her teacup to her lips. She had stopped midsip. "I didn't want to push you into naming the father." She sipped her tea. "Why in heaven's name don't you want to tell Adam? Phone him, Sam. He will be over the moon. I guarantee it."

Sam sat shaking her head like a lost schoolgirl. "No, Karen. It's not that simple. You don't know Adam's past. When he was younger, he was married. His wife died in childbirth, and so did his baby. I don't know how he will react, and this is not the time to pickle his mind. He needs to concentrate on the job, not me."

Karen Lowe finished her cup of tea then sat on the edge of the seat. "How far on are you? You don't look pregnant. Are you sure?"

Sam stood up. "It's time for a sleep before we get going. I'm not sure how long I have been expecting. We were on a flight from Switzerland when I first realised I was pregnant. Don't ask me how I knew. I just did. When we landed, I did a test and have done two more since then. At first I was devastated but I am starting to come to terms with my dilemma. It's official. My career is over. I am going to be a mum."

❖ ❖ ❖

Khanjar made his way to the communications room in the basement of his house. Faaris was perched on the edge of his chair, waiting for him.

"Well, Faaris, I can see from the twinkle in your eye you have another master plan for me to consider."

Faaris leaned across his desk and lifted a small Dictaphone-type unit. "Please listen to this, leader of the light." Khanjar listened while Faaris played the recording to him. "The recording is from two US Navy Seahawk helicopters that seem to be engaged in a search mission for a missing British army Lynx helicopter. I have used the recordings of the Americans talking over the radio and with a bit of creative electronic editing, I have come up with this message."

Faaris again played the recording. "Delta Xray Two, this is *Nimitz* control. Confirmed report received. Hostile terrorist aboard stolen Lynx. Mission parameter change. Destroy terrorist helicopter."

Before Khanjar could say anything, Faaris continued with his sales pitch to Khanjar. "I transmit this message to the helicopter, then use a super boosted signal to destroy all communications on board the helicopter. Once it receives our doctored message and its comms is destroyed, no one will be able to contact the helicopter to stop it attacking the British."

Khanjar was silent while he thought through the consequences of the plan Faaris had put forward. "Why use the second helicopter? I take it from your message Delta Xray Two is the second helicopter?"

Faaris was encouraged by the fact that his leader had not dismissed the plan immediately. "From listening to the warmongers' radio transmissions, I deduced that the first helicopter carries an officer or some other person who is directing the search. I fear, lord, if we send the message to that helicopter, the person directing the search will command the crew to disregard our message."

Faaris watched as Khanjar paced up and down the basement stopping only to massage his forehead, deep in thought. "Very well, my young warrior. Send your message, but only if the Americans find the Lynx, and they have to give chase. I will be in my study. Please keep me informed of the situation."

❖ ❖ ❖

I awoke with a jolt. My heart was racing and although the Lynx cockpit was freezing, I was sweating profusely. My sleep had not been restful. My time in Kuwait still haunted me in my dreams. To my surprise, the pilot seat was vacant. A quick check through the partially frosted cockpit windows found Captain Malden some distance away by a little stream.

Fiona Malden was deep in thought by the stream. I walked up behind her. She turned when she heard my footsteps clambering over the uneven, rocky terrain. "Good morning, Adam. Did you sleep well?"

I drew level with her before giving my answer. "No, Captain, I didn't. I am afraid too many demons from the past come back to haunt me."

Malden nodded thoughtfully. "I know what you mean. I was having a similar problem." Malden folded her arms across her chest and proceeded to kick a pebble into the water. "Adam, you really don't think the Americans will do anything stupid if they find us, do you?"

I gazed into the water, trying to see through the surface reflection for any sign of life. "I am not sure, Fiona, but what I am sure about is this: after you drop us on Arran, refuel at Prestwick, and head back to London. Don't speak to anyone about dropping us off, especially over the radio. The Americans have the best surveillance systems in the world, and you can bet your life they will be listening. You need to speak face to face with Neil Andrews."

Fiona Malden unzipped the top shoulder pocket of her flight suit, removed a folded piece of paper, and handed it to me. "Adam, if things do go wrong, can you make sure my mother gets this? Her address is inside."

I took the paper from Fiona Malden before commenting on it. "I shouldn't think you need to worry about your mum reading it. It's just another taxi ride."

Malden shook her head and continued to examine the bottom of the stream. "You are probably right, Adam, but there again, I am sure my husband thought that the day he died as well."

We were just about to head back to the chopper when the water at my feet exploded in a fountain of spray. For a fleeting second, I thought someone had opened fire on us. A second glance told a different story. Lying at my feet was Gary Harding. He was flat on his stomach with his head buried in the running water of the stream, gulping the freezing water down greedily. For what seemed like hours, he continued to drink. Finally, he surfaced and wiped the water from his flushed face. He sat on the frozen grass, the heat from his body thawing the immediate area around him. Fiona Malden had not seen the damage that had been inflicted on the young lad, so she was none the wiser. While Gary recovered from his drinking spree, I teased up what was left of his torn, blood-soaked T-shirt. My eyes were telling me lies. I had to bend down and screw up my eyes to make out the white scar tissue where yesterday there had been an exit wound you could have put your fist through.

"Jesus Christ." I could not help voicing my shock and amazement at the scene before me.

Fiona Malden was staring at the lad's stomach, but she was at a loss to see what all the fuss was about. "Am I missing something? It looks like an eighteen-year-old's belly to me."

I was busy explaining to Fiona Malden about the wound Gary had received when Smithy appeared. He was not looking his best and was carrying his wounded arm stiffly. "Bloody hell, guys, it's brass monkeys out here. What the hell are we up to?"

Gary lifted his shirt for Smithy to scrutinise. Smithy was silent for a few seconds before sharing his thoughts. "Good god, Mac, no wonder the Americans are after him. Imagine if you had an army of soldiers who could repair themselves. They will stop at nothing to acquire the technology."

Fiona Malden started to walk back toward the Lynx. "Well, guys, the sooner I drop you off, the better—before someone decides to end my career prematurely."

Ten minutes later, Captain Malden was going through her preflight checks prior to takeoff. "Keep your fingers crossed, guys. I have never had to start a Lynx without ground crew after leaving it this length of time. We might be walking to Scotland yet. Guys this is important I am going to fly below the radar for a bit. I need you to all keep an eye out for power lines telephone cables and also any other aircraft. Put the headphones on, and shout out if you see anything."

There was a high-pitched whine as the twin Rolls Royce engines were coaxed into life. Fiona Malden let the engines warm by bringing the rotor speed up slightly. The Lynx started to twitch and rock gently like some giant animal waking from hibernation. Fiona Malden increased the power and the Lynx left the ground, hovering only feet from its overnight resting place. With only a slight forward movement of her hand, Fiona made the Lynx respond, and it crept forward at walking pace.

"OK, gents, here we go. Please, if you are going to throw up, not all over me please. It tends to break one's concentration." Malden smiled to herself and pulled down the antiglare visor, leaving only the lower part of her face visible.

Fiona Malden shredded the Lynx through a narrow valley that opened out onto one of the main lakes of the Lake District. It was on the tip of my tongue to ask Fiona which lake we were on but decided against breaking her concentration. This was a mission, not a sightseeing trip. The Lynx skimmed so close to the water that the downwash of the helicopter's rotors disturbed the surface of the lake, leaving a wash similar to that of a speedboat. At the head of the lake, Fiona pulled back gently on the column while increasing the angle of her left wrist on the collective control. The Lynx lifted effortlessly as its pilot judged the rise at the head of the lake to perfection, clearing the high ground by only a few feet.

I glanced over my shoulder at Smithy and Gary Harding. Neither seemed to be phased by our low-level aerobatics. Both men were busy looking for problems. In my element, watching Fiona Malden throw the helicopter about,

I had forgotten the duty that Fiona had given to all of us. I returned my gaze to the horizon.

❖ ❖ ❖

In the cockpit of Delta Xray One, Dan Milner piloted the Seahawk. His crew and guests were studying the ground below for any sign of the missing British army chopper. In the distance, the Solway Firth estuary was spread out in front of them. Milner had spotted movement directly in front and below them. He double-checked his observations before saying anything to his crew. As he watched, the tiny speck of movement grew larger. Skimming the water was a Westland Lynx helicopter decked out in green camouflage. It had to be the missing aircraft. Unfortunately for the Lynx, it had been caught crossing the water, rendering its camouflage useless. Dan Milner radioed in his find to the *Nimitz*, then informed Delta Xray Two who was following five miles to their rear of his find.

Steve Newman had just received the message from Delta Xray One that his commanding officer, Captain Dan Milner, had just spotted the missing British chopper and was changing course to intercept the machine. Steve passed the message onto his crew. His tactics now went from searching to hunting, and he throttled up the big navy chopper, heading to intercept his team leader to give support in the chase. Steve picked up bad static in his headphones. Then he received a priority message from the *Nimitz*. He was genuinely shocked to hear that terrorists had managed to get their hands on a military helicopter. His first thought was the safety of his friends and colleagues aboard the *Nimitz*. Just as he reached for the radio controls to contact Milner for instructions, there was an ear-piercing squeal from the radio. His gauges momentarily fluctuated. For a second, Steve Newman could hear nothing. The ringing in his ears was still there although the comms were completely dead. Newman checked his gauges. More than half of them were dead. He cursed to himself.

He was about to go into action, and his chopper was severely compromised. He had no navigation or communication systems. If he went by the book, he should turn round and head back to the *Nimitz*. Steve Newman had a huge dilemma. Backup his commanding officer, or turn tail and head home, leaving his boss with no immediate backup. Newman decided there was nothing in the rulebook covering this situation and pointed his machine in the general direction from which his boss had last reported in.

❖ ❖ ❖

Fiona Malden was the first to spot the black dot above us at one o'clock. She turned left, skimming the surface of the Solway Firth heading for the closest landfall in an attempt to outrun the big chopper.

I watched as the grey silhouette grew closer. It was now on our left-hand side, just above us and at ten o'clock. The distance between us had shrunk to around two miles. I looked over at Fiona Malden, but her visor was down, masking her expression. She lifted the nose of the Lynx as we cleared the water and skimmed over the tops of the trees bordering the Solway Firth. I looked to my left. The big chopper was now at nine o'clock and closing fast. It was close enough now that I could see that it was a US Navy Seahawk.

I was still eyeballing the American chopper when Fiona Malden banked steeply to the right, following the contour of the hill and taking us out of visual contact with the American chopper. As soon as we were out of sight, Malden lifted the nose steeply, throwing off speed and turned the Lynx through three hundred and sixty degrees heading back round the hill the way we had just come. On the other side of the hill, Fiona Malden again set the Lynx on the deck skimming over green fields and hedgerows at suicidal speeds. Smithy shouted down the comms that he had spotted the Americans on our right at two o'clock some miles ahead and heading away from our position. Out of the corner of my eye, I caught the slightest hint of a smile from the partially covered face of Fiona Malden. It seemed to me that although Malden's nerves were on a knife's edge, she was enjoying doing what she had practiced and trained others to do for years. Dead ahead of us sat a village. Malden did not slacken off or change course. She passed over the village at over two hundred miles per hour, only feet above the rooftops. To my left, the village church-spire-cum-clock-tower flew past in a flash.

In a bizarre moment in time, I noted that its clock had stopped at ten past twelve. I knew this because I checked Malden's watch, and it showed eight fifteen. I was brought back to reality as again Smithy yelled down the comms that the Americans had changed course and were still ahead of us but had turned our way.

Malden reached across while I was trying to make visual contact with the American chopper and handed me a plastic-coated map. The comms burst into life in my ears. "Adam, I am kind of tied up. See if you can find out where we are and plot me a course north, but make the course through hills and woodland. Oh, and Adam? Do it quickly. We are about to have company again."

❖ ❖ ❖

On board the Seahawk code-named Delta Xray One, Areli Benesch and Colonel Brent Cussack were deep in conversation. Cussack wanted to try to force the British chopper to land while Areli was content to follow the helicopter to its final destination. Cussack was worried that if it landed at a military base, a confrontation with the British military could not be avoided. The pilot again spoke to Cussack over the intercom, asking Cussack what his directive was.

Cussack was silent for a moment. "OK, Dan, get on its tail, and don't let it out of your sight. I don't want it dropping its cargo in a field. But don't get too close. Apparently it might be carrying some pretty nasty chemicals." The comms went dead, and the big Seahawk banked left on a course to intercept the British army Lynx helicopter again.

❖ ❖ ❖

I was studying the map furiously for some type of escape route from the approaching Americans. I lifted the map up so that Fiona Malden could study my planned route. "OK Fiona, on our left, over that rise, I reckon Loch Ken must be over there. That would give us good cover for a bit. There is only one bridge crossing Loch Ken. If we dodge that, we can follow the loch, then cut left again for Girvan on the coast."

Malden did not reply but swung the Lynx left following my directions. As Fiona Malden tuned I spotted the outline of the US Navy chopper bearing down on our position. Her turn had scrubbed off some speed, and the big American chopper gained further ground on us.

Malden looked across and smiled at me. "Well, Captain Macdonald, we are about to see if our American friends are going to behave. It's party time." The navy chopper had closed the gap to one hundred metres. Suddenly below us the trees and ground fell away to the shores of Loch Ken. Fiona banked right and at the same time pushed the nose of the Lynx down, putting the chopper into a headlong dive toward the loch. At the last moment, Malden pulled the nose up. To my horror, right in front of us stood an arched railway bridge. I braced myself for the inevitable collision as the helicopter piled into the side of the bridge. Fiona Malden levelled out the Lynx, and for a second, the dark underbelly of the old bridge flashed past, its stone parapets only inches from the throw of the rotor blades. I was conscious that I had stopped breathing. Only the sound of Gary retching in the rear of the chopper told me we were still alive. Something caught the corner of my eye as Fiona Malden banked hard right and applied full throttle, the screaming Rolls Royce engines lifting the Lynx clear of the loch, heading up a gully toward the horizon on the east side of the loch.

A huge grey mass exploded into the waters of Loch Ken. The unfortunate Seahawk had not had the same luck as our machine and had belly-flopped into the loch. The American machine was a much bigger and a slightly less manoeuvrable helicopter than the British Lynx. The minute Dan Milner had followed Fiona Malden's dive, he was doomed. He had made the mistake of thinking he could carry out the same manoeuvre as the Lynx. He had no room to get out of the way of the looming bridge, and the big machine was too big to fit through the tiny gap. In the end, he had opted for ditching in the water under the bridge rather than hit the structure.

We were just starting to clear the summit that we had climbed as my breathing returned to normal. In the commotion, I had been gripping the map so tightly I had punched holes in it with my stressed-out fingers. Smithy was trying to contain Gary's vomit while Gary stared into space. I had just returned my eyes to the map when Fiona Malden flung the chopper violently on its side. Her actions were so rapid and so forceful that my helmet cracked off the doorframe, making me see stars.

The heavy machine gun fire came from nowhere. For a second, it did not register that the shooting was being directed at us until shells started exploding as they scored direct hits on our Lynx. For a split second, we seemed to hang in midair as the shock of the shells hitting us sent jarring vibrations through the fuselage. One shell entered the cockpit and started ricocheting off the frame. By some miracle, none of us were hit. Fiona Malden cursed like a trooper as she tried to regain control of the damaged Lynx. Malden banked left, away from the murderous gunfire. Her new path took her back high over Loch Ken.

❖ ❖ ❖

Steve Newman watched as the British Lynx headed west over Loch Ken. He was about to give chase and finish the job when his side gunner reported to him that the team leader's chopper had ditched in the loch below. He was torn between going to the rescue of his team leader or catch the Lynx before it could attack the American battle group. He had no comms of any kind and was forced to abandon the chase and go to the aid of his boss.

In the waters of Loch Ken, both Brent Cussack and Areli Benesch had been very lucky. They had been seated with their backs to the bulkhead. This position had cushioned them from the huge impact the navy chopper had suffered. The second the chopper had came to rest, the pair had sprung into action. Areli grabbed the arm of one of the unconscious crew who was face down in the water. She turned him on his back and kicked backward to the nearby shoreline. Cussack headed for the pilot and copilot who were lifeless below the surface, trapped in their seats. Cussack tried in vain to free the pair, only surfacing for a quick gasp of air. His attempts were to no avail. Both men were pinned by their legs. Cussack concentrated his efforts on the pilot as the copilot had suffered massive internal damage and was pinned to his seat by a submerged tree branch. His attempts to save the pilot still proved to be in vain. Captain Dan Milner had broken his neck in the impact and been killed instantly. Cussack spent the next twenty minutes, aided by the arrival of Delta Xray Two, looking for the missing crewmen. Cussack gave up and headed for the bank to join Benesch and the sole survivor of the Delta Xray One crew. Cussack collapsed on the beach. He had nothing left. He had drained his energy reserves looking for his fallen comrades. He thought to himself as he sat regaining his strength, that he was not in a good place but Colonel Southern had the short straw. He had the dubious task of dealing with Admiral Holister when he found out about the loss of his Seahawk and the death of his men.

❖ ❖ ❖

Fiona Malden had climbed to the west of Loch Ken and was heading in the direction of the coast. I watched as she lifted her antiglare visor. Her pale face studied her banks of dials she was looking for any tell tail signs that her machine had been mortally wounded.

I turned my attention to the two very quiet bodies behind me. To my relief we had all survived the attack unscathed. "Are you OK, Captain Malden?"

Malden answered without her gaze leaving her dials. "Don't worry about me, Mac. It's this girl here you need to worry about." Fiona Malden patted the dash of the Lynx as if it was her pet dog. "She does not take kindly to being shot at. I am going to stay up here until we reach the coast. If she behaves, I will take a chance and cross the sea to Arran."

Minutes seemed like hours as the Ayrshire coast appeared in front of us. Fiona Malden made one final check of her dials and indicators before declaring herself cautiously optimistic we would be OK.

Captain Malden reduced her height as we passed over the coastal town of Girvan. We were once again skimming the surface as Malden turned north-west, pointing the nose of the Lynx between the little island of Ailsa Craig and the southern tip of the Isle of Arran in the misty distance. We were in the middle of the Irish Sea when I heard the metallic clank from the back. There was a vibration for a second, and then it was gone. Fiona Malden's eyes met mine. We did not need to speak. Fiona's face said it all. She was busy rechecking gauges when the grating started. I watched as Fiona Malden's gaze left the dials and started looking for the best place to head with a sick helicopter.

A few miles to the west of the Ailsa Craig, a tiny speck bobbed up and down with the swell. Fiona pointed the Lynx toward it, and as if on cue, warning lamps and buzzers started to go off in the cockpit. The speck had become a small fishing boat. We were less than half a mile from the little boat when Fiona Malden brought the Lynx to a hover and shouted at us to jump. I watched as Smithy and Gary Harding hit the water twenty feet below us. Smithy had had the presence of mind to take the emergency life raft with him. As it hit the water, it exploded into action. I watched as both men scrambled on board. There was a lurch and a shudder as the Lynx gearbox started to tear itself to pieces. Fiona Malden started slowly to move forward, taking the pressure off the failing unit. She was screaming at me to jump.

"Ditch it, Fiona. I will stay in case you need a hand."

Fiona Malden was giving me daggers as the Lynx bucked and shuddered in its death throes. "Get out, you stupid man! I'm not ditching with you on board. Jump now. Go for god's sake, go."

I hit the water feet first with my knees slightly bent, as you would do with a parachute jump. My life jacket inflated and brought me back to the surface in a cloud of bubbles. The freezing Irish Sea was almost too much for my body to stand. The shock had stopped my breathing in its tracks. I looked back to see the raft forty metres or so behind me. I was about to turn and head back when a terrible silence enveloped me. For a split second, all I could hear was the wind and the lapping of the waves. I turned just in time to see the Lynx fall from the sky and hit the water with a tremendous crash.

As I watched the Lynx bobbing up and down, there was a loud pop and the emergency flotation devices were triggered. Normally, this would have been a good thing. The system was designed to allow the crew some time to abandon the helicopter before it headed for Davy Jones's locker. I watched in horror as the Lynx tipped over so that the pilot's side was totally submerged. I could see that the flotation device on the right side of the cockpit had been damaged by the gunfire. It was a further few seconds before my frozen brain registered that there was no sign of movement from the cockpit.

It seemed to take forever for me to reach the stricken chopper. My frozen hands would not open the pilot's door. I could see Fiona Malden face down in the freezing water. I tried again. The door would not budge. Panic took over, and a huge rush of adrenalin surged through my body. I put one foot on the screen and one foot on the side panel, and I used my legs to push. The suction finally gave way, and the door drifted outward. I grabbed Malden's harness and wrenched it open, pulling her free, turning her on her back so her face was clear of the water. I had lost all sense of direction but kicked away from the wrecked chopper. My frozen mind was losing control, and hypothermia was starting to raise its ugly head.

I had just started to think of Smithy and Gary in the life raft when powerful hands grabbed me under the armpits and dragged my sodden body over the side of a boat.

I watched in a haze as Fiona Malden was pulled aboard and laid next to me by the same strong hands.

An old man's craggy face stared into mine. Then his lips started to move. It took a few seconds for my brain to work out he was talking to me. With a tremendous effort, my numb brain started to make out bits of the one-sided conversation. "Did you call the coast guard, son?"

Fiona Malden stirred next to me, then turned onto her belly, and started to throw up violently. The old man seemed to vanish as if he were only some part of a bizarre dream. My senses were starting to come back quickly now. Fiona Malden was propped up between piles of lobster pots. She was almost transparent with a tinge of blue, and she was shaking violently.

Suddenly Smithy was by my side, shaking me by the shoulders. "Mac, Mac! Can you hear me? Are you OK?"

I staggered to my feet and looked around, getting my bearings and my sea legs. I staggered toward the old man who was standing at the stern of the fishing boat. I held out my hand as I approached. "Good morning. I believe we owe you one for pulling us out of the drink."

As I approached, the old man's face was full of concern, but as I spoke to him, he broke into a beaming smile. "Good to hear a good Scots tongue. A thought ye were all foreigners."

I smiled at the old man's observations. "They are all from England."

The old man's smile widened. "Aye, that's what I said, foreigners!"

I decided I needed to change the subject and fast. "Do you think you could do me a couple of very big favours? I will make it worth your while."

The old man's smile subsided, and he studied me intently. "My water-logged friend, I will be glad to help if a can, son."

I patted the old guy on the back and pointed to the northeast. "Do you think you can get us to Arran, my old friend?" The old man scratched his head.

He had a puzzled look on his face "Son, should we no be headin back tae Girvan and reporting this to the authorities, Ma name is Alan, by the way."

I pointed to the partially submerged side of the RAF Lynx. "Alan, can you see the bullet holes in the side of our machine? If we head back to the main-land, I fear that the chopper isn't the only thing that will be full of bullet holes, if you catch my drift."

Old Alan studied the side of the Lynx, then winked at me. "Better get the hell out a here, son, before some bugger takes a pot shot at ma boat."

Alan spun the crank handle of the old fishing boat, and her engine splut-tered into life. We started to pull away from the crash scene when I had a thought. I asked Alan to pull his boat round to the far side of the stricken and listing Lynx. Old Alan and the rest of his new crew watched me as I threaded my way through the lobster pots to where Captain Fiona Malden sat. I reached down and unclipped her Browning side arm. I checked it, then opened fire on the remaining flotation devices. With a whoosh and a splutter, the Lynx evened up. Then, in a pool of aviation fuel, it vanished forever below the gently lapping waves. Fiona Malden staggered to her feet to watch the Lynx descend into its watery grave. Fiona wiped away tears before speaking. "Poor old girl didn't deserve to go that way. You wasted bullets, Mac. She was heading that way anyway."

Fiona was right. It would only have been a matter of time before the chopper sank. "I know, Fiona, but if the Americans get here quickly and find your chopper, they will put two and two together. This way we know we can hide between the lobster pots and have a good chance of getting away with it."

I replaced the safety catch on the Browning and handed the weapon back to Malden. "No, Mac, you keep it. My specialty is flying helicopters. I can see what your specialty is. Let's hope for all our sakes, you don't have to use it."

Smithy and the others had formed a huddle between the lobster pots in an attempt to keep the wind off their frozen bodies. I decided to join our host for the trip to Arran.

"Alan, do you know much about the west side of the isle of Arran, north of Blackwaterfoot, beyond the King's Cave?"

Old Alan watched me out of the corner of his eye while he steered his fishing boat toward the southern tip of Arran in the distance. "Aye, son, I know it well. I supply many of the local guesthouses along the coast and a couple of the hotels." Alan was of retirement age, but he obviously supplemented his old-age pension with a bit of fishing on the side.

"Is it salmon you supply to your customers?"

I was not prepared for the reaction this last sentence elicited. Alan turned and glared at me. "As long as you are on my boat, son, dinnae say that name again. If ye have tae talk aboot that fish, please refer to it as a queer fish. It's bad luck tae call a queer fish by its proper name."

I had heard tales about how superstitious fishermen could be, and Alan had just proved it to me. I decided to comply with his wish and spent the rest of the trip listening to the old man's tales of the sea.

CHAPTER 10

ARRAN

As we approached the west side of the island, I guided old Alan into the bay that was the home of my little cottage. Although frozen to the marrow, I could feel my spirits lift as my little white cottage came into view. Alan ran the bow of his fishing boat up onto the beach, and Smithy helped Fiona Malden and Gary Harding out of the boat and onto to my private little beach. I asked Alan to wait while I sprinted up to the old cottage and turned over the old curling stone to reveal my spare door key.

Two minutes later I was back down at Alan's boat, cash and gifts in hand. Alan refused point black to accept any money for his efforts. "Son, I'll no take yer money." I had suspected this would be the case and had come armed with two bottles of navy rum. I handed them over to Alan. "Now yer talking, son. I'm sure a could find a home for them, lad, and don't worry. Mum's the word. Yer secret is safe wae me."

While the others busied themselves getting the fire lit, I watched as old Alan headed south and back to the Irish Sea.

Since buying the cottage on Arran, I had only visited it once to drop off a few of my things and arrange for a local lady to drop past once a week and keep the place tidy. Sam and I had spent a year getting to know each other in the comfort and beauty of the glass house, and I had neglected this picturesque little cottage. It was strange that fate rather than planning had brought me back.

Fiona, Gary, and Smithy sat around the fire draped in spare blankets I had provided for them.

I was sitting in a dream-like state, thinking of the past when Fiona Malden appeared in front of me. She was speaking to me, but I was still half asleep, half dreaming. Fiona stood in front of me and let the blanket slip to the floor.

She had removed her sodden clothing and was standing in her bra and pants. Her ample breasts were directly at eye level and were threatening to break free from the purple lacy bra. I became aware of Fiona's presence and looked up at her. She was looking down at me, hands on her hips. "I thought that might get your attention. You were away in a world of your own. Penny for your thoughts, Captain Macdonald."

I smiled at Malden and stood up. "Come on, Captain Malden. We better see if any of Sam's clothes fit you before Smithy blows a gasket. He isn't used to soldiers dressing like that."

Fiona followed me into the bedroom, and I showed her some clothes Sam had dropped off. Fiona Malden was bigger in every way than Sam, so jogging bottoms and a blouse were the only things that fitted, and even then, the blouse only buttoned halfway to accommodate Fiona's bust. I headed for the kitchen to make coffees, and Fiona tagged along behind me in her new attire. "You didn't answer my question, Mac. What were you thinking of before I disturbed you?"

I sighed while continuing to make the coffee. "OK, I can see I am going to get no peace from you until I tell you. I was thinking how fate has again brought me here. This little house used to belong to a girl I met on the beach near here. Fate brought us together then too. I was thinking I have had some good times here and some bad times as well."

Fiona moved to the opposite side of the tiny galley kitchen so she could see my face. She folded her arms, which forced her chest upward and caused the already stretched blouse to bulge in all the right places.

"So, Adam, did this girl end up your girlfriend? Come on, Adam, spill the beans." I smiled at Fiona. For sure, she was no shrinking violet.

"Fiona, one can you please keep your breasts under control? I am finding it very hard to concentrate on pouring the coffee, and two, grab those two cups and follow me." I marched out into the living room with the cups and handed them to Smithy and Gary. "Sorry, guys, it's black coffee tonight. We don't have any milk; we will do a shop tomorrow."

Fiona Malden followed at my back and handed me one of the mugs as we all gathered around the now roaring fire. After we had drained the mugs and watched the fire die down, talk turned inevitably to our predicament. Not surprisingly Fiona led the way. "Mac, looks like you are the natural leader, so what is your plan?"

I had been waiting for this question all day since we had arrived at the cottage. "Well would you believe me if I said nothing, let me explain. Sam and Karen were going to shake off their tail, then head for our house where there is also a transmitter. Once Sam destroys that, she knows to head for here. I want to wait for her, as she is the true spy among us. She will know how best to proceed from here. We dare not try to contact Vauxhall Cross through conventional channels. It is almost guaranteed that the American intelligence network will be waiting for exactly that call. Hopefully, they think we went down with the chopper, which will give us some breathing space until Sam gets here."

Fiona Malden put her cup down and sat forward. "Listen guys I know I am only the pilot, but can someone bring me up to speed on the full story? After all, if I am going to die, I would really like to know bloody why!"

Smithy was giving me a hard stare as if to say *the floor is all yours.* "OK, Fiona, for a start, you are not going to die, but right, you need to know what we know. An Israeli terrorist called Areli Benesch escaped from Porton Down with deadly chemicals that could end life as we know it. Sam, Smithy, and I have had dealings with this woman previously and were tasked with finding her and recovering the chemicals. During our investigation, we discovered Benesch had stumbled across Gary here and his invention. We think Benesch has contacted the Americans and informed them of Gary's incredible scientific work. We are not sure yet of America's intentions, but it looks like they are using the hunt for the dangerous chemicals to mask their real hunt for Gary and his scientific breakthrough."

Fiona Malden mulled this over for a few seconds before replying. "So if we handed Gary over to the Americans, we would be free to go looking for the chemicals?"

Gary Harding's face was a picture of horror. "No, Fiona. Gary is a British citizen. I think their plan would only work if Gary were spirited away, and the Americans could deny any of this happened. Anyway, Benesch is in collaboration with them. Who is to say the Americans don't already have the chemicals?"

Day had turned to night, and our thoughts moved onto the sleeping arrangements for the night. I suggested that Fiona and Gary use the double bed while Smithy and I made use of the couch and the floor. Fiona Malden rejected this, saying that the two men who had been wounded should have the bed. After all, she was one of the lads and needed no special favours. I grudgingly agreed but asked Smithy to accompany me outside on the pretence of collecting some wood for the fire. We left Gary and Fiona making up makeshift beds.

Smithy followed me over to the old boathouse and played a torch on the padlock while I undid it. Inside the boathouse sat a brand new speedboat that had never seen a drop of water. It had been one of the things I had dropped off on our last visit. I pulled back the tarpaulin covering the boat interior and lifted out an army holdall.

In my time on the training side of the SAS, I had amassed a few toys, many of which had left with me—a privilege very few of the regiment had the chance of doing. Normally, weapons and munitions were signed out and signed back in, but during training, things go amiss. As the training officer, it was my duty to supervise this. I handed Smithy an MP5 with three clips of ammo, a Beretta pistol, three clips, and two grenades. I lifted a Glock, two clips, and two grenades.

"So, Mac, that little spiel in the house was bollocks, I take it. You are expecting trouble?"

I locked the boathouse up while speaking to Smithy. "Hopefully, it will go just as I described it, but if it doesn't, we will be ready. If the shit hits the fan, get Gary out the bedroom window. The gorse bushes at the back will give you good cover. I will cover the front door and hopefully give you a bit of time to get away."

Although it was dark, I could sense Smithy smiling. "Bollocks, Mac, and you know it. If American Special Forces arrive, we won't have a snowdrop's chance in hell of getting out."

I stopped and surveyed the horizon and the dark shapes of the hills on the Mull of Kintyre. "You let me worry about that. Just stay on your guard at all times. Oh, and by the way, it's a snowball's chance in hell, not a snowdrop's."

Smithy shook his head as he followed my gaze out to sea. "Anyway, Mac, you have bigger problems closer to home to worry about tonight. I've watched Malden and you getting very cosy. Do you think you will be able to fend off her advances tonight when you are alone in the lounge?" I pulled away from the view to look at Smithy; he had a beaming grin from ear to ear.

"She isn't interested in an old goat like me. I will put a good word in for you, Mr Smith, if you like."

Smithy's smile broke into a chuckle. "Mac, you are one hell of a soldier, but you really have no clue about women, do you? Put a word in for me by all means, but I'm telling you now—she has the hots for you, old son."

Smithy's words were still ringing in my ears as Fiona Malden reached across and switched off the table lamp, drowning the room in darkness. For a few minutes, there was silence. Then Fiona broke the spell. "Come on then, Mac. Tell me about the girl you met here, were you lovers?" In the darkness, I smiled to myself. I could still hear Smithy's chuckles. He might just have a point.

"No, Fiona, our relationship never had a chance to get that far. Kay was murdered before I had a chance to get her off the island. I found her body at the foot of a cliff just along the coast from here. She knew too much and paid the ultimate price."

I think Fiona Malden knew from my voice it was not wise to pursue the question further, and for a few seconds, there was silence again. "Adam, you would be far more comfortable on the couch with me than rolling about the floor. I won't tell Sam, honest."

For a fleeting second, the temptation was overpowering. Fiona Malden was a striking-looking woman, and I had never been chased by the opposite sex before. I found it quite flattering, and then my brain took over from my genitals. Sam's piercing grey eyes filled my head, and I longed for her to be here with me again.

"Fiona, cards on the table. You are a very lovely lady, and if I were single, I would be on that couch like a shot. But we both know that it wouldn't stop there. The two things that stop me crossing the room are one, I am in love with Sam, and two, I am not about to mess with an MI6 assassin."

There was a loud sigh in the darkness from the other side of the room. "Well, you can't blame a girl for trying, Mac. Sweet dreams, honey."

❖ ❖ ❖

Neil Andrews was having the day from hell. He had been summonsed to the Cobra meeting to give an account of the situation so far and to explain the possible loss of a Lynx helicopter along with definite crash and subsequent deaths of an American aircrew in the vicinity of the missing Lynx's last-reported position. If initial reports were correct, and the Lynx was down, he had just lost his best team in one fell swoop. To say he was not a happy man would have been the understatement of the year.

He would have to regroup and fast before the PM decided enough was enough and replaced him.

He was about to contact Peter Kent and Robin Alder, his two most experienced agents, and give them the job of finding the missing chemicals when Jean, his PA, informed him she had Robin Alder on the phone for him on line one. As soon as the news had broken about the crash, he had dispatched Alder to snoop about the area and see what he could come up with. He listened to Alder's report without commenting.

"Sir, it looks like the American pilot crashed trying to avoid a bridge after flying at low level. I was about to leave when I bumped into a local farmer up here. He took me to a field where he swears he saw two helicopters in a gun battle. One small, grey-an-green, and one grey. I fobbed him off, telling him it was a NATO training exercise, but after he left, I had a dig about and discovered 7.6 millimetre shell casings all over the bottom of the field. Looks like the Yanks have a bit of explaining to do."

Andrews was having trouble controlling his rage. "Good man, Alder. Team up with Kent, and I will send you both new instructions very soon."

Andrews had just replaced the receiver when Jean patched through a second call. Air Chief Marshall Sir Steven Britain had never spoken to Neil Andrews before and was unprepared for a fired-up MI6 director in full flow. "Sir Steven, you must have read my mind. I was just about to pick up the phone when you called. I take it we have no news on our missing helicopter." Andrews paused only for breath, not letting the air chief marshall get a word in before continuing at full speed ahead. "Sir Steven, I have grave information that I was going to pass on at the Cobra meeting, but I think we need to act now. It has come to my attention that our Lynx had been fired upon by the American helicopters. They have gone too far. We need to send them a message and not one on paper. Steven, I want you to put the wind up them. We need to let them know if they try any more nonsense, they will pay a terrible price."

Sir Steven Britain was silent for some time before picking his words. He had received the letter from the PM advising him to assist MI6 in any way possible. He was not entirely sure that this request was covered by the letter.

"Director, with the greatest respect, any hostile reaction at the moment could end in disaster. We are both struggling to cope with the loss of our people, all the more reason to wait and look at things rationally. I think we should run this past the prime minister first."

Andrews exploded down the phone. "Good god, man! They were not just people. They were friends and colleagues, and they were my best team. They were in an unarmed helicopter, and they were blown out of the sky. Get the lead out of your arse, and get some planes in the air. I am not asking you to attack the Americans, just send them a message that if they try anything else, we will do more than debate it over tea and bloody biscuits in Number Ten."

Andrews knew he had rattled Sir Steven Britain and pressed home the advantage. "If Dowding had hesitated like this at the start of the Second World War, we would all be speaking German."

"Very well. I will send your message. On your head be it."

❖ ❖ ❖

Rear Admiral Holister was just finishing off an entry in his diary when there was an urgent knock on his cabin door. He was informed that his presence was required immediately on the bridge. He entered the bridge and could tell instantly from the faces that for a second day running, something bad was afoot.

The radar operator was supplying a running commentary to the assembled officers. Holister listened without comment. "Two unidentified aircraft, inbound speed Mach two point two and closing. Firing range within two minutes."

Holister glanced at the chart then barked an order to his team. "The USS *Kidd* is closest. Ask them to visually identify them. Ask the *Kidd* to attempt contact."

The radar operator continued his commentary. "Bogies have dropped to sea level, speed Mach two. Firing range in sixty seconds."

The XO turned to Holister. "Permission to bring the ship to action stations, sir."

Holister gave him a withering stare. "Yesterday, we shot the shit out of a British helicopter. The goddamned last thing I need is a spooked gunnery officer giving the order to fire. What if the plane is a Brit and for the second day in a row, we fire on them. No. We wait for positive confirmation, or if they lock their missiles on us."

There was an uneasy silence for a few seconds, and then the communications officer passed the information that the USS *Kidd* had just identified the aircraft as RAF Typhoons.

The assembled crew watched from the bridges as two black specks transformed before their eyes. The Typhoons passed between the *Nimitz* and its supply ship, level with the bridge at Mach two. The sonic boom as the warplanes smashed the sound barrier caused broken windows and general alarm among the younger members of the crews who had no previous experiences of the sheer raw power of an aeroplane breaking the sound barrier at such close quarters. The American sailors watched as, above the battle group, six Tornado fighter-bombers passed at high altitude.

The assembled group on the bridge watched as Holister once again consulted the charts. For a second, there was silence on the bridge as Holister considered his options. He pointed to a position fifty miles south of the southern tip of Ireland. "Gentlemen, plot a course for this position, then pass it to the rest of the group. I want us ready to move in fifteen minutes. I have a few things to discuss with our guest, Colonel Southern. You have the bridge." Holister marched off the bridge, heading for Southern's cabin.

Holister dismissed his marine outside Southern's cabin before knocking and entering without waiting for a reply. Southern sat with Areli Benesch on one side and Brent Cussack on the other side. "Sorry for the intrusion, Colonel, but I have little time for chat. I have decided to pull the taskforce out of the area and lower the risk of escalating the situation further. As you will have heard, the Royal Air Force has just sent us a warning. I will have a Seahawk ready and waiting to take whoever wants to go to Machrihanish Air Base. If not, you can come with me on a tour of the Irish coast. I will only return if the situation demands it. I for one do not want to go down in history as the admiral who caused a conflict between two friendly nations. The chopper leaves in ten minutes." Rear Admiral Holister was gone as quickly as he had arrived, leaving Southern with a dilemma.

Southern asked Benesch to grab her gear and head for the chopper. He waited until she had left before talking to Cussack.

Southern could not let the Vokxin travel back unguarded. If it ended up in a CIA lab, they would find out that it was the very chemical they were still supposed to be hunting for, and he would have a lot of explaining to do. He could not risk taking it with him. He had already been lucky not to release the chemical during his car crash.

"Colonel Cussack, I need you to do a job for me. I need you to go to Alaska, no questions asked." Southern crossed to his locker and extracted the vial from the back of the locker. Cussack looked at the vial he had been handed. He was bewildered as to Southern's latest orders. Southern sat down opposite him. "Brent, pin your ears back. I have a bit of news for you."

Southern poured a glass of water and took a sip before continuing. "The vial I have given you contains the Vokxin we have been looking for. Treat it with great care. Opening it would be catastrophic for the planet as we know it. I want you to take it to our dangerous chemicals holding facility, Area Charlie One, in Alaska." Southern held up a hand. "Let me stop you before you ask the next question because I know what it will be. Benesch gave me the chemicals the moment we arrived. The real mission is not to recapture some cold-war chemical that no one in his right mind would ever release. Benesch stumbled on a young scientist who has probably made the biggest breakthrough in scientific history. She was going to hand him over at the soccer ground, but MI6 beat us to the prize. Colonel, I need to buy time in the UK so we can acquire the scientist and his work. America needs this technology to keep it at the top. Just as we acquired the German missile scientists after the Second World War, we will bring this young scientist and his work to the US. Letting the powers-that-be think we are still looking for this Vokxin will give me the excuse to keep looking in MI6's back yard for our target." Southern stood up and gathered his things ready for the trip to the Scottish mainland.

Cussack lifted the vial. "OK, Colonel, you sort things out this side of the water, and I will make sure this nasty little chemical makes it to Charlie One safely."

❖ ❖ ❖

I awoke with a start. Outside, the pebble drive had been disturbed. I was soaking in sweat from no doubt another one of my dreams that had continued to haunt me since the Gulf War. The room was in total darkness. Outside, the grey dark of a winter dawn penetrated the thin curtain material of the cottage. I reached under the cushion that I had been using for a pillow and retrieved the Glock I had placed there the night before. I checked the pistol's action quietly and tried to make my way noiselessly across the living room to the front door. I pushed the door, and it moved. It was off the catch. Should I try to warn Smithy before I proceeded? The footsteps in the gravel by the front door made my decision for me. There was no time. I sprang forward pulling the door open on my way past, landing on my side, half in and half out of the door.

In a split second, I spotted the figure blocking my view of the sea. The woman's gasp and my brain recognizing the woman's outline stopped me only milliseconds before I fired. I removed my finger from the trigger and let the Glock fall the few inches to the ground.

Fiona Malden recoiled in shock. We both knew how close she had come to being shot. "Jesus, Mac! What the hell are you doing?"

I rolled onto my stomach using my left arm to prop up my head before speaking. "Captain Malden, would you please in future tell me before you go walkabout? I think that the situations we have found ourselves in demand a very high level of caution, don't you think?"

Fiona Malden sat down with her back against the wall of the cottage. I watched as she tried to rearrange her windswept hair into some sort of order. For a few seconds, we sat, both recovering from the initial shock of our close disaster. I watched Fiona's as the dawn grew stronger and light highlighted her short, jet-black hair and alabaster skin. She was a dead ringer for a youngish Liz Taylor. For sure, out in Civvy Street she would scrub up rather well, I thought. Why she would be interested in an old fossil like me, I wasn't sure.

Fiona was first to break the silence. "I couldn't sleep, Mac, sorry. I didn't want to wake you up. I was thinking, while I wandered along the beach, I could give one of my team a call and let him know we are OK. No one would find out that way."

I said nothing. I got to my feet, then walked across to where Fiona Malden crouched against the wall. I took her hands and pulled her to her feet.

At five foot nine, she had to stand on tiptoe for her jade-green eyes to be level with mine. She stared into my eyes, wondering what was coming next. "Fiona, look at me and tell me if you think this face is kidding. If you so much as touch a phone, I will break your fingers. Do we understand each other?"

For a second, Fiona Malden threatened to break into a smile, but as she studied my face, I could tell that she had got the message. She pulled away in shock as she realised this was no empty threat. "Sorry to get in your face, Fiona, but you don't know the type of people we are dealing with. The woman was a top Israeli agent, and the CIA are arguably the most efficient intelligence agency in the world. I know this from personal experience. Sam almost lost her life trying to guard me from them."

Fiona Malden turned and looked out over the Kintyre peninsula, arms folded. "So your girl was willing to give her life for you. Now you have got to admit, Mac, that's kind of romantic, don't you think?"

I smiled at Fiona Malden's naivety. "Fiona, I will admit it drew us together and formed a bond between us, but romantic? No, getting your arse shot off is never romantic."

In due course, my other two houseguests roused themselves but were none too happy at my offer of dry bran flakes with no milk. It was clear to see a trip to the local shop was going to be required, sooner rather than later.

It was agreed that Gary and I would wait at the cottage while Fiona and Smithy would use the two mountain bikes and rucksacks I had stashed in the old boathouse to travel the few miles south to the village of Blackwaterfoot. I knew from previous trips, most things could be acquired from the handful of well-stocked local shops. A quick forage into the feet of a pair of waders produced my emergency supply of cash.

Fiona made a grab for the cash. "I'll take that, thank you very much. You give it to Smithy here, and he will come back with beer, crisps, and men's magazines. Don't worry, boys. I will look after you." Smithy gave me a wink as he jumped on the bike and headed off, leading the way toward Blackwaterfoot.

I made a quick detour to the kitchen before heading off in search of Gary Harding. I found the young scientist on the beach in front of the old boathouse staring out to sea. As I approached from the cottage, I could see that he was far away in a world of his own.

"It's a lovely view don't you think?" Gary Harding almost jumped out of his skin.

The last few weeks of his life had driven the lad's nerves to breaking point. I handed Gary a can of cola I had picked up from the kitchen. "Sorry, Gary. I didn't mean to startle you. Sorry, the cola is all I have left in the house. We will get a proper breakfast going when Smithy and Fiona get back."

Gary opened the can without speaking; he studied the top of the can, avoiding eye contact. "I am sorry for causing all this bother, Mr Macdonald.

I wish I had never bothered trying to get rich quick. I should have got on with helping Professor Ferry, and none of this crap would have happened. I'm sorry."

I felt genuinely sorry for the lad. In the space of a few weeks, he had been transformed from spoiled genius to a hunted fugitive. "Gary, you have nothing to be sorry for, lad. Look at it this way. If you did not have your invention to bargain with, you would have been dead. Benesch was only ever going to use you to escape. Once you had served that purpose, she would have killed you. Your invention saved your life. Just think how many more lives it could save if we get it into the right hands. Listen to me. When Sam and your friend Karen get back, we will get you back to your folks. You can finish your work, be a very rich man, and help millions of people into the bargain."

Gary was still avoiding eye contact. "Mr Macdonald, I have many tests to do with DNA before I can be sure of the effects on humans. This has all happened too soon. Do you know what will happen if the Americans get their hands on me? I fear instead of allowing me to lead the research, they will want to cut corners, and because I carry the modified DNA, I will be treated as a glorified lab rat."

Gary Harding's fantasy of getting rich quick had come crashing down around his ears. From the look on the lad's face, it was clear to see all he wanted was to wake up the next day and find all this had been a bad dream.

"Mr Macdonald, if they come for me, please don't let them take me. Put a bullet in my head and finish it."

I watched as tears welled up in the young lad's eyes. "Gary, if we are clever, it will never come to that. Anyway, I have to wonder, after your last little display, whether a bullet in your head will have the desired effect."

Gary was visibly shaken by that last comment. "Oh, god no. What kind of monster have I created?" It was clear to me that Gary Harding like most genius types walked a fine line mentally, it would not take much to push him over the edge.

❖ ❖ ❖

The road from Adam's cottage started off with a few twisty bends, then climbed steadily toward the south of the island for a couple of miles before descending into the little costal village of Blackwaterfoot. Smithy set the pace with Fiona Malden tucked in behind him.

Fiona knew after only a few minutes of the incline that she could not match the pace of the younger man. She decided to kill two birds with one stone. She struck up a conversation to slow the pace and find out if Smithy had any interesting information on Adam Macdonald.

"Slow down, Mr Smith, before you kill me. It's been a long time since I did my battle fitness training, you know. I just sit on my bum in a helicopter these days."

Smithy took the bait and slowed down, pulling alongside Fiona's bike. Normally, Smithy was a quiet guy, but when it came to the ladies, he was not so shy. He made an exaggerated swivel with his head, checking out Fiona's rear view. "Well, Captain Malden from where I am, it looks like sitting on your bum has had no ill effects. It still looks pretty good to me."

Fiona Malden took the compliment in her stride. She was used to the endless chat-up lines from her male colleagues. She was more than capable of holding her own. A life in the army had taught her well. "So are you going to tell me what you and Adam were talking about last night when you went for your cosy little chat outside?"

Smithy decided to continue his verbal probing of Malden's armour. "We discussed tactics, and I warned him you had the hots for him." Smithy took his eyes off the road for a second to see if he had scored a direct hit on Fiona Malden's psyche.

He was somewhat surprised to find Fiona Malden smiling back at him with a devilish twinkle in her eye. "Well spotted, Mr Smith, but I think you need to try harder to cover up your jealousy."

Smithy was lost for a reply. Malden knew she had stopped Smithy in his tracks and said no more for the moment, letting the silence work in her favour. Smithy wanted to object, but he knew this would only make him look more insecure and convince Fiona Malden that she was correct in her observations.

He decided the best course was to move the discussion on. "Take my advice, Fiona, and forget Adam Macdonald. He is pretty well hooked up with Sam O'Conner. Let me tell you, Fiona, do not mess with that lady. I've seen her in action, and her bark is nothing compared to her bite. Trust me."

Fiona Malden thought for a moment before continuing the conversation. "So are all the stories about Adam true?"

Smithy pulled ahead for a second to let a car overtake them before returning to Fiona's side. "Depends what you have heard, Fiona. I don't know much about Mac myself. I know he was a top MI6 asset in Ireland during the troubles. Last year, the IRA sent a hit team over to eliminate Mac. I was part of a close protection detail sent to guard him. The shit hit the fan. Two of my unit were killed in action, and my boss was badly wounded; only Mac and I escaped in one piece."

Fiona Malden was so engrossed in the story that she barely noticed that they were on the descent into Blackwaterfoot. Adam had told them to watch out for a small humpback bridge over a stream that ran out into the tiny harbour of Blackwaterfoot. They knew they had arrived as the little bridge came into view next to a swing park. They propped their bikes up on the fence by the little swing park and headed off into Blackwaterfoot to scour the area for food to take back in the rucksacks to Adam's cottage.

After a hunt around the local shops, Fiona packed Smithy off with a shopping list to the local butchers. Fiona had told Smithy she was going to get bread and milk, and she would meet him back at the swing park. Fiona had omitted one small detail that she knew Smithy would not approve of. Before heading into the shop, Fiona popped two letters into the postbox, one to her mother and a second letter that Gary had pleaded with her to post. After all, Adam had said nothing about letters. Smithy returned to the swing park to find Fiona and her rucksack full to overflowing.

Smithy was for heading off right away, but Fiona had not recovered fully from the first trip and plonked herself down on one of the swings. She patted the swing next to her, gesturing Smithy over from his bike. "Come on, Mr Smith. I'm not as fit as you. Give a girl a chance to sit down for a bit before we tackle the hills again."

Smithy sat down, taking in the views out to sea from the little village park.

"So, Luke, you were in the SAS. Did you ever come across Adam when he was a captain there?"

Smithy smiled inwardly. It was clear to see Captain Malden had no intention of forgetting about Adam anytime soon. "Yes, Adam was in charge of training at Credenhill. He was my training officer when I first joined the Special Forces. One of the trainers, Sergeant Hunter, told me a story once that Adam had saved his life in Kuwait and had taken on and beaten a complete Iraqi republican guard unit. The Mac is a legend, even in Special Forces circles. The word is that he was blocked from receiving the VC by the government for some reason."

Malden was deep in thought for a few seconds. Her manner changed noticeably, showing a much more serious side. "Smithy, tell me what happened when my aircraft ditched. I can only remember coming to in the fishing boat. Nothing before that."

Smithy hesitated for a second. He knew what he was about to tell her would do nothing to help reduce her interest in Adam Macdonald. "Mac was the closest when the chopper went down. He could see you were in trouble and managed to rip the door loose and drag you out. By the time we got to you, both of you were in a shit state. Mac was on the edge of consciousness, and you were out of it."

Malden caught Smithy's eye. "So when were you going to tell me Mac saved my life?"

CHAPTER 11

BRUCE ELLIS

Only a few miles away from Blackwaterfoot on the Kintyre peninsula, the US Navy Seahawk touched down feet from the main control room. Lieutenant Commander Saul Bartowski watched the Seahawk land from the control room. He had been forewarned of the arrival of Colonel Southern and had deployed his SEALs at various points around the base to ensure his commanding officers safety. To Bartowski's surprise Colonel Southern arrived with a woman in tow.

True to form, Southern wasted no time and seconds later appeared in the control tower with the small, dark-haired woman by his side. "Good day, Commander. Can you tell me the whereabouts of our Delta team leader please?"

Bartowski had met Southern before on the odd occasion and was not put off by his brisk manner. Saul Bartowski ambled across to the north-facing windows of the control room and pointed north. "Sergeant Franklyn headed that way with his unit this morning, Colonel Southern. I would imagine he will be back soon, before the weather closes in tonight."

Southern exploded. "Who the hell gave them permission to leave the base?

From the back of the control room, a silent figure stood watching Southern's behaviour. He said nothing for the moment, weighing up how best to introduce himself to Colonel Southern.

Bruce Ellis was the replacement for the late Scott Tomlin, who had been killed by Benesch at the football ground. Unknown to Southern, although Scott Tomlin had been the rising star in the CIA, Bruce Ellis was his team leader at Langley. Bruce Ellis had cut his teeth in the NYPD, working as a homicide detective. His arrest count was impressive and had made him known to the FBI, who recruited him before he was transferred to homeland security. Ellis had spent the last two years with the CIA heading up the team that was charged with finding Osama Bin Laden.

It was not lost on Ellis how important this new mission must be for the president, to have him taken out of the biggest manhunt in the history of the world to replace his fallen understudy. Ellis had boarded the CIA Gulfstream while it sat in its hangar. He was shocked to find the president on board and waiting for him. He listened while the president explained the situation he was about to be thrown into. The president was not happy about the amount of information that was fed back to him and sensed a cover-up somewhere in the chain of command. Bruce Ellis was tasked with finding out the full story and reporting back directly to him and him alone.

Ellis stepped out from the shadows at the back of the control room. He had used the bodies in front of him for cover while he had studied Southern and the Israeli woman. "Good day, Colonel Southern. We meet at last. I have studied everything ever written about you, so I feel I already know you well. Forgive me. I should have told you first and foremost that Langley has sent me here to replace poor Scott."

Southern was taken aback by the stranger's comments. He had made damned sure in his career that there was nothing written about him. He had covered his tracks well, or so he thought. "And do you have a name, sir? For I have been told nothing of a replacement?"

Ellis knew he had Southern on the back foot and pressed home the advantage. "Forgive my ignorance. I am Bruce Ellis, and I am not surprised you don't know about my arrival, sir. I was briefed on the situation, and I have to say I think the general consensus of opinion back home is that there is a communication problem as no one has heard anything back from the UK. Could that be the case, sir?"

Southern had taken an instant dislike to the new arrival. He was not used to having the spotlight turned on him by anyone. The situation was made worse by the fact he had not handpicked Ellis, and he did not know his agenda. "Please return to your quarters. I will let you know when I have a task for you."

Bruce Ellis smiled and pointed to Benesch while studying Southern. “No problem, Colonel. Will I lock up the Israeli woman while you contact Washington and tell them you have captured her?”

Southern was furious with Bruce Ellis but outwardly maintained his calm. “Since you were briefed, there has been a change to the mission here. Miss Benesch is no longer a suspect. In fact, she is to be congratulated. She spotted the scientist removing the chemicals and raised the alarm. We are now hunting the scientist. Your information, unfortunately, is badly out of date. As I said if you make your way to your quarters, I will let you know when I need you.”

Bruce Ellis made his way past Benesch and Southern on the way to his room. He left his final comment until last. “Very well, Colonel Southern, for the moment, you are the boss. Oh, and you were right about the unfortunate part of your statement. It was the president himself who briefed me. If he doesn’t know what’s going on, then I agree with you, it’s very ‘unfortunate. Probably more for some than others.” Ellis left the room, closing the door before Southern could reply to his thinly veiled threat.

❖ ❖ ❖

Sam had planned to leave for the glass house early to beat the commuter traffic around Edinburgh Airport, but her plan failed miserably as she encountered her first taste of morning sickness. Although she avoided actually being sick, the thought of sitting in a moving car was too much to handle at the moment. She had dispatched Karen Lowe to the restaurant to get her breakfast while she made do with a glass of water and an extra half hour in bed. Eventually, the nausea passed, and Sam gingerly moved about the room to make sure she was well enough to move. She wandered past the full-length mirror and paused to look at her side view for any signs of her stomach starting to swell. Although little exercise and an intermittently ravenous appetite had filled out Sam’s frame, she was not chubby, and her stomach showed no signs of the impending expansion. Sam battled with the turmoil of thoughts inside her head. She was unhappy that her finely tuned figure was about to be replaced with a shape better suited to Mr Blobby. She knew she had to concentrate on the task at hand, but she could not stop her mind wandering off on tangents. One minute she was angry with herself for letting this happen, and the next she was filled with a sense of achievement and awe. She was a mess, and she had to get herself sorted out before the hunt for Benesch began in earnest.

Karen Lowe was given the job of driving Sam's Beetle while Sam's stomach adjusted to the motion. Sam used the time in the passenger seat to think through the situation.

She had already decided not to contact Neil Andrews until she had removed the incriminating handgun with the transmitter from the glass house. It would be far better if she waited until she rejoined the rest of the team at Adam's little cottage on Arran before contacting Andrews for an update on Benesch.

Sam only let Karen drive as far as the Stirling services before she proclaimed she was fit to drive and replaced Karen Lowe behind the steering wheel of her Beetle. From there on in, the pace of the trip increased as Sam pushed the Beetle hard. It was the BBC two o'clock news on the radio that almost caused Sam to crash just before Tynedrum. The news presenter explained that during a NATO training exercise, both the American navy and the British army had lost a helicopter in unrelated freak incidents. Sam had to stop the car. She was no fool. She knew a cover-up when she heard it. When it was announced all on board the Lynx were missing, she was physically sick by the side of the road. For the rest of the trip north, she kept telling herself that she could not contact Vauxhall Cross until she had removed the bugged handgun and moved away from the glass house. The thought of bringing up Adam's child alone haunted her, but she kept telling herself Adam had more lives than a cat. He would have survived. He had to survive.

Sam and Karen arrived at the glass house just as the winter sun had reached the horizon. Sam stood outside the glass house watching the sun cast its last shadows over the little islands of Rum, Eigg, and Muck. Her mood was not good. She sensed almost a sadness surrounding the cliff-top site as she watched the sun fall below the horizon. Karen was too gobsmacked by the glass house to notice the view. "Good god, Sam. How much does MI6 pay that you can afford a pad like this? Are you sure you don't rob banks in your spare time?"

Karen was trying hard to lighten the mood that had enveloped them since hearing the BBC news that afternoon. Sam said nothing and opened the front door, showing Karen into the garage area off the ground floor. A whirlwind tour of the glass house ended with Karen in the kitchen preparing an evening meal for them both while Sam stood outside on the balcony alone with her thoughts and a glass of fruit juice. Karen had removed the glass of vodka Sam had poured herself before heading outside.

Karen gave the chicken risotto one more taste before heading for the balcony. "Sam, that is the food ready. Better get it while it is hot."

Sam half turned toward her. The tears running down her cheeks were exaggerated in the light coming from the lounge windows. "I'm fine. I don't feel like eating. Sorry!"

Karen put her arm round Sam's shoulder and herded her back in through the lounge toward the kitchen. "You might not be hungry, but you have to think of your baby."

Sam was about to object but hesitated. She was already starting to hate this mothering crap.

Over supper, Karen let Sam do the talking. The conversation drifted to Adam. Karen noted the change in Sam as she relaxed. "So Adam is the one. When did you know he was the man for you? Was it instant, or did he win you over?"

Sam's eyes glazed over as her thoughts transported her back to her first encounters with Adam Macdonald. "I'm not sure when I first realised he was Mr Right. Not right away. He was a puzzle to me, not what I had expected. He was a real live hero, a legend in the military. I didn't know what to expect. I mean, there are not many men the IRA fear. Even my own sister, who had worked with Adam, fell for him, so much so that she gave her life for him. I expected him to be some kind of Herculean Rambo figure. I was shocked and puzzled to find a polite and somewhat reserved retired officer. Tall, dark, and handsome, yes. Rambo, no. I am still not sure if I have found the true Adam. He is deeper than the ocean. That's why I am not sure how he will react to the news that he is about to become a father—that is, if he is still alive."

❖ ❖ ❖

David Southern sat by himself. He studied the report compiled for him by Langley before making a final decision about his next move. The report stated that satellite images and British search-and-rescue conversations concluded that it was more than likely that the British Lynx helicopter had crashed somewhere off the west coast of Scotland and that there were no survivors. There was a nagging feeling that this was still unfinished business. There were too many unanswered questions. Was the scientist on board? Why, if they were dead, were MI5 and MI6 still hunting around that area of Scotland? Also, who had sent the dummy message to the navy chopper telling them to attack the Brits? Who had sent Bruce Ellis to try and undermine his investigation? All these thoughts were still tumbling around in Colonel Southern's mind when Benesch, accompanied by Bruce Ellis, sat down at the table in the quiet corner of the canteen that Southern had commandeered for his office. Southern wasted no time with small talk. The quicker he could get Bruce Ellis out of his hair the better. "Ellis, I want you to investigate the missing British helicopter. We must be sure the mad scientist and the deadly chemicals are at the bottom of the sea and not lurking about Scotland somewhere. I will have a chopper drop you off at Prestwick Airport as this was the destination on the original flight plan. Good luck and keep me posted."

Ellis nodded, stood up, and headed for the exit without another word. Southern waited until he had left the canteen before speaking to Benesch. "I trust him even less than I trust you, Are you sure this trip is worth the effort?"

Benesch cut him in two with her glare. "My American friend, you are correct not to trust me, as I will never trust you. But you must remember we both have the same goal, so for the moment we work as a team, correct?" Benesch unfolded a map and traced the coast of Scotland with her fingertip until it came to rest on the west coast just below the Isle of Skye. "Here is where I found the British agents before, and here is also where the radio signal is coming from. We must investigate it. My gut tells me this."

Southern shrugged. He had little option. The trail had dried up, and he was running out of time and favour with his superiors in Washington. "Very well. Take as many Delta men as you need. Leave in the morning, and keep radio comms on."

Bruce Ellis contacted the American embassy the next morning, and after a few minutes explaining what he wanted, the embassy placed a call to air traffic control in Prestwick advising them they had an air accident investigator in Scotland who might call to ask some questions about the American military accident. The coordinator seemed puzzled as he had already spoken to air crash investigators but complied with the embassy's wishes that he do everything in his power to assist.

The coordinator did not have long to wait. Twenty minutes after the call, an American arrived and introduced himself as Special Investigator Bruce Ellis. Tim Matheson was senior controller at Prestwick and had been on duty during the helicopter incident. Both men pored over the charts Matheson had produced.

"So Tim, this is the last time you spotted our aircraft on radar?"

Matheson frowned. "It is difficult to be accurate, Mr Ellis. As I have already explained, there were three military helicopters in the area. I am not blessed with all military operation details, but watching the radar that morning, all three helicopters at some point dropped below radar contact. To me, it looked as if they were engaged in some sort of exercise. Given that there was a NATO exercise going on in the Irish Sea, I think that must have been the case."

Bruce Ellis was not interested in the American choppers. He already knew all the details from his contacts at the Pentagon. He needed to know about the British chopper, but he did not want to draw suspicion to his actions. After all, the Americans should have nothing to do with a missing British army helicopter.

Ellis asked a few more questions about the US choppers before changing to the British chopper. "Tim, there is no way that the last contact from the British chopper was actually our second Seahawk returning to the carrier?"

Tim Matheson thought for a second before shaking his head and placing his finger on the chart. "No, there is no chance of that. Here is the last radar contact for our Lynx. Your Seahawk attended the crash site. It was recorded some fifty minutes later crossing the Irish Sea twenty miles further south. No, this was without doubt the last time our chopper was picked up by radar."

Bruce Ellis noted the position and also the position of the downed American chopper. Drawing a straight line from them both would mean that the British Lynx would have passed over the costal town of Girvan. This would be his next port of call. "One more thing, Tim, and then I will get out of your hair. Was there any radio chatter that you monitored between any of the choppers?"

Tim Matheson smiled at Bruce Ellis. "Mr Ellis, even if there were, we would not be able to pick it up. We did monitor some heavy radio interference around the time of the crash, but I am sure you know as well as I do that the military have encoded equipment. I think you should ask your navy that question."

Ellis arrived in Girvan just after lunchtime. He parked his hire car by the harbour and found a nice little restaurant only yards away.

Over lunch, he got talking to the waitress and casually dropped the helicopter crashes into the conversation. The waitress had seen nothing but pointed to the harbour.

"If anybody saw anything, it will be the boys in the boats. Everybody knows if you want to hear about anything in Girvan, ask a fisherman. Now, sir, is there anything else I can get you?"

Ellis thanked the waitress, paid the bill, and left a big tip. Then he headed out of the door toward the harbour wall. Ellis surveyed the harbour area before deciding on a chubby little man on the far side of the harbour. He was sitting on the bow of a white, weather-beaten fishing boat watching the world go by.

The little man watched Bruce Ellis as he made his way round the harbour wall. Before Bruce Ellis could say a word, the little man introduced himself. "Hello there. You look a wee bit lost. Can a help ye?"

Ellis smiled openly at the chubby fisherman. He knew instinctively that he had struck gold. "I sure hope you can. I wondered if you can recall seeing or hearing about anyone who witnessed the missing army helicopter passing near here?"

The little man's demeanour changed noticeably. He studied Ellis with searching eyes. "And who would you be that needs to know a thing like that?"

Bruce Ellis jumped the couple of feet from the harbour wall onto the deck of the fishing boat, extending a hand to the fisherman. "My name is Ellis. I am a special investigator with the Air Investigation Joint Task Force. Pleased to meet you, sir."

Ellis was talking rubbish, but he was pretty sure the fisherman would not further question his made-up story.

"Ah, I see why you need the information now. And I might just be able tae help yer investigation." The fisherman pointed to the wooden lip of the hull just along from where he sat. "Sit yerself doon." He waited for Ellis to perch himself on the edge of the boat before continuing with his account. "It must have been aboot eight thirty for I had just sat down tae mend ma fishin net when a heard the machine comin fae over there. It passed right over the top o where we are noo, headin out tae sea. It was goin like the wind. It was just about out o sight when a heard it make a clankin noise. I tried tae look oot, but ma eyes are no whit they used tae be. That was the last I heard of it until the news came that it was missin. I told the local bobby, but he said I was probably still pished. Cheeky young whippersnapper."

Ellis had understood the majority of the conversation, but he was not used to the local Scots tongue and quizzed the chubby little man on a couple of points, just to be clear. "Sorry to ask, but what is a 'bobby'? And 'pished'? When you heard the noise, did you not take the boat out to have a look?"

The chubby fisherman started to chuckle at the American's pronunciations of the Scots words. "Sorry, son. A 'bobby' is a policeman, and 'pished' means drunk as a skunk, or alcoholically inebriated, tae be politically correct. Tae answer your last question a could nae go out. Ma boat is broken, son. Am waitin for a new crankshaft, an a was the only stupid bugger here that morning."

Ellis was a skilled interrogator. He knew there might be some tiny morsel of information that he had not extracted from the fisherman, so he kept pushing. "So was anyone out fishing in the area where the chopper was headed?"

The chubby little fisherman was quiet for a second before replying. "I never saw anyone oot there."

Ellis watched as the fisherman's eyes darted about, looking everywhere but at him. "Are you sure about that? Because there is a reward for any information that will help us."

Just as they spoke, old Alan chugged into the harbour, heading for his usual berth. The chubby fisherman caught him out of the corner of his eye then turned away, looking at Ellis. "Listen. Ye did nae hear this fae me, but old Alan over there was in the pub, fairly pished. He let it slip he saw the machine come doon next tae his nets. The old bugger knew he had said too much and clammed up when folk started tae ask him about it, said he was jokin."

Bruce Ellis thanked the chubby little man and pushed a handful of twenty-pound notes into his podgy little hand. His first impression of the little man had been correct; he was on the road to discovering the truth.

He had old Alan summed up before they had exchanged their first words. This old man had that look of steel in his eyes. He would be a much harder nut to crack than his fellow fisherman who had just informed on him.

"Hello there. I was just talking to a friend of yours who says that you might have seen what happened to the army helicopter."

The old man recoiled as though he had been struck by a black mamba. Ellis noted this with interest. The only thing that made him different from anyone else around here was his American accent. Could it be the old man somehow knew that the British chopper had been attacked by the Americans?

Old Alan regained his colour and his composure quickly. "Sorry, son, you sneaked up on me. My mind was far away. What was that ye said about a helicopter?"

Ellis knew before he went any further that the old man would tell him nothing willingly, so he changed tactics. If he couldn't get any information out of him, maybe he could trick him.

"It's OK, Alan, isn't it? We know you got to the chopper. We just need to know if you got the pilot out and where you dropped him off." Old Alan's face was pale and cast in stone. Ellis continued with his fairy tale, adding more detail to try and confuse the old man. "Sorry, Alan, but the joint task force needs your help. You see, the satellite that caught you attending the chopper went out of range before we could find where you had dropped the pilot."

Ellis produced a folded up map from his jacket pocket and handed it to the old man. For a few second the old man looked down at the map, Ellis held his breath. In his jacket pocket, his fingers were firmly crossed.

Old Alan folded the map back up and pushed it forcibly into Ellis's jacket pocket. The two men were only inches apart. Alan's steely eyes stared into Ellis's. "You must be mistaken, sir. I have no idea where yer missin helicopter is or the people on it. Now if you don't want tae buy ma fish, be off with you."

Ellis knew he had pushed his luck far enough and backed off without any further conversation. As he looked back, he saw the old man glancing across the water to the northwest. Then, as if conscious of being watched, he turned away and started marching round the harbour. The cold sea wind had eaten right into Ellis's bones, and he headed back to the restaurant for a well-deserved cup of coffee and a regroup of his thoughts.

Bruce Ellis had just ordered when the commotion from the harbour started. He was just in time to see old Alan land a perfect punch on the little chubby fisherman's nose. He marched away, taking strides a man half his age would have been proud of, leaving the chubby little man on his knees, holding a bloody nose.

Bruce Ellis's attention was broken by the waitress who was busy pouring his coffee out. "Take no notice, sir. It's just two daft old men fighting about their catch, I bet." Ellis returned to the table. The coffee did wonders, and he started to go over in his head what he had found out that day.

He knew that the chopper had passed over Girvan at the right time, and that the old man had made contact with it. The fisherman's fear of the American accent, and the fact he had slipped up confirmed this. Old Alan had stated he didn't know what happened to the people in the helicopter, but how did he know there were multiple people in the helicopter? Ellis had only ever mentioned a pilot to him. And then there was his glance northwest after he had thought Ellis had left. Ellis spread the map out and followed the old man's line of sight. He studied the island to the northwest. Could his target be on the island of Arran?

Southern listened to Bruce Ellis as he reported in. He said little, agreeing Ellis should continue with his investigations once he reached Arran.

Southern called Sergeant Al Franklyn to report to his makeshift canteen office. When Franklyn appeared, there was an uneasy silence. Benesch had left that morning with four of his best men but had not requested Franklyn's company. He was not happy that he had been upstaged by the Israeli bitch, and he wanted Southern to know it.

"Franklyn, I want you to take your most trusted soldier and interrogate a witness for me. Ellis found him in the town of Girvan on the Scottish coast but was unable to get him to talk. I am sure you can persuade the old man to help us in our investigations. Here are his details. It would appear that Ellis doesn't have the balls to get the job done. So one man's failure is another's opportunity to prove himself. A navy helicopter from the fleet will be here in ten minutes to pick you up and drop you at Prestwick Airport. Get into your civilian clothes, and get me a result, quickly please."

Franklyn saluted and headed for the canteen door. "Sergeant, remember he is an old man and only a witness. Be careful."

❖ ❖ ❖

Sam had woken early, and after a few minutes of nausea, her stomach had settled down. A sudden notion to go for a run grabbed her, and she swiftly scribbled a note for Karen Lowe, leaving it on the kitchen worktop on her way to grab the lift to the garage area.

Outside, Sam found it was a chilly but calm morning. Sam paced herself, not pushing too hard. She had no idea if pregnant women should be out jogging. She had an idea what Karen Lowe would say about it, but at that moment in time, she couldn't give a damn. Sam planned her day as she ran. First, she would take a gentle jog down to the Invermorroch Hotel in Arisaig to pick up any mail that had been left for them. Then a gentle jog back the four miles to the glass house to shower, eat, and swap her Beetle for Adam's Freelander. She loved her Herbie dearly, but in her present state, maybe the superior ride of the big 4x4 would help her travel sickness.

She was sure if they got a move on, they could catch the evening boat for Arran. She smiled as she worked out that she would be in Adam's strong arms by nine. As soon as the warm feeling arrived, it passed. Was he alive? And she had still to tell Adam about her little secret. A feeling of dread enveloped her and threatened to strangle her. The tears came in floods and soaked the front of her jacket. She had to stop just before the Invermorroch and pull herself together. She swore at herself for being such a soft-hearted reject.

Margo Kidd had just finished cleaning the front windows of the Invermorroch when Sam appeared by her side. "Missed a bit." Margo turned to see who had commented on her handiwork to find Sam standing, smiling at her.

"Ann, my goodness, where have you been hiding? Paul reckoned you had emigrated, it has been so long since we last had a visit. Come in, lass, come in."

Margo poured Sam a fresh orange, then joined her on the barstools, brandishing a large glass of wine. "Well, don't keep it to yourself. What have you been up to?"

Sam explained to Margo that they had been on a trip to Oslo, combining a winter holiday with an article on explorers. Sam explained that she had visited the Amundsen Museum while Alan had spent time poking about Oslo. Sam could tell from Margo's expression she had no clue who Amundsen was. Sam was fairly sure her cover story had worked, and Margo had swallowed it hook, line, and sinker.

What Margo said next almost made Sam fall off her barstool. "I explained to your Asian friend that you had been away for some time, and I didn't know when you would be home."

Sam tried to maintain a calm outward composure, but inside she thought her head was about to explode. Who was this Asian gentleman? Could it be one of Neil's men? Sam doubted that. It was true MI5 and MI6 were actively recruiting from the Asian community, but it was unlikely. Out in the sticks here, there were few Asian people. It was far more likely that an Asian MI5 or MI6 recruit would be deployed in large Asian communities rather than up here. Sam listened as Margo described a rather handsome, distinguished, middle-aged gentleman with an impeccable command of the English language. Sam was shocked to find that he had appeared this morning and had breakfast with Margo and Paul, leaving only twenty minutes before Sam had arrived. Sam said her good-byes, promising to call back and arrange a night out. Sam jogged away nonchalantly until the hotel was out of sight. Then she broke into a sprint. She had to get back and warn Karen before it was too late.

CHAPTER 12

KHANJAR

Karen had awoken to find a note in the kitchen saying that Sam had gone for a run. Although Karen was concerned, she was not surprised. In the short time that she had known Sam, she already knew Sam was her own person, and no one could change her mind once she had it made up.

Karen wandered out onto the balcony with a cup of tea, only to be driven back indoors by a sea wind that whipped around her loose T-shirt and jogging bottoms. Karen studied the view from the living area. As she watched, the fast-moving clouds changed position sending the low sunlight dancing in different directions over the sullen sea changing the mood in an instant from sunny to overcast. As Karen watched, there was the ring of the doorbell. Sam had warned her not to answer the door, and she stood still listening to the wind whipping at the big picture windows. There it was again; whoever was ringing the bell was persistent. Suddenly Karen felt a pang of anxiety course through her body. What if Sam had fallen or been knocked down, what if she had miscarried! Karen charged down the spiral staircase. There was a young innocent looking Asian lad standing on the other side of the privacy glass door trying to look in.

Karen opened the door to the youth. He stood with his hands behind his back smiling sweetly at Karen. "We have been looking for you everywhere. Nice to meet you at last!" Before Karen could move, the smiling youth sprang forward, placing a pistol against Karen's forehead. The smile had vanished and was replaced by a look of pure hatred. "Get on your knees where you belong, secret-service bitch."

Karen had started to comply when she was forced onto her knees by the youth who produced a large cable tie. Karen thought her arms were going to be dislocated as they were forced back and tied behind her back. Her peripheral vision picked up movement as a second man appeared by her side. His dark piercing eyes studied their new captive. "Where is the gun, bitch? No bullshit, or you will suffer pain you can only dream of in your worst nightmares."

Karen was terrified but she had to stay strong, somehow she had to warn Sam before she walked into a trap. "Listen, the gun is next to the toaster upstairs in the kitchen. I have played ball, so when my friend arrives shortly let her go, or better still, don't answer when she calls. You don't need her. You have me, and she has nothing to do with the secret service. It will only complicate things if you take her hostage."

Smiler grabbed her arm and flung Karen forward. She could not put her hands out to save herself and went headfirst into the tiled floor of the garage. It almost knocked Karen out, and she struggled to remain conscious. Smiler was by her ear, screaming at her. "You deluded, stuck-up cow. We will decide what happens here, not you. Shut the fuck up, and I might just let you die quickly once you have answered our questions." Smiler raised his clenched fist high above his head.

Karen saw it coming and tried to curl up in a ball. The blow never came, and Karen opened her eyes to find a third man had entered the room. The latest arrival was huge, a middle-aged giant, his jet-black (but shading to grey) hair swept back at the temples. He had grabbed Smiler's arm in midpunch and was glaring at him. He did not have to say anything. Smiler knew his place and retreated to the corner of the room to wait further instructions from the new arrival, who was obviously in charge.

Like his comrade, he studied Karen with dark inquisitive eyes, saying nothing for a few seconds. "Tell me, girl. Where does the door at the far side of the garage lead to?"

Karen knew better than to cross the giant. She was sure one flick of his huge wrists would snap her neck like a twig. "It leads to the gym. The other door is the office." Karen neglected to tell him about the third door, which led to the shooting range. Hopefully, Sam could get in there and pick up a weapon.

The giant picked Karen up by the tethered arms and marched her across the garage to the gym. He opened the door, then launched Karen across the room. Karen landed on her face once more and tried to get to her knees. The kick caught Karen in the stomach and spun her over like a leaf in the wind. She was badly winded and struggling for breath as the giant dropped his face next to hers. "Did anyone give you permission to move? No, I think not. You are lucky you are still breathing, whore. Enjoy your last few breaths before Khanjar sends you to meet your god."

Karen watched as the giant attempted to call someone on his mobile phone. As she watched, he flew into a rage. Whomever he was calling was not available.

Phal had tried to call his master, but the poor signal had stopped the call. Phal warned his two young accomplices about the dangers of underestimating the MI6 woman and departed, looking for a signal so he could reach his mentor.

Karen had managed to prop herself up against the far wall of the gym while she recovered from her beating. She watched as Smiler approached her and stood looking down on her. "You do not look like a government agent, bitch. You look like a schoolteacher. Tell me what you do for the British secret service."

Karen made eye contact with Smiler before replying. "I am an assassin, and I get rid of vermin that threaten our country, If I look like a schoolteacher, all the better for my cover."

Karen was not finished. She knew the next comment would get her beaten, but she had to keep the spotlight off Sam. "In fact, now I come to think of it, both of you would fit into the vermin category."

Karen watched as the rage returned to Smiler's face. His friend joined him. Karen knew this was going to hurt. Smiler made a move forward but was stopped in his tracks by a voice from the gym door.

"Gentlemen, you are making a big mistake. I think you are looking for me. Karen is a scientist who is helping me with my inquiries. She was trying to take the heat for me. I am a computer analyst with the security services." Sam walked into the room and offered the two young men her hands. "I am sure the government will pay you a huge ransom to get me back."

Smiler grabbed Sam's hands, forcing them back behind her back and securing them with a zip tie. He noted that she was a different animal from the first woman he had tied up. Her arms were taut and conditioned. She was no computer geek, but he was not sure what to do. He would wait for his uncle to make the decisions. Phal would know what to do.

Karen waited until the two young men had walked to the door before whispering to Sam. "What the hell are you doing? Why did you give yourself up like that? You could have raised the alarm."

Sam never took her eyes off their captors while she spoke to Karen. "I needed to know what the situation was before I decided what to do. And by the looks of things, your mouth was about to get you into big trouble. Have you seen any more, or is this it?"

Karen leaned closer so that the two men could not pick up her voice. "There is at least one more. He is older, a giant of a man, and they mentioned Khanjar. He may be here as well."

Sam raised an eyebrow at the last comment. "Good. I have been dying to meet Khanjar and his Al Qaeda friends. Do as I tell you, and do not make eye contact with the two young bucks."

As Sam talked, Karen was watching Sam work her hands back and forward in slow deliberate movements. Bit by bit, the tie strap moved down Sam's hands until it fell off.

Sam never flinched, keeping her eyes on her two captors at all times. "Don't worry, Karen. They are amateurs. See how they cross each other's line of sight? Look how they handle their weapons. Very soon they will make a big mistake, and I will be there to take advantage of it."

Sam did not have to wait long before her chance arrived. Sam heard the beat of the helicopter blades first and for a second her heart missed a beat. Their two guards heard the noise and Smiler left to go to the garage windows to find out what the situation was. Sam hissed at Karen to get down on her belly and leapt forward, covering half of the gymnasium floor space before her remaining guard spotted her. Sam knew she could not hesitate. Every fraction of a second was vital to her attack. Sam watched as her target started to raise his handgun, but Sam knew he was too late. Her flying sidekick hit with full force on the side of the jaw. Sam landed just behind him as he started to fall. He had fired, but it was too little, too late, and his shot smashed into the wooden gym floor two feet from Karen's left ankle. Unconscious, he landed on his gun, which discharged into his abdomen. Sam, for the moment, was oblivious to this. Her next target had just entered the gym at a run. For a fraction of a second, he was thrown by the fact Sam was not where he had left her. That gave Sam the time to cover the short distance to him. Sam grabbed the handgun he was carrying with her left hand, forcing it upward and outward, using her momentum to even up the natural muscle imbalance between man and woman, driving him backward, off his balance. Smiler was wiry and strong, but Sam made sure she maintained her advantage. She used her right hand to drive her thumb into the corner of Smiler's eye in a gouging motion. Smiler screamed as his optic nerve was torn from the mutilated eyeball. He staggered backward, away from the madwoman. Sam's kick came from close quarters and hit Smiler under the chin, breaking his jaw in two places and snapping his spinal cord at the base of his skull. His body went into convulsions as Sam grabbed for his discarded handgun. Karen screamed a warning to Sam as the light in the doorway was blocked by the arrival of Phal.

Just as Sam's fingertips touched the handgrip of the gun, it was kicked from her grasp by the foot of a hard-charging Phal. Sam knew in a millisecond she was in grave danger and rolled sideways, away from the feet of Phal. The giant tried to check his charge, but his bulk carried him past Sam before he could attempt a second strike. Phal turned like a whirlwind, pulling a curved dagger from the waistband of his trousers.

Sam knew from his lightening reactions she was in trouble. She was busy looking for something to defend herself with when Phal stopped dead in his tracks.

Although the Sig Sauer was silenced, in the closed area of the gym, the bark of the powerful handgun was still loud, and Sam's attention was drawn immediately to the menacing figure of Areli Benesch standing in the doorway of the gym, holding the weapon with both arms raised. Sam glanced back across the gym just in time to see the giant frame of Phal fall backward, like a felled giant redwood tree. Benesch stepped into the room, followed by three soldiers in full American battle dress.

Karen watched in horror as Areli stepped over the doomed body of Phal and, as cool as a cucumber, shot him in the forehead at point blank range. Karen was so close to this horrific scene that the spent shell casing from Benesch's gun hit her on the forearm.

Benesch gave Karen the once-over, then headed across the room to Sam. "We meet again, Samantha. Are you going to tell me where my young scientist friend is? Or will my new friends have to drag it out of you?"

Sam smiled sweetly at Benesch. "Come on, Areli. You know better than that. I tell you, and you will probably put a bullet in me."

Benesch returned the smile, but it was anything but sweet. "My dear British agent, your friends tortured me almost to death. Either way, I have sworn an oath that I will put a bullet in you, your boyfriend, and Neil Andrews also, before I leave this country." Areli pointed toward the body of Phal. "What were your friends after?"

Sam shrugged her shoulders. "Al Qaeda, who knows? Probably to kidnap and torture for the publicity."

Areli was pleased with this answer. She had captured her sworn enemy and destroyed an Al Qaeda cell into the bargain. Her new American friends would be happy with her day's handiwork.

She turned to her three Delta soldiers who had accompanied her into the house. "Signal the helicopter to return, and then bring the two women to the front of the house for extraction."

Sam used this time when Areli was talking to her soldiers to walk over to Karen. Sam had noticed that during the struggle one of the gunmen's stray bullets had hit the wall mirror behind Karen, leaving shards of razor-sharp mirror strewn all over the gym floor behind Karen's position. Sam sat next to Karen then leaned back, picking up a long sliver of mirror. Sam gave Karen a reassuring hug while cutting through the zip tie that held Karen's hands behind her back. Sam whispered in Karen's ear. "Do nothing stupid. Walk in front of me, and keep your hands behind your back. I will let you know what to do."

As the group exited the glass house by the garage, the chopper could be heard making its approach to the cliff-top site. Benesch led the way. Areli had left one Delta guarding the entrance, and he ushered them out while checking the skies for the approaching chopper. A second Delta soldier led the two captured women out while the remaining two Delta operatives followed Sam and Karen.

Both Sam and Benesch caught the glimpse of movement at the same time and started to spin round as the others were still searching the skies for the helicopter. The noise of the arriving helicopter had drowned out the approach of the black Mercedes. Benesch threw herself to the ground. Back in her native Israel, drive-by shootings and bombings were commonplace. Benesch, like most Israeli security personnel, had grown a sixth sense. Sam's lightening reactions saved her as she threw herself at Dr Karen Lowe, rugby tackling her to the ground as the first volley of shots passed over their heads cutting to pieces anything that was unlucky enough to get in the way. Sam watched as the lead Delta soldier was hit in the back and thigh. He fell within inches of Areli Benesch, his body protecting Benesch from the murderous gunfire coming from the Mercedes. Sam made sure Karen was flat on her belly then started weighing up the situation. The Mercedes had two gunmen with Kalashnikov automatic rifles. Sam only had a shard of broken mirror glass concealed in her waistband; she needed a weapon and fast. One Delta had ducked back into the garage and was returning fire from the house, while the other two had no option but to return fire from an exposed position. Almost instantly, one of the Delta troops who was caught in the open was hit in the neck and shoulder. Sam could tell before he even hit the dirt he would be dead. She crawled on her belly toward the dead soldier, keeping him between her and the Kalashnikov. Sam knew if she kept flat, she had a good chance of not getting hit. If not operated by a skilled marksman, the Kalashnikov had a bad habit of rising up when fired, so the safest place was with your face in the dirt. The Mercedes gunfire was now concentrated on the soldier in the garage, and Sam watched in horror as the bulletproof windows of the glass house took round after round of AK-47 punishment. Sam pulled the dead Delta commando over, unclipping his side arm and checking it, while still keeping one eye on the Mercedes.

The side panel of the glass house finally gave way with a crack, leaving the Delta troop in the open. He was cut down in a hail of bullets trying to get across the exposed garage floor.

Sam could see things were starting to happen in slow motion. Just as the chopper appeared overhead, Sam was aware of a person standing over her.

Areli Benesch had been watching the proceedings closely, and her training was telling her to take out the biggest threat. Areli processed the biggest risk. To her, Samantha O'Conner was a bigger risk than two gunmen. She knew Sam would not hesitate to kill her, and she had just watched Sam arm herself. She was the most lethal opponent Areli had ever encountered. She had to die.

Areli took aim just as her last Delta soldier was gunned down.

Sam reacted a fraction too late, and in her heart, she knew it. Benesch had out-thought and out-manoeuvred her. For a split second, their eyes met.

Suddenly Areli was falling to her knees. For a second, Sam was at a loss to understand what had happened. Areli continued to fall in slow motion, blood spraying from her left ear.

Sam realised she had been shot, and she traced the possible route of the bullet to find Karen Lowe on her knees next to the last Delta soldier to die, still holding his Glock at arm's length and staring wide-eyed at what she had just done.

Sam's senses returned first. Luckily for them, the Mercedes gunmen had transferred their attention and gunfire to the now hovering helicopter.

As Sam watched, one of the aircrew was hit and fell from the chopper, landing a few feet from Karen Lowe. Sam knew the minute the helicopter did a runner, she would have the full attention of the gunmen again. She used the dead body of a soldier to steady her aim and emptied the full magazine into the Mercedes. The passenger window exploded, and the Kalashnikov in the front of the Mercedes fell silent. Suddenly, the mayhem around Sam and Karen was gone. The chopper banked away steeply over the sea and headed southwest while the second machine gun fell silent. Sam was about to reload and head for the Merc when Karen moaned and fell over.

Sam changed direction and dived over the dead American soldier to where Karen now lay.

Karen had been hit by a bullet intended for Sam. It had taken a deflection off the dead soldier's body armour, fragmented, and buried itself high in Karen's left leg. "Sam, oh shit, I'm so cold. Am I finished? God, I think I am dying."

Sam ripped Karen's blood-soaked tracksuit bottom open and checked out her damaged leg. It was a mess, but if Sam could stop the bleeding—and as long as Karen's artery was intact and the shock didn't kill her—Karen would make it. Sam ripped the boot off the closest dead soldier and unthreaded the lace. Sam worked fast, threading the lace round and round Karen's thigh.

"Karen, speak to me. Keep talking, girl. Talk about anything. Keep the mind working. Come on. You will be fine, just work with me. Come on, Karen. Speak to me." Karen was on the edge of consciousness. Sam put her leg against Karen's and pulled hard cutting off the circulation to the damaged leg. Karen sat up bolt upright and let out a howl any self-respecting wolf would have been proud of. Before Karen could collapse back into unconsciousness, Sam pulled her to her feet, screaming at her to keep her awake. "Stand up, you stupid bitch. You're not dying on me. Come on! Open your fucking eyes." She struggled to keep Karen on her feet. Sam was sobbing openly, but the fire in her belly would not let her give up on the girl. "Come on, Karen. Do it for me. Please, Karen, stay with me."

To add to Sam's frustration as she fought to keep Karen with her, a body was ejected from the big black Mercedes, and the car sped off as Sam watched helplessly.

❖ ❖ ❖

Khanjar threw the big Mercedes through the twisty costal bends south of Arisaig. He had to get clear of the area before his enemies regrouped and sent troops against him. He had made a big mistake when he decided to investigate the signal on the west coast. He was not sure what he had stumbled onto.

It must have been some type of safe house. He had not expected such stiff opposition and, as a consequence, had paid a heavy price. Three of his best men had perished, and he had lost Phal, his right-hand man. Khanjar cursed in his native Arabic. These devils would pay for capturing his son and for killing his friend and colleagues. He dialled the number of his home, and within seconds, the phone was picked up. "Get Faaris on the phone now."

There was a short pause, and Khanjar used the time to thread his way through the midmorning traffic of Fort William on his way south. Faaris eventually materialised on the other end of the hands-free phone system. "Tell me, my young friend. Are you sure that you can do all you say you can to the infidels' communications and still remain in hiding, without giving our position away?"

There was a small silence before Faaris replied. "Lord, you must remember I worked for the American fools. It was I who put the very searches in place they will use to find us. Have no fear, lord. They will not defeat my systems. I have access to every search system in the American arsenal."

Khanjar smashed his fist into the steering wheel. "Then it is time for you to wage war on our enemies. You have my permission to do everything in your power to attack them. Good luck, my friend. I will be with you as soon as possible."

❖ ❖ ❖

Sam's head was in turmoil. She knew her chances of keeping her beloved glass house a secret were nil. No matter how she played the scenarios in her head, none of them worked out with the glass house still secret. All she could do now was to play the damage-limitation game.

Karen was chalk white and shaking like a leaf, but she had recovered slightly. Sam fed her painkillers and rechecked her tourniquet. It seemed to be doing the job. "Karen, I need to know if you can hold out for a little while. It is important that I do a few things before we get you to hospital. Do you think you can sit for a bit while I get them sorted?"

Karen's bloodshot eyes met Sam's, and Sam could see the determination in her eyes. She said nothing but nodded, knowing Sam would never have asked this of her unless it was of vital importance.

Two minutes later, Sam was dashing about like a madwoman. Karen watched her charge into the office with a large suitcase and a second holdall. She emerged five minutes later dragging the case behind her. Sam had her fingers and her toes crossed as she pulled the dust cover off the car that sat parked in the corner at the back of the garage. Particles of glass and plasterboard sprayed onto the tiled floor as Adam's pride and joy was revealed to Karen. It sparkled in all its glory in the middle of what had become a miniature war zone. Sam pulled the driver's door open. She did not want to leave the car here, but she would have no option if the battery were flat. On the first attempt, the big V8 turned but refused to fire. This heartened Sam. At least the battery was OK. Her second attempt scored a bull's-eye, and the big green Aston Martin V8 Vantage roared into life. There was no time to waste. She loaded the case and holdall into the boot and reversed the big sports car through where the garage doors used to stand. Clear of the garage, she stopped and ran back to where Karen was propped up against the wall. "Karen, I will be back in ten minutes. Are you still OK?"

Karen looked up at Sam and tried to give her a reassuring smile. She waved the Glock she had shot Benesch with. "Go. I will be fine. I have my insurance policy with me, go."

Sam racked her brain as she sped down the drive and onto the coast road. She needed to have her act together before she reached Arisaig and the Invermorroch Hotel.

She didn't have time to think. When she arrived, Paul Kidd, the owner, was painting a window frame and waved as Sam pulled up in the big Aston. "Travelling in style today I see, Ann. Margo's inside."

Sam paused by Paul's side. "Well, Paul, it was actually the owner of this fine establishment I was looking for."

Paul put the brush down and turned, giving Sam his full attention. "Fire away, Ann. I am all ears."

Sam patted the bonnet of the big green Aston Martin. "I was wondering if you could put this old girl in one of your lockups for safekeeping for a while. We are having some alterations done, and Alan would kill me if I got as much as a speck of dirt on his baby. I would happily pay the rent for a while. Do you think you can help me out, Paul darling?"

Sam gave Paul a seductive smile, pulling on all her feminine charms to win him over. Before Paul could answer, Margo appeared in the doorway. "Absolutely no problem, Ann. Isn't that right, Paul?"

"Oh, I think we can manage that for you. Looks like Margo has already made up my mind for me, as usual."

Sam and Margo watched as Paul reversed the Aston Martin into the first lockup at the back of the hotel. "I am glad you popped in, Ann. I was worried. Did you hear that racket this morning? Sounded like guns and helicopters everywhere. I thought it was coming from your direction, but Paul reckoned it was further away on Skye. You must have heard it?"

Sam turned to face Margo. "I was just going to tell you about that. The army decided it would be a good thing to practice beach landings in the bay just below us. What a bloody racket they were making. I think at least one of the helicopters was American. Bloody inconsiderate. What if I wanted a lie-in? They might have warned us they were playing soldiers."

Margo nodded in agreement. "Yeah, Phil the postie says he saw a big American helicopter pass over him on the Morar road. Must have been the same lot that were on the beach. So what alterations are you getting done at the big house?"

Sam made a show of checking her watch. "Bloody hell, is that the time? Sorry Margo, must dash. The joiner is due, and you know what they are like to get your hands on. Here, I will pop back soon. Bye for now." Sam handed Margo an envelope with enough money to pay for the car storage for a year and set off at a jog before Paul or Margo could object to the large payment.

On the outskirts of the village, Sam stopped and entered a beautifully maintained old-style phone box complete with phone book. Sam had come prepared and fed the phone before dialling the London number. The phone at Vauxhall Cross was answered immediately. Sam said only two words—words which all her life she had dreaded having to say. "Red Vixen. I say again, Red Vixen."

There was a pause as the person on the other end of the line checked the code. "Understood, Agent O'Conner. Putting you through now."

There was a click as the call was escalated up the chain of command. "Hello Samantha, this is Jean, Neil Andrews's PA. The director is in a Cobra meeting with the PM. How can I help?"

Sam cursed under her breath but regrouped. "Jean, take some notes. Then get hold of Neil. Here we go. I am making my way to Fort William. I can't remember the name of the hospital, but I will be there in an hour with a gunshot victim. I need medics ready to go. Dr Karen Lowe has been shot but is for the moment stable. I need a cleanup squad to a big house on the coast three miles northwest of Arisaig, multiple bodies, four Al Qaeda, five US military, also Areli Benesch."

There was a stunned silence on the end of the line. "Wait, Sam, I will try and get the director."

Sam slammed down the phone and set off at a sprint for the glass house. She had no time to waste on political etiquette. Karen needed her help now.

Sam was relieved to find Karen conscious, if somewhat pale. A quick recce of the glass house garage revealed one thing—Sam's Herbie was going no place. The back window and wing had been hit by machine-gun fire. To Sam's relief, Adam's Freelander was intact. Sam acted as a mobile crutch for Karen, and between them, they managed to deposit Karen in the passenger seat. Sam grabbed a few bits and bobs and loaded the Freelander up. Her last action before leaving was to inspect the bodies; her last port of call was Areli Benesch. For a second, Sam looked into the still, staring eyes of the Israeli assassin. She had been a formidable opponent. Sam frisked her lifeless body, making sure she had no chemicals on her person. Sam's last action was to close the eyes of the assassin for the last time before heading south to Fort William.

❖ ❖ ❖

Neil Andrews's blood pressure went through the roof when he found that Samantha had not waited on him. Jean read out the notes that Sam had given her. Neil needed to know what the hell had happened in Scotland. He was in imminent danger of following his predecessor out of the door at Vauxhall Cross, and he needed some answers now.

Neil paced up and down, planning his next move while Jean stood in attendance, waiting for the inevitable orders that would follow this period of reflection. "Right, Jean, get Kent and Alder along with a cleanup team to the house Sam talked about. Send the chemical team up as well, better safe than sorry. Get the commanding officer at Hereford on the blower, but first get me the US ambassador. It's about time we cut the bullshit. If it gets me sacked, so be it."

It only took Jean a few minutes to locate the US ambassador and patch him through to Neil's office. "Good afternoon, Mr Ambassador. Sorry to bother you, but I need some answers, and you either need to tell me or get someone on the phone who can, even if it means getting your commander in chief out of his bed early."

There was silence for a second. The US ambassador knew that he was talking to the MI6 director, but he was not used to such abrupt manners. "Fire away, director. I will help if I can."

Andrews sat down on the edge of his desk. There was no easy way to say this, but he was going to say it anyway. "We have confirmed at the time our Lynx helicopter went missing, it was being fired on by a US navy helicopter. We have the spent shell casings to prove it. Also one of my agents has just reported to me that a US covert raiding party has been attacked in the north of Scotland with heavy loss of life. My question is, sir, what in god's name do you think you are doing? The time is two thirty seven. You have until five to come up with an explanation for your actions." Andrews slammed the phone down before the ambassador had a chance to reply.

❖ ❖ ❖

At almost the exact same time, Faaris completed his final online checks, then activated his computer programme. Faaris had worked with the American air force in Iraq before becoming radicalised. He had been smart enough to carry on after Iraq, building up a vast knowledge of American, British, and Saudi

Arabian military-communications systems and computer weapons. When it had been decided he should leave the American forces, Khanjar had arranged for his fake kidnapping and ransom before a body double was beheaded on TV. Faaris had spent his time since then hidden away in his basement lab in the Scottish wilderness.

Although Faaris could not have known this, his actions could not have come at a worse time for the two nations' security forces. The American military was the more affected. It lost all military communications within a thousand-mile radius of the United Kingdom. Admiral Holister suspended all operations until the source of the problem was located. In stark contrast, Colonel Southern ordered that nothing would change and forces under his command would continue with the mission.

❖ ❖ ❖

Bruce Ellis, for the second time, parked his hire car by the harbour wall in the costal town of Girvan. He was having problems contacting Washington, so he decided to use the time to have another go at getting the crusty old fisherman to open up to him about his involvement with the British helicopter. Ellis walked over to the harbour wall and peered over the side to where the old man's boat had been anchored. He was just quick enough to duck back out of sight.

The old man was in residence, and he had company in the form of two nasty-looking visitors. Ellis walked along the harbour wall until he was directly above where the old fisherman's boat was moored. Ellis stayed well back from the edge while he listened to the goings-on below. It was clear from the raised voice that the old man was not happy, and the other thing Ellis learned was that the two men were Americans. Without warning, the boat's single-cylinder engine chugged into life, and the voices tailed away as the fishing boat made its way out to sea. Clear of the harbour, the fishing boat only travelled a few hundred metres before it was enveloped in the early morning sea mist. Ellis looked around for another boat that could follow the old man, but there were only a couple of boats left and not a soul in sight. Bruce Ellis contented himself by searching for the Americans' car. It didn't take much detective work. The van rental was the only vehicle in sight. He placed a transmitter under the rear bumper and headed for the coffee shop to try and get some heat back into his bones while he waited for his American friends to return.

Bruce Ellis waited in the café for two hours, but there was no sign of the old man or his boat. Just before lunchtime, Ellis clocked the American's rental van as it reversed away from the harbour. Ellis noted that it was occupied by only one male. Ellis drained his coffee cup and made a beeline for his own hire car. Using the tracker, Ellis followed out of sight until his tracker warned him the target vehicle had stopped by the seashore a few miles ahead. Bruce Ellis reduced his speed and approached with caution. He was in time to see the second male appear from the direction of the beach. The minute he was in the van, the driver sped off in the direction of Ayr.

Bruce Ellis was no fool and did not like what he was seeing. He pulled his rental car into a viewing area not far from the point where the second American had been picked up and headed back to that point to begin his study of the area. It didn't take him long to find what he was looking for. Ten feet from the pebble beach, the old man's boat lay partially submerged, rocking gently with the incoming tide. A quick search revealed little other than the fact that the old man was missing. Ellis tried once more to contact Washington but was out of luck. His next call was to the American embassy in London. He was informed that the secure comms link to the White House was down and that they were in the same boat as Ellis.

The only thing left for Ellis to do was to tail the two Americans until he found out what their agenda was.

❖ ❖ ❖

Another day had passed, and still there was no sign of Sam. There was not an hour that passed without one of my three companions asking me what we were going to do if Sam didn't appear at the cottage soon. In the short time we had spent together, we had bonded, and we had come to know each other a little better. Fiona had taken Gary under her wing, treating him like a kid brother. Out of earshot, Smithy and I talked over some scenarios we might find ourselves in if the Americans or Benesch came calling.

Behind my little cottage, the cliff path climbed along the edge of the hilltop forest before descending to a series of beach caves. The path then clawed its way back up the hill before descending through the forest and finally coming out in a forestry commission car park next to the main road. Smithy and I had run the route a couple of times to give Smithy a chance to map out the route for future reference. Fiona had volunteered to teach Gary a few cooking tips while rustling up our evening meal. After the meal, I wandered outside with a cup of coffee, drawn by the last glimmer of the sunset over the Mull of Kintyre peninsula. It was a cool evening with just the occasional wisp of wind. Spring was on its way, confirmed by the cackle of geese as they passed overhead, heading for the Scottish mainland. As darkness enveloped me, I wandered along my little beach, deep in thought. How long could I justify waiting for Sam before getting my friends off the island? I had expected Sam's arrival a couple of days ago. I was torn between the fact that I needed to find Sam, and equally that I need to get my team to a place of safety. I wandered over to the boathouse and deposited my empty cup by the door. I busied myself by checking the kit I had arranged for Smithy and myself. If nothing else, the army had taught me the good old saying well. "Fail to prepare, prepare to fail."

If the shit hit the fan, at least the kit I had assembled would give us a fighting chance. I had listened to the soft footsteps approaching from the rear, so I was not unduly startled when a voice from the darkness behind me started to speak.

"I have watched you check those rucksacks a dozen times in the last two days, Mac. Do you think a mouse might run off with your grenades?" Fiona Malden stepped out of the darkness to be by my side.

"Well, if it isn't the lovely Fiona. Where have you left the other two?"

Fiona Malden turned leaning back against the boathouse wall so we were face to face. "Oh, I left my slaves doing the dishes while I popped out to keep you company."

I bent down and rummaged in the rucksack. I found what I was looking for and stood up facing Fiona. "Good girl! I was hoping you were going to pop out and visit me. I have something for you."

Fiona's eyes widened, and a half smile formed on her lips. "Sounds interesting, Mac. You have my full attention. I hope you are not going to disappoint me again, Captain."

I could see the devilment in Fiona's eyes and decided on a bit of my own devilment. Without speaking, I took Fiona's right hand and lifted it to waist height. Fiona's big eyes were still staring into mine inquisitively as I placed the Glock in her hand.

Fiona looked down at the feel of the handgun and gave a low moan. "Mac, you sure know how to dash a girl's hopes. I bet Samantha would be happy with this, but I would have preferred roses or chocolates."

I stood behind Fiona and lifted her hands into a double-handed firing position, gently moving her fingers to the correct placement. "You need to feel the weapon. It's lighter than the Browning, so you will tend to overcompensate at first. There is no safety catch as such. The safety mechanism is on the trigger." I could feel Fiona relax, her body resting, her back and shoulders against my chest.

"Hmm, I am starting to change my mind, Mac. You make a good teacher. Keep this up, and I might change my mind about the roses and chocolates. What were you saying about feeling the weapon? No wonder Sam fell for you."

Fiona rested her head on my shoulder just as Smithy came to my rescue. "Dishes are finished. Anymore cups out here?"

Fiona Malden sighed and dropped the Glock to waist height as she turned. "Smithy, did anyone tell you your timing is terrible? Mac was just showing me how to handle a weapon."

Smithy burst out laughing as he picked up my mug from the boathouse door. "Fi, you're a big girl. I am sure you can work that out for yourself."

Gary Harding appeared by Smithy's side. "We have a party out here or what?"

Fiona Malden shook her head. "You guys are unbelievable. Can a girl not get a lesson without the whole team arriving?" Malden headed for the cottage door. "It's OK, Gary. Mac was just showing me his weapon!" The look on Gary's face made Smithy and me burst out laughing.

❖ ❖ ❖

Bruce Ellis followed the van to the car park in front of Prestwick Airport where he watched as the same navy pilot who had dropped him off made contact with the two thugs in the van. It didn't take a brain surgeon to work out who had sent the heavies to visit the old man. He had never liked Southern, but now he was going to make it his mission to bring him down. He had given Southern the old man on a plate, and Southern had taken it too far. Ellis felt that he had a hand in the old man's fate. He continued his surveillance of Southern's two heavies, who for some reason continued after speaking to the pilot.

Ellis followed them to the ferry terminal at Ardrossan, then joined the queue for the evening Arran ferry. Ellis's hunch about Arran being the place the old man had tried to keep secret had proved correct. It would appear that the old man had talked to the two heavies before he went missing.

❖ ❖ ❖

Sam had left Karen in good hands at the Belford Hospital. She could not bring herself to speak to Neil Andrews just yet; she needed to find out about Adam for herself. It had been Neil Andrews who had broken the news of her sister's assassination many years ago. Now that she was carrying Adam's child, not to mention that he was the only man she had ever truly loved, the news of his death would have been too much to bear in public. If it was true, and Adam was dead, she would lock herself away until she came to terms with it.

She had left a note for Andrews, and together with Karen's testimony, that would be enough to keep Andrews off her back for a while.

Sam checked her watch one more time. If she was quick, she could just about make the evening ferry to Arran. She fiddled with the radio controls, looking for a station that had a news spot. Sam was just in time to catch the hourly news bulletin on Radio 2. Sam wanted to hear if there was any news about the missing Lynx, but she was out of luck. The only local bit of news was that a Girvan fisherman's body had been found washed up on a west coast beach.

Bruce Ellis heard the same news as he waited in the queue for the evening ferry, and he was past fury. Southern and his thugs were going to pay for this. All he needed was for the bloody comms to start working so he could follow up on a few leads, then report to the president. The slippery bastard was not going to get away with it this time.

CHAPTER 13

CAPTURE

Colonel Southern had just received the news that Benesch and her team had been wiped out at the west coast signal origin. Southern put two and two together and got five. It had obviously been a British secret-service trap. Southern could sense his time on British soil was coming to an end. He had one last chance at grabbing the young scientist before the comms returned and he had to report the loss of life to his superiors. Southern searched through Areli Benesch's kit before he came across what he was looking for. Southern opened the container that housed the Diavokxin. Three of the ten cut-outs were vacant, but the other seven vials were intact.

Colonel David Southern was the master of turning a defeat into a victory. He would have one more attempt at grabbing the scientist now that he had their location. Then he would report to Washington that he had recovered the two chemicals and that he had transported the global killer to the chemical-warfare lab in Alaska for safekeeping. Also that during a gun battle, Benesch had fought to the death against US Special Forces. He reckoned if he was lucky, he could score brownie points and capture the scientist. The only snag was that for his story to work, he needed everyone other than the scientist eliminated so they could not challenge his version of events.

❖ ❖ ❖

For an hour, I tinkered around in the boat shed, checking over my new speedboat, which had never been used. I contemplated repeating history and ferrying us all across the water to the Kintyre peninsula, but I had no idea what to do once there. Although it would get us off Arran without trace, there was the problem of transport when we reached the far side. If Sam arrived, she would suss it out when she found our new boat missing. My thoughts turned to Sam. Had she heard about the missing Lynx? If so, she would be frantic. No, I needed to stay put for another day before deciding on an alternative course of action.

I had just finished checking over the state of charge of the boat batteries when I heard footsteps by the door. "Adam, are you coming in? Smithy has got the kettle on for a brew." Fiona had learned her lesson from the other morning and gave me good warning before ending up looking down the wrong end of a gun for the second time in a week.

"Come in, Fiona. It's OK. I won't try to shoot you this time."

Fiona Malden appeared wearing my heavy wax jacket I had purchased from a Brodick store to fend off the west-coast weather that afflicted Arran from time to time.

"Have we said something to offend you, Mac, that you are loitering out here in the cold?"

I finished replacing the waterproof battery covers on the speedboat before replying. "No, Fiona, I just needed a bit of space to think round a few problems. That's all."

Fiona Malden glanced over her shoulder as she walked toward me. "Mac, just a word of warning, and don't get too panicky. I am going to give you a kiss. Just go with it."

I was pinned between the boat and the bench at the end of the workshop. There was no escape. Fiona pressed her warm body hard against mine. Her lips were warm and inviting, but all I could think of was what Sam would do if she walked through the door at that moment. The kiss only lasted for a second. Then Fiona backed off.

"When exactly, Captain Macdonald, were you going to tell me that you saved my life? Smithy told me you ripped the door off the Lynx to get me out. The kiss was just my way of saying thanks. Pity you are hitched, Captain, otherwise I think I might have been a bit more generous than just a little kiss." Fiona ended the sentence with a very saucy wink.

"Fiona, you need to get yourself a man who can make an honest woman of you."

Fiona Malden chuckled to herself as she turned and walked to the door. "No, Adam, what I need is a new helicopter. I am getting withdrawal symptoms."

As Fiona reached the door, I watched as she stopped dead in the doorway. When she turned back to look at me her expression had changed dramatically, and her complexion had paled. I came alongside her just as I heard the noise of a helicopter in the distance. "What's wrong, Fiona? Why has the chopper got you spooked?"

Fiona was chalk white. "Mac, you need to trust me. I've got a really bad feeling about this. That is the noise of a US Navy Seahawk fitted with engine mufflers. American Special Forces use them. It may sound miles away, but trust me, that thing is getting close."

I exploded past Fiona, telling her to lift the two rucksacks placed at the door. Smithy was halfway across the living room, coffee in hand, when I burst in the door. I didn't need to say anything. Smithy put the cup down and screamed at Gary to get his shoes and jacket on.

I checked Fiona Malden out for shoes and clothing before handing her a Glock and asking her to go and help Gary to get ready. Smithy and I huddled together at the gable end of the cottage, out of sight from the sea where the helicopter seemed to be approaching from. "Smithy, we will go with plan A. You take Fiona and head back the farm road as a decoy. I will take the lad and head straight up through the forest until I come to the little loch. Then I will rejoin the trail and meet you on the road, all going well."

In the gloom of the half moon, I could make out Smithy's expression. "All going well! Adam, this is going to be a turkey shoot, and you know it!"

Smithy was right, but the officer in me came out. I could show no fear. If that happened, it would pass through the others, and what little chance we had would be snuffed out in an instant. "What's wrong, Mr Smith? Too much of a challenge for you? This is exactly why you joined the SAS. Time to man up, soldier."

Smithy hesitated for only a second. "OK, Mac. This looks like another one for your legendary military actions. I suppose I will go down in history with you. Promise me this, Mac. If I bite the dust tonight, bury me next to your mate Sergeant Ferris. I never met the guy, but it seems unfair that he is stuck up on that hillside all by himself."

Before I could answer, Gary and Fiona appeared by our side, both chalk white.

"Right, you two, listen up. Gary, you are coming with me. Fiona, you are going with Smithy." Fiona Malden was about to protest, but I had been waiting for this. "Fiona, before you say a word, you are a serving army officer, and I need you to help Smithy create a decoy so we can get Mr Harding here to safety. No ifs, no buts, just do it."

Fiona Malden looked crestfallen but nodded and stepped back behind Smithy. The wind brought the sound of the chopper to us again, and Smithy was off. "Remember my request, Mac."

I was about to reply but decided no matter what my reply was, it would not help the situation. I led Gary up the steep cliff-side path without stopping or looking back until we reached the highest point. We left the path and headed in through the trees of the hilltop forest. It was a split-second decision, but I needed to know what we were up against. I placed Gary three trees in, with his back to the trunk of a big spruce tree facing away from the shore and dared him to move a muscle until I came back for him. Hopefully the tree would shield him from night-vision technology.

❖ ❖ ❖

Lieutenant Commander Saul Bartowski watched from the cockpit of the Seahawk as the heat signatures of his targets split up, leaving the little cottage abandoned. His original plan was to circle round and land his men on the main road where the track to the little cottage met the road. He had been warned by Southern to treat his suspected targets with respect as they came with reputations second to none. Bartowski changed his plan and ordered the pilot to drop them on the beach in front of the cottage. Once on the beach, he ordered the chopper pilot to take off and circle until he set a flare off for the chopper to return. The comms were still down, much to Bartowski's frustration. He had wanted to contact his commanding officer in Coronda, California, to verify his latest orders.

He was very uneasy about carrying out covert operations in the United Kingdom. He did not feel that it was his place to order his men to open fire on allied forces without a very, very good reason. His mind clicked back into business-as-usual mode the minute his feet hit the pebbled beach.

❖ ❖ ❖

I watched as the dark sinister shape of the big American chopper hovered only inches above the beach. It only took seconds for its superbly trained and deadly package to deliver itself on my own little beach. It was hard to comprehend what my eyes were telling me. I watched as eight Navy SEALs and their commanding officer deployed right in front of my little cottage. I should have been legging it through the forest, but I needed to know how their leader was going to commence operations, and how many I would be up against. The leader did not make me wait long before the answer became clear. He deployed four of his men to track Smithy and Fiona.

He led the other four troops at a jog in our general direction. It was my worst nightmare. To be that sure of our positions, he must have night-vision technology. I reckoned he would be at my position in the next ten minutes. I had to do something to slow them down and give Gary and me a fighting chance of escape.

I rummaged around in my bag of tricks and produced a ball of twine. I tied the twine between the two trees I had sat between. It would be obvious that the grass had been trampled down here. I set the twine at ankle height then left to pick up Gary and get the hell out of here.

After only a few hundred metres, it was obvious to me that we were in big trouble. Gary may have been the next Albert Einstein, but an orienteering champion he was not. I needed to think of something and fast before our faceless friends arrived to say hello.

❖ ❖ ❖

Bartowski arrived on point and spotted the trampled area where someone had crouched in the long grass. Bartowski noted that from this position the beach below was in full view. Bartowski signalled for his men to follow him into the forest. His boot touched the twine, and Bartowski froze to the spot. The SEAL behind him spotted his sudden stop and followed the twine to its final position before giving the all clear. The fact that there was no booby trap did not make Bartowski feel any better. It might just have been twine, but it was a warning of what might lie ahead, and thermal imaging in this situation was more dangerous than helpful. Bartowski reluctantly gave the order to remove the imaging system and continue single file. The SEAL unit was forced to cover the forest terrain at walking pace, each man watching for the slightest movement ahead of them. Not a twig snapped as the team edged forward.

Suddenly the eerie silence was broken well and truly by the sound of gunfire below and to the right of their forest position. It was clear from the gunfire that the other SEAL unit was not getting all its own way. The sounds of M16's, handguns and MP5s echoed around the trees that surrounded the five-man team. Bartowski cursed to himself as he was forced to listen but could do nothing. He did not have his usual luxury of satellite imaging or even comms with his other men. He was fighting blind and deaf. He was pretty sure his targets had few weapons, but he could not be certain. Suddenly the trees opened out onto a small lake, or as the locals called it, a loch. Bartowski split his men and took two men around the left side of the water closest to the gunfire while he sent the other two around the right side. The two men on the right encountered heavy undergrowth and became unintentionally separated trying to claw their way through the mass of bushes and thorns.

❖ ❖ ❖

I watched as the to men worked their way through the dense undergrowth. I had picked this route for that very reason. I had climbed high into the tree that bordered the little loch. The climb had almost done me in, and it wasn't helped by the fact that my rucksack was weighing me down with its hurriedly sourced contents, trying to pull me back to terra firma. The first man passed underneath me, but I let him go. It was the tail-end Charlie I was interested in. On the branch in front of me sat the reason for my agonising climb, the boulder I had lugged up the tree in my backpack. I watched tail-end Charlie approach and judged his speed to coincide with the trajectory of my caveman-designed weapon.

The boulder fell with absolute silence and accuracy, hitting the soldier right on the top of his skull with a sickening crunch. Luckily for me, the wind from the sea helped the forest around me to drown out the noise. I could have done no more damage if I had hit him with a sledgehammer. His body and crushed skull fell forward into a dense bush. I held my breath, waiting for the rest of the SEALs to start investigating why their buddy was not speaking to them on comms.

To my astonishment, the fallen soldier's buddy, who was leading the way, turned to look for his comrade behind him but then continued clambering his way through the undergrowth. I let the first soldier continue before climbing down and checking my victim. I relieved him of his M16 and two spare magazines but was surprised to find no comms equipment on his body. This explained why his partner had continued. He had no idea he had lost his wingman.

❖ ❖ ❖

On the far side of the forest by the track, Smithy had decided to take advantage of an old ruined cottage in the next field. It could have been no more than a hundred and fifty metres away. Smithy put his mouth close to Fiona Malden's ear. "Fi, I want you to follow the hedgerow down to the shore. Then when you are level with the ruined cottage, cut over the field and wait for me in the ruin. Understood?"

Fiona nodded and was about to leave when Smithy stopped her. "When you cut over the field, stay low and move very slowly, but if you hear gunfire, run for it in a zigzag fashion. Got it?"

Again Fiona Malden nodded, then set off without waiting any longer. Smithy clicked of the safety catch on the MP5 and checked that it was on single shot before settling down in the shallow ditch by the side of the dirt track to see who would come his way.

He had watched the big chopper hover on the other side of the cottage but he had no idea how many men it had dropped. If Fiona could get to the ruin unnoticed he would be able to keep their attention away from Captain Malden giving her a chance to escape, he had lied to Fiona Malden he had no intention of heading to the ruin, his job if it happened was to draw the fire from the Americans. Smithy was no fool. He knew by doing this he had almost certainly signed his own death warrant.

The seconds ticked by as Smithy waited.

To him it seemed like hours not minutes. The mud of the ditch soaked through his clothing, making his forced frozen position an uncomfortable wait. Slowly, out of the gloom, Smithy picked up movement on the opposite side of the track. He counted as three bodies moved slowly and deliberately toward him on the far side of the road. Smithy decided to wait until the first soldier had passed, but as the first shadowy figure drew level, Smithy was forced into action. As if on cue, Fiona Malden made her run for the old ruin. Adrenalin had taken over from brains, and she sprinted in a straight line for cover. Smithy listened as the lead soldier gave the order to bring down the threat to their left. The second in the queue crouched, took aim, and was hit in the neck and head by bullets from Smithy's MP5 before he could squeeze the trigger. Smithy had milliseconds before the next soldier in line fired on him, and both weapons were discharged at the same time. Smithy caught a bullet in the arm and fell back into the ditch while the SEAL dropped his weapon and curled up in agony, hit in the stomach at close range by Smithy's MP5 round. Fiona Malden had made the cover of the old ruin but, to Smithy's dismay, opened fire on the track with the Glock Adam had given her. Smithy cursed as he worked his way along the ditch. With a handgun at that distance, it would be a miracle if Fiona hit anything. Fiona was setting herself up as a target. She had ruined his plan for her escape.

Smithy's eyes were out on stalks as he looked for the third SEAL, who had escaped his attempted ambush. He had to find him before he decided to get rid of the target in the ruin.

❖ ❖ ❖

I had placed Gary Harding in the hollow of a tree trunk before climbing my tree. Gary again had been dared within an inch of his life to move or make any noise until I returned for him. I made my way slowly and almost noiselessly to where I had left Gary. The shooting north of our position had now stopped. I dreaded finding out what the outcome had been from that little encounter. As I approached the hollowed-out oak tree, I could hear the American voice dead ahead. The Navy SEAL had found Gary and was ordering him to stand up. For a fleeting second, I thought about challenging the American soldier to surrender, but I knew in my heart he would never do this. He was younger, fitter, and battle ready. He would shoot me before I had time to react. I had no option. I needed the few milliseconds that a surprise attack would give me to make sure I still had the upper hand over my American friend. Just as I brought the confiscated M16 up on target, he spun round bringing his own weapon to bear on me, but the milliseconds saved me, and the M16 bullets hit him in the neck and chest, splitting his body armour, sending him crashing to the ground, mortally wounded in the neck.

Gary was up and ready to go so I cut left onto the forestry path and the opposite direction from the other three SEALs who were still trying to navigate their way round the far side of the small loch. I knew from previous exploration of the area, the three stranded SEALs would take a good fifteen minutes to make their way back to the forest trail. We had to make the most of this time and head for the road where we would hopefully meet up with Smithy and Fiona, then flag down the first car and get the hell out of the area.

❖ ❖ ❖

On the opposite side of the Atlantic, the president paced up and down in the situation room. The assembled military and security personnel were treading on eggshells. The president had not slept for the last twenty-four hours. His command and control structure was in tatters. His eyes and ears of the world could watch their potential enemies, but they could not communicate this, as the entire military comms infrastructure had collapsed. For all the president knew, North Korea could have invaded the south, and Russian ICBMs could be on their way to Washington. The monitoring systems would have picked this up. They just couldn't tell anyone. The president stopped opposite the head of the NSA cyber terrorism unit. "Bill, care to tell me how the hell the NSA could give its own computers a virus?"

Bill Masterson undid the top button of his shirt before replying. The temperature in the room seemed to have increased, and Masterson was sweating profusely. "Mr President, it would appear from initial investigations that the viruses were introduced to our systems years ago but were designed to only become active when we tried to hunt down this jamming signal that has appeared. The hunter programmes were designed by one of our top computer programmers, and we are struggling to understand how they operate. It may be some time before we can debug the systems."

Bill Masterson could not see the president, who was standing behind him, but he could feel the president's eyes burning into the back of his skull. "Debug the system, Bill. This is not some office PC, for god's sake, Bill. If our enemies find out what has happened, it could be disastrous. May I suggest you get the man who designed the programmes to start debugging them? We need the system back on line yesterday. Do I make myself clear, Bill?"

Bill Masterson's face was bright red, and his head looked as if it could explode at any moment. "Mr President, the situation is crystal clear, but the problem is Faaris Nejem, who designed these programmes, is dead, and the truth of the matter is that we are now not sure of his motives. He may have penetrated our inner circle to plant these viruses. We just don't know for sure."

The president was just about to reply when there was a knock on the situation room door, and the president's PA was let into the room by the big marine standing guard at the door. "Sorry to bother you, Mr President, but this letter just arrived by courier, and it is marked top secret and urgent." The president took the letter and opened it while the assembled room sat quietly awaiting the next round of interrogation by the president.

The president finished reading the note, then shook his head. He didn't know whether to laugh or cry. "OK, guys, listen up I need to speak to operations commander at Charlie One in Alaska, and I need to speak to Admiral Holister urgently. I don't suppose any of you guys has a spare pair of homing pigeons?"

❖ ❖ ❖

Smithy had spied his missing Navy SEAL working his way along the hedgerow between Adam's cottage and the field adjacent to the old ruin. He was going to outflank Fiona Malden and attack from the rear of the building. Smithy was wounded and needed to end this before his target was out of effective range of his MP5. Smithy leaned his wounded body against a fence post to steady his weapon and give him the best chance of a kill.

The sniper's bullet that killed Luke Smith was fired from the tree line some twenty feet above and three hundred metres away. It was a perfect headshot. The sniper had waited until Smithy silhouetted himself. As he used the fence post, his upper body had became fully visible. The one soldier Smithy knew nothing about and had taken no precautions against had killed him.

Fiona Malden knew instinctively that something terrible had just happened and clambered over the crumbling, collapsed wall of the derelict cottage to be met with a hail of bullets from the hedgerow. Malden fell backward into the ruin.

❖ ❖ ❖

Sam cursed her luck. Only twenty minutes from the cottage, she had heard the slapping noise as she reached the summit of the String road that threaded its way across the hilly centre of the Isle of Arran. Sam struggled with the large spare wheel as she watched a car slow down then pull away, leaving Sam to change her own puncture.

In the hire car, Bruce Ellis slowed down, admiring the rear view of the leggy blonde who was struggling with the spare.

Normally, Ellis would have stopped to lend a hand, but tonight, he had other things on his mind. He was not sure what he would find on Arran, or if his letter would ever reach the eyes of the president, but he had to try. He had to stop Southern's thugs before they committed any more atrocities. He cursed his luck. He needed communications, and he needed them now.

❖ ❖ ❖

Al Franklyn studied the map of Arran while directing his corporal to the car park closest to the little house that the old man had finally given up the location of. Franklyn was desperate to get to the house and steal the glory from the SEALs. He wanted to make sure his Delta team was credited with finding the missing chemicals, not the SEAL team who had not put in the legwork to find the missing chopper crew. Franklyn needed something to appease Colonel Southern; his last words were ringing in his ears—*Be careful! He is an old man.* How was he to know the old guy had a dodgy heart? If only he had held him under the water for a little less time.

The forestry commission car park loomed out of the darkness on the left and Franklyn instructed his driver to park the van. By the looks of the map, the cottage should be about a mile to the northwest.

❖ ❖ ❖

I was about to lead Gary Harding out into the car park when I heard the van approaching.

I wanted to jump out and get the driver to take us to Brodick, but my sixth sense kicked in, and I dragged Gary back into the bushes as the van pulled up and stopped. I watched as two nasty-looking characters pulled a holdall from the back, then proceeded to load magazines into two snub-nosed M16s before heading off down the opposite track in the general direction of my little cottage. I gave it a few seconds, then checked out the van in the forlorn hope the driver had left the keys behind.

Gary joined me by the side of the van as I searched for the keys. "Are you going to hotwire it, Mac?"

I smiled at the comment but started to remove my rucksack. "No, Gary. Modern vehicles are not that simple. Unless you have a key or a computer, they are bullet-proof. You go and wait for me by the road while I make sure our friends don't come after us in the van."

I had no time for a work of art, so it had to be crude but effective. I worked quickly, cable-tying my three grenades to the chassis below the passenger's and driver's seats, wedging them in so that the blast would be deflected upward. I then ran twine from the drive-shaft bolts to the grenade release pins. If the van moved, the rotation of the drive shafts would pull the pins on the grenades. I calculated the blast might not kill the driver and passenger, but for sure they would not be winning any dancing competitions after tonight. It was time to get the hell out of there before my remaining SEAL friends navigated the loch and made our lives very difficult.

We had only walked a few hundred metres when the car's headlamps blinded me as it pulled up by our side. "Sorry to bother you, sir, but we badly need a lift. I will pay you handsomely if you could drop us both off in Brodick."

The stranger seemed to be checking us out before giving us his verdict. I did not want to use it, but I held a Glock behind my back just in case the driver needed a little more forceful persuasion.

Before the driver could reply, a voice came from the darkness. "Put the handgun on the deck using your thumb and forefinger only, then take three steps back in front of the car headlamps, and get on your knees, hands on your head. That goes for you too, kid. And you, driver. Do not attempt to drive away. Your life may be in great danger if you do."

My night vision had been destroyed by the car headlamps. I could only make out vague shapes moving in the darkness. To attempt anything would have been madness. It could only be my Navy SEAL friends. I warned Gary about trying anything mad.

As I placed the gun on the ground, the driver spoke for the first time. I was shocked to find he was an American. "Buddy, if you want to stay alive, you better start talking to me. Are you part of the British chopper crew that went missing?"

I was puzzled but answered the question as I walked back and got down on my knees. "Yes, I am one of the four people your navy decided to shoot down, thank you very much!"

I was aware of a second body coming up close behind me, which confirmed my suspicions this had to be the second of the three SEALs who had been tracking us. Without warning, the car door opened, and the driver of the car stepped out onto the deserted island road. "Hold station, soldier. That's an order." For a second, there was total silence. It appeared that the SEALs were not expecting the intervention of the mysterious American driver.

"Identify yourself, sir." There was a huge amount of doubt in the SEAL's voice. This intervention had obviously not been planned and had thrown a spanner in the works.

"Special Agent Ellis, Central Intelligence Agency. I am ordering you to turn these men over to me for questioning."

I watched as the SEAL stepped forward to examine a piece of paper held out by the driver. "I am Lieutenant Commander Saul Bartowski, sir. Your letter means nothing to me. How do I know what the president's signature is like? You could have written that yourself. You have no jurisdiction here. This is a navy operation."

Ellis was having none of it. "Commander, you are in the same boat as me. Neither of us can contact our commands, but I am telling you now, sir, you have been duped. You have been sent on this mission by Colonel Southern, who has overstepped his command. Your mission is flawed and in great danger of causing an international incident."

I listened as the argument continued. I needed to play for time. My only hope was either the Americans fell out and shot each other, highly unlikely, or my young friend Smithy had untangled himself from his pursuers and was about to flank my American friends. Eventually they agreed to move the argument back to my little cottage where the chopper had been arranged for the pickup.

The SEAL commander spoke as he kept a watchful eye on the surrounding area. "Bumped into two Delta guys back in the woods. We will wait here, as they have transport to take the prisoners back to the beach. You can follow on behind." His remark was directed at the car driver, but I decided to throw my oar in the water for what it was worth.

"Commander Bartowski, I think you had better do what your CIA friend says. If you don't, and he is right, the only thing you will be in charge of is security at your local shopping mall. You had better drop that prisoner crap as well. I am a serving officer of her majesty's secret service."

Bartowski didn't like what I was saying and marched over to me until our noses almost touched. "Listen here, secret-service man; you killed two of my men in the woods. That makes it personal. When we get back, you'll pay for that!" We were still staring each other down nose to nose, like a pair of prize fighters when there was a muffled explosion behind us in the forest.

"Well, Lieutenant Commander, it sounds like I just got another two of your guys. I wonder what the Pentagon does with sloppy SEAL commanders these days."

My comments were too much for the SEAL team commander to bear. He went for my throat, but I was ready and smashed my forehead into his unprotected nose. The big soldier staggered backward, his nose badly damaged. I was praying Smithy was in the vicinity just waiting for the right moment, but before I could do anything, the butt of a rifle hit me hard in the back of the neck. The last thing I saw was the road coming up to meet me as I started to lose consciousness.

I came to propped up against the whitewashed wall of my cottage. At first, only a few of my senses worked correctly. I was aware of someone sitting next to me, but I was trying too hard not to lose consciousness again to pay attention. The person was having a conversation with someone close by, but the words were just tumbling around my head like a half-finished crossword.

Lieutenant Commander Bartowski had split what was left of his raiding party into two in an effort to speed up the recovery of his fallen comrades. He had been forced into having to leave the CIA agent to guard the two prisoners. The commander was approached by his master chief. "Sir we have recovered all our men and one enemy body, one of their bodies is unaccounted for. Permission to take the men and sweep the field to the north, sir."

Bartowski glared at him. "Negative, Master Chief. We are running out of time. Signal the chopper. Oh, and by the way, don't refer to them as the enemy. God knows what is going on here, but enemies is wrong, Send the signal."

He was not in a good place. He had lost men, and the CIA guy was getting to him. If the CIA guy was correct, he could be in a lot of trouble. He had been told if the downed helicopter crew was present, he must capture and return the young scientist to Machrihanish and eliminate any other targets. Bartowski had decided in the absence of proper communications, he would return the scientist and his bodyguard to the base and await confirmation from Washington before carrying out what in his mind was murder pure and simple.

The grey dawn of another day had started to lift the darkness around my cottage when my thoughts finally started to make some sense. My head was bursting, and I had to constantly fight the urge to throw up. My hands had been cable tied, and the CIA guy was standing guard over us. Gary sat next to me, as pale as a sheet and sobbing openly into his untied hands. The Americans obviously did not think he was any kind of threat. Looking at him, I tended to agree with them. On the far side of the path leading to the beach was a scene more fitting for Afghanistan than the Isle of Arran. A row of body bags lay ready for the arrival of the American helicopter.

I watched as one of the black-clad American soldiers made his way to the beach, to my surprise he fired a flare high above the coastline. It would appear that the Americans were in big trouble with their communication systems. It went some way to explaining the high body count. If they could not communicate, they could not work as an efficient fighting unit.

The big American navy chopper appeared within minutes and hovered millimetres from the ground as the gruesome task of loading the dead bodies commenced. I watched as the SEAL leader supervised before heading up from the beach to the little cottage flanked by one of his men.

Our only chance now lay with Smithy. If he escaped, he could contact Neil Andrews. Bartowski stopped and spoke to the CIA guy before heading in my direction.

"I want you both to follow the man who has been guarding you to the chopper." The big guy turned and looked me directly in the eye. "No funny business. I will have no problem shooting you in the back if you try to escape. Do I make myself clear, prisoner?" By the look in my American friend's eye, it was clear he was hoping for just that scenario.

I looked around helplessly for any sign of the cavalry arriving, but only a solitary sea gull called in the gloom to its fellow gulls. That was the only thing moving around the beach at this early hour. It looked like my luck had finally run out.

As we reached the beach, I saw that only a few feet from the waiting, chopper one final body was laid out on the grass dune among the seaweed and pebbles.

My knees buckled, and I fell onto my knees next to the body of my friend and fellow soldier, Smithy. He had been shot in the head. He had died instantly. I was looking at the body of a young man who had saved my life on two separate occasions. He had been one of the very best soldiers that Credenhill had ever produced.

The tears ran to the tip of my nose then dropped onto the sand, forming a tiny damp patch. The churning in my stomach started to burn so much that it hurt almost as much as my head. I knew this feeling all too well. The despair started to turn to a cold, terrible fury that cleared the fog from my muddled brain.

My grieving was cut short by an arm on my shoulder, trying to get me to stand up. I spun round, ready to strike double-handed the man who had disturbed my time with Smithy. Bruce Ellis staggered back in the soft sand just out of reach of my arms. He was pointing his Beretta at my head. I decided to cool it for the moment. My time would come.

Bartowski arrived, face flushed. "Get the prisoners on the goddamned helicopter, this isn't some goddamned CIA field trip. Move it!"

I did not move but pointed to the body of Smithy. "His name is Luke Smith. I thought you might like to know when you killed him, you crossed the line."

Bartowski screwed up his face and pushed me forward with booted foot. "Spare me the bullshit, and get on the chopper, asshole."

Throughout the time we had been captured, Gary Harding had said nothing to me, but now he stumbled alongside me as we approached the big dark grey helicopter. "Mac, get ready to escape when I give you the signal." I was shaking my head at Gary as he was pulled up aboard the chopper. "No, Gary. Behave yourself. That's an order."

I was lifted bodily and thrown onto the floor of the chopper, then hoisted up by the arms and placed on a bench seat opposite Gary Harding.

The last SEAL to board was Lieutenant Commander Saul Bartowski. He looked down with glee as Bruce Ellis extended a hand to be helped on board. Bartowski leaned out of the door, shouting down to him, "Overloaded, CIA man! See you around, buddy."

Bartowski signalled to the pilot, and on his command, the pilot throttled up and started slowly to lift the big machine up into the sullen grey sky.

❖ ❖ ❖

Sam cursed as she walked the last few hundred metres of the road. Her luck had deserted her, and nothing was going right. She had discovered that her evaluation that the Land Rover had survived the firefight at the glass house unscathed had proved to be incorrect. She had jacked the car up and removed the puncture to find that a stray bullet had hit the spare tyre and boot floor. She had wasted valuable time. She had packed everything away when she heard the faint gunfire in the distance. Foolishly, she decided to jog across the island. Sam was a mile from the car when she realised she had left the Glock with the bug in the glove box while she had struggled with the spare tyre. She pondered the risk of carrying on unarmed. She could not understand why she was so indecisive and absentminded. She finally decided to turn back and set off jogging back up the hill to the car. Now, even though she was armed, Sam's jogging plan failed when she developed what she thought might be a stitch, but she couldn't be sure. This baby nonsense was driving her mad. She abandoned that plan finding a bench by the side of the road Sam curled up letting her stitch recover. Some hours later Sam was woken by the grey dawn and opted for walking and thumbing a lift. Again, Sam was out of luck. The mountain pass was surprisingly quiet, even by Arran terms. Sam counted the number of cars that passed her on the String road on one hand. Not one car stopped for a damsel in distress.

Sam's mind was doing backward flips as she arrived at the road end to Adam's little cottage. She hadn't been sure the exact direction of the gunfire she had heard some hours ago, but she suspected it had come from the Machrie vicinity. Sam could hear the rotor beat and slightly muffled noise of a helicopter in the direction of Adam's cottage. Sam didn't know whether to laugh or cry. If there was gunfire, there was a good chance that Adam Macdonald was the source or the cause of it. Trouble followed Adam round like his shadow.

Halfway down the dirt track to the cottage, Sam could hear the chopper clearly now, god knows what the pilot was up to the engine was working hard but the helicopter seemed to be stationary. Sam removed the Glock from her ankle sock checked she had a round in the chamber and tucked the gun in the back of her waistband for easy access. Sam was treading carefully now, moving slowly step by step, checking for any movement in the improving light of the morning.

Ten metres in front of Sam, a body stumbled out of the ditch and fell headfirst on the road. Sam went for the Glock, bringing the muzzle to bear on the motionless body in front of her on the pebbled road. Sam edged forward, watching for any movement on either side of the road. Three metres from the body, Sam realised she was looking at the body of a woman. Her clothes were soaked through with a mixture of blood and mud. The woman was alive but had lost a lot of blood. Sam's heart missed a beat when the woman's head rolled to the side, revealing her face. It was the Lynx pilot who had brought them south from Edinburgh Airport. Sam wanted to sprint down the lane to the cottage to find Adam, but she could not leave the woman in this state. With some effort, Sam managed to get the woman on her feet and moving toward the cottage. Only seconds from the cottage, the engine note of the helicopter increased to a low, pitched howl as finally the machine lifted into the air, revealing itself at last to Sam. The big grey beast swung out toward the sea as Sam stopped and looked on. The two women were so close that the rotor wash from the big navy chopper threatened to blow over the unsteady pilot that Sam had found by the roadside. Sam was so busy watching the chopper, the car was almost upon them before Sam realised and pulled the army pilot out of the way of the charging car.

The car skidded to a halt, and the driver's door flew open. Bruce Ellis had been fast, but Sam was faster. He found himself looking down the wrong end of a Glock. Sam screamed at him, "Both hands on the car roof now, do it now, or I will drop you where you stand."

Bruce Ellis was not sure what to do next, but he was pretty sure the unhappy lady with the gun was not joking.

"Is there something wrong with your fucking hearing? Put your hands slowly on the roof. Now!" Sam backed up her screamed threat by placing her finger on the trigger of the Glock, releasing the safety mechanism. She watched as slowly the driver's hands came into view, his right hand holding his Beretta handgun. He gently placed the gun on the roof of the car, then took a step back with his hands on his head.

"OK, lady, you win. Now you have to listen to me if you want to get your people back safely."

Sam could feel a glimmer of hope run riot inside her brain. "OK, I'll take the bait. What people are you talking about?"

Bruce Ellis pointed to the chopper that had just departed. "The scientist and the soldier are on that chopper."

Fiona Malden was too far-gone to look, but both Sam and Ellis watched as the chopper headed southwest, headed for Machrihanish. Sam wanted to ask the next question but was afraid of the answer. When the question came it was almost a whisper. "What is the soldier's name please?"

It was as if time stood still. Sam wanted to scream at the American to hurry up with the answer. When it did come it was bittersweet in the extreme. "The guy on the plane is called Adam, and there is a dead soldier on the beach called Luke."

Sam continued to watch the progress of the navy helicopter in the distance, but it was through tear-filled eyes.

❖ ❖ ❖

My eyes were glued to Gary Harding. I was willing him not to do anything stupid. Against these guys, he had no chance. They were some of the best-trained men in the American military. Gary stared into space as if in a trance. He was pale and sweating badly. I tried to engage Gary in conversation, but a punch on the side of the head from the nearest SEAL warned me to keep quiet for the moment. Suddenly without warning, Gary stood up. The SEAL who had whacked me started screaming at Gary to sit down. Gary looked directly at me and raised his arm in a weird stop gesture. On the palm of his hand written in ink was one word: *Diavokxin.* I looked at Gary in horror. He was smiling at me as the big Navy SEAL forced him to sit back down, but there was something wrong with the smile. Clenched between his teeth was a glass vial. Gary bit down on the end of the glass tube before I could react. The glass popped and sprayed its content directly into the face of the big SEAL, who staggered back coughing. Gary launched himself forward over the bulkhead toward the pilot.

To stay in the aircraft was certain death. Flinging myself out at this height with my hands tied was also almost certain death, but I liked the odds better and charged for the open side hatch, holding my breath. I smashed both my tethered fists into the jaw of the only SEAL blocking my escape route. He tripped over one of the body bags, leaving my escape route free. I had my feet on the edge as the chopper started to bank hard right, but my leap into the unknown was halted abruptly as someone grabbed my collar and pulled me back into the hard-banking Seahawk. I was powerless to fight against gravity and the force pulling me backward.

All hell was breaking out in the chopper. Bodies were falling in every direction as the Diavokxin did its hellish work. Luckily, I was the only one who had been briefed on the Cold War chemical. As long as none of the chemical entered my lungs, I was OK. All around me, men had inhaled the chemical, and it was only a matter of time until they died. They were in effect the walking dead. Suddenly the Seahawk reversed its spiral and banked hard to the left in a spiral dive. From the chopper's erratic actions, I could tell the pilot was either dead or dying. Banking in the opposite direction threw me toward escape once more. I managed to half turn to find Bartowski holding onto my collar, his other gorilla arm anchored to the seat back. It seemed that if he was going to die, he was going to make damned sure I was going with him. I was running out of time as the chopper lost altitude, and my lungs used the last of the untainted oxygen. I decided I had one last attempt left in me. I used every ounce of strength left in my body to pull against the tie wrap holding my hands together. With a crack, the tie wrap snapped. This had a double effect. As my hands flew apart, my elbow caught Bartowski right on the point of his chin. I was falling away from the doomed chopper. I was disorientated and unable to get into any kind of position for hitting the water. I hit the water in a cartwheeling motion, and everything went black.

❖ ❖ ❖

Bruce Ellis spoke to the young woman as they watched the chopper. Bruce could see that the information he had just given her was having a profound effect on her state of mind. Tears were running down her face and dropping onto her clothing. "Listen, I don't know who you are, lady, but I can help. I really can. We need to get to the air base pronto!"

Sam gasped then pointed helplessly as the Seahawk stood on its tail, then banked to the right. Something was wrong, something was very wrong.

Sam was thinking on her feet. "You really want to help me, fine. Help her down to the cottage, then follow me to the old boathouse." Before Bruce Ellis could answer, Sam handed over the injured woman, then took off down the track past the cottage to the boathouse. Despairingly, she watched the helicopter in its final death throes as she flung the boathouse doors open. She had only seen the boat once on its delivery and had never set foot in it. Seconds later, Bruce Ellis appeared in the doorway and stood staring as Sam pulled back the cover.

There attention was taken from the boat as a large thud and shattering of metal reached their ears. The chopper was down.

Ellis knew what was coming, but one look at the desperation in the woman's face stopped him from objecting to the next course of action.

CHAPTER 14

THE AFTERMATH

Before the boat was even floated off its trailer, Sam turned the ignition key, praying there was life in the battery. The big fuel-injected Suzuki engine burst into life on the first time of asking, and Sam wasted not one second. She slammed the throttle against the stops. The back of the speedboat sat down in the water, the nose lifted as the engine's 150 horsepower was delivered in one huge burst.

They were off. Ellis clung to the passenger seat for dear life as Sam hit the incoming waves head on at full speed.

The crash had happened a couple of miles southwest of Arran. Sam knew that the chances of surviving a helicopter crash were slim. She wondered what the odds were of surviving two. She turned her attention back to the horizon, her tear-filled eyes trying to pick out any debris on the watery horizon. Several times Bruce Ellis thought his spine would snap as Sam showed the big speedboat no mercy. Ellis wanted to lean over and pull back on the throttle, so he could tell Sam she was wasting her time, but he let her be. Looking at her, he realized she needed to know that she had done everything humanly possible when all hope was eventually lost.

❖ ❖ ❖

PC Brian Morrison trundled down the cottage lane from the main road. He was new to the island and was enjoying working with the friendly islanders. It was light years away from his last Glasgow beat. He was quite happy to deal with the occasional theft or road accident. He had had more than his quota of stabbings, drug raids, and bloody football crowd control. He was looking forward to this posting, as his maximum service was due shortly. He relished the thought of finishing his police career on the peaceful little island just off the Ayrshire coast.

PC Morrison had arrived at the office to find that there had been various reports of gunfire and explosions. He checked the map and traced the suspected area from around the King's Caves to the little village of Machrie. PC Morrison was pretty sure that it was a farmer on a shoot, or at worst, something to do with the NATO exercises that were reportedly taking part off the west coast. He decided that if nothing else, it would get him out of the office, and he went off to take a look at the area just in case he was wrong, and the Russians had decided Arran was a good place to start the invasion of Britain.

PC Morrison pulled the Honda CR-V up outside the little white cottage. He was not hopeful of finding anyone at home as there was no cars present. A quick reccie of the property found an abandoned hire car hidden behind the empty boat shed. PC Morrison tapped on the door of the cottage, and it swung open to his touch. The hairs on PC Morrison's neck stood on end as his eyes adjusted to the gloom of the cottage. Propped up against the sofa sat a female. She was covered in blood and was holding a blood-soaked towel against her side.

When she saw the uniform, she relaxed, her left hand dropping a Glock onto the carpet by her side. "I would be very grateful if you could call me an ambulance, I don't think I can last much…" Fiona Malden's head flopped to the side as she passed out.

Brian Morrison checked the woman's pulse. She was still alive, just. Her pulse was weak. Brian Morrison charged into the kitchen. He needed to call his office, but first he needed to stop the woman bleeding to death. He grabbed a roll of cling film and proceeded to wrap the woman's waist tightly, pulling the cling film round and round until he was satisfied that the bleeding had been stemmed. He used the same cling film to lift the handgun away from the woman's side. It only took him seconds to call for assistance. Then he decided to have a walk around the property just in case there were any more nasty surprises. As PC Morrison walked past the empty boathouse on the beach, he noticed gulls swooping down, fighting each over something. PC Morrison looked down at the body of the young man before reaching for his radio. "Hi, Sergeant. It's Morrison again. You better add coroner to the list of visitors. I have just found a body on the beach. Might be an idea to give forensics in Glasgow a shout. I think we are going to need them. This guy has been shot in the head." PC Morrison found a discarded boat cover on the beach and used this to cover the body of the young man until forensics could get to him. So much for a quiet life.

❖ ❖ ❖

I came to in a watery hell. For a few seconds, it was only animal instinct to survive that kept me from drowning. My brain function started to return, but with it came the pain. My left side was not working, and when I tried to kick my legs to keep me afloat, the pain in my back was incredible—so much so that I attempted to scream, but the seawater entered my mouth and muffled my scream. Only by using one arm and my lower leg was I able to remain afloat. Even if I could swim, I had no way of knowing which way. The waves swamped me, and with every wave, my lungs burned more. The grey of the water turned into the grey of Sam's eyes, and the freezing seawater became warm. I was drowning, and all I wanted to do was see Sam one last time.

❖ ❖ ❖

It was Bruce Ellis who spotted the dark shape as Sam spun the boat round for the umpteenth time. Adam was lifeless as Sam and Ellis pulled his waterlogged body on board. Sam sobbed uncontrollably as she started CPR. Ellis wasted no time and gunned the boat toward the misty Arran shore. Adam was grey and totally unresponsive. Minutes seemed like hours as the boat charged toward the shore.

The ambulance crew had just started treating the wounded woman in the cottage when a madwoman burst in the door of the little cottage. Sam could not believe her luck when Ellis had slammed the boat onto the beach to find an ambulance waiting for them.

Bruce Ellis had taken over CPR while Sam sprinted to the cottage. Sam led the paramedic with his defibrillator down to the beached speedboat. Bruce Ellis held out little hope of success, but Sam was more positive. She had witnessed at first hand the incredible willpower that Adam Macdonald possessed. On the third attempted resuscitation, the paramedic picked up Adam's pulse. It was weak, but it was steady.

It was then that Sam spotted the legs protruding from under the tarpaulin. Sam collapsed after lifting back the cover to discover the body of Smithy. She could take no more. Her world was being turned upside down. Eventually, she found an inner strength from the depths of her soul, rallied, and placed the cover back over her dead friend. She had to stay strong for Adam and the baby. Smithy was gone, but Adam, for the moment, clung to life. He needed Sam, not some blubbering idiot.

Sam supervised the loading of both Fiona Malden and Adam into the ambulance. Adam was still unconscious, but some colour had returned to his face. Outside the ambulance, PC Morrison hovered, waiting to question two of the three new arrivals. His sergeant had headed to Brodick to meet the ferry and the imminently arriving forensic officers from Glasgow.

PC Morrison stopped the man who had arrived in the boat but could get little information from the American, who was just a passer-by here on holiday. He took contact details from the American and advised him not to leave the island until the investigating team had interviewed him. PC Morrison turned his attention to the woman who was about to leave in the ambulance. Sam reluctantly stepped out of the ambulance at the police officer's request. "Sorry to hold you up, but I need to know a few things before I decide if I can let you leave. Can you tell me the identity of either the woman or the body I found on the beach?"

Sam popped her head back into the ambulance to ask where they were headed then turned her attention back to PC Morrison. Sam pointed to the pocketbook and pen that Morrison was brandishing. "For a start, officer, you can put those away. I can tell you now you will be wasting your time. I could tell you the woman in the ambulance is an RAF pilot and the dead man on the beach is one of my MI6 team, killed by an American raiding party. If it were not for the Official Secrets Act, I could tell you that the man in the ambulance is also an MI6 agent who has just been in a helicopter crash, and that the man you just let go is most likely a CIA agent, but you would think I had lost my marbles, so let's save us both a bit of time, Just call this number and ask for Neil Andrews. Tell him Sam and Adam are alive, then say 'Red Vixen.' Then do as he tells you if you value your job. Tell him we are on our way to NHS Cross House in Kilmarnock."

PC Morrison used his own mobile phone to contact the number the girl had given him. He was not sure why, but for some reason, he had the terrible feeling he had stumbled upon something that he was going to have no control over. The young woman was as cool as a cucumber. She did not seem to be spinning a yarn. Brian Morrison recited the phrase, then went pale when he was told he was being put through to the director of MI6. Sam watched as he answered questions, then finally, with a shaking hand, he handed the phone to Sam. "He wants a word with you, miss."

Sam took the mobile from the police officer. "Hello, Neil. Sorry to disturb your lunch, but we are in a spot of bother here. Can't stop to chat. Need to get to hospital. Speak to you soon." Sam clicked the phone off and handed it back to the PC. "Listen, officer, if you want to get into the good books, find the American you let go and hand him over to Neil Andrews. He will be very happy with you if you can do that." Sam jumped into the back of the ambulance and popped her head back out just before the ambulance pulled away. "He might even forget that you let him escape in the first place!"

PC Morrison mulled over the situation as he paced up and down outside the little cottage. He had two options: stay here and wait for his superiors, or try to catch the American. Morrison checked his watch. If the Claonaig ferry were on time, it would be sailing in around forty minutes. If the woman were right, this small ferry on the north of the island would be the quickest way back to the mainland. PC Morrison made a split-second decision and headed north for the little ferry. Morrison reckoned if the American was not there, he still had time to get back before he was posted AWOL.

❖ ❖ ❖

Bruce Ellis was just about to drive down the on ramp to the ferry when his path was blocked by the big police 4x4. The big policeman who had questioned him at the cottage stood by the car, tapping on the window with his baton. "Please step out of the car, sir, so we can have a word." Ellis stepped out and was immediately frisked by the big Scottish policeman. The gathering crowd gasped as PC Morrison removed a handgun from the breast pocket of Ellis's jacket. Ellis decided discretion was the better part of valour and allowed the policeman to cuff him and place him in the back of the police car.

It looked like the American embassy was going to have a busy time extracting him from the clutches of the British justice system.

❖ ❖ ❖

Sam arrived at Cross House hospital and was immediately separated from the two casualties and taken to an empty office to wait for initial tests on Adam and Fiona. The nurse who showed Sam to the office promised to come back and keep Sam up to date on the casualties. Sam collapsed in the big comfortable armchair in the corner of the office. She had been up all night and was absolutely shattered. Sam still couldn't come to terms with her pregnancy. Normally, she would still have plenty of life left in her, but she didn't even have enough strength to take her jacket off and was asleep within seconds of sitting down.

Sam came to when she was gently shaken awake by a tall, grey-haired, distinguished-looking gentleman. He held out a cup of steaming coffee for Sam as he spoke to her. "Hello there. You must be Samantha. Forgive me for waking you up, but I thought you might like a cuppa and some information on your friend's conditions."

Sam straightened up in the chair and accepted the coffee that was being handed to her. "Sorry about that. I am just so damned tired these days. Please tell me how Adam is."

The doctor seated himself on the corner of the desk next to Sam, moving his name plaque out of the way to do so. Dr Cameron Kennedy crossed his arms and frowned slightly as he started to speak. "Unfortunately, Adam has not regained consciousness yet. We gave his lungs a wee clean out to get any seawater away. We also gave him a top-to-toe check over. When Adam wakes up, he won't be skipping out the door, I'm afraid. Adam has a broken collarbone and a damaged disc in the base of his spine. We really need Adam to wake up so we can do some further tests with him. Basically, Samantha, we need to know if Adam can feel his legs."

It took a few seconds for Sam's groggy brain to register what the doctor was telling her. "God, no. Not crippled, not Adam."

Dr Kennedy got up from the desk and started pacing back and forth. "Samantha, at the moment, that is the least of Adam's problems. No one knows how long Adam's brain was starved of oxygen when he was underwater. Let's get his head working first. Then we can worry about his legs."

Dr Kennedy could see how upset Sam was and decided to change the subject for the moment. "The woman who was brought in with him is doing slightly better. The bullet that hit her side passed straight through without hitting any major organs. She also has a broken wrist, but her main problem was loss of blood. She should be fine, but she will need reconstructive surgery around the exit-wound area."

Sam checked out the name plaque on the desk before answering. "Dr Kennedy, how long before you will know about Adam?"

Kennedy continued to pace up and down before answering. "It's very hard to say, Samantha. I would like to see him regain consciousness in the next forty-eight hours. Any longer than a couple of weeks, and the signs will not be good."

Sam went to stand up, but her legs would not do what they were told. She went down headfirst on the carpet and came to with Dr Kennedy on his knees next to her. Kennedy helped Sam back to the chair, then handed her two pills and a glass of water. "Sorry, doc, but I don't think I should. You see, I'm pregnant."

Kennedy removed the pills and knelt next to Sam. "When was the last time you had the baby checked?"

Sam shook her head. "Sorry, doc. I have been kind of busy."

Sam reckoned Dr Cameron Kennedy must be one of the top dogs at the hospital. Ten minutes ago, Sam had told him she was pregnant. Now she was having an ultrasound. Ten minutes after that, she was wheeled back into Dr Kennedy's office carrying the report from obstetrics. Dr Kennedy sat at his desk and studied the report. "Well, Samantha, a bit of good news for you."

Sam found herself sitting on the edge of her wheelchair, holding her breath, waiting for the baby news. "We think you are just short of sixteen weeks, and the baby is doing fine. I have to confess, until you told me, I would never have guessed you were expecting. First-time mothers, especially women who exercise, tend not to show so much due to their strong abdominal muscles, which mask the pregnancy. I suspect over the next couple of weeks, that will change and you will start to show more. Rest is what you need, my dear, and lots of it. Does the dad know about the baby?"

Sam looked at the carpet, avoiding the doctor's eyes. "No, not yet. I plan to tell him the minute he regains consciousness."

There was an uncomfortable silence for a few seconds, "Ah, well, try not to get too stressed. It's not good for the baby. And Adam is in good hands. It's early days yet. I will arrange for a room close to Adam to be made available for you so you can rest. On a different note, when you were in obstetrics, I had a phone call from your boss. He will be here in an hour or so. I recommend you use the time to get something to eat and grab some sleep before, if my first impressions are correct, Attila the Hun arrives."

Sam smiled to herself. Yes, Attila the Hun was not a bad description of Neil Andrews in full flow. And Sam was sure Neil would be in full flow.

Sam was fast asleep when the door to her room was thrown open, and the light switched on. "Plenty of time to sleep when you're dead, O'Conner. Rise and shine, Samantha!" Neil Andrews was at the foot of the bed, accompanied by Peter Kent. Neil Andrews moved round the bed and sat down at Sam's feet. "OK, Sam, let's hear it from the top. I have the PM waiting for my report. This better be good, or we will all be heading for the job centre on Monday."

Sam was feeling worse than when she had fallen asleep but pulled herself together. The last thing Neil Andrews needed to know at the moment was that Sam was expecting a baby. "How is Adam?"

For a split second, Neil Andrews's face gave away his anxiety, but he masked it while glancing across at Peter Kent. "He is still out. I need to speak to him the moment he wakes up. Right, young lady, report please."

Sam's face was a picture of concentration as she pulled together a report of the last few days out of contact with Vauxhall Cross.

"OK. Adam and I decided to split up to confuse our pursuers. I took Smithy's bugged gun and placed it on the back of a lorry going south. Karen and I headed for my house, where I knew my marked gun was. I needed to get rid of it before my own home was discovered. Unfortunately, my house turned into the OK Corral. Some Al Qaeda thugs turned up. I was in the middle of dealing with them when Benesch and her new American buddies showed up and crashed the party. We were all about to be loaded on an American chopper when more Al Qaeda showed up with machine guns, and all hell broke loose. Benesch was killed in the gun battle, and so were the Americans. At least one Al Qaeda escaped in a big black Merc. I suspect it was Khanjar, as there was talk of him when the other Al Qaeda thugs first showed up. Benesch was looking for Gary Harding. I suspect that the Americans have the Vokxin and Diavokxin already and are just looking for Gary Harding to complete the treble."

Neil Andrews stood up. "OK, Sam. Peter will stay and ask you a few more questions while I go and have a word with the pilot. She may be able to shed some light on what happened on Arran." Neil Andrews left without another word and made his way back to the nurses' station.

Peter Kent waited until Andrews was well out of earshot before speaking. "Jesus Sam, what the hell have you been up to? That house! Where did you get the cash for that pad? I've said nothing to his lordship, but if Andrews finds out, there will be a lot of awkward questions for you to answer, girl!"

Sam was weeping. Her hormones were again rioting. Sam cursed inwardly. Now more than ever she needed to be calm, not some blubbering wreck. "Sorry, Peter, Smithy's dead. The bastards shot him."

Peter Kent was not normally affected by losing a team member. It came with the territory, but he had been fond of the young guy. "Who shot him, Sam?"

Sam wiped away a tear that had reached the end of her nose. "The Americans, I think."

Dr Kennedy was just going over some medication changes with the nurse on duty when Neil Andrews appeared by the desk. "Hello there. Could someone point me in the direction of the young lady who was bought in with gunshot wounds?"

Dr Kennedy put down his folder and gave Neil the once-over. "Hi, I am Dr Kennedy. You must be Director Andrews. Nice to put a face to a voice. Fiona is conscious but very weak. Normally, I would not allow visitors just yet, but as you have already pointed out to me, the situation warrants special measures. Please follow me, and I will stay just to keep an eye on Fiona."

The two men arrived at the door to Fiona Malden's room, but Neil Andrews raised a hand before Dr Kennedy entered. "By all means, doctor, go in and check on her, but you will not be present when I question her. You do not have the clearance for what may be disclosed. Please take a seat out here, and I will call you if I need you."

Dr Kennedy was about to object, but he was pretty sure he would be overruled and pointed to a chair further down the corridor. "I will wait there until you are finished, not too long please." He doubted if Andrews even heard the last sentence as he was already halfway through the door.

"Good morning, Captain Malden. I hope you are on the mend?" Fiona Malden's eyes were sunken in her skull, and her skin had a yellowish-grey tinge. It seemed to take a few seconds before she realised who was speaking to her. "Sir, I'm sorry about the Lynx. I did everything I could, but they hit the gearbox. I had no option but to ditch in the sea. Sorry!"

Neil Andrews placed himself on the bed at the same spot as he had sat on Sam's bed. "Don't worry about the helicopter. That can be replaced. Captain, I need to know a few things. If you can help me out, that would be great. Who fired on you? Who escaped the crash? How did you end up here?"

Fiona Malden painfully pulled herself up to a seated position before replying. "We were fired on by an American Navy Seahawk. Their waist gunner caught me as I climbed out of a valley, I think somewhere in the Scottish borders. I had Captain Macdonald, Luke Smith, and the scientist lad Harding on board. We all survived when I had to ditch my Lynx off the Scottish coast northwest of the Ailsa Craig. We were picked up by a fishing boat that dropped us off in a little bay on the west coast of Arran. Captain Macdonald has a little cottage on the coast, and we holed up there, waiting for Captain Macdonald's partner to join us. It never happened, and we were discovered by the American Special Forces. We split up. I am not sure what happened to Captain Macdonald and the scientist lad, but we engaged the Americans. I think Luke was hit, but I'm not sure. I was shot, fell, and banged my head. When I came to, the Americans were leaving. I can't remember much after that. Sorry, sir."

Neil Andrews stood up and started pacing back and forth. "Captain Malden, can you remember who opened fire first?"

Malden shook her head. "Sorry, sir. It was dark, and I wasn't sure who was in what position. Can you tell me who made it, sir?"

Andrews ducked the question. "You rest, and I will be back shortly with the full picture once I put the pieces together."

Neil Andrews had just stepped out of Malden's room when he was met by both Dr Kennedy and Peter Kent's partner, Robin Alder. Dr Kennedy excused himself and entered Fiona Malden's room to make sure she was OK.

Alder approached Andrews with an unexpected problem. "Sir, there is a policeman outside who spoke to you on the phone. I think he has lost his marbles. He reckons he has captured a CIA agent and has him in his patrol car. He wants to know where you want him."

Alder was smiling, but Neil Andrews for the moment was taking nothing for granted. He ordered Robin Alder to lead the way to where the policeman was waiting. PC Brian Morrison was introduced to Neil Andrews and led him out to the police Honda CR-V, where he found a man handcuffed to the steering wheel. Neil Andrews opened the passenger door and leaned into the cabin. "Good day, sir. The constable tells me you are an American agent. Has he been taking drugs, or is there any truth to his claim? What I mean, sir, is do you have any way of proving who you are?"

Bruce Ellis smiled at the stranger as he replied. "Buddy, do you have any way of proving who you are? For all I know, you could be the hospital janitor." Bruce Ellis removed his smile and continued without any more wisecracks. "If I am not who I say I am, then how would I know about your nasty chemicals you let somebody walk away with from your chemical warfare lab that doesn't exist? Listen, buddy, you need to let me go. I know what's going on here, and I can stop it. I'm not your enemy. We need to work together to stop this madness before any more of our people are killed."

Andrews asked him to hold on a second and walked over to the big police constable. "Well done, officer. I am very impressed. Not many officers would have tackled him single-handed. Can you release your prisoner into our custody? No need to fill out any paperwork. It will all be taken care of. I will personally talk to your commanding officer."

Brian Morrison wore a beaming smile from ear to ear. He hated paperwork and was glad to get rid of his American friend. "That's very good of you, sir. It was no problem. An American CIA agent is child's play compared to some of the nuggets I have had to deal with in sunny Glasgow. I'll get him out for you now. With a wee bit of luck, I can catch the last ferry back tonight." The big constable busied himself releasing Bruce Ellis. Then he handed Neil Andrews the American's handgun.

"One last thing, PC Morrison, when you get back to Arran can you keep an eye on the cottage where the shootings occurred, and let me know if anyone has an unhealthy interest in it."

PC Morrison left, promising to call if anything out of the ordinary happened on the island.

Neil Andrews was not sure whom he had found, but the American was far too well informed to be ignored. He dismissed Alder, sending him to get coffees while the pair stood outside, weighing each other up like two gunfighters at high noon.

"I am Neil Andrews, director of MI6. Can I have the pleasure of your name and position please."

Bruce Ellis smiled, patting Andrews on the back. "Hi, Neil. I am Special Agent Bruce Ellis. I was sent by the president to find out what was happening this side of the pond. Oh, and by the way, I already knew you were Neil Andrews, but you are acting director, and will only get the job full time if you sort this mess out, am I right?"

Andrews was taken aback by Bruce Ellis's statement. "OK, Mr Ellis you have just succeeded in getting my full attention. Can you please tell me every last detail you know about this 'mess,' as you call it."

Ellis shrugged his shoulders. "No problem. Let's go get that coffee, and I will tell you what I know."

Dr Kennedy allowed Neil Andrews to use his office. Andrews wanted some time to study his American friend and asked Robin Alder to keep an eye on Sam in case she decided to go walkabout again. Bruce Ellis made himself comfortable at Dr Kennedy's desk while Neil Andrews, true to form, had already started pacing up and down.

"OK, buddy. Pin back your ears. Here is what I know so far. There are a few blanks, so feel free to fill them in on the way, and maybe we can figure this out. Colonel Southern was given the task of coming across here with a task force to regain control of the chemicals that your dudes had lost. The president was concerned that not enough info was finding its way back to Washington, so the boss dispatched me to check on things. I did a bit of digging about. I was myself concerned when I found Southern hanging around with the person he was sent here to find. A word in the ear of our flight coordinator found that Southern was sending his number two to our very own chemical weapons store in Alaska, which also doesn't exist. Put two and two together, and you have got to think Southern has found the chemicals. Southern seems to have an unhealthy interest in the chopper crew that one of our choppers shot down by mistake. As yet, I haven't figured out what he is after, but he has killed people and put his career on the line for it."

Neil Andrews stopped pacing and turned to face Bruce Ellis. He was furious because of one of the comments made by Ellis.

"Shot down by mistake? Do your helicopters usually shoot down unarmed aircraft?"

Bruce Ellis realised he was treading on eggshells and decided it was better to defuse the situation. "Listen, Neil. I am sorry. I did not mean that to come out the way it did. We have been suffering severe communication problems. The pilot of that chopper swears that he received a message that the chopper was carrying the terrorist and was ordered to shoot it down. Hell, things have got so bad that the only way I could contact the president was to send him a courier-delivered letter."

Neil Andrews had heard whispers from GCHQ that the Americans were having comms problems. Indeed, some of the US-based systems used by the British army had failed, so it seemed the American was telling the truth. "I know exactly what your Colonel Southern was after. Benesch took a scientist hostage, then discovered he had a made a huge scientific breakthrough. Benesch joined forces with your colonel to have him spirited away so your people could recreate his work, but the only fly in the ointment was that our people had grabbed him back. I hope that fills a few blanks for you, Mr Ellis."

Ellis nodded. "Yep. I wondered where the scientist was going to come in. I take it that it was not your boffins who have been playing with our comms?"

Neil Andrews shook his head. "No, nothing to do with us. Tell me, Bruce, what kind of dealings have you had with Al Qaeda?"

Bruce Ellis smiled at Neil Andrews. "Neil, until this shitstorm happened, I was leading the team that is hunting for Bin Laden. I don't think you can tell me much about them that I don't already know."

Neil Andrews let out a low whistle. "My, my, your president must have been worried to remove the man in charge of the manhunt of the century. So you will be acquainted with Khanjar, his real second in command, and not al-Zawahiri, as thought by the vast majority."

Bruce Ellis nodded without replying. Neil Andrews drained the remains of his coffee cup before continuing. "Good, then you will know of the attempted dirty bomb attack in London. What you may not know, because we kept it close to our chest, is that it was carried out by Khanjar's son. He was captured and used against Khanjar. Unfortunately, when Benesch escaped, she contaminated the facility, killing Khanjar's son in the process. As you can imagine, if Khanjar found out his son had been killed, there would be major terrorist activity. In short, Bruce, our handguns have been bugged, and I have lost good agents. Your guys have been told to attack us, and comms have been tampered with. I don't think we can rule out Al Qaeda. They would love to see us destroy each other."

Neil Andrews went on to explain about the Al Qaeda attack at the glass house and the loss of life and death of Benesch.

Ellis listened, taking it all in before changing the subject. "I take it the guy we pulled out of the water was one of your men. Do you think the guy will make it?"

Neil Andrews stared out the office window. He did not want the American to see the concern written all over his face. "Adam is still in a coma. Who knows? Even the doctors don't know. One thing is for certain. Unless Adam wakes up, we will never know what happened to your Seahawk and its passengers."

Sam was in her own little world as she sat by Adam's bedside, watching the heart monitors steady blip work its way across the screen, never faltering. She was so far away she never noticed the nurse slip in to check on her patient. For a few seconds, Nurse Russell watched the pale young woman. "Talk to him, pet. They can hear, you know. You can help bring him back. Just let him know you are here waiting for him."

The nurse checked a few things and slipped out as quietly as she had arrived.

Sam drew closer to Adam with the intention of whispering in his ear. She stopped and looked at the peaceful expression on Adam's face. For a man approaching forty, only the wisp of grey hair by his temples pointed to his age. His jet-black hair and tanned features looked more in keeping with a man approaching thirty. Only a few laughter lines around his eyes gave away the fact that Adam had seen his fair share of life, some good some bad. Sam longed for him to lift his eyelids so she could look into his hazel, almost golden, eyes once more. She twirled a lock of his dark hair playfully through her fingers as she prepared to speak to him.

" I am sorry, Adam. I never planned to tell you this way, but you need to know this. Adam, you are going to be a dad, and we both need you to come back to us. You can't miss your child growing up. Adam, darling, listen to me. You need to fight this. You need to fight like you have never fought before. Please, Adam, for me, please!" Sam was sobbing in between huge gulps for air. Her tears fell on Adam's cheek and ran down onto the pillow. Sam's despair turned a corner. Her raging hormones kicked in, and suddenly, she transformed from a weeping wreck into the killer that had been installed in her psyche by the secret service. She had been trained in dozens of methods to kill her enemies, but none of them would be final enough for whoever had caused their world to implode around them. Sam managed with a huge struggle to contain the murderous rage, and once again returned to her vigil by Adam's bedside, wiping away her tears while telling herself to get a grip. The next two hours passed, and Adam showed no sign that Sam's plea had got through to him.

Sam made the trip to the coffee machine with Robin Alder in tow. She handed Alder the first cup and waited for her own. "Robin, I take it Neil has asked you to keep an eye on me. That's the reason you are following me around like a collie dog!"

Robin Alder smiled but avoided eye contact, concentrating on his coffee cup. "Well spotted, Sam. Hey, nice pad by the way. You are a dark horse. Anyone else would have been raving about a house like that, but you never mentioned it once. Spill the beans! How did you end up with a pad like that?"

It was Sam's turn to avoid eye contact. "I could tell you, Robin, but then I would have to shoot you. Official secrets and all that. You know how it is."

Sam turned and headed back to Adam's room before Alder could ask any more about the glass house.

Sam slipped quietly back into the room then stopped dead in her tracks. Next to Adam's bed sat a woman in a wheelchair. She was holding Adam's hand and smiled as Sam entered the room. "Hi, Sam. You might not recognise me out of uniform, but we have met before. I am Fiona Malden, the pilot who picked you up from Edinburgh Airport."

Sam studied the new arrival in the blink of a second—short, dark hair and paler than normal skin. Sam could not ignore the fact that she felt threatened by her presence. Sam's stare moved from the woman to her hand as she held onto Adam's hand. Fiona followed Sam's gaze and removed her hand. "Sorry, Sam. I was just trying to give Adam a bit of friendly support. Do you know where Smithy is?" Sam collapsed in the spare chair at the foot of the bed without replying. "Sorry to be a bother, Sam, but it's Colditz in here. They won't tell me anything. I had to bribe the nurse by promising her son a tour of my helicopter the next time I'm at Prestwick to get her to tell me about Adam and bring me here for ten minutes. So where is Mr Smith?"

Sam noticed something that stopped her from replying.

Before Fiona Malden could say anything, Sam charged to the door and screamed for the doctor. Within seconds, the nurse and a junior doctor appeared to find Sam staring at the EEG monitor. It was intermittent, but along with Adam's heart monitor, there were seconds where the readings fluctuated. The junior doctor studied them. "I need to get Dr Kennedy's opinion, but I think our patient is dreaming, and dreaming is good. It shows brain function."

The nurse tried to remove Fiona Malden, but she declared that if she were not allowed to stay, she would discharge herself. The nurse backed down and allowed Fiona to continue her bedside visit for a little longer.

Sam and Fiona sat in silence, both watching the monitors. It was Sam who spoke first. "Fiona, I never answered your question. Smithy is dead. He was shot and killed in the attack. Gary Harding, we think, was with Adam when the American chopper crashed and is missing, presumed dead."

Fiona Malden wiped away a single tear and shook her head in disbelief. "The Americans lost a second Seahawk. What a bloody mess. After all this madness, Gary is dead. Heads should roll for this."

Sam agreed but was a bit more streetwise when it came to these things. She had a feeling that somehow this would all be swept under the carpet. The British government needed to keep a low profile after they were found breaking international treaties, and the Americans had not covered themselves in glory with their handling of a situation that had turned into a disaster for both countries.

I was fighting against a current that kept dragging me under the water. I could see the daylight on the surface above, but I could not reach it. My body had no feeling, just a huge fatigue that tried to get me to stop fighting the current.

As I watched, the surface above me changed into Sam's smiling face. My body wanted to stop swimming and study Sam's face, but my brain told a different story. I needed to keep swimming if I wanted to see Sam's real face again. My mind played tricks on me, and I was sure I could hear Sam's voice talking to another woman. I kicked for the surface once more, but the fatigue threatened to overpower me. I kept telling myself—just one last push. I could almost touch the surface. I just wanted to sleep but deep down, I knew if I stopped, it was over. The thought of this terrified me and spilled over into anger. I kicked once more.

Suddenly, I couldn't breathe. Something was in my mouth. Everything was brilliant white. I was aware of people around me, but I couldn't understand what they were saying. My confused mind couldn't understand where the water had gone. I was still fighting to get to the surface, but hands were pushing me back.

I fought back, trying to push against the hands, but the pain in my back and shoulders was too much. I fell backward, expecting to hit the water. Instead I found a pillow and the clear voice of Sam telling me I was OK. I found a nurse on my chest trying to remove tubes from my throat. For a second, everything went black. Then I was gulping huge mouthfuls of air in between throwing up.

I thought I was hallucinating. Sam was holding my hand, tears running down her flushed cheeks while in the background a short-haired woman hovered. A man appeared in front of me, talking to me, trying to tell me where I was, but my numbed brain could only focus on Sam. I studied her haunting grey eyes and her flushed cheeks. She had regained some of her old figure and was radiant. I could not drag my eyes from her. I had been so close to never seeing her beauty again. Without warning, images of the recent past events started to flash in front of my eyes. I was fighting for my life as the helicopter went into its final death spin.

Suddenly, I was once more on the beach in front of my little white cottage, staring down at the body of Smithy. I lifted myself up using my elbows. The determination helped clear the fog from my brain.

"Sam, Smithy, oh god, Smithy!"

Sam came closer to the bed. "I know, Adam. He's gone. You need to rest. Lie back, and let the doctors check you out."

For the first time, the words got through to me, and I sat back against the pillow, exhausted and devastated by my recollections. The last conversation Smithy and I had come back to me in a flash. "Sam, don't let them bury Smithy. His last wish was to be buried next to my old mate, Ian Ferris. You need to get hold of Neil Andrews for me."

Sam puffed up the pillows behind me and gently pushed me back onto them. "Oh, I don't think that will be a problem. You just lie back and rest. Now that I know you will be OK, I will leave you here with Fiona. I'm sure she can watch you until I get Neil for you." Sam bent down and kissed me on the forehead before heading for the door. Sam turned before leaving giving me a nervous smile and strangely, a wave. I was still groggy, but for some reason, her body language worried me. I could not put my finger on it, but it felt wrong.

Sam bumped into Robin Alder in the corridor. "Great news, Robin. Adam is awake. Can you do me a big favour and find Neil Andrews? Adam is asking for him. I don't want to leave his side for the minute."

Robin Alder put the half empty coffee cup down, smiling at Sam. "No problem, Sam. Trust Adam to be right back to business the minute he comes round. Back in a second."

Sam watch Robin Alder make his way to the end of the corridor, then turn right out of sight. Sam grabbed her bag by the chair and headed for the exit. Outside, Sam spotted a taxi that had just dropped off a couple and was about to pull away. Sam gave her six-million-dollar smile to the driver. "Hi there, would you be a gentleman and help a damsel in distress? I need to be at Glasgow airport in forty-five minutes to catch my flight? Would you be a darling and take me, please?"

Sam's hourglass was running out, and she knew if she was going to go through with this, she had to do it soon, before it was too late.

An hour later, Sam sat down in the departure lounge of Glasgow Airport. She had purchased a case and some new clothing. She studied her ticket to Heathrow and the times between her arrival and connecting flight. She was relieved to see that she had enough time between flights to sort out a few things that needed attention.

The last few hours had been non-stop from the moment I had woken. The tests and scans were endless. I was wheeled back into my room. The nurse that delivered me promised to return shortly with pain-relief medication. I found that my room was not empty. In a big armchair in the corner of the room, Fiona Malden sat studying a newspaper. Before I made it to the bed, Fiona started reading an article to me. "You've got to read this bullshit to believe it, Adam. Listen to this. 'It has emerged that the recent training accidents suffered by both British and American forces during military exercises off the west coast of Scotland may have been more than just freak accidents. The Ministry of Defence have refused to comment, but a reliable military source has confirmed both countries have started a witch hunt, looking for an Al Qaeda terrorist cell that has targeted the training exercise, which so far has allegedly lost three helicopters and over twenty military personnel. If these figures are correct, this will be the biggest loss of life in a military exercise since the Second World War.'"

Fiona Malden folded the paper, putting it down by her feet. "Anyway, enough of that tabloid bullshit. How are you feeling, Adam?"

I ducked the question. "Have you seen Sam or Neil Andrews? Sam was going to get Neil, and I haven't seen either of them." Fiona shook her head, so I changed direction. "Do you think you are well enough to go and get me a phone of some type?"

Fiona slowly pulled herself to her feet. "No, I probably should be in bed, but I am fitter than you, honey. I will go and see what I can drum up for you."

True to her word Fiona Malden returned with a mobile phone in her hand. "It seems your friend Neil has had all phones banned in this part of the hospital, but Nurse Cowan was naughty and ignored him. You tell me the number, and I will punch it in." I gave Fiona Malden the number for Credenhill admin. She waited until it started to ring then held the phone to my ear.

❖ ❖ ❖

Sergeant Bob Hunter was just about to leave the base. Bob had been looking forward to a spot of fishing when the duty officer summoned him to the admin building. Bob cursed under his breath. He had been minutes away from escaping the confines of the base. Bob had his fingers and toes crossed, hoping that this was not a call to assist on a job.

"Sergeant Hunter, I think it is about time for me to call in that favour you owe me."

Bob Hunter was silent for a few seconds before forming his reply. "Well, it has to be Adam Macdonald. He is the only man I know that I owe a favour to."

It was good to hear big Bob's voice. We had been through the mill together, and over the years, we had built a relationship based on comradeship and trust. "It's OK, Bob. Don't sound so worried. I'm not going to ask you to get up to any mischief. Does that expanding waistline of yours still fit into your dress uniform?"

Bob wasn't daft. He knew if it was dress uniform, it was bad. "That sounds ominous, Mac. What's the story?"

I cleared my throat trying not to let my feelings carry down the phone. "It's young Smithy, Bob. He bought it during an undercover op." I was struggling to keep my voice calm and my tears from breaking to the surface. "Smithy asked to be buried next to Sergeant Ferris, so I need yourself and half a dozen of our guys up here to lay the lad to rest in a manner befitting one of ours."

It took only milliseconds for Bob Hunter's reply. "We'll be there. Just give me the details. What a bloody sin. Smith was one of our most promising newbies. I remember the CO going nuts when he found out the spooks had grabbed him for themselves. Bloody shame."

I said my good-byes to Bob and promised to get him details about the location and time of the funeral.

Fiona Malden had sat quietly holding the phone to my ear. " Fiona, still no sign of Neil Andrews or Sam?"

Fiona switched off the phone before replying. "No, the hospital was very quiet when I was out looking for a phone. Adam, where is this guy Ian Ferris buried? I know it's none of my business, but I can't stand the thought of just a few guys going through the motions. If it's not too far away, I would like to attend the funeral."

I decided it was better to give Fiona a bit of background info rather than just the name of a place. "Ian Ferris was my sergeant during the Gulf War. When he retired, he became a gamekeeper on the Menamar estate in an area they call the Sma' Glen, south of Aberfeldy.

When I retired from the army, Ian spoke for me and managed to get the estate owner to sell me the western gatehouse to the estate. Unfortunately, Ian got mixed up with a hit man who was looking for me and was murdered by him.

We buried him on the highest point of the estate looking down on the area Ian prized most, the nesting site of his beloved golden eagles. Ian served with the SAS in many conflicts and was awarded the Victoria Cross for his actions during the Falklands War. He was and always will be an SAS legend. Smithy was one of the burial party who arrived from Hereford to honour him. It must have been then that Smithy decided he wanted to be put to rest in the same place as my friend Ian."

I shuffled to the corner of the bed and gingerly put my feet onto the cold floor. "Come on, Captain Malden, make yourself useful. I need you to be my crutch until I get my balance back."

Fiona Malden's look was one of horror. "What the hell do you think you are doing, you silly man? Sit down before you get us all into bother."

I smiled at Fiona but totally ignored her advice and started to stand up. Fiona hobbled round the bed to try and grab me. The pain came in a burning stabbing feeling from my left leg up my back and burned into the base of my skull like a branding iron. I wanted to drop to the floor and curl up in a ball. Two things stopped me—my desire to get mobile and find someone who could answer my questions. The other was one of pride. I did not want Fiona to see that she was right and that I should have followed her suggestion to sit down.

I gritted my teeth and swallowed up the waves of pain as they hit me. I groaned and stood to my full height just as Fiona Malden reached my side, helping to steady my wavering frame. "Jesus, Mac, sit down before we both land on the ground." This did nothing other than to make me redouble my efforts, and jerkily, I made my way to the door.

I was halfway across the room when the door opened. Dr Kennedy led the way followed by Neil Andrews and Dr Karen Lowe.

Dr Kennedy spotted me and charged into the room, taking the weight from Fiona Malden. Against my will, I was walked slowly backward and sat down on the edge of the bed by Dr Kennedy and Fiona Malden. Neil Andrews watched me with an amused expression on his face while an ashen Karen Lowe looked on from the door.

"Well, Mr Macdonald, I see that your director's description of you was spot on. He said you would need a lot of watching. Tell me, just where did you think you and your accomplice were off to exactly? By the way, I am Dr Kennedy, and my job is to sort you out, so a little cooperation would be appreciated. Now can we have you back in bed, please? We need to rest that badly bruised back of yours."

"All due respect, doc, I need to speak to Neil, and I don't think he will want too many people hearing what I have to tell him."

Neil Andrews sensed a Mexican standoff was not far away and intervened before Dr Kennedy found out how stubborn his patient could really be.

"Dr Kennedy, would you do me a big favour and give Dr Lowe the once-over for me while I have a word with Adam? She has had a long trip from Fort William, and I would be happier if you had a look at her gunshot wound—better safe than sorry. I promise I will get your escapee back in bed for you."

Dr Kennedy nodded and left, taking a silent Karen Lowe with him.

Andrews waited until the door was closed before continuing. "OK, Adam, the floor is all yours. Fire away."

I was going to tell what I knew but just not yet. I folded my one good arm over my pinned-up arm. "Not quite so fast. Neil. There is a deal to be struck first. Young Luke Smith wanted to be buried next to Ian Ferris. I want your word that this will happen before I kiss and tell."

I watched as the veil came down behind Neil Andrews's eyes. "We will get that sorted. Now let's hear your report, Adam."

"Just let me make one thing clear before I start. As god is my witness, if you go back on your word, Neil, director of MI6 or not, I will break both your legs." I paused for effect. "If you are thinking about ignoring my request, ask yourself—does the jaw still hurt?"

I watched as Neil Andrews's face flushed with anger, but I could see the fear in his eyes. He knew me too well.

"OK, back to business. We got jumped by a US Navy SEAL team. I overheard one of their unit call the leader 'Bartowski.' I took four of them out before my luck ran out. Gary Harding and I were loaded on board a Seahawk and were shipped out when Gary Harding committed suicide by releasing Diavokxin in the chopper. I managed to break free before I inhaled the chemical and jumped as the chopper was going down. The rest is a bad dream. What have you done with Sam?"

CHAPTER 15

ASSASSIN

Sam wandered along the huge curved structure, giving the impression of a tourist on her first visit to Charles de Gaulle Airport, lost in the architecture surrounding her.

In truth, Sam was not sure if she had picked up a tail. Charles de Gaulle was crawling with French DGSI officers, not to mention Interpol, and no doubt half the world's security services.

Sam was no fool and had visited the French capital on hundreds of occasions during the course of her career. This trip was different, but old habits die hard, and Sam did a double sweep of the waiting area before buying a magazine and plonking herself down to study the various travellers dotted around the area. Sam had ruled out two suspects when her eyes were drawn to the page in the magazine she picked up. Ironically, it was an article on illegal abortion clinics in France. Sam carefully read the first few paragraphs.

Although the morning sickness had tailed off, Sam still had problems maintaining her concentration.

Sam was furious with herself. Her mind had wandered, and she had lost sight of two passengers she was not sure about. Time was running out, and she needed to get on with it while she still could. Sam did another sweep of the terminal before deciding she was not being tailed and headed to the Hertz car rental desk to pick up her prebooked hire car.

Again Sam had to reprimand herself when she found herself marvelling at the huge curves and glasswork instead of looking for potential threats.

Sam picked up her Hertz rental car with little fuss. Her French was perfect, and the girl behind the Hertz desk complimented Sam on her fluency, adding that she thought Sam must have spent a long time in Paris to pick up local accent. Sam kept her reply short. Again, force of habit cut the conversation short. The last thing Sam needed was the girl remembering her vividly and giving a good description of her.

Sam had only driven the rental Clio for a few minutes after leaving the airport before she swung left and headed along the Avenue Jacques Daguerre. Sam turned into an industrial site filled with small works units. Sam checked the numbered units and stopped two units away from her ultimate goal.

Sam rummaged in her travel bag producing sunglasses and a baseball cap. She headed for the end unit, pulling on disposable gloves as she walked. The front door to the unit was covered by a barred metal gate. Sam, on a previous visit to the unit, had arrived early and watched Alex Dupond, the owner of the unit search for his keys. Then, when he was unable to find them, Sam watched him lift the hinged side of the iron gate clear of its mountings and swing it to the side, lock still intact.

Sam followed his actions and the gate lifted clear, leaving the locked inner door. Sam used her elbow to smash the single pane of glass. Then she climbed into the printing office.

Alex Dupond and his printing business was an MI6 front. In reality, it supplied agents who had just arrived in France with new identities and, if needed, weapons to carry out their mission.

Alex Dupond kept the local authorities sweet by printing political leaflets for all the major parties. His operation had gone on for years undetected, but his security measures were at best poor.

Sam ignored the wailing alarm and headed for the back rooms and Alex Dupond's office. The back wall of Dupond's office was dominated by a large mirror, and Sam found herself checking out her profile to see if the baby was showing yet. The wail of the intruder alarm made Sam tear herself away from the mirror and get on with the job.

Sam pushed the desk back to reveal a floor safe. Sam rummaged around in the desk drawer, coming up trumps. She inserted the big key in the safe, and with a click, it opened to reveal three Glocks and two Berettas, various boxes of shells, and two small boxes containing NLB7 nerve agent and delivery devices.

Sam emptied the contents of a gym bag she found in an office cupboard on the floor and quickly loaded the two Berettas, all the ammo, the nerve agent, and a belt containing money and throwing knives into the gym bag, followed by a couple of plastic folders. Sam deliberately steered clear of the more favourable Glocks as she had no way of telling if these had also been bugged.

Ten minutes later, Sam was on the road again headed for Dijon. En route, Sam's mind wandered back to Adam. She was desperate to find out how his recovery was going, but she knew she could not contact him. If he found out what she was about to do, he would go berserk. If she got on with it, she would be back in the UK before Adam forced Neil into sending out the search parties.

❖ ❖ ❖

Neil Andrews and Robin Alder stood outside Adam's room. Neil kept his voice low, so no one other than Alder could hear the conversation. "Tell me one more time how you managed to lose her?"

Alder could feel his cheeks flush as he tried in vain to hold his own against his boss. "Sir, I was asked to contact you, but by the time your PA had tracked you down, she was gone. Peter Kent told me to hold the fort here while he finds Sam."

Neil Andrews fought back the urge to strangle Robin Alder with his bare hands. "So, Robin, what you are telling me is that you found it necessary to tell Peter Kent about your little mistake but thought it better not to share the information with me. After all, I am only the director of MI6. Why bother me with little things like that?"

Alder wanted to reply, but he knew whatever he said would only infuriate his boss further. "Did Samantha drop any hints to you as to where she might be headed?" Again Alder was about to speak but decided a shake of the head would probably do the least damage.

I could hear the murmur of voices in the corridor, and despite Fiona Malden's attempts to make me sit on my butt, I was up again and grimaced my way to the door trying to put the pain in my back to the back of my mind.

Outside, I found Robin Alder and Neil Andrews. I could tell the minute I saw Neil Andrews's face that something was afoot. "Well, well. If it isn't Batman and Robin in the flesh. The dynamic duo, so to speak. Neil, you need to contact Menamar estates in Perthshire about the funeral arrangements. The man you are looking for is Kiron Al Ahdal. He is the estate owner. I don't think you will have any problems. He is a nice bloke."

I had been watching Neil Andrews as I spoke to him, and a strange expression had come over him as I talked about the funeral. "Kiron Al Ahdal. Tell me, is he a Saudi Arabian who studied at Cambridge, do you know?"

I was still looking at the amazed look on Neil's face. "I am not sure of his nationality, but the last time I spoke to him I did notice he was wearing a Cambridge tie, if that helps."

"Good god, Adam. Talk about coincidences. Kiron was my roommate when I was at Cambridge, before the secret service got their teeth into me. It must be him. There can't be many men with names like that who went to Cambridge."

Fiona Malden appeared by my side. "Come on, Adam. Back to bed. The director is going to sort out the funeral arrangements, and you need to do your bit if you are going to be fit enough to travel to the funeral."

Neil Andrews closed the door to Dr Kennedy's office, unlocked his briefcase, and placed a small laptop on the desk. He switched it on, watched it boot up, then he punched in a code number, and waited. It took a few minutes for the prime minister's staff to extricate the prime minister from a function he was hosting. Andrews watched as the PM made himself comfortable in front of his matching laptop.

"Good evening, Prime Minister. How can I help you, sir?"

Even on the small laptop screen, Neil Andrews could tell that the PM was in a more relaxed state than he had seen him for some time. "Andrews, I spoke to the president this afternoon. The Americans have the Vokxin and

Diavokxin under lock and key. It would appear that Colonel David Southern was acting out without the authorization of the White House and has been detained pending a court-martial for his actions. The president has placed Special Agent Bruce Ellis in charge of American affairs in the UK and has asked our help in clearing up Southern's mess, as well as helping them gather evidence for his court-martial. Bruce Ellis will also be heading up a team of CIA and NSA officers. It would appear the cyber attack on American communications is possibly coming from the UK, Ireland, or Iceland. I want you to give him any assistance required, as both our countries have bridges to mend."

❖ ❖ ❖

Bruce Ellis was shown to the second door of the two-cell block located within the main structure of the Machrihanish Air Base main complex. It took a few seconds for his eyes to become accustomed to the gloomy surroundings of the cell, which had no natural light and relied on a solitary low-wattage bulb for illumination.

Colonel David Southern stood in the corner of the room, decked out in his full dress military uniform. "Good evening, Colonel. I trust you are being treated well?"

Southern scowled at Ellis before replying to his question. "Tell me, pretty boy, when the Russkies were knocking on our back door, and you were still running around in diapers, who do you think had your back covered? And this is what I get as a reward. Son, sometimes you got to stretch the rules if you want to come out on top. So if a few unfortunates get hurt in the process, that's life, buddy. If we want America to remain the number-one superpower, someone like me has got to make the hard decisions. And to answer your question, no, I am not being treated well. God damn it, I'm the project leader, not the criminal."

Bruce Ellis could feel his blood pressure increasing. He had never been a David Southern fan but the longer he knew him, the more he despised him.

"Colonel Southern, the sad thing about that little propaganda speech of yours is that you actually believe the shit you are shovelling. You are going home to a court-martial. You can look each and every relative of the American servicemen you condemned to death by your actions in the eye and tell them that. They won't need to put you in jail for the rest of your life. They will tear you apart with their bare hands.

The game's over, Colonel. Luckily I had a chat with the flight controller who scheduled the flight of Colonel Cussack. He has given a statement confirming your hidden agenda. When the president found out the truth, he placed me in charge of winding down this op. You better get used to this type of accommodation because you will spend the rest of your life in it."

Southern stared directly into the eyes of Bruce Ellis. "I am sure you would love that, son, but it's not going to happen. You have my word on that."

Ellis turned and walked out. He was finished wasting his breath on the man. Ellis walked past the guard by the door as his eye caught sight of his side arm holster. It was empty!

A single shot came from Southern's room.

It was over. Ellis found the colonel's body in the corner, his lifeless eyes staring upward. Colonel David Southern had kept his word and found the only way out—taking his own life, preferring to be judged by a higher authority.

❖ ❖ ❖

Sam stood naked in front of the full-length mirror in her bedroom. She had filled out, and her ribs were no longer visible. She was not sure about her tummy. It seemed a bit swollen, but even a trained eye would find it hard to say for sure she was pregnant. Sam was tired. She had been travelling all day, stopping at Dijon that night to recharge her batteries for the next day's travel. Madame Dubois, the landlady of the bed and breakfast, had supplied Sam with an ironing board and iron. Sam waited for the iron to heat up so she could finish her preparations before hitting the sack for the night. Sam pulled on a baggy T-shirt and collapsed on the bed as the iron was taking an age to heat up.

Sam's mind wandered from pillar to post, changing moods on the way. She wondered how Adam was and longed to phone the hospital for an update.

Only her secret service training stopped her. She was jealous that the pilot Fiona got to sit and comfort him while she was here. Then the darkness and fury returned. There was one person who had gone unpunished for his part in this bloodbath.

Sam knew, left up to her superiors in MI6, they would find a way to forgive this animal.

If Sam was to deal with Karl Muller, she was going to have to do it on her own and now, while she was still fit enough to carry off the operation without giving birth in the process. Sam knew the risks involved. If Muller had replaced the bodyguards that Smithy had dispatched, it would be a formidable task to get to Muller. Sam mulled over the problem. She couldn't fake her way into the castle. Muller knew her face. To walk in the front door would be nothing less than suicide. A hiss from the iron told Sam that the iron had eventually reached a workable temperature. Sam removed a secret compartment of her purse and laid out on the bed half a dozen passport-sized snaps of herself. She unclipped a plastic folder that had been removed from the printers and laid out three half-finished identity cards. She inserted three of her pictures and folded the open plastic covers over the photos, using the iron to seal and shrink the cards until they became perfect copies of the real thing. One was a normal Swiss driving license for a thirty-year-old called Rhona. The second was for an inspector in the French DGSI, and the third was for an agent of the Swiss FIS. Sam studied the workmanship of the cards before placing them back in the hidden compartment of her purse. Sam stripped, rebuilt, and checked the action of the Berettas before finally getting her head down for the night.

At first, although Sam was dead on her feet, sleep would not come. The words Adam had drilled into her kept popping into her weary head. "Fail to prepare, prepare to fail." Sam's thoughts turned back to Adam and the first time Sam had kissed Adam. It was Christmas Day on the beach in front of her beloved glass house, under the seaweed Sam had held up, declaring that it was mistletoe. Sam fell asleep thinking of this moment with a smile on her lips.

❖ ❖ ❖

Peter Kent watched as Neil Andrews walked from the hospital reception to the waiting, chauffeur-driven, armoured Jaguar that had arrived to take Neil Andrews to the airport. Once more Neil Andrews had proved that the only person he really cared about was himself. His new job had been secured, and although a trail of destruction littered his native country, he was hotfooting it back to the seat of power in Westminster without a thought for the people he had talked into getting involved in the mission.

Peter Kent watched the Jaguar leave, then turned and headed to Adam Macdonald's room.

Fiona Malden was trying her best to convince me Sam would be here shortly. Karen Lowe was sitting on the end of my bed and had joined forces with Fiona. "Don't worry, Adam. Neil Andrews will have her filling in paper work or something, you'll see."

Just at that, the door opened, and we were joined by Peter Kent. "Well, I'm sure you will be glad to hear that our leader has just departed for London."

Peter was smiling as he said it, but I was not in the same frame of mind. "Peter, I need you to tell me two things. Cut the bull, and tell me the truth. Where has Sam gone? And has Andrews sorted the details for Smithy's funeral?"

Peter's smile vanished. He must have known the question had to come but it did not make the answer any more palatable. Kent sat down in the corner of the room as he slackened his tie. "No point beating about the bush. Adam, she has vanished. I don't need to tell you how good she is at that. I traced the cab she took from here to Glasgow Airport where she got a BA flight to Heathrow, but she vanished at Heathrow. I have three analysts going through the CCTV footage, but I am pretty sure they won't find her."

Peter Kent and I didn't agree about many things, but he was right this time. I had watched Sam, and she was a pro. If she didn't want to be found, she wouldn't be.

Peter Kent continued. "Slightly better news about the funeral. I did hear him on the blower to a guy called Kiron, and he mentioned Smithy, so I take it they were talking about the funeral. They were on the phone for ages. It was the first time for a long time that our boss smiled. He seemed to be reliving old memories, but I think the funeral is fine although I have no idea when. Listen, Adam, the real reason I popped in was just to tell you that Robin and myself are leaving. Neil wants us to help the Yanks find their rogue radio hacker. If I hear about the funeral or Sam, I will get a message to you."

I awoke the next morning to find my two girlfriends, Fiona and Karen, already in my room and getting ready to try and feed me my breakfast. I was grateful that although both girls had been wounded, they still felt the need to help me. I had a guilty conscience. I really just wanted to be left alone. The fact that we had lost Smithy and Gary was just starting to sink in, and my actual girlfriend had decided for some reason to abandon me. I was busy trying to think through what Sam might be up to when Fiona Malden interrupted my train of thought.

"Adam Macdonald, you have been holding the same spoonful of cereal in your hand for the last five minutes. If you don't hurry up, Karen and I will feed you like a baby."

Karen Lowe joined in, trying to lighten the mood. "Adam, tell us about the man Smithy wants to be buried next to. Why did he want that?"

I pushed away my breakfast tray with my good arm, gathering my thoughts on Ian Ferris. "I have already told Fiona a bit about Ian, He joined the Argyll and Sutherland Highlanders and then he was selected for the Special Air Service. He had distinguished himself in more than a few conflicts before the Falklands came along, but Ian became a Special Forces legend during the Falklands conflict. He was given the task of taking an Argentinean gun emplacement, but during the skirmish, his unit ran out of ammo, a problem endured by the majority of the army. Not wanting to let the enemy know the ammunition situation, Ian Ferris led his men into the gun emplacement where he fought hand to hand with an Argentine sergeant. Although he had been shot, he managed to overpower the enemy sergeant, shooting him with his own pistol, then shooting the machine gunner, allowing his men to overrun the position, capturing the rest of the gun crew in the process. Ian was awarded the highest military decoration for his bravery, the Victoria Cross. He was about to retire when the Gulf War came along, and I was put in charge of his team. Ian and I became friends, and after I retired, Ian looked out for me, getting me a house close by to the estate he worked for. I got mixed up last year with some bad people, and one of them traced me to the estate, where they killed Ian and almost killed Sam and me."

I paused, remembering the moment. "We buried Ian on the hill overlooking the estate. I did not notice at the time, but it must have had a profound impact on Smithy who formed part of the burial detail. Not a bad place to be buried. I might end up there myself one day. You never know."

I was about to lapse back into my own little world, but Karen Lowe was having none of it. "So what about you, Adam. Do you have family?"

I was not prepared for that question. It had caught me off guard. "Yes, but we don't keep in touch. We have gone our own ways."

Karen was staring at me, waiting for me to continue, while Fiona made her way to the big armchair and lowered herself into slowly before joining in on my interrogation. "Come on, Adam. You can't leave Karen hanging like that. Spill the beans, man."

It was clear to see I had been backed into a corner with no manoeuvre. "Do you girls not have examinations to get, or some type of physiotherapy? Don't let me detain you."

Fiona Malden shot a sideways glance at Karen Lowe before continuing her verbal assault. "Nice try, Captain, but you have got us curious, so please continue. Our treatment can wait."

I sighed and sat back against the pillow Karen had just fluffed up for me. "OK, I can see I am going to get no peace until I tell you. My mother died when I was twelve, and my father brought myself and my younger brother up by himself, or at least he paid for the boarding school. The last time I set eyes on either of them was at my brother's wedding. Paul, my brother, could sell sand to the Arabs, and the last I knew he was selling thermal insulation door to door. He blamed me for ruining his wedding. That is why we went our own ways. The reason I ruined his wedding is because I knocked out my father before the wedding started, and it put a damper on things. So there you have it."

I thought I had got away with it until after a few silent seconds, Karen asked the six-million-dollar question. "So what caused the fight with your father?"

I felt that I had to justify myself to the girls. "There are a couple of things you need to know that had just happened to me. I was stationed in Northern Ireland working undercover and had just witnessed the death of the girl agent I was working with. My head was not in a good place. My father approached me and started giving me an earful about my appearance. In Ireland, you had to fit in, and I was scruffy for a reason. I decided to let my father know that it was not disrespect and that I was working undercover. My father took it the wrong way, which in hindsight was not unexpected, taking into account that he was a Church of Scotland minister. To my horror, he started ranting about the devil's work the British were doing in Ireland." I shifted uncomfortably in my bed. "That was like a red rag to a bull, and the red mist descended. We ended up screaming at each other outside his church door. I told him to back off as I had just lost my friend and colleague and was not in the mood for it. Then he went too far. He suggested that it was god's will that Mary was killed, and she had it coming to her."

I could remember the moment so clearly, feel the anger even now. "I went off like Vesuvius. My left uppercut hit him right under the jaw. That was the last time he ever saw me. I can remember standing over him as the congregation poured out of the church. I was screaming at his unconscious body, 'That was god's will too, you hypocritical old bastard!' So you see, I don't think they will be in a mad rush to see me again."

❖ ❖ ❖

Sam tucked into her second pain au chocolat as she mentally ticked off her to-do list before reaching her target in Switzerland later that day. Madame Dubois placed a third pain au chocolat in front of Sam. Normally, Sam would have refused all three, but this morning she was ravenous and becoming strangely attached to the French delicacy. After she washed down all three pastries with strong sweet coffee, Sam was ready for the road and her assault on Switzerland.

Sam crossed the border unchecked and headed for a motel on the outskirts of Basel. The receptionist took little notice of Sam as she recorded the details of the Swiss driving license Sam had given her as identification for the week's rent of the room that had been booked in advance.

Sam had decided although this type of operation, done correctly, could take months to set up, she would give herself just one week to complete the mission and get herself out of Switzerland.

Sam was not one for the grass growing under her feet, and after sorting her accommodation, she headed into Basel where she dropped her hire car and continued on foot to Nauenstrasse on the opposite side of the city from her hotel. Sam had decided to swap her hire car for a local vehicle from Europcar.

It would draw less attention than a French hire car and throw the local police of her tail long enough for her to get out of Switzerland. Sam watched as the girl checked her driving license and confirmed the address that MI6 had placed in the system. Sam had no intention of handing over a credit card for security of the vehicle. It was a far too convenient way to be traced, and Sam did not want to announce to the world she was in Basel. The young girl was trying to tell Sam she could not continue with the hire, but Sam was having none of it. She produced a fistful of notes, declaring that her cards had been stolen and that until they were replaced, she was dealing with cash only. A quick visit to the manager's office produced the result Sam was hoping for, and twenty minutes later, Sam left the forecourt, her identity still hidden. Sam pushed the BMW she had hired hard. She wanted a quick reccie of the gun dealer's stronghold before heading back to her hotel.

Sam pulled up at the road end to the castle and was checking the area for CCTV cameras when the little delivery van appeared from the direction of the castle.

Sam's gut instinct kicked in, and she stepped out into the road, holding up her hand for the little van to stop. As Sam walked round to the driver's side, she could see that it was a young girl who was driving. Sam produced the FIS identity card and waved it in the girl's face. The girl was already pale but lost more of her colour when she saw who had stopped her. "Please step out of the vehicle. You will accompany me to my vehicle where I have some questions for you." Sam led the girl to her BMW, placed her in the passenger seat, then joined her in the car.

Before Sam could speak, the girl launched into conversation. "Is this about Mae Ling? She has left you know. After the incident, she couldn't work. Her nerves are gone. Those animals need to be taught a lesson. Are you going to question them? Because if you are, you better take a gun and a big dog with you, Acussa scumbags!"

Sam had come across the Acussa before in her travels. The Hong Kong commissioner had called in MI6 many years ago to try and stop the Triad splinter group, the Acussa, who were systematically taking over the country's black market. Sam had been working with Peter Kent at the time. They had managed to get a mole into the Acussa in the form of a young prostitute. The plan had been to let the girl feed information back to them. She had been picked because she was the younger sister of a murdered rival gang leader. The plan had worked until the girl had managed to tease her way into the bed of the Acussa warlord. They found him tied to his mirrored bed, cut to ribbons with a razor blade. They found the girl in the toilet. She had run a bath and cut her own wrists before the Acussa could deal with her.

Sam listened as the girl described how her friend had been held against her will and gang-raped before being dumped by the roadside to find her way back to Basel. Her boss, who was also her uncle, had demanded the police take action, but it seemed that Karl Muller and his new bodyguards were untouchable.

After the girl's abduction, her uncle, the owner of the Hungry Dragon, had refused to serve or deliver food to the gun dealer or his men. Kara, the young delivery driver, was almost in tears as she explained how her boss had been taken round to the back of his business and beaten to within an inch of his life and then told that his wife would be next if he missed even one delivery. Sam's temper and her blood pressure started to boil as she remembered how close she had come to suffering the same fate as Mae Ling.

"Kara, can you tell me how many of the Acussa stay at the castle?"

The young girl wiped away a tear and sat for a few seconds thinking. "I'm not sure. Usually, two of them meet me at the door. After Mae Ling, my boss told me to leave food at the door and get away as quickly as possible. I normally see two of them, but I did see one by the big helicopter, and they have a servant man, but he is not Acussa. I am sorry that is all I can tell you, madame."

Sam thought for a second. "Kara, how often do you deliver to the Acussa?"

"Mostly every second day, but sometimes more at weekends. I will be back tomorrow. They always order on Fridays."

Sam weighed up what she had just been told before deciding on her next course of action. "OK, Kara. I will meet you here tomorrow. This is a covert mission, so you cannot tell anyone, and that includes your boss. Do you understand?"

Back at her hotel, Sam ordered room service. The fewer people who saw her, the better, and Sam was not in the mood to socialise that evening. Mae Ling's fate had got to Sam. Deep down, she knew it was more to do with the fact she had almost suffered the same fate, but poor Mae Ling hadn't had Adam or Smithy to help her. She was missing Adam and worried about his injuries. It would appear that Karl Muller could pull strings with his Swiss hosts as well as literally get away with murdering British agents. Sam slept badly that night. She was not stupid. She knew she had bitten off more than she could chew, but she was damned if she would let that jackal and his scum-bags sit in his castle on the hill and get away with it.

Sam watched every hour pass as she waited for the evening and the food delivery of the Hungry Dragon. Sam had only been parked up for twenty minutes when the little van pulled up behind her BMW. A wide-eyed Kara approached the back of the BMW.

Sam jumped out to greet the young woman. "OK, Kara, here is what I need you to do. I need your jacket and baseball cap. I am going to do the delivery tonight. You are going to lock yourself in the BMW and listen to the radio for half an hour." Kara nodded but said nothing. Sam could tell she was scared out of her mind. "Tell me, Kara, how do they pay for the food? Do I need to collect money?"

Kara shook her head as she watched Sam pulling on her bright orange jacket. "No, they pay over the phone when they order. Just drop the food and run. That is what I do."

Sam pulled her blond ponytail through the back of the baseball cap and put on a pair of glasses with clear lenses to change her appearance slightly. Sam studied herself in the wing mirror of the BMW before heading off. The jacket was one size too small, which made Sam's chest more prominent. Sam decided that was fine. It might distract her Asian friends.

Sam made sure Kara had the car keys and was locked in safely before jumping in the micro van and heading up to the castle.

Sam parked the van far too close to the helicopter for comfort—deliberately to evoke a response from the castle inhabitants—before jumping out and strolling toward the main door.

Halfway across the large courtyard the main doors sprang open and two large Asian gentlemen wearing white T-shirts with "Security" emblazoned on them met Sam just before she reached the foot of the stairs leading to the front doors.

Sam was not sure what if any other languages they spoke but opened up the conversation in French. "Nice tattoos, guys. They must have cost a fortune, not to mention a bit of pain!" Sam watched as her two thugs were caught off guard for a second. The bigger of the two recovered first, peeling back his T-shirt sleeve over his huge overdeveloped bicep to reveal a naked woman draped over his shoulder. "I like this one, blondie. What do you think?"

Sam knew they were watching her to judge her reaction. She pushed a carrier bag of food at each of them as she replied, "Six meals as requested, chef put extra bean sprouts in for the six of you. I have put in six pairs of chopsticks. Will that be enough?"

Sam was aware of the second Acussa trying to manoeuvre himself behind her and altered her position so she could deal with him if required.

"Tell me, blondie. Did Mae Ling tell you she joined us for dinner? Would you like to join us?"

The second Acussa was running his fingers through Sam's ponytail, and Sam could sense the danger. "Sorry, my tattooed friend, but you do not get to touch the merchandise." Sam ducked under the arm of the second Acussa and started walking backward toward the van, keeping an eye on the two thugs. It had taken all Sam's self control to stop her from breaking the Acussa's arm when he touched her. "I do not know who Mae Ling is. I just started today. Catch you later, guys."

Sam had chanced her luck and did not want to push any further. Time to get out while she still could.

On the way back down the hill, Sam drove slowly, mapping out the terrain around the castle approach road. Back at the BMW, Kara was overjoyed to see the safe return of Sam. "Kara, to your knowledge, have the Acussa ever ordered any more than six potions?"

Kara thought for a second, her face etched with concentration. "Madame, I think you may be correct. I can never recall more than that."

Sam thanked the young girl, reminding her not to breathe a word of this to anyone, not even her parents.

As Sam headed back to her hotel, she was deep in thought. Normally, this would just be the start of a MI6 operation. Initial contact would be followed up by eavesdropping on the target, gathering local info on the target, plus any other information that could be dug up through other friendly intelligence agencies, followed by weeks of surveillance documenting the target's movements. Sam had given herself a week. She had no backup, and she could not talk to any other agencies because she knew most of them used Karl Muller to supply them with weapons and information on their enemies. Just like her boss, they would not lift a finger to help her.

Sam was up bright and early, and after a breakfast spent gorging on fresh fruit, Sam headed to the local Internet café where she ordered a café latte and croissant while she busied herself, first checking the location on the west side of the Hungry Dragon. Having noted this, she tucked into her croissant while she surfed the net for any information regarding Operation Pandora and the resulting aftermath.

Sam came up with only a few things that she already knew. Only conspiracy theories floated about regarding the military exercises. Sam concluded the only way she was going to find out what was happening back in the UK was to finish the job she had come here to do and head back to Scotland and Adam.

Sam spent the afternoon shopping for some very specific clothing. No matter how hard she tried, she found herself studying the shop mirrors to see if her tummy had changed in any way. It was early evening when Sam strolled into the Hungry Dragon. As well as the delivery service, the Hungry Dragon had a busy but well-organised restaurant. Sam ordered a meal while she watched the comings and goings of the restaurant staff. By the time Sam had finished her main course, her bladder was telling her there was no room for a big meal, a baby, and a bladder. Something had to give, and Sam made her way down a narrow corridor to the toilets. En route, Sam found what she was looking for hanging on a coat peg next to the customers' coats. Sam had a quick check to make sure no one was looking and stuffed the bright orange jacket and baseball cap in her handbag and continued on her way to the toilet.

An hour later, Sam had parked the rental BMW some distance away and pulled the rucksack over her black Gore-Tex hooded jacket. Sam tucked one of the knives in her belt and checked the action of her Beretta before sliding a newly loaded magazine into the handle. She loaded the Beretta into the rucksack and headed up a wooded trail that would take her close to the back of the castle grounds. Sam had no plans for an assault yet, but she needed to do a bit more reconnaissance before she finalised her full-on attack plan.

Sam had clicked the timer on her wristwatch as she had set off. She stopped after some time, checking the raised woodland to her right. Sam had checked local maps on the Internet and knew that the path was at its highest point closest to the castle. The path dropped away to the left, eventually finding its way to a series of waterfalls that were popular with the locals and tourists who used the area for the sport of canyoning.

Sam slowly worked her way up a small rock face, stopping only a few feet from the top to work out how high she had climbed. She was surprised to find she was over twenty feet up. For a fleeting second, Sam lost concentration, thinking of what would happen to the baby if she lost her footing and fell from this height. She pulled herself together and climbed the last few feet, rolling over the top but remaining on her stomach. She knew from the maps she had only about fifty metres of cut meadow to the walls of the old castle. To Sam's right, the grass tapered away to nothing as the wall of the back of the castle merged into the southern part of the rock Sam had just climbed. It was impassable and had obviously been built there for that very reason.

Sam watched for movement near the castle. Sure enough, one of the Acussa guards strolled past, not looking at anything in particular. Sam had waited until dusk for this very reason. Her black clothing merged with the shadows and acted like an invisible cloak. Sam waited until he had vanished round the corner and legged it across the grass, dropping behind a stone balustrade before vaulting over onto a raised stone courtyard. Sam followed the contour of the building round until she came to her first window. A quick look inside found the window was at the end of a hall. It had double-lock bolts at either side, and Sam concluded the only way in was to smash it. Sam was halfway around the wall to the next window when she heard the muffled footsteps coming her way. Sam pressed herself against the wall and sank back into the evening shadows. Sam stood next to a black drainpipe and held her breath, not daring to move as the Acussa walked past, his white T-shirt standing out against the gloom of the evening. He turned without looking in Sam's direction and headed back while Sam consulted her wrist-watch again.

The second window revealed the kitchen, and as Sam watched from the partial darkness, the butler Sam had met previously walked into the kitchen. Sam watched with interest as he removed his suit jacket, revealing a shoulder holster that sported a Glock and second magazine. It would appear the butler was more than just a butler.

Sam traced her footsteps back into the undergrowth and worked her way slowly clockwise toward the front of the building. She checked for trip wires and infrared beams, but there were none. Sam concluded that the wildlife around the castle would cause too many false alarms, and Karl Muller instead had put his faith in his gangland bodyguards. Sam had made her way to almost the front of the castle and was held up in the undergrowth just behind Karl Muller's Bell helicopter. She was about to change her position when she heard the Acussa guard making his way across the forecourt, heading in her general direction. Sam held her breath. Her fingers rested on the hilt of her knife as she watched the tattooed figure open the side door of the helicopter and reach inside, reappearing with a six-pack of bottled lager.

Sam watched as he pulled the top off with his teeth and spat the cap into the undergrowth, glancing back at the castle door to make sure his guilty secret was not discovered.

Sam checked around her feet to find the forest floor littered with bottle tops. Sam waited until her lager-drinking guard had finished his bottle and had returned to his patrol around the castle grounds. Sam had seen enough for the evening, and as the guard had headed to the back of the castle, Sam, after grabbing one of the lager tops, took the opportunity to leave by the front drive. Since Sam had arrived, the light had completely gone, and Sam did not fancy finding her way down the rock face in the dark.

It was getting late, and Sam was fairly confident she could get back to the main road using the drive without being discovered by anyone visiting the castle. Sam was five minutes from the castle when she heard the sound of the helicopter. It would appear Sam had been wrong. Someone was just about to arrive at the castle and judging by the time of night they wanted to do it on the QT.

Sam turned and sprinted back up the road slowing to a crawl as she made her way into the undergrowth again opposite the main doors. She was just in time to see an Asian man and his chopper pilot enter the front door ushered in by Muller's trusty butler.

Sam cursed that she did not have a camera with her. She had never seen the man before, but she was sure his presence here at this late-hour meeting with Karl Muller was a sinister development. Sam wondered if she had just been the first MI6 agent to lay eyes on Al Qaeda's second in command, Khanjar.

Sam's intuitive decision to turn back paid dividends, as if on cue, six Acussa, led by the big guy Sam had spoken to, made their way out the front door, taking up positions around the perimeter of the house. Sam was fairly sure this was the full team sent out to enforce a secure perimeter for their guest, even more proof that whoever the Asian gentleman was, he was important.

Sam waited until the closest Acussa took itchy feet and wandered across to his mate for a chin-wag before she very slowly edged away from the house. Sam was aided by a rain shower, which covered a lot of the noise as she made her way slowly through the undergrowth, getting well clear of the castle before joining the road.

❖ ❖ ❖

Karl Muller could tell that Khanjar was not his usual calm and collected self. He noted also that his bodyguard was not his usual one. Muller was on his guard, as he had not requested the meeting. Khanjar had insisted that it happen now, leaving Muller quaking in his boots.

Had Khanjar found out that it was he who had informed on his son? Muller mulled over the idea of handing over Khanjar to the Americans. He wondered how much the Americans were willing to spend to apprehend the Al Qaeda second in command. He could kill two birds with one stone, so to speak.

After a few seconds, he dismissed the idea. If he was found out, which he almost certainly would be, there would be no corner of the planet that Al Qaeda would not turn over looking for him.

"Good evening. I trust your flight went well?"

Khanjar was not in the mood for small talk and wasted no time coming to the point. "My friend, I would like to purchase more of the Russian limpet mines that you supplied me with previously. I would need them delivered to the same address as before, but I need them very quickly."

Karl Muller tried to keep the excitement out of his voice. He needed to play it cool, but he knew he had struck the jackpot. "You will be glad to hear I have the perfect thing for you. I have just purchased—at great expense—two cases of state-of-the-art, American-made limpet mines. They have the strongest magnets known to man and contain two pounds of hyper-weapons-grade plastic explosive, twenty times more powerful than C4. One mine is the size of a cola can but is capable of sinking a battleship. One placed on the hull of a tank will completely destroy it."

Karl Muller did not wait for a reply and wheeled himself away from the desk. Pulling the doors open of a wall cabinet. He removed a can of cola from a wooden box and tossed it across the room, forcing Khanjar to catch it.

Khanjar looked at the can in disbelief while Muller chuckled at his bemused expression. "I had the Coca-Cola artwork done myself, had to glue the ring pulls on, but unless you pick one up and feel the weight, you would never know." Muller returned to his desk. "I have no problem with credit. Feel free to take them with you."

Khanjar placed the limpet mine on the desk and studied it before replying. "I see, my friend, we have come to the evil part of the deal, where you once again try to empty my organisation's wallet. Very well. How much? But you must include delivery in the price. I do not want to run the risk of being found with them."

Muller ran his hand over his chin trying to decide how much to charge. "These are no ordinary mines. I had to go to great lengths to acquire them from my American contacts. I can deliver them to your address. They can be detonated by timer. Simply turn the base ninety degrees in any direction. The timers are set for ten minutes. Beware. Once placed on a metal surface, they will detonate instantly if removed. I will also supply you with a satellite phone so you can detonate them remotely from any place in the world. My price to you is four million US dollars."

Khanjar winced at the price. He had paid two hundred thousand dollars for the limpet mines that he had used previously, but he knew in his heart he could not refuse. His plan depended on having the mines ready to use that week, or it would not work. "You drive a hard bargain, my friend, but time is not on my side so I will send one of my men with the money. Please arrange it so."

Muller could not help himself. If he could find out what Khanjar was up to he could add another million to his profits. "So I take it you are going to sink the British fleet with your purchase, or do you fancy attaching them to the prime minister's Jaguar?"

Khanjar regarded his guest with cold eyes. "If I were a sailor, I wouldn't want to be on a navy ship in Devonport any time soon." Khanjar made eye contact with Muller before he swept out of the room heading for his helicopter.

Khanjar watched from the co-pilot's seat as the helicopter cleared the top turrets of the castle then swung north headed for a refuelling stop in the North of France before hoping over the channel. Khanjar had drafted in his younger brother as he was running low on skilled men. His brother Hani was a military pilot who had seen many hours of conflict in the Middle East.

"Well, little one, we have been given the tools to deal the British forces a knockout blow. I will give them the ultimatum. Release my son, or pay a terrible price."

Hani checked his altimeter before speaking. "Brother, are you sure that they will not find our man?"

Khanjar was smiling at his younger brother. "Do you not know me, brother? I have hinted that the special mines are to be used in Devonport against the navy. I have a hunch that my friend Muller will sell this info to the British, who will increase the security around their ships. They may take their eye off the ball. If they reduce the security around their scrapped nuclear subs, nine of which still contain nuclear fuel rods, it will help Magdi who has clearance to enter with his company to carry out routine maintenance to the mothballed submarines. With reduced security, he will place the mines on the hulls of the nine submarines while they search the active navy ships for our mines. If this comes to pass, it will also confirm that Muller was the leak who caused the capture of my son. Brother, I swear if this happens, I will return to Switzerland and make the traitor watch while I cut his heart out."

Hani was looking across at his big brother. "Brother, you do know that if your plan succeeds, everybody in the Plymouth area will be contaminated with radioactive waste, including Magdi."

Khanjar shrugged his shoulders in reply to Hani's question. "If that comes to pass, Magdi will join our heroes in dying for our cause. It is a plan that our leader is aware of and fully supports."

❖ ❖ ❖

Back in her hotel room, Sam was putting the final touches to her plan. She had decided to wait for a couple of days and do a bit more reconnaissance. She had just packed her stuff away and was running a shower when there was a knock at her door. Sam dived across the bed and removed a Beretta from under the pillow tucking it in her dressing gown before approaching the door with caution. Sam peered out of the peephole in the door. Her heart jumped into her mouth.

Sam was still in shock as the voice from the other side of the door confirmed she was not hallucinating. “Come on, Sam. Open up so you can pour me a coffee.”

Sam opened the door, and Bruce Ellis walked into the room. “Hello, Samantha. I think we need to have a friendly chat while you make the coffee.”

Sam resigned herself to the fact that she had been caught red-handed. “Not before you tell how the hell you found me.”

“Come on, Sam. You are dealing with the CIA. One of our analysts at Langley spotted you on CCTV. You see, although I have been put in charge of European ops, I still head the team looking for Bin Laden. They picked up chatter that something was going down in Switzerland. So they stepped up surveillance and found the lovely Samantha wandering about Basel. Now I have told my story, and it’s time for you to come to the party. What has Neil Andrews got you doing for him in Switzerland? Or do I need to call him and ask him?”

Sam made it up as she went along. The best lies were always partially true, so Sam decided to distort the truth rather than offer an out-and-out lie. “You will have heard that our handguns were fitted with a transponder. I am here to find out who put Karl Muller up to it. That is all.”

Bruce Ellis mulled this around in his head for a while before coming to a conclusion. “So why are you here on your own? Where is your team?”

Sam had been waiting for this question. “Neil Andrews doesn’t trust anyone. He wants me to find out what I can on my own, just in case we have a leak at MI6.”

Bruce Ellis relaxed a little. Sam’s story was working. “OK, Sam. Here is my burner phone number. Word has it Khanjar may be in town. You let me know if you spot him. I will be in town for a couple of days. Buy you lunch tomorrow, and we can compare notes.”

Sam showed Ellis out. Her head was pounding, her plan was in tatters, and if Ellis contacted Neil Andrews, the game was over.

Sam woke around six. She was not going to let this latest setback stop her. She was under no illusion that Bruce Ellis was going take her word on the situation or that he was going to trust a lunch date. He was CIA. Sam knew the minute she stepped out of the hotel she would be followed by a team of CIA agents and tailed everywhere she went. Bruce Ellis would not allow her to assassinate Karl Muller, not when he knew who Khanjar was.

Sam had other ideas, and by seven, she was packed and out of the room. She did not cancel the room even although she knew she was not coming back. For sure, the CIA would check to see if she had checked out. Sam drove the BMW through morning rush-hour traffic, noting that the cars two and three back followed the same route. Sam parked the BMW in a shopping centre car park and dropped the keys down a drain. She had watched as her two target cars had driven past. Sam legged it with her holdall out the emergency exit and straight into a waiting cab. She watched with amusement as one car had stopped by the exit and its driver and passenger were walking along the pavement while tyres squealing could be heard from inside the car park as the second tail attempted to get out onto the road in a hurry.

Sam gave the two men a little wave as the taxi pulled away.

Four streets away, Sam stopped the taxi driver and paid him handsomely, asking him to go to the airport to pick up her husband. She explained to him she had a lawyer's appointment and couldn't accompany him. The driver couldn't have earned that money in a week and eagerly took down the fictitious name and flight Sam gave him. Sam watched as the taxi sped off to the airport, knowing the Americans had the cab number and would have it tracked to the airport. Sam pulled on specs, a baseball cap, and a black hoodie and worked her way through the streets, trying to avoid CCTV cameras. Ten minutes later, she was reunited with her little Renault. Sam sped off, away from the city, watching for more tails but after half an hour's driving, she was confident for the moment she had shaken off her American tail.

It was time for Sam to do a bit of shopping. First stop was a charity clothes shop where Sam bought and changed into a flower-pattern dress and raincoat. Removing all her makeup and putting her hair up in a bun made Sam look like a fifty-year-old schoolteacher. Sam headed for an off-license where she purchased a six-pack of beer. Then she went to a local garage where she bought a petrol can, a gallon of petrol, and some sandwiches. Sam had time to kill, and she wanted to stay well away from Basel and Muller's castle. Sam pointed the Renault south, heading for a quiet spot she knew from previous trips to Switzerland.

Sam set a steady pace, not wanting to draw attention to herself, stopping at a café to make a call to Fred—an acquaintance she had made on previous trips. Sam had contacted him from Heathrow, but now she had to change her plans. After a few nervous minutes, the phone was answered. "Hi, Fred! It's the girl with no name. How are we today?"

Fred reacted as if Sam were his long-lost niece. "Ah, my favourite girl! Your flight is all arranged. We leave at ten, three days from now, my pretty one."

Sam put on her pleading voice. "Fred, I don't know what I would do without you, but I have a big problem. The photo shoot has changed again, and I need to be in London by tomorrow afternoon. You couldn't be a darling and see if we can get a flight for early tomorrow morning?"

Fred tutted down the phone, but Sam knew he was teasing her. "Oh, I think as it is you, I can rustle up something. It may cost you a bottle of schnapps for the flight coordinator, but I will work on him, and if that doesn't work, he is my brother-in-law. I will get my sister to beat him up with a rolling pin. I will be ready to leave at nine. Will that do you, my dear?"

Sam thanked Fred before hanging up and checking the roadside café car park for new arrivals. To Sam's relief, no other cars had arrived for the moment Sam was on the loose.

Sam arrived on the banks of Lake Zug and was happy to find that the waterside car park was almost empty. Only a silver Alfa Romeo estate sat at the bottom of the car park. Sam was amused to see that it sported British number plates, although there was no sign of its driver. Sam concluded that the owner was either sightseeing or possibly fishing.

Sam munched on her sandwich, washing it down with bottled water. In the turmoil of the morning, Sam had forgotten how hungry she had become.

After lunch, Sam once again checked the deserted car park before embarking on her next task. Sam opened her holdall, removing one of the NLB7 dispensers. Carefully, using a pair of nail scissors, she prised the top of each of the lager bottles. Sam pulled on a pair of disposable gloves she had picked up from the petrol station. The last thing she wanted was to let the NLB7 enter her system through a cut and end up comatose in the car park. Sam delivered three drops into each of the bottles of lager before replacing the caps, using the butt of her Beretta to tap the side of the caps to resecure them to the bottle. The NLB7 was normally injected into the bloodstream, inducing an instant coma like state. Sam had no clue if it would work if swallowed. Sam rechecked her watch. She still had plenty of time. A quick look around the car park proved that no one was in the area. Sam stripped down to her underwear. Rummaging around, she pulled on skin-tight black cycling trousers, a black T-shirt, and black hoodie, followed by black running shoes. She pulled her hair back into a tight ponytail and, for the hundredth time, stripped and checked both Berettas, unloading and reloading the magazines to prevent any fouling during rapid-fire situations. Sam checked her watch. She wanted to get going, but she knew she would be far too early and sat back, telling herself to relax.

It was the shout that brought Sam back from a deep sleep. Sam sat up, startled. Much to her relief, it turned out to be the owner of the Alfa Romeo returning. He carried his fishing rod, while his collie dog tried to catch his own fish.

Sam rubbed her eyes and watched as the noisy new arrival coaxed his dog into the car and left. The car park seemed strangely lonely, and Sam fought back the urge to find a phone so she could hear Adam's voice one last time. She smashed the steering wheel with her hands. She needed to snap out of it and get the job done, then get the hell out of Switzerland.

That murderous feeling she knew so well returned. She would avenge Smithy and all the other agents who had lost their lives because of this scumbag. Sam started the little Renault and shot out of the car park. Next stop, Muller's castle.

❖ ❖ ❖

Neil Andrews could not believe what he was hearing. "Bruce, how long ago did you lose contact with Sam?"

Bruce Ellis was furious with his team. He hated admitting to Neil Andrews that he had lost Sam again. "Early this morning. She vanished into thin air and sold us a dummy. We spent the morning checking the airport. Neil, tell me she isn't going to do anything stupid with Karl Muller. He is the gateway to Al Qaeda. I need him to get to Khanjar and then Bin Laden. If I report to the president that Muller is at risk, no matter who it is, I know I will be told to deal with them. Neil, you have got to call her off."

Neil thanked Bruce Ellis and hung up.

Neil Andrews's brain was doing backflips. He had said nothing to Bruce Ellis, but he had just paid Muller half a million pounds for info that just might save hundreds of thousands of lives. He had sent every available man along with every free MI5 agent to Devonport to search everyone involved with the maintenance of the British fleet based there. If Khanjar managed to get limpet mines on a carrier, or god forbid, another nuclear sub, it would be disastrous. Now he had his wayward agent just about to kill their best source of information in Europe. Neil had no doubt now that this was what Sam was up to. On top of that, he was just about to leave for Luke Smith's funeral and a business weekend with his old friend from university.

All he needed now was the PM to call him. He considered cancelling his weekend, but the thought of spending it with naval top brass made him decide to head north. There were too many cooks already involved with the search. He was confident Peter Kent would keep him up to speed with developments.

❖ ❖ ❖

Magdi marched past the Ministry of Defence police officer who stood at the entrance to the dock complex. He thought he had made it, but the police officer called him back. "One minute while I check your pass."

Magdi was shaking in his boots but held his nerve. "No problem, boss. Where have all your mates gone to?"

The police officer ignored him. He was happy with the pass but turned his attention to the cardboard case Magdi was carrying on his shoulder. "What's in the case, mate?"

Magdi smiled. "The only thing that keeps me and the lads going, full fat cola and lots of it."

The MOD policeman gave the case a glance and was about to wave him on when a thought popped into his head. "How about a tin of cola for a thirsty policeman who has no one to relieve him?"

Magdi had come prepared for this and pulled a can of cola from his jacket pocket. "For you, mate, no problem. Better take this one. I just pulled it out of the fridge. The cans in the case will be warm. They have been sitting in the back of the works van, mate."

Magdi phoned Khanjar from a pub in Plymouth. "Hello, K. Just to let you know, mate, the cola has been delivered, four cans each, and nine old timers got the lot." Magdi hung up without waiting for a reply. He had done his bit and needed to get out of Britain fast. He knew if the scrap subs exploded, the spooks would leave no stone unturned looking for him.

❖ ❖ ❖

Bruce Ellis was not sure why he had done it, but he had just ordered his team back to the UK to continue the search for the source of the communications jammer. He was about to contact Washington but stopped short.

He cursed, jumped into his hire car, and headed for Muller's castle.

CHAPTER 16

PAYBACK

Sam had come across her first mistake as she arrived at the foot of the stone wall. She could not climb holding the petrol can. A bit of improvisation was called for, and Sam managed to squeeze it into her backpack, but this caused problems of its own. Sam struggled to climb as the weight of the backpack threatened to pull her off the rock face. Slowly she worked her way up the twenty-foot rise, poking her nose over the top gingerly in case any of the Acussa guards were around. All was quiet, so Sam clambered over the edge, staying flat on her belly while she studied the windows of the castle.

Despite falling asleep, Sam had arrived too early, and dusk was still some time away. Sam followed the shade of the trees, which were swaying in the wind. It looked like this part of Switzerland was about to be hit by a storm. Sam was happy. The wind through the trees masked any small noises she made as she worked her way round the perimeter of the estate, coming up behind Carl Muller's helicopter. Sam sat watching the front of the old castle for some time before making her next move. Slowly, Sam crawled to the side of the chopper and tried the door handle. It clicked and opened outward noiselessly, revealing a half-empty vacuum pack of bottled lager. Sam substituted her doctored lager for the remaining bottles and retreated into the undergrowth to wait.

For some time, Sam sat with her back against a big oak tree, facing away from the castle and using a makeup mirror to keep an eye on the front door. While Sam waited, she removed the jacket and cap that she picked up from the Hungry Dragon and placed them at her feet. She checked both Berettas and unloaded two spare magazines, making sure the spring action was smooth. It was then that Sam noticed the tremble in her left hand. Sam had worked hard with her physio to get her arm back in action after a lunatic had tried to cut her throat with piano wire. Only Sam's lightening reactions had saved her life as she managed to get her hand between the wire and her jugular vein, but the damage to the nerves in her arm had been severe. Sam had thought she had won the battle and restored her arm to good working order. Now she watched as her hand shook uncontrollably.

The crunch of feet coming across the gravel courtyard toward Sam focused her mind on her situation. Sam watched as the Acussa checked toward the castle, then swung the chopper door open and helped himself to a bottle of lager—two gulps and the bottle was empty. He tossed the bottle into the undergrowth and marched round the back, checking the perimeter.

Sam watched as he left. She had no idea if NLB7 would work taken orally, normally it was injected straight into the bloodstream, and its effects were instantaneous.

The big guard reached the corner of the castle. Sam watched as he stopped dead, swayed a little, then went down like a felled tree. It was show time. Sam reckoned that there would be three guards on patrol, with three off duty. She needed to take out the other two quickly.

Sam knew the one thing that would bring them running was if something was wrong with the boss's beloved helicopter. Sam splashed half the petrol over the interior of the chopper then retreated to the woods where she pulled on the Hungry Dragon jacket and cap, grabbed her petrol and rucksack, and tucked both Berettas in her waistband before flinging a match into the cockpit of the chopper. Sam heard the whoosh of igniting petrol as she ran to the corner of the castle, checking on her Acussa friend. He was out of it. As a precaution, Sam took his Glock and threw it away from him, dropped the petrol and rucksack, and started to stroll toward the front door of the castle.

As predicted, Sam was halfway across the forecourt when the big wooden front door burst open, and two tattooed Acussa guards ran out of the door, one dragging a fire extinguisher with him. The lead Acussa was the same one who had been playing with Sam's ponytail.

He stopped in his tracks, looking at the girl from the restaurant, who had a beaming smile from ear to ear. It was too late. In their confusion, they had dropped their guard. Sam removed her hands from her back revealing the Berettas. The first Acussa reached for his side arm but had been outwitted and outgunned. Sam's first shot hit him high in the chest, and his side arm spun out of his hand. The second Acussa fared no better. He was still trying to untangle himself from the fire extinguisher when Sam's shot hit him just above his ear, killing him instantly. He died even before his body hit the pebbled forecourt.

Sam ran back, recovering the rucksack and petrol, and headed to the front door, checking her charge before entering the lion's den. Inside the hall, Sam had a dilemma. Where next? She could not afford to dither and made for the kitchen. Just as she charged in the door, she met the butler who was halfway round the kitchen, a carving knife in his right hand. He stopped dead, calculating his next move.

"Put the knife down gently. Do it now and step back."

The butler complied, stepping backward, away from the bench. Sam could tell he was as slippery as an eel. "Where are the other three Acussa?"

The butler was making all the right noises. "Either next door or upstairs asleep. Listen. I'm MI6. I have been planted here to keep an eye on Muller."

Sam watched as he dropped his left hand by his side. Sam fired hitting him square in the chest. She ran past him as he collapsed forward onto the kitchen table, his blood starting to pool in front of him. "Sorry mate, I'm MI6, and if you are MI6, you are a traitor. Nice try. See you in hell."

Sam cautiously stepped out of the kitchen and was about to turn left. She was sheltered from above by the overhang of the staircase, but something caught her eye. The front room door was half open. She caught sight of an Acussa who was framed in a mirror further back in the room. He had compact machine gun of some type. He had no idea Sam had seen his reflection. Sam emptied a full magazine into the door, moving toward the door as she fired. There was a thud as his body slumped behind the door. Five of Sam's shells had hit their target. There was movement above Sam. She spun round, discarding the empty Beretta, firing at the movement she had detected in her peripheral vision. The tattooed figure had been crouching behind the banister waiting for Sam to show herself. Her shots were slightly off, but her first shot split the wood of the banister. The Acussa reared backward, his cheek and nose punctured by flying splinters. He fired on Sam as she lay on her back on the floor, in full view of her enemy. One shot sparked off the marble floor, but his second caught Sam in the shoulder. She fired again. This time, the Acussa's luck had run out, and he took two bullets, one in the stomach, and the second hit him in the throat. He collapsed. His limp body careered down the stairs, landing at Sam's feet in a heap.

The adrenalin was coursing through Sam's veins, and for the moment, she was intent only on finishing the job. Her wound was numb. Sam wasted no more time, grabbing the rucksack and charging up the staircase two steps at a time.

A check of all the rooms proved fruitless until she came to the double doors of Muller's office.

Karl Muller had been fast asleep in his bedroom, which was annexed to his office and en suite bathroom. When the gunfire started, at first Muller thought that he was dreaming and took a few seconds to wake up. He tried to contact Simon his butler, but no one answered the intercom in the kitchen. Muller's physical condition meant it took him some time to get dressed and pull himself into his wheelchair. He was making for the office door to lock it and sound the alarm when the door burst open.

Sam stepped into the room and locked the door behind her, wheeling a protesting Muller away from the door. Sam pulled off the baseball cap and jacket, tucking them in the rucksack. Muller suddenly realised who the girl was. "You! What do you want with me?"

Sam took the opportunity to replace the magazines in both the Berettas while he was talking. "You have one chance to save your skin, Muller. I want to know everything you know about Bin Laden and Khanjar. Tell me now, and I may spare your sorry life."

Sam watched as Muller started to laugh. "My dear woman, give up now. I have some of the most ferocious Asian guards money can buy, not the fools you and your friend got rid of previously. You are in big trouble."

Sam bent down, looking into the gun dealer's eyes, her cold stare piercing his very soul. "Look into my eyes, Muller. Do I look worried to you? Your men are dead, scattered like seeds in the wind. It is you, my friend, who is in trouble. If they were still alive, do you not think they would be trying to break down the door?"

Muller's heart sank. He knew she was correct. "It will be only a matter of time until the authorities get here, and they will lock you up for the rest of your stupid life. I will tell you nothing."

Sam walked over to the door, returning with the fuel can. "Very well. I came here to kill you, so the information would have saved your life, but not to worry, my treacherous little friend."

Sam unscrewed the fuel-can lid and, to Muller's horror, started pouring the petrol over him. "No, no don't! Stop!" Sam flung the can into the corner of the room and watched Muller's screwed-up face as she produced the box of matches from her pocket. When he saw the matches, Muller almost jumped out of the wheelchair. "No, please, I have money, lots of money, anything you want, but please no, not this. Stop, please." Sam lit the match. Muller screamed at her, "No, I can tell you nothing about Bin Laden. Please spare me, please."

Sam stepped closer with the match. "Khanjar. Tell me about Khanjar, or burn."

"OK, OK, Khanjar was here. I sold him two cases of American limpet mines disguised as cola cans. He told me he was going to attack Devonport naval base with them. You will find CCTV pictures of him in the top drawer of my desk. I can tell you no more now. Please spare me. I am only a gun dealer."

Sam extinguished the match and examined the pictures in the top drawer, showing them to Muller who confirmed the pictures Sam had were of Khanjar taken covertly while he arrived. "Tell me, did you give Khanjar the information about the bugged handguns you sold to the UK? How often does Khanjar tell you his targets?"

Muller was sobbing and shaking badly. "I gave him a computer to track the guns, and he never talks about his missions normally. I normally only get intel about his missions if I bug the sitting room he is in."

Sam frowned. Something didn't smell right. "How is he going to detonate the mines?"

Muller was trying to pull himself together. "He has a satellite phone that will remotely detonate the mines."

Sam had heard enough from the whining wreck. She pushed firmly on his neck, injecting the NLB7 into his bloodstream.

Sam was acutely aware that she had not taken care of all the Acussa. One was still out there, and in her headlong rush to take the castle, she had had no time to check on the state of her downed Acussa opponents. Sam knew that walking out onto the staircase could be very dangerous to her health.

Tong pey, the leader of the Acussa, had been in the bath when the shooting started. He cursed as tried to pull clothes on over his soaking wet torso, even more when he realised he had no weapon at his disposal. He had watched as his colleague was gunned down on the balcony. He had only missed being hunted down by the girl from the Hungry Dragon when he climbed into the loft space to evade capture.

He had used the time the girl spent with his employer to regroup, arm himself, and check on his men. To his dismay, every man was down. Only Bojing, his second in command, was still active, although badly wounded. He had taken a shot in the chest just above his heart and was bleeding badly. Tong pey was not sure how long the man had to live and was prepared to put him out of his misery when the time came.

Tong pey knew two things for certain. The only way out was the front door, and the only way down was the staircase.

He placed Bojing on one side of the door while he took up position on the other side. When the girl tried to escape, she would be dead before she hit the bottom step. His weapon of choice was the Uzi 9mm machine pistol, a murderous weapon. He was going to turn the Hungry Dragon girl to Swiss cheese for what she had done to his men.

Sam looked out of the office window, but it was as she thought. The window looked out over the forest and had a sheer drop down the cliff wall. Only a paraglider would be able to escape from here. The castle was not unlike Colditz, which the Germans used as a prison in the Second World War for that very reason. The only way out was the stairs.

Sam opened one of the glass cabinets and removed an Israeli-built assault rifle. She wrapped the long carrying strap around Karl Muller, anchoring him to the chair, then tucking the weapon under his frozen arm. Sam could only imagine what was going through Muller's head as he watched Sam truss him up like a turkey. As a final touch, Sam placed the bright orange Hungry Dragon baseball cap on his head. She checked both her Berettas and looked around the room. There was enough military hardware here to start a small war. Unfortunately, without ammunition, they were about as much use as a chocolate fireguard.

Sam steeled herself for what she thought was about to come. Crouching down, she unlocked both the door, which swung into the room. Sam listened. Only the popping and banging of a burning helicopter met her ears.

Sam whispered in Muller's ear, "Time for a little trip, my friend. Let's see if you can flush out some of your Acussa friends for me." Sam used all her strength to push the wheelchair at speed to the top of the stairs. At the last second, Sam flung herself on her belly and skidded across the marble floor toward the banister, Berettas at the ready.

Bojing and Tong pey had watched the office doors open silently and were targeting the top of the stairs. It was the orange baseball cap that came into view first, travelling at speed. Both men opened fire at the same time, and all hell broke loose. The Uzi carved a line in the plaster wall, finally coming into contact with the flying wheelchair. Muller was cut to pieces as shell after shell smashed into his frozen body.

Sam opened fire with both guns the second the Acussa gave away their positions. Bojing was hit three times. First in the stomach, and then, as he tried to straighten up, Sam hit him again in the neck and chest, shooting him clean through the heart.

Tong pey was just too fast, but Sam managed to wing him as he ducked outside, evading the murderous fire Sam was putting down on the front door. Tong pey screamed in fury as he examined the bullet hole in his upper thigh. He ripped his T-shirt off making a field tourniquet to stop the bleeding. This done, he turned his attention to his Uzi, reloading and ready for the final fight.

Sam used the cease-fire to check the state of her weapon. She had no more full magazines left and checked the magazines she had discarded, coming up with only ten rounds of ammunition.

❖ ❖ ❖

Bruce Ellis saw the black smoke from the main road as he thrashed the Audi hire car round the bends approaching the castle. Only a few seconds from the castle, he heard the chatter of a machine gun. He removed his Glock, getting ready for whatever he might find at the castle.

Tong pey heard the Audi engine scream as it emerged onto the forecourt of the castle. Instinctively, he opened fire on the charging Audi. The Audi was out of control. In a hail of bullets, it smashed into the already mortally wounded helicopter, causing the overheated fuel cell of the chopper to burst.

The explosion was huge, sending parts of the helicopter's rotor blade flying across the forecourt. One large piece lodged itself in the stone of the castle wall just above Tong pey's head.

He ducked just as a man appeared from the undergrowth behind the helicopter. Tong pey saw the Glock and raised the Uzi, but he had been distracted and was too late. Two bullets took out Tong pey at the same time.

Bruce Ellis shot him in the head while Sam, halfway down the staircase, had a partial shot and hit him under the arm, her bullet passing straight through his heart. He collapsed, his weight pushing against the Uzi trigger. It went off, firing in an arc as he fell, carving a line across the marble floor and covering Sam in marble dust but mercifully missing her by inches.

When Bruce Ellis entered the hall, he found Sam sitting on the bottom step of the marble staircase. Her black top was torn at the collar and was encrusted in dried blood. She was visibly shaking, not lifting her head as Ellis sat down next to her.

"Well, you British girls really know how to throw a party!" Ellis waited for a reply, but Sam was silent, still trying to come to terms with the fact she was still alive.

It took Sam a few seconds to come to her senses. Bruce Ellis was still sitting beside her, surveying the carnage. Without speaking, Sam stood up and climbed the stairs, returning with her rucksack and second Beretta. She handed Bruce Ellis one of the photos she had.

"Before Muller's men shot him, I had a word in Karl Muller's ear. He swore to me he knew nothing of Bin Laden. These are pictures he took of Khanjar. I need to go and try and stop Khanjar, the guard by the corner on the castle grounds has been drugged. Maybe your chaps at Guantanamo might be able to loosen his tongue a little."

Sam started for the door, but Bruce Ellis stood in her way. His Glock was pointed at her forehead. Sam stopped in her tracks and made eye contact with Ellis. "Bruce, you and I know we are not enemies. These clowns that lie around us are the enemy, but our bosses turn a blind eye because it suits them. If you think I am truly evil, pull the trigger. If not, get out of my way. I have a job to do. Find Bin Laden, and I will be at your side if you need help." Sam raised her hand and gently pushed Bruce Ellis out of the way while her eyes burned into his soul.

Ellis watched helplessly as Sam marched to the boundary of the castle grounds, then vanished into the gloom of the night.

Sam made heavy weather of negotiating the cliff she had climbed earlier. She was shattered, and her right shoulder had seized up as the adrenaline faded and her wound became sore and stiff.

At the bottom of the cliff, Sam stopped for a breather and to gather her thoughts. Sam was about to move on when it happened. At first it was a strange sensation, like someone had switched on a washing machine in her belly. Sam was just starting to think, "Baby?" when she received her first kick. It was as if someone had turned on an emotion tap in her head. She walked down the path slowly, waiting for the next kick, the tears streaming down her face.

To Sam, it was at last confirmation that she had a baby to look after. Reality struck home. Sam couldn't believe what danger she had just put her unborn child through.

When Sam reached the Renault, she should have fled the scene, putting as much distance as possible between herself and the investigation that was sure to happen. Instead, Sam sat in the driving seat, holding her belly, trying to will her little one to move. It was the wailing police car passing Sam's parking space that brought her back to her senses. Sam did not want to bring up her child in a Swiss prison and set off in the little Renault to find her friend Fred and her way home to the UK.

Sam arrived at the little airfield in the middle of the night and reclined the seat, trying to catch a few hours sleep before her flight.

Although Sam was shattered, sleep would not come. Her brain was racing, and her shoulder was killing her. Muller's comment kept coming back to haunt her. Why had Khanjar told him he was about to attack Devonport? The only conclusion Sam could draw was that he was trying to draw British forces away from the real target.

Sam wondered if Muller had tipped off Neil. Khanjar must have known of Muller's little sideline in information.

Sam longed for the night to be over. She wanted to be in Adam's arms, telling him all about the baby kicking. Sam was suddenly filled with guilt—to start with, for not telling Adam about the baby. Then the terrible dread returned. What if Adam did not want a child? Bringing a child up on her own was not part of any game plan Sam had ever had.

Sam was woken by a gentle tapping on her side window. Fred was at the door smiling as Sam came to and stepped out to greet her friend.

Fred hugged her, giving her a squeeze, which brought the fact back to Sam that she had been shot. She held onto the scream, giving Fred a peck on the cheek. Fred held her at arm's length, studying her with a concerned look on his face. "Young woman, are you sure you are well? Forgive me, but you look terrible." Sam shrugged off Fred's comments and fell in beside him as he made for the admin building and canteen.

"Forgive me, but we will have company on the flight to London. Madame Chemolie, a friend of my wife, will be accompanying us to do a bit of shopping." Fred rolled his eyes in mock disgust. He showed Sam to a seat and returned with a plateful of small rolls that the locals called *burli*, fresh butter, and a choice of honey or various cheeses. Although Sam was starving, she had one more pressing problem. She was finding more and more that she needed a toilet close by. Sam excused herself and made for the toilet. On the way back, she stopped by the pay phone and made a collect call to Vauxhall Cross.

Neil Andrews's PA had just arrived at work and was hanging up her coat when the switchboard put a call through. She was surprised that it was a collect call, but when Sam gave the appropriate code, Jean accepted the charges. Sam gave Jean the details of the flight that was due to arrive at Stansted soon, although Sam was not sure when. Sam asked for a car as she was wounded and a doctor to be at Vauxhall Cross to have a look at her. When Jean tried to get Sam to go to hospital, Sam flatly refused. She stated it was vital that she get to Vauxhall Cross as quickly as possible.

Sam returned to Fred, who was pouring her thick black coffee. "Young lady, listen to Fred. You need to eat more, or you will be no use to the photographers." He winked at Sam as he said it. "Come eat. We must wait for the phenomenon that is Madame Chemolie anyway. Plenty of time to get you fed, my girl." Sam tucked into the burl, smothering them in thick, sticky honey, and demolishing four of them before topping up with more coffee under the watchful eye of Fred.

An hour later, Madame Chemolie made a sweeping entrance as her white, chauffer-driven stretch Mercedes pulled into the airstrip. Fred led the girls past his normal twin-engine Piper Seneca and onward to the hangar.

Inside sat the pride of the airfield—a Falcon 900. Sam was the first to speak. "Fred, have you been robbing banks again?"

Fred and Madame Chemolie looked at each other, smiling at her innocent comment. "Young lady, you are closer to the truth than you think. The jet is mine, and this will be our first real trip in her. As for the bank, I didn't rob it, but I do own it." Madame Chemolie led the way up the stairs to her new toy."

Sam entered the cabin of the luxury jet and was ushered through the café-crème leather and walnut wood panelling to a large armchair opposite Madame Chemolie. "Wow, this must have cost a fortune. Do you trust Fred with your pride and joy often, Madame Chemolie?"

Madame Chemolie was busy studying her hair in a mirror, looking for any stray hairs that had outwitted the hairspray. "To answer your first question, thirty-three million Euros to be exact, and Fred I would trust with my life. He was a display pilot with the Patrouille de France. Please, not my Sunday name. You may call me Maria. May I have the pleasure of your name, my dear?"

Sam was shattered and in no mood to act out the part. She broke a golden rule. "Thank you very much for the use of your jet. My name is Samantha."

Madame Chemolie watched Sam for a few seconds before speaking. "Tell me, Samantha, what your business really is. Fred tells me you are a photographic model. I don't think even Fred believes that."

Sam struggled to think of an appropriate answer. "Do you mind if I take the Fifth Amendment on that one, Maria?"

Madame Chemolie smiled, basking in the glory of being right. "Samantha, tell me one more thing. When is the baby due?"

Sam almost fell off her Connolly leather chair. Madame Chemolie was watching her closely and burst out laughing at Sam's expression of horror. "My god, how did you know that? Do you have some sort of clairvoyant powers?"

Madame Chemolie shook her head. "Only the powers of a woman who has had four children of her own. Your body hides it well, but your actions give you away. You keep holding your tummy as if you are checking it is still there."

Sam smiled at the old lady. "I think the baby is due sometime in November, but I have been too busy to get proper checks done."

Maria scolded Sam for not taking proper care of herself, but as the flight progressed, the two women warmed to each other, so much so that Maria passed Sam her business card, explaining to Sam how lucky she was. The French and Italian heads of state had asked for her number but were politely refused by the Swiss banking tycoon. "You, my dear, may call me anytime."

As Fred nosed the Falcon 900 into its allotted bay at Stansted, a black Range Rover with two police motorcycle riders pulled alongside. Fred was shocked to find when he spoke to the driver of the Range Rover that he was here to pick up Sam and not Madame Chemolie.

Sam tried to pay Fred the usual amount for his services, but Madame Chemolie was having none of it. "Samantha, you were my guest. There is no way that you will pay for the flight. Frederick is my pilot. When you come to visit me, and you will, call Fred. He will pick you up with the Falcon. My dear, go and have your baby and be happy. Au revoir, honey."

As Sam got to the cabin door, Fred was standing, wagging his finger at Sam. "So Samantha is your name. Godspeed to you, my dear. It looks as if the photographer is in a hurry to get you. He has even sent a police escort." Fred winked at Sam as she passed by on her way to the Range Rover.

CHAPTER 17

THE BURIAL

Sam was freezing. Even with the heating on she could not keep herself warm as the big Range Rover and its police escort cut its way through the traffic heading south to the centre of London. When they arrived at the side ramp of Vauxhall Cross, a reception party was there to meet them. One look at Sam's colour and the doctor whisked Sam into a room to examine her. They were followed by Jean who, in the absence of her boss, had organised Sam's arrival.

Sam attempted to remove her jacket to let the doctor have a look but the time spent inactive had caused her arm to seize up.

With a little help from the doctor, Sam was able to peel her jacket off. Her T-shirt was a different story it was glued to her back with congealed blood and the doctor had literally to cut it off her. Sam winced as he removed the final bits of material around the wound. The bullet had passed clean through mid-way between Sam's shoulder and neck on her right side. Jean gasped as she was not used to fieldwork and never seen the aftermath of a gun battle before. Dr Adams worked swiftly, cleaning in and around the wound so he could have a better look at the damage. "Well, Samantha, you have been a lucky lady. The bullet doesn't seem to have fragmented, and it would appear to have missed arteries and nerves possibly nicking the top of your collarbone, we will know once we have transferred you to hospital for some x-rays."

Sam wanted to shake her head but her neck was too painful. "No, doctor. No x-rays. Just sort it."

Dr Adams was not used to being challenged by his patients. "Sam, I'm not asking you I'm telling you. You are going for an x-ray!"

Sam grabbed him by the throat. "Listen carefully, doctor. I'm not in the best mood. I am pregnant, and there will be no x-rays or medication. Clean the wound, and stitch it. No anaesthetic. Just do it, and do it fast."

Dr Adams was about to explode, but Jean intervened, removing Sam's hand and walking the doctor over to the corner of the room where she carried out some swift negotiations with the unhappy doctor.

Sam watched as he left the room. Then Jean approached Sam with care. "Sam, the doctor will do as you say on one condition. He is concerned about your blood loss and has popped out to get some equipment. He wants you on a saline drip to help the blood loss. Sam, bloody hell, does Neil know you are going to be a mum?" Sam had broken out in a cold, clammy sweat. She wiped her face with the back of her hand before making eye contact with Jean. "No one knows, Jean, and it's going to stay that way. Do we understand each other?"

Dr Adams stitched Sam up without saying a word. Sam was determined she was not going to make a fool of herself and dug her nails into the chair as the needle was threaded through her skin. At last it was over, and at Sam's request, Dr Adams checked the baby's heartbeat, confirming the baby seemed fine. He checked the drip and announced he would be back in an hour to see how his patient was doing.

Sam sat back, her ordeal over. The baby was fine. That was her only thought. She was just about to drift off to sleep when Jean appeared with a mug of tea, a tray of biscuits, and some clothing for Sam to change into once the doctor had finished with her.

Jean watched as Sam tucked into the tea and biscuits, letting her have her fill before speaking. "OK, Samantha why the mad charge to headquarters? What do you have that is so urgent?"

Sam put her cup down. "Jean, I need to speak to Neil urgently. It's Khanjar. I am sure he is up to something big. He has thrown us a dummy. Tell me, did Neil receive a call from Karl Muller this week?"

Jean was avoiding eye contact with Sam. "Sam, you know I can't possibly discuss that with you. It's more than my job is worth."

Sam exploded. "Jean, cut the bullshit. This is very serious. Do we or do we not have men checking for limpet mines on the ships in Devonport naval base? Because if we do, I will bet my baby's life they are looking in the wrong place, and we are about to be hit by a major terrorist attack elsewhere. Khanjar gave this information to Karl Muller to throw us off the scent. Now, for the love of god, Jean, answer the fucking question."

Jean was not sure if it was because Sam had convinced her or the fact that she might just have her baby right here, right now that convinced her to admit Neil had spoken at length to Muller before authorising a bank transfer to his account.

"Jean, we need to get Neil right now!"

Jean was shaking her head. "He has gone for the weekend. I had already tried to contact him when I found out you were on your way here. He has either switched off his phone, or he has bad reception up north."

Sam turned and stared at Jean. "Why is Neil up north?"

Jean had forgotten Sam had been out of the picture for some time. "Sorry, Sam. It slipped my mind to tell you. It's Luke Smith's funeral on some godforsaken mountain in, I think, the Perthshire hills. I made all the arrangements for Neil. At least the poor lad is getting a good send-off. Neil has flown north along with a burial detail from Hereford. They are all meeting up for the service at Neil's friend's estate. Adam, Captain Malden, and Dr Lowe are also attending the funeral."

Sam handed Jean the teacup without speaking and then, to Jean's horror, started removing the needle from her arm.

"Oh my god, Samantha, stop! What are you doing? Wait for the doctor, please."

Sam handed a shocked Jean the needle while she held her finger over the puncture wound. "I am going to get dressed. I need you to get me a mobile with Neil's number on it. Then I need a car to take me to Heathrow or whoever has the first flight to Edinburgh. Then I need a hire car waiting for me and make sure it is a bloody fast one. No lectures, Jean, just do it."

Jean decided to comply with Sam's request and was just about to leave the room. "Jean, before you go, have a rake in my bag. You will find a picture. Can you get it to our analysts quickly, please?"

Jean pulled the picture from the bag and studied the black-and-white snap of a man entering a large stone doorway. "Who's the chap, Samantha?"

Sam paused for effect. "No one in particular. I believe he goes by the name of Khanjar."

Jean had been walking toward the door while Sam was speaking. She turned to glance at Sam open-mouthed when she heard the name and walked clean into the doorframe before regaining her composure and dashing out the door toward the computer rooms.

Left alone with her thoughts and with no need to put a brave face on for the moment, Sam slowly removed her blood-soaked underwear, finally giving up on the idea of replacing her bra as it proved an almost impossible task. Sam slowly and gently pulled a black T-shirt over her head, struggling to get her right arm through the sleeve. By the time Sam had managed to pull on the black jogging trousers, she was drenched in a cold sweat.

Jean finally reappeared, carrying a mobile phone. "OK, the car will be here to take you to Heathrow in twenty minutes. You are booked first class on BA flight ED122. You should get into Edinburgh around nine thirty. I have booked a room at the Hilton for you, and there will be a car ready for you after breakfast. I requested a Porsche, but the hire company is having a few problems getting one. They promised me they would have it sorted for tomorrow morning. I took the liberty of contacting your colleague Peter Kent as he is in charge of coordinating the search at Devonport for the limpet mines. He will be calling you on the mobile any time now. I will leave you for the moment, as I have to go and explain to Dr Adams that you are a headstrong lunatic who won't be told what to do. Oh, by the way the picture thing? That was pure class. That's why you are Neil's number one. Well done, Samantha."

Twenty seconds after Jean left the room, the mobile phone started to vibrate in Sam's hand. The display simply stated the word "Kent." Sam hit the key and before Peter Kent could say a word, Sam was barking instructions down the phone to him.

"Peter, it's Sam. Listen. Khanjar has pulled a fast one. It was him who leaked the information about the limpet mines at Devonport. He does have limpet mines, but you can bet your last dollar they won't be at Devonport. It must be another naval target someplace."

Kent listened to Sam's story without interrupting. He had taught Sam and knew how good she was. "OK, Sam, I hear you, but all the other bases are being checked. We have even had divers checking our ships abroad, and the big commercial ships at all the busy ports have been checked."

Sam was racking her brain. "Peter, whatever it is, I get the feeling it's big. He has gone to a lot of trouble to wrong-foot us. He has lost a few men lately. Maybe it has forced his hand into a major attack while he can still do it. Have the nuclear subs been checked at Faslane? He could be having a second go at them."

Peter Kent was one step ahead. "No, Sam. They have been checked and ordered to put to sea as a precaution. There is nothing in Faslane."

Sam had to end the conversation as Jean had arrived to escort Sam to the waiting Range Rover. The trip to the airport was the stuff of nightmares. Sam would have killed to have her police motorcycle escort back instead of crawling along at walking pace. Once at the airport, Sam did something she had never done before. Faced with a huge queue at the security gate, Sam pulled a police officer to the side, showed her ID, and was ushered through a side door into duty free. On the plane, no matter how Sam sat or moved, she could not get comfortable. Her shoulder was killing her, and her mind was racing, trying to guess Khanjar's next move before it was too late

❖ ❖ ❖

Sam was not the only one not getting any sleep. Sam's phone call had started alarm bells ringing in Peter Kent's head he was studying an aerial photo of the naval base along with an attendance log of everyone who had visited the base while his colleague Robin Alder studied CCTV footage of the base. While Alder checked the images, Kent bounced ideas off him some feasible, some ridiculous. "OK, Robin, let's rewind. We know he has limpet mines. We also know he has a fascination with all things nuclear. His attack on the sub in Scotland and his attempt to explode a dirty bomb prove it. So let's circle every ship that is nuclear powered and put the spotlight on every one of them." Kent spent the next hour going over the movements of each ship before admitting defeat for the umpteenth time that night. Robin Alder stopped on his way to put the kettle on and studied the red-circled ships.

"Excuse me, sir, but you may have missed a few." Kent spun round to find Alder with his finger on an area not marked in red ink.

"They are decommissioned subs, Robin. They are just shells."

Alder was shaking his head, his eyes becoming wider as he spoke. "Not all of them, sir. The MOD have not completed the decommissioning program. There are still intact nuclear subs in that area." Kent picked up the phone and called the duty officer in charge of the security on the base. The call only took a few seconds and when finished, Kent hung up, a haunted look on his face. "Get your coat on, Robin. The guard has been reduced to a skeleton staff as men have been diverted to help search the fleet for the mines. There has been a team of outside contractors working on the decommissioned subs this week, carrying out routine maintenance on the old subs. We need to get down there ASAP."

❖ ❖ ❖

Sam was woken by the hotel alarm call. She had finally fallen into a deep sleep and was feeling the better for it. All she wanted to do was get down to breakfast. She was ravenous.

Her first attempt at jumping out of bed failed miserably as she tried to sit up but her arm seized. She felt like an eighty-year-old falling back on the fluffy pillows. Gently she pulled herself up and headed for the bathroom where, with some difficulty and the use of the mirror, she managed to change the dressing on her wound. She spent another twenty minutes trying to dress with the same result as her previous attempt. The bra was a step too far, but she managed her top. Sam studied her profile in the mirror. The bump at the top of her tummy just below her ribcage now protruded further than her ribcage.

In front of her eyes, her body was changing to make room for her little one. Sam decided it was time they both headed for breakfast. While Sam waited for her cooked breakfast to be prepared, she called Neil's number, but as before, it came up unobtainable. Sam gave up and tucked into the full cooked breakfast that had just arrived followed by three cups of coffee. Sam was just draining the bottom of the cup when her mobile phone started to vibrate. To Sam's dismay, it was not Neil but the hire car company. The receptionist from the hire car company was full of apologies. They had not been able to get their hands on a Porsche at such short notice, but she assured Sam that the driver would be at the hotel in thirty minutes with her hire car stand-in.

Sam signed out of her room and carried her bags into the seating area by the reception. She tried Neil again but to no avail. Her mind wandered back to Adam. How the hell was she going to break the news to him that he was going to be a dad?

Sam's mind was still on this when a young woman approached from the reception area. "Hello, I think I have a hire car for you, that is, if you are Samantha O'Conner." Sam shook hands with the girl then followed her out the door to the car park. The girl handed Sam the keys of a Volkswagen. Sam's heart sank. The last thing she needed just now was a puddle jumper.

Just as Sam was about to make a comment the girl pointed at a Blue Scirocco R parked in the first bay. "Sorry it's not a Porsche, but it is the fastest thing we have in the fleet at the moment."

Sam thanked the girl, signed the paperwork, and turned the key in the ignition. From the noise the coupe emitted when it started, it looked like the car meant business, a fact backed up as Sam joined the motorway slip road for Perth and opened the throttle watching the speedo needle touch one hundred miles per hour before it reached the end of the slip road. Sam was glad to see that her new chariot had followed the latest car craze, and the gears were controlled from the steering wheel, taking the pressure off her damaged shoulder.

Fifteen minutes later, Sam was about to rocket past Stirling services. She was in two minds about whether to stop. But severe indigestion and a complaining bladder were telling Sam she needed to stop and sort it out. Her mind was finally made up when her phone, which she had left in her coat pocket, started ringing. Sam changed down with the paddles on the steering wheel and took the slip road off the motorway heading for the services.

Sam checked her phone the minute she stopped in the car park. It had been Peter Kent who called. Sam combined a toilet break with a search through the store for indigestion tablets. Sorted once more and back in the privacy of the hire car, Sam called Peter Kent.

"Sam, thank god you answered. You were right, girl. The shit has hit the whirly thing down here. We have found the mines. They are on the hulls of nine scrap nuclear subs parked up in Devonport. When the shout went up about the limpet mines, they pulled men from the security of these old boats to help find the mines on the navy ships. If they go up, the southwest of England will be decimated with radioactive waste. Sam, I have someone here who needs to speak to you."

Sam was in a state of shock. Khanjar had played a blinder this time. He had made a dirty bomb on a massive scale.

"Hello, Samantha, It's Bruce here. Wow, you guys really know how to get yourselves deep in the shit! Listen, girl. We need to find Khanjar and fast. We put tracking devices in the mines and let them be stolen from our navy warehouse. Our plan was to let Khanjar or Bin Laden buy them from Muller, then when he took them home to momma, we had a duplicate remote, and we were going to have us a fireworks party. Unfortunately, after your little party in Switzerland, the Swiss were not keen to let me go, and I had no chance to get the message back to Washington that their package was on its way. When I finally got out and checked, our Al Qaeda friends had planted them on your subs." Sam inhaled sharply, while Bruce continued. "The mines can be set off in three ways. Once the magnetic base is in contact with a metal hull, pulling the mine off will set it off instantly. Once a cylinder is placed, if you rotate it, you set a ten-minute timer before it explodes. Also, it can also be detonated remotely from, say, a satellite phone anywhere in the world. Sam, all he has to do is press a button. God knows why he hasn't already done it. We are still trying to identify him from the photo. I have nine CIA personnel looking for the communications terrorist. If you need them, they are yours. We will keep trying to identify him. Happy hunting, Sam."

Sam was about to hang up when Peter Kent came back on the phone. "Sam, you need to get Neil to switch his bloody phone back on. The PM is going berserk. Poor Jean and Bill Mathews from MI5 have been summonsed to the Cobra meeting. Find him, Sam, and bloody fast."

❖ ❖ ❖

As the convoy of Range Rovers, Discoverys and Jaguars pulled up in the drive of the Menamar estate, I gazed out of the side window of the Range Rover I was travelling in. On the hill to my left out of site stood the grave of my good friend Ian Ferris. The thought of revisiting the gravesite to bury another one of my friends did nothing for my already sullen mood.

We had met up with the guys from the regiment at Prestwick Airport and travelled in convoy. Fiona Malden had remarked that she had never felt so safe or important being escorted by SAS and MI6 agents. Karen Lowe remarked that even the queen would not have this amount of protection. I smiled at the naivety of the young scientist. In my later years with Special Forces, I had been taken along by the royal protection squad to advise them on various bombing scenarios and the level of protection at some venues was staggering.

I watched as Neil Andrew met Kiron Al Ahdal on the steps of the Menamar House. I smiled as the two old friends embraced each other like lost brothers. I had only met Kiron on two occasions—once, when Ian had introduced his boss during my purchase of the estate's lodge house, and sadly a second time, after Ian's death when I could no longer bring myself to stay in a place with so many bad memories. Kiron had been kind enough to buy the lodge house back, leaving me free to move in with Sam.

Truth be told, the main reason for my sullen mood was because my girlfriend was still AWOL despite Neil Andrews's best efforts to try and track her down. It was not so much that Sam couldn't look after herself—after all she had been a MI6 agent for years before our paths crossed. It was Sam's inability to walk away that concerned me. The girl had a knack of always biting off more than she could chew. It was like playing Russian roulette. Sooner or later, Sam would run out of luck. I was hoping whatever she was up to, this would not be the time.

I watched as the girls clambered out of the Range Rover in front of me. Karen had recovered the fastest and stepped out with too much bother. Fiona was on the mend and carefully let herself down onto the gravel driveway. It was my turn. My shoulder was strapped up and since it was immobile, it was painless. My back was another matter. The trip from Cross House had been a long one, and my back had seized up. Fiona held back, waiting to help me out of the big 4x4, sensing I was apprehensive about my mobility.

Slowly my feet touched the gravel path. As the weight was transferred from the seat to my feet, a white-hot pain shot from the base of my spine to my shoulders, causing me to take a sharp breath, which in turn increased the pain. I wanted to sit down and not ever move again, but my pride and determination forced me on.

The look on Fiona Malden's face said it all. "Mac, take it easy. We have a wheelchair with us if you need a rest."

I smiled through gritted teeth. "Fiona, I will be fine, but would you do me the honour of taking my good arm and helping me walk across until I say thanks to Kiron for allowing us to put Smithy to rest here."

Kiron and Neil had seen my slow progress and met us halfway across the drive. "Adam, it's good to see you again, Neil tells me you have had a rough time of it. I hear you fell out of a helicopter. You must tell me the whole story. But first, can you introduce me to this beautiful woman who is draped over your arm."

I watched Fiona blush at the compliment paid to her by Kiron. "But of course Kiron. This is Captain Fiona Malden, a good friend and colleague of mine. I would like to thank you for letting us bury our friend next to Ian."

Al Ahdal gave a slight bow keeping his eye on Fiona. "My friend, it was the least I could do. My estate was at its best when Ian looked after it. His attention to detail was second to none, and any friend of his is a friend of mine, but please young lady, Fiona, if I may, the captain title intrigues me. Please put me out of my misery and tell me about it."

I was surprised to see Fiona Malden was blushing furiously. "No great mystery, Kiron. I am a helicopter pilot and a captain in the army."

Kiron was smiling from ear to ear, and I could see mischief in those dark eyes. "I trust, my lovely captain, it was not you who dropped Adam from the helicopter?" All four of us chuckled at the comment before Kiron continued. "Fiona, I would love to take you away from the army. Come and work for me."

Before Fiona could reply Neil Andrews butted in. "Listen, guys. The minister is already by the graveside waiting. I think we should get up there."

Kiron had supplied two estate Defenders one was a pick up which hauled the guys from Hereford up the hill we had the pleasure of being thrown all over the place as Kiron piloted the second Defender to the top of the hill. Fiona squeezed my hand as she felt me wince at every jolt. It was my turn for devilment. "So Fiona, I think Kiron has a bit of a crush on you. How do you fancy joining his harem?"

Fiona winked at me and whispered her reply. "He would do, honey, but only if he gave me a new Bell 429 as a wedding present."

At the top of the hill, I had a new pair of hands to get me out of the Land Rover. "Come on, Mac. It's my turn to give you a hand."

Bob Hunter held out his arm, steadying me as I emerged from the rear cabin of the Defender. As I regained my balance, Sergeant Hunter and the rest of the burial detail came to attention. I was not in uniform or serving but it was a nice gesture that did not go unnoticed by the rest of the small band of mourners on the top of the hill.

"As you were, guys. Thanks for making the trip to honour young Smithy." I stopped speaking. It was all I could get out without choking on my words.

Fiona Malden stood by me and squeezed my hand. Thankfully, the minister took control of the situation.

Fiona whispered in my ear. "Wow, Neil Andrews is the director of MI6, but the guys never even acknowledged him. It is you they respect. You really are a legend, aren't you?" I said nothing. My thoughts were with my departed friend.

Smithy could have been a legend too, if only he had lived. He had been the best shot I had ever trained. This combined with his lightening reactions had made him the best student the Special Forces had trained for some time. Which, considering the competition, was quite an accolade.

❖ ❖ ❖

Sam had visited Adam's lodge house but had never been to the actual Menamar house. Sam used her hire car's sat-nav to guide her along the twisty Perthshire country lanes. Sam was just about to question the sat-nav's ability to get her to her target when the large stone pillars of Menamar house appeared on Sam's left. Sam powered the Scirocco up the drive, coming to a large gravel courtyard in front of the big front door. Although various vehicles were parked there, the big house was eerily quiet. Sam could see in the distance what she thought was a group of people on the hill.

Sam was about to set off up the hill when her bladder reminded her she was expecting. Sam made for the big front doors, which were ajar. As Sam entered the front door, she chuckled to herself. Standing on either side of the door were two curling stones. This seemed to be a Scottish thing. From guesthouses to cottages, everybody seemed to collect these stones. Sam wondered how many of the occupants actually played the game.

Inside the hall, Sam shouted, but the large house seemed deserted. It looked like Sam was going to have to find the bathroom on her own. Sam picked the first door she came to. This only led into a garage.

Sam was about to close the door and continue her hunt when something caught her eye.

The dusty black car was difficult to make out in the gloom of the windowless garage, but the shiny metal on the rear wing was what had caught Sam's eye. She moved into the garage to get a closer look.

Sam's blood ran cold as her brain did the maths. The shiny metal was where the paint had been blasted off the back wing by three nine-millimetre bullet holes. This Mercedes was the car with which Al Qaeda had attacked the glass house. It was Sam herself who had peppered the car with bullets.

Sam was panicking big time. She had come to a funeral and had no weapons with her. Her first reaction was to get the hell out of there and call in the cavalry. Sam being Sam, she talked herself out of it. She needed to know more. This was the perfect opportunity to snoop around while the house was empty.

Sam closed the door to the garage and headed quietly across the hall to the next door. This led into what looked like the main lounge. There was nothing of interest here. It had been set up to receive the mourners on their return from the burial. Sam left and headed down the long hallway. Another door on the right loomed. Sam entered, finding a library-cum-study decked out with large brown leather chesterfield couches. At the top of the room sat a very large Georgian desk. Sam focused her attention on the desk. The owner was a careful man. The desk drawers were locked. Sam also found a floor safe next to the desk, but again, the owner had locked it.

It seemed whatever secrets the house held they were well locked away from prying eyes. Sam was busy trying to pick the lock with her good arm when she noticed the picture on the desk in front of her.

It was like an electric shock. Sam had been so busy looking for evidence, she had not seen what was right in front of her nose. The owner of the house must have been very proud of the picture to have it front and centre on his desk. It had been taken at a Buckingham Palace garden party, and it showed a man bowing to the queen. The revelation that Sam had come across was the fact that the man was the same man that had visited Karl Muller that fateful night not so long ago. The queen had invited Khanjar to lunch!

Khanjar was the owner of Menamar. Khanjar was Kiron Al Ahdal!

Sam picked the phone on the desk up to call someone, but it was dead. Sam's head was pounding. She needed to tell MI6. She fumbled in her bag for the mobile phone, but there was only incredible static from the phone. It had suffered the same fate that presumably Neil Andrews's phone was suffering. Something was jamming the signal.

Sam wandered down the hall to where the staircase descended into the basement. At the bottom of the stairs, a door was partially open, revealing a light. Sam moved quietly down the stone stairs, so slowly her leg muscles ached with the effort. Just outside the door, Sam stopped and observed the room. The room was large, probably the full size of the building above. Rows of large computers were linked by cables that resembled huge spider webs hooked to the ceiling of the room. One man decked out with headphones sat by his four computer screens. He was immersed in his work. Sam could make out one screen that was using a satellite to spy on a naval base. It didn't take rocket science to work out which base it was watching. Sam turned her attention to the man. He was young and fit. Sitting on his desk next to his right hand was a Glock.

Sam weighed up her chances of overpowering the unknown man. Sam was wounded and unarmed. For all she knew he could be a martial-arts expert as well as having a gun. It may only take a push of a button to fire the limpet mines. Sam had to make sure if she went in it would be decisive. At the moment, it wasn't looking good. She needed a plan and fast—before the funeral party and Khanjar returned.

Faaris was watching the Americans' latest attempt to find the source of the signal that was blocking all their military communications. He chuckled to himself. He was feeling particularly pleased with himself that morning.

What he had planned made his boss's attack on the submarines look like chicken feed. He had finally gained access to the command and control computers of the Iranian army. He had the programme all set up to upload to the Iranian computers. All he needed was the blessing of his boss. Once sent, it would transfer the blocking programme to Iran.

Faaris could just imagine what the American generals would do when they found out that the Iranians had been attacking their computers.

He sat back in his high-back chair at exactly the same time as the curling stone made from the finest Ailsa Craig granite smashed into his skull. Slivers of bone penetrated his frontal lobe, killing him instantly.

Sam gasped in agony as the effort she had put into swinging the heavy granite piece tore the stitches in her wound. Sam cursed to herself as she searched the basement for any more of Khanjar's men. Not knowing what to do, Sam decided switching the computers off by cutting the power at the mains seemed to be the way forward. Sam traced the cables to a large circuit breaker on the far wall and flung the switch with her good arm, plunging the basement into darkness. This done, Sam groped her way to the front door. She was not finished yet, not by a long way. She checked the magazine of her newly acquired Glock, then went in search of transport.

❖ ❖ ❖

The service had finished, and we were breaking up to head back down to the big house for the reception when the howl of a big diesel engine broke the silence of the occasion. I, being the slowest, was the last of the party and was still by the graveside. The Range Rover appeared, bouncing from rock to rock before pulling up as the driver slammed on the brakes in front of the already parked Land Rovers.

To everyone's amazement, a very pale Sam stepped out of the big beast.

Neil Andrews was the first to regain his tongue. "Ah, our long-lost Samantha has returned. Sorry, Sam, you have just missed the service."

I was growing increasingly worried. Sam looked on the edge. I had never seen her like this before. Something was wrong, seriously wrong.

Sam was speaking but not to us. She directed her comments to Kiron. "Your son has been moved to Devonport. The game is over, Khanjar."

Sam's focus was firmly on Kiron as she spoke. Then she raised her hand, pointing a Glock at Kiron's head. "Let me see your hands. Do anything now, and you will condemn your son to a terrible death. Let me see your hands. Do it now, and do it slowly."

Everyone's attention was focused on Kiron's hands, but they stayed firmly put in his pockets. His face was one of thunder. Neil Andrews had had enough. "Sam, for god's sake, put the gun down. I can vouch for Kiron. I have known him since university. You are mistaken."

Sam's eyes never left Al Ahdal as she threw the photo at Neil's feet. "This was taken last week at the home of Karl Muller. Want to ask your pal to explain his way out of that, or has the cat still got his tongue? What do you say, chicken shit? Where's your fancy dagger now the tables are turned?"

Two things happened at almost the same time.

I was aware of movement on my left. The driver, one of Kiron's men who had driven the honour guard up the hill in the first Defender, was on my left between myself and the grave. He started to move at the same time as Khanjar exploded into action pulling the satellite phone from his pocket, screaming at Sam to drop the gun.

Sam fired at the same time as I grabbed the driver, and the gun that he had produced from his jacket. It was an uneven match at that point. I was nothing more than a cripple. I had no hope of winning in an uneven fight, but I had to do something before Sam ended up dead. As we struggled, we both lost our footing and went headlong into Smithy's grave as the driver's Glock went off.

Sam had baited Khanjar into action, taking the double gamble that one, he did not know his son was already dead, and two, he would hesitate when it came to killing his own son, giving Sam the vital second she needed to strike. Sam's eyes were glued to Khanjar's hand holding his satellite phone, watching where his fingers were. The bullet hit Khanjar in the right eye socket as his finger searched for the send button. It never reached it. The phone went spinning helplessly out of his hand, falling into a clump of heather.

Everything was in darkness. My body was numb. Suddenly, I spotted movement in front of me as Khanjar's driver struggled to free himself from the position he had landed in. My opponent reached down the side of the coffin, trying to retrieve his weapon, which had landed in the gap between the coffin and the side of the grave. He was making heavy weather of it and was holding his stomach with his other hand. If he reached the gun, I was dead. One last lunge at my opponent to try and knock him off balance worked better than I had anticipated, and I came crashing down on him as his head and neck were jammed by the side of the coffin. There was a sickening crack as his spinal column was snapped clean at the base of his skull, severing his spinal cord, killing him instantly. It felt like hours, but it could only have been minutes before daylight returned as I was hoisted upwards from the bottom of the grave. Big Bob and one of his men pulled me out of the grave. Karen Lowe was comforting a clearly shocked minister while a group had gathered around Sam who was fighting her way through. We met in the middle of the small crowd. To my amazement, Sam was crying like a baby as she threw herself into my arms. Also to my amazement, my strapped-up collarbone first withstood the fall into the grave, then the charge by Sam.

Neil Andrews stood alone, still staring at the picture Sam had thrown at his feet. We held onto each other while all around was madness.

Sam used her sleeve to first wipe away her tears, then to brush away from my face some of the dirt I had collected on my trip into Smithy's grave.

Back at the big house, Neil Andrews had come back to life. Finding his phone was now working, he was speaking to the PM and half the MOD.

Sam's phone came to life, vibrating in her pocket as we sat on the steps of the big house. Sam held the phone so we could both hear the conversation. "Sam, it's your best buddy at the CIA here. Girl, I don't know how you managed it, but we just got our comms back. We traced the source of the jamming to the same position as the signal from your phone. I take it we owe you one."

Sam winked at me before replying. "Bruce, you better believe you owe us. You could start by sending your people across to defuse the limpet mines you lost track of. I have a confession to make. I had to eliminate Khanjar. Both his friends here are dead as well, so I'm afraid this hunt for Bin Laden is a dead end, my friend."

The phone was silent for a second while Bruce Ellis digested the latest information. "What the hell, Samantha. We will get him. You have my word on it. As for your limpet problem, we have guys in the air on the way to you. Sit tight. The cavalry is coming. Got to go, girl. The big boss is on the other line for me. Bye for now."

Sam put the phone away then sat looking toward Smithy's and Ian's graves, tears welling up in the corner of her eyes again.

"So, madam, care to tell me where the hell you vanished to?"

Sam wiped her eyes before replying. "Oh, I bumped into Karl Muller. It seems we had a difference of opinions. He thought he should live. I thought he should die."

Sam was staring directly at me. Her grey eyes were hauntingly beautiful but cold as ice. She did not elaborate. She didn't need to. I had seen these eyes before. Sam the assassin was alive and kicking.

Fiona Malden broke the spell. "Bloody hell, Mac, you guys are unbelievable. Mac, you have only been out of hospital for a matter of hours, and you still mange to shoot a terrorist in the stomach and break his neck into the bargain. As for this lady, no one will mess with you, girl. But listen, Sam. Don't listen to this one. He will tell you he is fine, but he is far from fine. You look after him, honey."

I watched Karen Lowe approaching. To my surprise, she took Sam by the hand and led her away. "Don't look so worried, Mac. It's girl talk."

I was about to follow when a voice came from behind me. "Mac, we are about to bugger off. Got a chopper picking us up at Leuchars in two hours, mate. Will you be OK? Just to let you know this will be my last shout. I am hanging up the uniform next week. Here is my number. Give me a call soon, and we will meet up for that beer we have been promising ourselves for years. One last thing, Mac, for the love of god, stop before we are digging a hole up there for you. Do you hear me? Anyway. We are out of here. We will speak soon, bud."

Suddenly, I was tired, more tired than I had ever been before. I caught Sam's eye and beckoned her over. "Listen, I don't know about you, Samantha, but I would kill just to have you all to myself in our glass house on the hill. Do you know if we left right now, we could catch the sun going down behind the islands while we sip vodka on the balcony? How does that sound to you?"

Sam looked back at Neil who was still talking on the phone. Fiona and Karen were in deep discussion, and Bob was busy rounding his troops up.

"Why, Mr Macdonald, so you can really chat a girl up when you want to. Sounds good to me. Let's get out of here."

Sam chucked a set of keys at me and pointed to the blue Scirocco parked in the drive.

"I hope you are you up to driving with one arm. My shoulder is giving me a hard time. You'll like it, I promise. Oh, by the way, the balcony thing. We might have to rethink that. I don't think we have a balcony any more, Adam."

CHAPTER 18

SAM'S SECRET

It had been two weeks since our return to the glass house. I was up with the sunrise, and my walks had increased gradually every day. My back still ached after walking, but it was a dull ache. Slowly my body was starting to repair itself. The story was much the same for Sam. I was glad to see that her appetite had returned with a vengeance.

The first thing Sam had done was to call her German friend at Huff. After seeing detailed pictures of the damage to the gable end of the glass house, he was able to put a repair plan in place that would entail two weeks of work. This had been scheduled to start today, so I decided to get my walk in before madness descended on the glass house.

On returning to the glass house, I found Sam tucking into a full cooked breakfast while gulping down a banana smoothie.

"So, young lady, care to tell me one more time why our transport situation is solely reliant on a stolen hire car?"

Sam frowned at me, probably for disturbing her breakfast. "Adam, we already went over this. You know why. You are just being mean."

I leaned over, attempting to nick one of Sam's sausages, but she was too fast and whisked the plate away from me, wincing as she did so because she had stretched her shoulder wound.

"Yes, you did tell me, but it was after you plied me with alcohol. By the way, I think that is why you fed me the vodka—so I would forget the conversation. Let me recap what I think you told me. Your Beetle was attacked by Al Qaeda because an American soldier was hiding behind it. My beautiful Aston Martin Vantage is lying in a smelly old lockup some place, but you think it's

OK. And my Land Rover Freelander that you thought was OK turned out not to be OK, so you left it on Arran someplace. You just don't know where you left it."

Sam rolled her eyes before replying. "No, Adam, I know where I left it. I had to abandon it at the top of the String. I just don't know where it will be now. And the Scirocco isn't stolen. I just haven't got round to taking it back yet."

With typical German efficiency, the Huff workmen turned up at ten to nine. Sam and the foreman wandered round the damaged areas of the glass house. For a few minutes, I followed them, but since I didn't speak German, I finally gave it up and wandered to the front of the building watching the to and fro of the white topped waves on the beach below.

After a little while, Sam joined me. She linked her arm through mine and rested her head on my shoulder as we both watched the world on the west coast of Scotland go by. After some time, Sam managed to make herself speak again. "Why don't we take a stroll down to the Invermorroch hotel? I need to speak to Paul and Margo. I promised our German friends I would find them accommodation."

It was my turn to roll my eyes. "Do you really need me to come with you? I am sure you can handle the negotiations on your own. I don't know if my ears can stand Margo this morning."

Sam stepped back and punched me playfully on the good arm. "Listen, Captain Chaos. They have been good enough to look after the Aston for you, so go and have a shower, and I will go over a few things with our builders until you are ready."

Sam was waiting by the hire car when I reappeared. "Where did the sling go to?"

I moved my arm gingerly to prove it was usable. "I have had enough of the bloody thing. I will be fine. I am strapped up anyway, and it will stop Margo asking awkward questions."

The afternoon was warm with a nice breeze from the sea stopping us from overheating as we strolled down the hill toward the little village of Arisaig. Sam walked with her wounded shoulder on the far side of me, her arm around my waist hugging me as we strolled along.

"So before we walk in here, what is the plan? We will have to explain what went on at the glass house and why we have people in rebuilding it. Try and explain that one Miss O'Conner."

Sam smiled up at me as we walked. "MI6 are professional liars, Adam. You should know that by now. I have already got that one in the bag. All you need to do is smile and agree with me. Before we left, I explained to my German builder friend that the glass house had been used in a film shoot, and that the American film company was picking up the bill for the repairs. I will spin the same yarn to Paul and Margo. You see? Not so difficult after all, was it?"

I was shaking my head in disbelief. "Do you really think the builders bought that load of old bollocks?" Sam started to giggle at my comment. "OK Samantha what is so funny about that?"

Sam was still giggling to herself. "Oh, I think they bought it. They even asked if you were the actor Gerard Butler."

Paul was outside cutting the boundary hedge, but he stopped as we approached. "Good God, if it isn't the talk of the village. Margo and I thought we might never see you again after all the rumours that were going about. You had better come into the bar until I call Margo. She will be desperate to hear what has been going on."

Sam squeezed my hand and winked at me as we entered the bar and propped ourselves up on barstools awaiting the arrival of Margo, the town gatherer of hot gossip. Margo arrived and gave us both a large hug before joining us on the barstools while Paul poured coffees for us all.

"Come on then you two, I can't wait any longer spill the beans, what the hell is going on at your house. It was show time for Sam. "OK Margo the last time we met I confess we were spinning you a bit of a yarn.

The truth is I was sworn to secrecy by the film company." At the mention of film company Margo almost fell off the barstool. "You see, Paul, I was right! There was something going on. Told you so. Sorry for butting in, Ann. Please continue."

Sam sipped her coffee letting Margo's imagination build up before continuing with her story. "Remember the tall Asian gentleman who came looking for me? He was the assistant producer. He was just checking in with me to make sure we had all our gear ready to move out before the filming started. There was a clause in our contract to say it was not to be made public knowledge to avoid crowds from arriving at the shoot."

Margo was mesmerised by Sam's story. "So what is the film called? Oh my god, it's Matt Damon, isn't it? He was here in Scotland for filming. It's the new Matt Damon film, isn't it?"

Sam smiled inwardly. She had Margo hook, line, and sinker. "Margo, we can't tell you anything about the film. The contract was quite specific, wasn't it, Alan darling?"

Sam turned looking at me for a reply. It took a fraction of a second to remember my alias was Alan. "Sorry, I was a million miles away there. Yeah, the contract is very binding, but we are being paid handsomely to keep it to ourselves. Let's just hope they will return our home to its former glory when they are finished with it."

Margo leaned across, passing a tray of nibbles around as she spoke. "Well, I can tell you the security people the film company employed were not very nice. Phil the postie told me that the road to your house was being guarded by two guys. I was worried about you both and decided I would pop up and have a word with them. They were very rude, eventually telling me to eff off. I got the impression they were not very nice people. When they eventually left, Paul and I chanced it and drove up to the house. You can imagine what was going through our minds when we found the house in ruins. We genuinely thought you had been killed or abducted. My god, is the film company going to pay for the house?"

Sam was smiling as she replied, "Oh yes, and then some. The old pad is getting the full makeover, thanks to the film company. In fact, that is one of the reasons we popped into see you both. The house was built by a German designer-house company, and we have six workmen who have just arrived to start work on the house. We were wondering if you could put them up for a few weeks while they rebuild our house."

It was Paul who spoke first, beating Margo for a change. "No problem! Things have been slow for this time of year, so it looks like the film company will be helping the local economy as well as yourselves. Tell them to pop in with their bags, and I will have six rooms ready for them."

Margo, not wanting to be outdone, decided she would have the last word on the matter. "Alan, will you tell your workmen we don't allow working clothing in the dining room? Now is there any chance the film company will be back for more filming? You know the Invermorroch would be happy to put up any movie stars, and Matt Damon can stay free of charge should it turn out he is in the film."

Sam had obviously decided enough time had been spent on the subject of the film and changed to a subject closer to my heart. "Paul, do you think you could put Alan out of his misery and reunite him with the real love of his life?"

Paul smiled. Reaching into his pocket, he pulled out the keys to the Aston Martin and handing them to me. "You must be mind readers. I was going to pop it out of the garage this afternoon and let it run for a bit to charge the old girl's battery. Alan, when you get a minute, you must take me for a run in her. I have been so tempted to give it a run myself, but knowing my luck I would have ended up on my roof, so I opted for just giving her a bit of a rev. What a lovely machine! I can see why you bought it. Even for the noise alone, it was worth it. Come on, Alan. Give me a hand to get her out of the garage."

I followed Paul out of the back door while Sam and Margo remained in the bar.

Margo waited until she was alone with Sam at the bar before speaking. "Come on, Ann. You can spill the beans about the film. It will be our little secret."

Sam had half expected the inquisition and was ready for her. "Margo, if I tell you, and it ever got out, the film company could cancel the contract. You must understand we can't afford to let this happen, at least until our house is repaired."

Margo backed down knowing she was getting nowhere. "OK, Ann, you win, but I think there is another secret you may have to come clean about."

Sam felt a whisper of dread creeping into her mind. "Oh and what might that be?" Margo patted her on the leg while making eye contact with her. "Come on, Ann. You can tell me. You have that glow about you and have put on some weight. I see you are wearing a loose top that almost hides your tummy. Have you and Alan decided when you are going public about the baby? We can have the baby shower here, my wee present to you. Just say the word, and I will arrange it for you. When is the wee one due?"

Sam was in a state of shock. She had been putting off telling Adam, but this had put the problem back on the agenda front and centre. The last thing Sam needed was Adam finding out this news from the village gossip. "Margo, you are spot on, but please for me, keep this between you and me. Alan and I have been working apart and with the movie and other things, I haven't got around to telling him yet. I would kind of like to be the one to do that, so if you could keep your detective work secret. We will meet up soon to sort out a wee celebration, I promise."

Margo grabbed Sam and pulled her toward her, giving her a big hug. Sam wanted to yell as her wounded shoulder was compressed but managed to control her pain. "Your secret is my secret, Ann. Come on. We better go and drag the boys out of the garage."

We left the hotel and headed for the main road. I watched as the big V8 engine temperature climbed off the cold. The turnoff for the glass house loomed up on the right, but I had different plans. The big Aston needed the cobwebs blown out of the exhausts. I slid the gear lever into fourth and started to accelerate. The engine changed from a low rumble to a snarl as the big engine sucked air in then launched itself forward, changing note again to a full-pitched howl.

All too quickly, Malaig arrived and the end of the road—literally, as the main road stopped and any further progress could only be made by ferry.

Sam had not spoken on the short trip. Sam knew from previous experience that trying to outshout the Aston's big V8 engine only resulted in a sore throat. But know that we had pulled up outside the local shops and switched the big car off conversation could be resumed. "Well now that you have got that out of your system what are we doing here." Sam half turned in the passenger seat waiting for my reply. "I thought we might replace our vodka stocks as we have run dry. We all know how much you like your vodka."

That evening after packing our house-building crew off to Paul and Margo's, Sam and I finished our supper then headed out onto the patched-up balcony to watch the sunset. I handed Sam her usual measure of vodka. For a while, we both said nothing. My back was sore from the day's activities, but I was content to be home again. I was not so sure about Sam. Since our visit to the hotel, she had been very quiet. She was staring out to sea, clearly in another world. I decided to be the first to break the silence. "Has the cat got your tongue? You do know we are on borrowed time before Neil sends his henchmen to pick us up now that he knows our hideout."

Sam returned from wherever her brain had wandered to. "Sorry, I was daydreaming. Neil will be too busy brown-nosing the prime minister and lording it because MI6 saved the day again to worry about his minions for the moment, but yes, sooner or later, he is going to come looking for us."

There was a stiff breeze brewing, so Sam and I decided to continue the conversation indoors. I lowered myself gently onto the fitted couch Sam put her glass down and joined me cuddling into my side. "Sam are you sure there is nothing wrong? You are very quiet. You know bottling things up won't help. If it's going to be just me and you in our own little pad, you need to tell me if something is bothering you."

Sam did not reply or look up at me after a few minutes Sam sat up to my surprise her eyes were tear filled and red. "Sorry, Adam, I'm not much fun tonight. Can't stop thinking of Smithy. I'm going to get an early night. The new glass for the house repairs should be here tomorrow. See you in the morning." I watched as Sam headed to the bedroom.

Sam did not go to the main bedroom, instead heading for the spare room with the single bed. Inside, the door closed, Sam examined her belly.

She had been about to tell Adam about the baby when he had come away with the comment about just the two of them. It had stopped Sam in her tracks. She needed to tell him. She just couldn't find the right time. Sam knew the longer she waited, the more difficult the conversation would be.

It was a gorgeous morning when I awoke. I had not slept well. Sam had chosen to sleep in the spare room. Something was going on with Sam, but she was keeping it to herself for the moment.

The smell of freshly cooked bacon hit me as I walked into the kitchen area. Sam was busy cooking eggs, bacon, sausages, tomatoes, mushrooms, and toast. Sam caught sight of me and came round from the hob to plant a smacker of a kiss on my lips. I was taken aback by the complete personality change that had happened overnight. "Morning, Captain, I've been thinking once we have the workmen sorted, let's jump in the Aston and take a run up to Camusdarach beach with a picnic. It's about time we had a little time to ourselves, and anyway, I have something to tell you over lunch." Sam must have seen the worried look on my face. "It's OK, Captain. Nothing to worry about, I promise. I just have a little project I am hoping you might be able to give me a hand with."

Sam's promise did nothing to calm my nerves. "Sam, I've seen your little projects before. What are you up to this time, which country's government have you planned to overthrow?"

Sam smiled sweetly at me. "I promise you, Adam. It's a much smaller project than that. Now eat your breakfast before the German crew arrives."

The morning went like clockwork. The glass for the gable end of the building arrived ten minutes after the workforce had appeared. The foreman had made both myself and Sam burst out laughing when he asked if Matt Damon had stayed here. Margo had already got to him. He could not understand what the joke was. Sam was busy trying to explain to him as I loaded the picnic into the back seat of the Aston Martin. I rejoined Sam just as the big black Range Rover appeared from nowhere.

Sam groaned as she realised who the rear passenger was. "Good morning Samantha, and of course, there is no show without Punch. Good morning, Adam."

Sam dismissed the foreman and came to join me by the big Aston Martin.

"Good morning, Neil. How are we doing this fine morning?"

Neil Andrews shook his head at Sam's question. "I would have been much better if I didn't have to keep chasing you pair of idiots all over the country. Who the hell gave you authorisation to take leave? The Americans have asked for you both to take part in a debrief. I have given my permission for this, so you need to get yourselves back to Vauxhall Cross for next Monday."

I did not have to look at Sam to know that she was starting to boil. She gave my hand a squeeze just as she launched her broadside at him.

"Idiots? You have the audacity to call us idiots? Mr Andrews, you have a very short memory. Tell me again what 'idiot' authorised the most dangerous prisoner in the UK to be housed in the same building as weapons of mass destruction? When you were telling the PM how good MI6 were, did you let him know about that little beauty? And another thing, which 'idiot' found Khanjar and saved the south of England from a nuclear disaster when the whole of the western world had been looking for him for years? There is only one 'idiot' standing here, and he arrived in a big black car five minutes ago and started talking out of his arse."

Sam's face was pure red. Even Neil was looking worried. "OK, people, we have got off on the wrong foot here. Sam, calm down before you blow a gasket. Neil, she has a point. I think you should engage your brain before you speak. It helps sometimes."

Neil Andrews was not happy. He knew how to wind Sam up, but even he had been shocked how easily Sam had gone off on one. "All right, Samantha, I admit the 'idiot' tag was a step too far, but let's look at the cold, hard facts here. Yet again, both of you went AWOL leaving me yet again to cover your backsides. Yes, Sam, you did find Khanjar but not before you had massacred a gang in Switzerland without authorisation from MI6 or the Swiss. Not content with that, when you did go AWOL again, you waltzed off with a hire car. I might add that to keep the peace with the rental firm, the department has had to buy the bloody car. So when you start back next Monday, you can bring your new company car with you. That is, if you can get your head into it."

Neil turned and started to walk back toward the Range Rover. He had decided the meeting was over. Sam let go my hand and flew at Neil before I could stop her.

She grabbed him by the shoulder and spun him round to face her. "OK, boss, you win, but we have a problem, a big fucking problem. My maternity leave has just started, six months paid, six months unpaid. Tell the Americans I will take the meeting in a year. Now get out of my sight for at least a year."

There was silence as Neil and I took in what Sam had just said. The wind had been completely taken out of Neil Andrews's sails, but he recovered first. "I am going to kill Jean. She knew. She knew all along. That is why she asked me to tell you she was asking for you. I will kill her."

Sam and I watched as the Range Rover vanished over the crest of the hill, heading toward the main road. I was still in shock. I turned to look at Sam, but she would not look at me. She turned away and started to walk back to the house, tears running down her cheeks.

I followed at a distance, trying to get my head round the new situation. I found Sam in the lounge looking out over the coast, a box of tissues sitting on her knees. I sat down quietly, trying to think of something to say.

I was mindful that having a baby was exactly the opposite of what Sam had planned for her life.

Sam was first to speak. "Adam, I am so sorry. I did not want you to find out this way. No one should find out about a thing like that in the middle of an argument. I was going to tell you over lunch. I'm sorry. I should have told you a long time ago. I don't know what is going on with my head at the moment. Neil just pushed the wrong buttons, and I lost the plot. It was out before I could stop it."

I watched as a tear gathered in the corner of Sam's eye and tumbled down her cheek before splashing on her blouse. I picked up a tissue and wiped her eyes for her. "Listen, don't think because I am not saying much that it's a bad thing. Give me a bit of time to let it sink in."

Sam reached over and took my hand then placed it on her belly. "This is why I slept in the spare room last night. Be patient and you will see."

For ten minutes there was nothing. "Bloody typical. Last night he was kicking me stupid, and today when his dad is here, nothing." Sam's stomach was as tight as a drum, but there was a definite swelling high up.

"You said 'he.' Is it a boy?"

Sam dried her eyes one more time, and for the first time since Neil had arrived, she smiled at me. "A figure of speech. It acts like a boy though, a real pest, kicks you at all the wrong times."

As if the baby had been listening, I felt movement under my hand. Sam could tell by the look on my face I had felt something.

I don't know when we both fell asleep, but I woke up as the waves crashed on the beach below. It was three in the morning. Sam was sound asleep. I listened as her breathing took on not a snore, but almost a low purr.

I marvelled how something so beautiful and peaceful could be so violent. I slid my hand under her hand onto her tummy, feeling for the movement of the baby. Everything was still. I picked Sam up and carried her through to the main bedroom, tucking her in before snuggling into her back with my hands wrapped around her belly.

I was first to rise and wandered through to the kitchen to get breakfast under way. Things started to come to me as I worked. Sam had never touched her vodka the night before last, and her appetite had changed—subtle things, but now they made sense. Sam had always had a volatile temper, but this explained her explosion at Neil. By the time Sam was up and about, I had already spoken to Markus, the German foreman. While Sam tucked into a late breakfast, I attempted to pack the Aston. My attempt failed miserably. I discovered that Sam had stashed the Russian drug money in the boot. I had to make do with stuffing things into the back of the big coupe. Back in the kitchen, Sam was just finishing her third coffee.

"Sam, don't go off on me, but just a thought. Is that much coffee good for a baby?"

Sam smiled to herself before replying. "Adam, if you had been with me the last few weeks, let me tell you, caffeine was the least of my problems. I take your point though. I will try to moderate my intake. Anyway, changing the subject, what is all the running about for?"

I readied myself for a tongue-lashing before replying. "We are about to vacate the premises and let the builders get on with it. You need peace and quiet, and I need to go and see what has become of my cottage. We can cut across and get the wee ferry to Arran this afternoon. You can put your feet up in peace and quiet, and I can go hunt for our lost Freelander—of course, that's only if it is OK with you."

Four hours later, we pulled off the road onto the farm lane that led down to my cottage. Sam was asleep in the passenger seat as I pulled up outside the cottage. The cottage had been left unlocked, and four coffee mugs still sat where they had been left that fateful night.

I left Sam sleeping while I tided away the cups and put the fire on to warm the cottage. After an hour, Sam joined me. It was too late to go shopping, so we dined out that evening. On returning to the cottage, I changed the dressing on Sam's wound. Then in return, Sam gently massaged my lower back in the area that had taken the brunt of the fall from the chopper. I was almost drifting off as Sam worked her palms into the small of my back. It was her voice that brought me back from the brink of sleep. "Adam, are you sure the young scientist lad died in the chopper crash?"

I did not reply. I was still thinking about it when she spoke again. "Don't you find it funny that the Americans are not interested in why one of their top military men went out on a limb to get his hands on the lad? I mean, Southern may have been deluded, but he wasn't a stupid man. Any self-respecting intelligence agency has got to be asking questions, but from the biggest agency in the world—nothing."

I slowly sat up using my good arm to pull me to a sitting position. "You have a point, but remember the Americans requested a meeting with us. Who is to say it wasn't about Gary Harding and his discovery? After all, we really don't know how much the Americans knew about Gary."

That night, with little to worry about, we both slept like logs. I was first to get up and decided a walk in the early morning sunshine was just what my stiff back needed to get itself working and ready for the day ahead. I scribbled a note for Sam and headed out.

I climbed through the heather to the cliff-top walk, stopping at the viewpoint. It was such a beautiful place, but a cold stab of pain from the past hit me and sent a cold shiver through my spine. Not two years ago, I had been happy in the fact I had found a partner to love, only to have my hopes dashed.

This was the very spot from which Kay, the previous owner of the cottage, had been thrown to her death. I watched as a gull glided on the air currents. I thought how quickly life could change for the better or worse. Here I was now with a partner who was expecting my baby. As I watched the gull, out of the corner of my eye, I picked up movement at the cottage. I turned to see a big Vauxhall pulled up by the cottage. I was too far away to make out who was in it or how many. Fear struck my heart like an arrow.

Sam was alone in the house, fast asleep. I took off back down the path as fast as my damaged body would carry me. My brain was racing as I travelled. For the life of me, I could not remember if I had left any weapons at the cottage. As I drew closer, it was apparent the occupants of the car were in the cottage or outbuilding. I gave the cottage a wide berth for the moment and headed for the boathouse a quick glimpse inside confirmed no one was present I slipped in and undid the cover of the boat. My heart leapt as my fingers found the slide of a Beretta. A quick check on the magazine and we were set.

I carried on back round to the front of the house on the grass until I was only a few feet from the front door. Any further movement would be announced the second I stepped onto the gravel. I stopped and listened. I could hear a man's voice talking. It was American. I was sure I had heard his voice before. Tucking the Beretta in the back of my trousers, I made my way to the front door.

Sam had a sixth sense when it came to these situations and called to me. "Adam it's OK. You can come in. It's only out friendly neighbourhood CIA agent, Bruce Ellis."

I walked in to find Sam sitting with Ellis in the living room. "Hello, Adam, glad to see you have made a good recovery. Sorry to bother you. I won't take up too much of your time, buddy."

I sat next to Sam on the couch. "Listen, did you see anything to do with this young lad's invention or whatever he was supposed to do? It's just I have this Harvard professor who seems to think the guy was onto something. As a favour, the president asked me to look into it. I know you guys have had it bad, so I will be out of here soon. Neil told me our meeting was cancelled, so I had a hunch—and admittedly a satellite photo—that you would be here. I have already spoken to Captain Malden and Dr Lowe. They couldn't shine any further light on the matter. So if you can confirm you saw nothing, I have done my bit and can at last head home for some R and R."

Sam and I played dumb. I got the feeling from Ellis it was much to his relief that there was nothing to investigate. "Hey, before I go, the two girls knew I was coming looking for you. Karen says hi, and she hopes you are in good health. Fiona Malden has a bit of news for you. She has just been told by her boss she is to be decorated for her part in the Pandora fiasco. The girl did good. She is getting the DFC and has been transferred to some secret squadron that they did not want to tell me about."

Ellis stood up to leave and then stopped, hesitating before speaking. "I really shouldn't be telling you guys this, but what the hell. Samantha, you have made the big time. Langley has a system for grading foreign agents based on their ability. Whoever thought it up must have been a bit of an Ian Fleming nut, or it was done tongue in cheek because the very top agents, of which there are five at the moment, are designated the double-Os. Samantha O'Conner has been classified as 005—treat only with extreme caution. Hey, you even have the Aston Martin outside. Way to go, girl!"

Sam followed Ellis out of the door and called to him as he was about to get into the big Vauxhall. "Bruce? Make that double-O five and a half!" Sam undid her dressing gown and made a show of patting her swollen belly. Ellis was still laughing as he reversed out of the lane, narrowly missing the postie in his van as he pulled up.

I was surprised to find that a rather large parcel addressed to myself had arrived. Sam watched as I tore open the envelope that had been taped to the front of the parcel. She watched my expression and said nothing when I set fire to the contents of the letter. "Just a few things from an old friend, Sam. Nothing to worry about." Sam watched but said nothing as I opened the parcel and placed the shoulder bag in the bedroom before rejoining Sam in the lounge. Sam never asked about the parcel or the contents of the letter. There was no need. She had already guessed.

Again, I was awake first and spent ten minutes watching Sam's belly rise and fall with her breathing. For some reason, my focus moved past Sam to the dressing table. In the gloom of the bedroom, it took a few seconds for my eyes to focus on Gary's shoulder bag. Sam still purred away as I made my way to the lounge with the bag. Curiosity had gotten the better of me. I emptied the contents onto the coffee table. Gary's chemical formula and test results were here, along with thee syringes with a urine-coloured liquid in them. This was accompanied by two DVDs. His father had revealed in the letter of explanation that he had received a note from Gary stating that in the event of his death, I was to be given all Gary's work.

I had a dilemma. Should I hand them over? Whom could I trust with this goldmine of information? Dr Karen Lowe was my choice, but as soon as I decided on this, I changed my mind. The minute I handed this over to Karen, I would be painting a big target on her back. As already proved, people would have no hesitation in killing for this information. I came to a snap decision. For the moment at least, no one would have this Pandora's box of information.

It took me five minutes to throw on some clothes, grab a waterproof zip bag from the cabin of the speedboat, and head out up the hill on the forest track. Further along the coast, there was a series of caves, the largest of which was named the King's Cave. For the benefit of satellite, I made a show of entering each cave. I found a natural fissure in the wall at the back of one of the caves and deposited Gary's work safely stored in the waterproof pouch. I replaced the research with some stones from the foot of the cave to give the impression the bag contents had not changed and continued my pilgrimage around all the caves. Then I returned through the forest to my little white cottage and the woman I loved.

For the sake of Sam and our baby, I and I alone would be guardian of Gary's own little Pandora's box.

The early morning mist was starting to clear as I crossed the lane leading to my cottage. I was startled to find a police 4x4 sitting in the lane. As I approached, the driver's door swung open, and a rather large police constable stepped out.

"Good morning, sir. I take it you are Mr Alan Hunter, the gentleman that was pulled from the sea?"

I smiled at the policeman. There was something very likable about the gentle giant of a man. "Yes, officer, you are correct. I was just out for some exercise to get these old bones of mine moving again."

Under the watchful eye of the constable, I turned my bag upside down, emptying the stones I had gathered onto the drive. "Helps make me work a bit harder if I carry stones with me."

PC Brian Morrison shook his head then moved closer to me, lowering his voice. "Your boss told me to keep an eye on the place. I take it Neil Andrews is your boss?"

I was smiling at the policeman's attempts to whisper. There was not a soul awake for miles. "Yes, my wife and I work for him. She is asleep in the house, so it's just as well you are whispering."

PC Morrison nodded knowingly. "Yes, I have met your wife. She gave me a good tongue-lashing when I tried to question her. I better not keep you, son. I for one would not want to burn her toast. I just dropped down to tell you we have a black Land Rover Freelander HSE sitting at the office unclaimed. I take it from the bullet hole in the boot floor that it belongs to yourselves. When you come to pick it up, ask for PC Morrison—that's myself—and I will get you sorted out. I will leave you to get on with breakfast. Good day to you, sir."

I sat on a big stone on the beach drinking a coffee. Today was going to be a beautiful day. A breeze from the Irish Sea ruffled my hair, but the morning sun warmed the air. Peace at last!

I was about ready to nod off when Sam sat down beside me. For a second she said nothing. "Adam, do you love me?"

I turned to look into those mesmerising grey eyes, studying her before replying. "Sam, I love you more than anything in this world."

Sam looked away for a second and then back again. "I like that answer. You are getting good at saying all the right things."

I pulled Sam to her feet with my good arm. "Come on, double-O five. Let's get some breakfast into you. We need to look after junior."

Sam stopped in her tracks. "I knew it! The minute Bruce came out with that idiotic story about agents being graded, I knew I would get no peace. You couldn't resist it, could you?"

I smiled at Sam. She always did look sexy when she was mad. "That's nothing, girl. Do you think Halfords will do a two-for-one deal if we get a child seat fitted into the Aston at the same time as an ejector seat?"

"Adam, I take it all back. You are still a big Scottish idiot! There is no hope for me. I'm in love with an idiot!"

The End…or is it?

22150668R10177

Printed in Poland
by Amazon Fulfillment
Poland Sp. z o.o., Wrocław